F Dinan, N

Things You Would Know
If You Grew Up Around Here

Things You Would Know If You Grew Up Around Here

Nancy Wayson Dinan

BLOOMSBURY PUBLISHING

NEW YORK • LONDON • OXFORD • NEW DELHI • SYDNEY

BLOOMSBURY PUBLISHING
Bloomsbury Publishing Inc.
1385 Broadway, New York, NY 10018, USA

BLOOMSBURY, BLOOMSBURY PUBLISHING, and the Diana logo are
trademarks of Bloomsbury Publishing Plc

First published in the United States 2020

ISBN: HB: 978-1-63557-443-2; eBook: 978-1-63557-444-9

LIBRARY OF CONGRESS CATALOGING-IN-PUBLICATION DATA IS AVAILABLE

2 4 6 8 10 9 7 5 3 1

Typeset by Westchester Publishing Services
Printed and bound in the U.S.A. by Berryville Graphics Inc., Berryville, Virginia

To find out more about our authors and books visit www.bloomsbury.com and
sign up for our newsletters.

Bloomsbury books may be purchased for business or promotional use. For information on
bulk purchases please contact Macmillan Corporate and Premium Sales Department at
specialmarkets@macmillan.com.

To Ben, James, and Paul,
who taught me how to be in a family

Things You Would Know
If You Grew Up Around Here

I think hard times are coming.

—Ursula K. Le Guin, 2014 National Book Awards

Things You Would Know If You Grew Up Around Here

This Drought Is the Worst Anybody Has Ever Seen

Even the oldest of the old-timers agree. It's been more than two years since the lakes were full, and now they're at less than 30 percent. Cattle are dying, so beef prices are skyrocketing. The towns at the bottoms of the lakes are rising up out of them.

The old-timers say it's not the apocalypse but the leading edge of it. They say that we're giving too much water to the rice farmers one hundred miles south; this area of the world was never meant to grow rice. The restaurants on the lake closed a long time ago. The boat ramps jut out into thin air.

They say an El Niño will fill everything back up, as if the warming of the earth is a good thing. But rain or no, we will be a desert one day. That is the direction this part of the earth is taking. Once we were at the bottom of the ocean. The dinosaur bones you find here are finned, the limestone the remnant of an ancient seabed. The coming storm will bring water, but it's temporary. The tide is on its way out.

BEFORE

2003

After Boyd's first day of kindergarten, she'd told her mother about Miss Davis, her teacher, and how the woman was sad. By the second week of school, Boyd told Lucy Maud that Miss Davis had lost a little girl. Lucy Maud had not known what to do with this information, so she'd stayed after one day when she picked Boyd up. Miss Davis wore a floral dress, pink flowers on a black background, and the belt had bagged at the waist. Through the window, Lucy Maud saw Boyd happily playing on the blacktop next to the playground, swinging a striped, segmented jump rope. One two, the rope clacked as it hit the ground. One two.

Miss Davis had been hanging letters on a bulletin board, but she stopped when Lucy Maud came in. "Have a seat," she told Lucy Maud, and Lucy Maud had folded herself into the offered chair, a foot off the ground, meant for kindergartners. She'd looked down at the table: the name tag read BOYD. One two.

Lucy Maud hadn't known what to say, hadn't, in fact, known what Boyd meant. So she just said what she'd come to say: "Boyd says you're sad. Did you lose a little girl?" How young she had been, how stupid. She hadn't considered how much this question would hurt. One two.

Miss Davis stopped, hand resting below that loose belt, cupping an absence. "What?" she asked, pale under the fluorescent lighting.

Lucy Maud, now aware that she'd asked the question too bluntly, that she was doing more harm than good, rose. "I'm sorry. I didn't think—"

Miss Davis was more than pale then, ashen, grief across her features, but it was a private grief, something she'd been unable to share. To the world, miscarriage is an unfortunate thing, a disappointment, something medical, but to the mother, a death to mourn alone. "How did Boyd know? It was this summer, and I've been so careful not to say anything." She pressed her eyelids closed, unsuccessful at keeping the tears at bay. "I'm sorry."

Lucy Maud stood to offer a tissue, saying *No no no, don't be sorry*, and now the jump rope was silent. Miss Davis took the tissue and gasped. Lucy Maud turned to see what Miss Davis saw: Boyd in the window, eyes big in her freckled face, called to Miss Davis's pain. Who could blame the woman for the fear that hardened her features? It was a monstrous thing.

There had been other times. Hurt children trailed Boyd for years. Anytime Lucy Maud let her out, they'd follow Boyd like some pied piper, giving her candy, toys, pencils, erasers, marching almost martially behind her. At the Texas State Fair in Dallas one year, Boyd, maybe ten, had convinced Lucy Maud to buy one hundred dollars' worth of skin care products, even though they didn't really have the money, and then had, at home, tossed the stuff in the garbage. "It doesn't work," Boyd said. "But the man needed money or else he'd lose his house." When Lucy Maud had pressed, Boyd had said two children, a boy and a girl. Boyd had said *maybe*; she'd said she *thought*. Lucy Maud had been unnerved, sure, but had dismissed it. What child didn't have a wild imagination?

The time on the road trip to Colorado when Boyd had said *Turn here*: the elderly couple broken down on the side of the road. The time at the grocery store, Boyd lingering on the greeting-card aisle, selecting a sympathy card for Aunt Jackie, two days before Kevin's brother Dillon had died in the car accident. The time Boyd, much older, sixteen, came to Lucy Maud and told her about her husband's girlfriend, back when Lucy Maud still thought she'd be married to Kevin forever.

All of these things, so easy to ignore. Simple explanations, really. Boyd was perceptive, maybe; maybe she paid attention. Paid so much attention that other people's trauma hurt her. A sort of sympathetic lightning rod. But no, that wasn't quite right. Boyd was like the forked stick of a dowser, positioned over dry earth, tuned not to water but to pain.

April 15, 2015

In the fourth year of the drought, Boyd erected a scarecrow. She was technically a senior in high school, but she'd been homeschooled since seventh grade when she had made that scene in the middle school cafeteria. Her mother had pulled her out of school, and her father thought it was fine—it was a better educational model anyway, he thought, and he told Boyd to read Thoreau by the edge of their lake.

Boyd hadn't started with the scarecrow, though. That year, when they were deep in the throes of the drought, their next-door neighbor, Carla, half a mile up the road, made organic soap for a living and had oils delivered in drums. An empty drum washed ashore one afternoon in March, floating because the lid was still attached, and by the beginning of April, Boyd had scrubbed it, coated it with waterproof paint, and set it at the corner of the house where the garage gutters drained.

But it did not rain, so Boyd had time to study the barrel. She did not like the green she had painted it, as the house was on a downslope and the green cut into the sky, so she repainted the drum, blue this time, the matte blue of the bluebonnet, of the vein in the crook of her wrist. One morning a scrim of water was on the lid, and she knew the mosquitoes laid eggs in nothings, in slips, in waters the depth of eggshells. She turned the barrel on its side, cut a hole, and lined it with wire screen to trap any mosquitoes that grew inside, and she built a stand so that it would not roll down the hill. Dew no longer collected on the top.

That was the year a mosquito could shrink a baby's head, the year we poisoned our children in Flint, the year we sprayed millions of gallons of water into the ground to loose the gas instead. That was the year we arrested looters, that year when the lake fell and towns emerged. There was a fire just east of the capital and the smoke dusted everything. The wind took the fire and unfurled it, a motion like the casting of dice.

Still no rain, so Boyd instead repaired the decaying network of gutters that lined the eaves of the entire house, so that one-half inch of rain would fill the fifty-gallon bucket. She did not wait for the rain but planted anyway, despite her mother's objections about the cost of water. She planted Big Boy tomatoes, Celebrities, yellow pear tomatoes, all from starts, all already bearing fruit on the branches. She planted rosemary and oregano, the fragrance attaching to her fingers, then to her clothes, then to linens and furniture and dishes until she tasted the herbs in meals when she had not added them, smelled them in her shampoo. She scattered a handful of pole beans across a cleared patch, the beans clicking as they hit the parched earth. "Be fruitful," she told the beans. "Multiply." She watered them into their new home with the hose, and still it had not rained.

As she worked, she thought about what she was, about the things she felt that were not her own, about the way she had even come to see clear thoughts that did not belong to her. She did not think about this vision in any specific way, no ordered questioning of who she was and what she was for, but she simply felt the keen difference between herself and everyone else she had ever met. Something told her that she was not alone, that at least one more person was out there who understood and processed the world in the way that she did. Her mother was not this person, nor was her father. Isaac was the only person who had never asked anything from her emotionally, never taken a strength or comfort from her to use for himself. But Isaac was not the person she sensed out there in the larger world, the one who would understand what Boyd was because that person was the same thing.

The new blooms on her plants would not fruit and she blamed the lack of bees. She took a paintbrush to the plants early one morning, spreading pollen from blossom to blossom, as Isaac's father, Ruben, had taught her to do. Isaac would return home soon from his first year at college, and Boyd did not yet know what they were, or if she would easily slide back to him, the way that she wanted. The grackles gathered and she built the scarecrow from an old pair of jeans and a pink lawn shirt with buttons in the shape of a cat's head, stuffing straw into the sleeves and the pant legs. She attached a pair of her mother's old Nikes to the empty holes at the ankles. "You are alive," she told the scarecrow. "Now scare all these birds off." Then she knelt next to the fissured earth, her fingers pressed into the dust, and said, "I wish I could fix you." Part of her felt that the cracks in the earth understood.

What is coming: when the drought breaks in the fourth week of May, when the rains finally come, they will break every river for hundreds of miles. Houses will float off moorings and children will never be found. When Boyd returns to her garden, the scarecrow will be missing one shoe, and footprints will be in the mud, circling, circling, displaying the brand's trademark Swoosh in the ball of the footprint. The other shoe, the one the scarecrow will still wear, will be crusted with mud.

But on this day, the garden made its first claim on her: when she rose from her kneeling position, she saw the bean tendrils had wrapped around her wrists. She hesitated, unwilling to break them, and when she pried the stems off, a bee stung her in the hollow of her neck. She slapped it and another stung her in the rise of her collarbone. When she was still again, the tendrils wrapped around her shoulders.

In the sky, the mockingbirds. In the earth, the stone.

Things You Would Know If You Grew Up Around Here

Where There's Quartz, There's Gold

This is what the old-timers will tell you, but it's not quite that easy. Quartz indicates gold, yes, but so much quartz is around here that it's not a reliable measure. Not all quartz indicates gold; you could search for a long time and find nothing. If the quartz has bleached areas, that's a good sign; the acid in certain minerals that would bleach a rock indicates gold. Likewise if the rock is rusted. If there's oxidized iron—any of the iron oxides or oxyhydroxides, not just the rust that we normally think of—even if it's not only in the quartz, you've got good conditions. Hematite, magnetite, and ironstone are all iron oxides, so that's something you're looking for. You're looking for slate; slate and quartz together—now, that's a good sign.

Gold is heavy, so it's buried deep. What rises to the surface are flakes, dust, grit. But you know how the world is today. You know how the Hill Country attracts a certain kind of people: individualist to the extreme, a little off, prone to believing in the apocalypse. You know how these Hill Country people feel about banks, about the stock market. They have six months' worth of canned goods in their pantry, six weeks' worth of water in rinsed-out milk jugs. That gold dust is worth a lot these days because people feel as if the world might end. Gold seems solid, substantial, able to hold its value. You can pay a semester of tuition at UT with a tiny sack of that gold dust.

May 20

The first night Isaac came home, he invited himself to dinner. Boyd didn't know if it was because of her or because he wanted to pan for gold at the edge of their lake, as he had the summer before, and the summer before that. Their late-night conversations left things open-ended, as they had always been with the two of them—both of them wanting to be together, but Isaac wanting to leave the Hill Country and Boyd wanting to stay. There was no good answer, and they both knew that.

Over the last four years, Boyd's mother, Lucy Maud, had become accustomed to seeing Isaac over her kitchen table, and when he'd camped on their lakeshore over the previous two summers, he'd often turned up unexpectedly right at dinnertime, and though he'd been uninvited, Lucy Maud had given him her share and had made herself a ham sandwich. She liked Isaac—she really did—and she noticed how relaxed Boyd was around him, how Boyd's body seemed to settle back, how Boyd seemed to slow down. But Isaac's ambition bothered Lucy Maud—she knew from experience how such naked ambition could be both powerfully magnetic and dangerously callous. But now Lucy Maud chased this thought from her mind, putting the dinner leftovers on a paper plate and covering it with foil, but it wasn't for Isaac. "Here, you two," she told Boyd and Isaac. "Take this to Carla." Boyd was still eating, twirling her fork in the last of the Alfredo sauce, humming to herself she was so content and happy.

Isaac took the plate from Lucy Maud. "We'll head up the road soon as Boyd's done."

Boyd shook her head. "Carla isn't up the road. It's Friday."

Lucy Maud, taking bread out of the pantry, and ham and mayonnaise out of the refrigerator, nodded. "It's Friday," she repeated, as if Isaac would know Carla the way that she and Boyd did. "Why d'you think I'm sending her some supper?" Boyd knew Lucy Maud was worried that Carla had started up her wandering again.

On Friday evenings, Carla would not be up the road at her house, making soap or knitting beanie hats and scarves. She still did those things, only not on Fridays, and one of the reasons she took this break on Fridays was because her soaps weren't selling well in the grocery stores, and she would never make a living on hand-knit beanies that took three hours to make and sold for ten dollars. If her soaps weren't selling, then she might have to return to Austin, to cubicle land, and the thought inspired in her little hippie heart the coldest sort of fear. Freedom, that's what that soap represented, and she was willing to risk a lot for freedom. And ever since she'd found out that the pioneer settlers had probably buried the victims of the hanging tree on her ten acres, she'd been convinced that the reason she wasn't selling soap was because her property was cursed.

So she'd set about trying to reverse the curse, but she didn't immediately fall into the pattern of her Friday vigil. Nobody had any idea where they'd buried those people, other than on that slope down by the water, the slope that was more than an acre, where a poured-concrete picnic table sat under a scraggly live oak, and where prickly pear bloomed nearly all summer long. The graves had never been marked, and the dragonflies sure weren't telling. The acre was sown with the black pebbles of deer scat and the powdery brown hills of fire ant mounds. Carla wasn't even sure *if* the convicts had been buried there; she just had what the sheriff and the city councilman had told her. A small part of her suspected that they had been pulling her leg; they were just the type to mess with a middle-aged woman living out here all by herself.

Still, she got a metal detector and walked all over that acre, finding nothing but marble and granite so shot through with iron that the stone was beginning to rust. She found some fishing tackle, long, long abandoned and ancient, and a beer can that had the old-fashioned pull tab removed. She'd knelt and unearthed it when the detector had started beeping, and it had been such a curious sensation to see that can, that link with at least thirty years ago, and maybe even more. The last hand to touch it might also be buried in the ground, and she thought then that the whole world was a graveyard and that they were all cursed. She never found the unmarked plots, and she guessed that the victims of the hanging tree had not been buried in lead coffins but had probably been tossed as is into rough-hewn graves. Nothing to set off the detector, so she had turned her attention to the tree itself.

Boyd and Isaac found her down there that night, on the far end of Boyd's family's property, headed toward the dam and away from the house, just as the sun was disappearing in a riot of coral and turquoise. The hanging tree was an ancient matriarch of a live oak, set in a grove of mesquite, and the big branches arced out over them like the tentacles of a sea monster. Boyd had a Maglite for the dark, though it hadn't yet come, and Carla was setting up candles in a row underneath the old live oak, whispering to herself. "Oh," she said when she saw them, then she stopped whispering and just started talking, now that she had an audience. "This one's for George Bluffton, who killed a Comanche over a saddle with silver hardware. They wouldn't have hanged him, but he shot the sheriff's horse." She set a dollar-store votive candle in the granite gravel as the night began to take over. "This one's for a different Comanche, blamed for the dead baby on Babyhead Mountain." The hanged Comanche got a tall votive, the kind the grocery store sold with the Virgin of Guadalupe and a rosary printed on it. Boyd saw the script on the side and felt an urge to read it aloud, but she said nothing and let Carla run the show. "This is for the woman Hettie Meyer, who killed her own children." This was a tall red pillar, twisted into the dirt until it stayed upright, though it canted to the side and would drip wax. Carla didn't seem to care and stood, dusting her hands on her broomstick skirt.

Isaac asked, "Is that all there is?"

She shrugged. "How the hell should I know?"

Isaac handed her the plate of fettuccine Alfredo and she ate it in silence, communing with the dead. Boyd wanted to lean on Isaac, but she wasn't sure he'd let her. The wind died down and the night got loud around them.

The moon rose behind the tree, huge in its low position in the sky, and Carla set the paper plate down and lit the candles one by one. Ten minutes before and the wind would have carried the plate away; now the plate rested lightly on the ground and did not budge.

"How's that going to get rid of the ghosts?" Isaac asked.

"No ghosts. Never have been ghosts. Only this bad luck until they're properly satisfied." Carla hugged herself, gripping her elbows. "Bet it's someone falsely accused." The lore went that a tree that had hanged an innocent man would wither to the ground within a summer, but this one had kept right on growing. In the daytime, it was a haven; to be under the branches and to feel the cool air of transpiration was the next best thing to air-conditioning, was the way to be a part of the world. The candles were no match for the dark, but the moon was more than enough. Boyd stared at the ground, watching the attenuated shadows cast by the golden pinpricks of light. No wind, and then, one, two, three, the candles were snuffed out.

"Carla?" Isaac said. But she didn't answer. Boyd could not see either of them; the dark had come on so silently and completely that she nearly stopped breathing. But not full dark: the moon was still in the business of casting shadows.

And the shadows on the ground, they were moving in a way . . . What was the word? *Swaying*? Is that how she would describe what the shadows were doing? Yes, swaying, ding-dong, like a bell, like a mast on a ship at sea. And there were more than three; there were perhaps twenty shadows moving on the ground, shuddering like cocoons, each chrysalis tethered to the tree shadow by a thin length of darkness.

"Boyd," Isaac said. "You got that Maglite?"

She remembered the flashlight, felt for it, clicked the button on its side. The shadows disappeared, pushed back and headed off. But she heard the movement of wings and shone the flashlight up into the tree, and lined up on every branch were birds of carrion—turkey vultures and buzzards and crested caracaras—hooked beaks and hooked claws and oily, oiled feathers. They clucked and tutted, and when Boyd shone the flashlight on them, they spread their wings and took languidly, heavily to the air, reluctant to leave the place to which they'd been called. Boyd heard Isaac's gasp and Carla's slight moan, but Boyd was silent. The night carried the smell of the lake, and, from far away, the sound of Lucy Maud's television, tinnily playing the theme song from *Law & Order*.

"What are they?" Isaac asked, his whisper only barely audible over the sound of the wings.

Boyd said nothing—she thought about mentioning the bean tendrils in her garden—but Carla made a sound as if she didn't know, then continued, "Well"—she bent to relight the candles—"they could be a couple of things. One, they could be because of the hanging tree, because we are asking this curse to be lifted. They could be a good thing. The curse could be flying off as we speak." She got the votive candle lit and handed it to Boyd, and then the pillar candle to Isaac.

"What's the other thing?" Isaac asked, cupping a hand around the flame, trying to keep it going in the windy night.

"Oh," Carla said, as if it weren't important, "carrion birds can be an omen, not so great."

"Oh, yeah?"

She turned to him. "Yeah. They could mean death." She smiled at him in the candlelight. She was just pulling his leg.

Boyd rolled her eyes, a gesture nobody else saw. "Or they could just mean there's a dead thing somewhere around here."

"Yeah," Isaac said, considering. "Probably that."

The three of them walked back to Boyd's house, letting the whole thing go, and, once there, Carla and Lucy Maud opened a bottle of wine and sat at the kitchen table over a game of rummy. Boyd walked Isaac out to his car, and here was the moment they'd both been waiting for, the moment they were alone for the first time since Isaac had left for his spring semester at UT. She leaned on the top of his car door, waiting for him to say whether he'd missed her or not.

"Crazy about those birds, huh?" Isaac drummed on the steering wheel. She couldn't tell if he was avoiding discussing their relationship or if he was truly preoccupied by what they'd seen.

She shrugged. "I've seen crazier."

He finally looked up at her. "Okay," he said, amenable, not ready to talk about anything serious. He shifted, then finally said, "Boyd, I'll be moving my stuff down tomorrow night."

She nodded. She already knew that. She'd take her camping stuff down tomorrow afternoon, then he'd be there later. They were going to have the whole summer together, panning side by side. They had plenty of time to figure out what they were to each other, but to Boyd the answer was becoming increasingly clear. She bit the inside of her lip. "See you then," she said, tapping twice on the top of the car door, signaling that it was time for him to go, then she turned back to the house.

In a second, he was behind her, his arms around her waist, and his face buried in the back of her hair. "Boyd," he said, then stopped.

Her breath hitched in surprise—he'd been so quick to get out of the car and cover the distance—and the relief that he was still Isaac, that he still felt for her what she felt for him. But really, it wasn't the same.

"Boyd, I—" He loosened his grip on her, the hug almost over. "I missed you. I just—I'm looking forward to this summer." In his statement was the acknowledgment that he was leaving things unsaid on purpose, things that she wanted him to say. There was a distance here, deliberate and unintentionally cutting.

She nodded, feeling his face against the back of her neck, then he let go. "Yeah. All right."

He got back in the car, and soon she was lit in his headlights. She lifted a hand in farewell, and he did the same.

"Crazy about those birds, huh?" he said again as he pulled away.

"Yeah," she said, but he didn't hear her.

Isaac wasn't ready for that serious conversation just yet, but was instead preoccupied with his own life as he drove from Lucy Maud's house to his father's. He'd be at the lake for two and a half months this summer, and to be honest, it wasn't his favorite thing. Something about the endeavor was elemental, rugged in a way he imagined his personality was missing, but really, it was a hot and dirty thing to do. He had noticed that most of the people he'd met who embraced ruggedness had not had any sustained experience with said ruggedness. He did it for one reason—it was a reliable way to pay his tuition and avoid student loans. He earned much more in a summer of panning than he did working at a minimum wage job. He was thinking about panning, then this made him think about Boyd, how something about her made him somehow better.

Isaac had been in middle school, sitting in the back of his father's classroom reading a choose-your-own-adventure book when he'd first become aware of Boyd. Ruben King coached the middle school social studies team, and two students had been on the team that year: a girl and a boy. The boy had been familiar to Isaac, a kid he knew from track, but the girl had been unknown, even though Isaac had been in the same classes with her. She had been so uninteresting to him that she had floated underneath his radar, even though, Isaac thought later, she had been a bit weird, something not quite right around the edges.

That day, the sun had slanted in low, even though it was only around four o'clock. The year was wrapping up, and it would soon be time for the Christmas break. The light, too, was cold, though the heater was on in the school, and he wasn't uncomfortable. He didn't feel the cold, he thought; he *saw* it. Then the girl dropped a book, a heavy novel, *The Clan of the Cave Bear.* He read the title in surprise; his father had read the book the previous summer, and when Isaac had asked what it was about, Ruben had said that Isaac would have to wait a few years to find out. Now, here was this girl who was in his same grade, reading the book. Isaac had studied her then, studied her brown hair and freckles and the way her pant legs were just a little too high and her shoes—brown ballet flats—were just a little too worn. That day, too, he'd noticed the way his father had responded to this girl, noticed how he treated her with respect, almost as if she were an adult.

Isaac saw the girl again a week later. By this time, he knew her name was Boyd, and he'd begun to notice her everywhere. That afternoon, he'd been at the H-E-B in Marble Falls. A man had been sitting at the picnic table out front, an old man with two long dark braids over his shoulders, a bandanna around his temples, a plaid flannel and Wrangler jeans and house shoes. Isaac, sitting in his dad's truck while Ruben ran in for some milk and cereal, watched Boyd emerge from the grocery store, walk over to the old man, reach into a plastic bag, and hand the man something. Isaac couldn't see what it was exactly, but the flat box looked like some kind of over-the-counter medicine. The man looked up at Boyd—Isaac was certain that he did not know her—hesitated, then took the box, sucking in his lips and nodding, looking, Isaac thought, as if he was trying not to cry. Isaac had watched them, Boyd in a black sweater and ripped jeans, and he imagined that Boyd had read the man's mind. Boyd had patted him on the shoulder and walked away, while the man had gaped at her as if she'd been something from another planet, or an angel. Now Isaac thought about that day, and how Boyd had been a central figure in his life for so long. Now that he had left the Hill Country, probably for good, she had receded in his life, and this thought carried with it a sharp sense of loss, but only when he turned his attention to it. His headlights scraped the dusty road as he drove on home.

BEFORE

2009

The teacher's son sat at the back of the class during those early practices, those days before she even knew his name. She thought that sometimes he watched her, but then she would turn to him and his gaze would be on his book. She caught nothing from him, no hint of what he was feeling, and this was unusual, because that year—seventh grade—she was beginning to feel everything. The other person on the social studies team, Paul, was quickly becoming an open book to Boyd, but not Ruben King's son. Boyd knew that Paul liked a girl named Amanda, who didn't like him back, and that he stayed up late into the night writing her name in his journal. Sometimes, Boyd knew, Paul dialed six of the seven digits of Amanda's phone number and then sat there, finger poised over the final digit, but never called. But Ruben King's son revealed nothing to her.

It happened on a windy day in April, a day almost at the end of the school year. Would things be different now, Boyd wondered, if, on that day, she had stayed at home? Would she have made it to the end of the school year, taken a break, returned to eighth grade perfectly fine? Would she have finished high school? Would she have even known Isaac, or at least known him in the way that she knew him now?

That year had been weird for Boyd anyway. That year, an innocence had begun to flake away, and Boyd had been shocked to discover that some of her classmates smoked pot. She caught their thoughts at lunchtime, and though later in her life this would be no big deal, in seventh grade, the idea of her classmates doing drugs came as a cataclysmic shock. Shocking, too, had been the first realizations about sex, the thoughts of a classmate about what her high school boyfriend had asked her to do in the back of his car, and another about what had happened at a party when the parents had been out of town. By the end of that year, by that April, Boyd had come to understand the world as a very different place from the one she had known just the year before. It was perpetually unsettling, and Boyd was on edge.

But that day, there had been the new girl, the one whose sweaters were too big and whose shoulders were always hunched. Where had she come from? Boyd tried to remember, but she couldn't. The girl had appeared sometime between the beginning of the year and April, and Boyd hadn't had a class with her. The girl was behind, maybe, maybe not too smart, and so she hadn't been in any of Boyd's classes, not even in PE. Until that day in the cafeteria, Boyd hadn't noticed the small girl in the big sweaters at all.

Boyd was sitting by herself at a lunch table—no big deal; she did it all the time. She knew that many of her classmates thought that this was a fate worse than death, but Boyd preferred it, and they'd long since stopped giving her looks. Her oddness and solitude no longer registered. This was a good thing.

Where had that girl sat all that time in between? Boyd did not know. Later she would think that the girl had eaten in the office with the counselor, a measured introduction to the world of school and other kids and the look and feel of normal lives and normal families. But the fact was Boyd did not know where the girl had been until this day, when she showed up at Boyd's table, standing awkwardly, asking with her big eyes for permission to sit.

At that time, Isaac sat with the athletic kids, though he never played football or basketball; he only ran track. In April, it would have been track season, though. She was only vaguely aware that Mr. King's son watched her, watched what she did when the big-sweatered girl approached her.

The eyes had been almost too much for Boyd. They had been sad— anybody could see the sadness that trailed that girl like a vapor—but what got to Boyd was the bravery she saw in them, the effort it had cost this girl to approach Boyd and merely gesture to the table, asking permission to sit down. That bravery nearly knocked Boyd back—the table was almost empty and Boyd was virtually an outcast. The girl did not need to ask Boyd for permission.

Boyd, sensing a disturbance, smiled thinly and waved her hand, saying, *Please, there's plenty of room.* And the girl—she exhaled then, a long breath that hitched in the middle. A girl who was accustomed to hiding what she felt, a girl who was perpetually afraid.

She sat down and picked at her lunch, chasing the canned corn around the tray with her plastic fork, saying nothing, not asking for Boyd's friendship or time or anything at all, just asking for a place to sit down. Relief came off the girl in waves.

But Boyd—something was wrong. She felt it first at the back of her throat and realized that she was holding her breath. A feeling from this girl—behind the relief and bravery, there was something else. This girl knew something of the world that Boyd had not yet once suspected. Until then, Boyd had known about selfishness, about pettiness, about the serious character failings of the human animal. But this girl—she knew about evil, and Boyd had never before encountered evil.

At first, Boyd did her best to hide the reaction. She didn't get anything real from the girl, not yet: no images, no thoughts, nothing to grasp. There was just the sense that the girl had seen something, felt something, *knew* something, that Boyd could not yet imagine. Then it started coming to her, just flashes: how old the girl had been when it had first occurred, what her father had promised to do if she ever told, how old the girl's brother had been when her father had started to go in that bedroom instead. And Boyd—she couldn't believe it, had never suspected, felt the broken body and the head on the pillow and the guilt and scheming to try to protect the little brother. Boyd, in the cafeteria on that windy April afternoon, amid the smell of cafeteria pizza and corn, had put her hands on the girl's forearms, had tried to take some of it away.

When her thumbs slipped underneath the girl's sleeves, Boyd felt a jaggedness run up her arms, as if she were being cut from wrist to shoulder with a serrated knife. Whatever traveled from the girl to Boyd had a sawing feeling, a sense that something was making its way in, a feeling as if her skin were ripping and as if she were dripping blood and tissue onto the school's linoleum. Boyd screamed, unable to process anything, unable to help in any way but to take some of the pain as her own. She continued screaming, cafeteria forgotten, while the girl looked at her, an exhaustion in her eyes. Not letting go, Boyd stood, knocking the girl's tray to the floor, and now other kids were also up, staring at her, and the lunchroom monitors ran toward her, and everybody watched, because it looked as if Boyd were hurting the girl, but Boyd was the one who was screaming.

But the first person to reach her had been the teacher's son, the one she would later know was named Isaac, and he wrapped his arms around Boyd in a way that broke her contact with the big-sweatered girl. Boyd was surprised by how large he was—in middle school, she still thought of the boys as boys, but Isaac was almost as large as her father already, and Isaac had a smell that was different from her own, oniony and sharp. He dragged her away as the other girl sat, stunned, and he pulled Boyd out to the hall where nobody else was, and he—a stranger—just kept his arms around her, even as she stopped screaming and started crying, and he stood there as other people walked by and stared, which surprised her, because he was popular, and she was not. He said nothing, only made soothing sounds, and his body blocked her from view. The ripping feeling that had traveled through her body was leaving her, but only gradually, and Boyd was convinced that the teacher's son was taking that feeling away for her, was doing for Boyd what Boyd had tried to do for the girl. Boyd had never been comforted like this and did not know what to make of it. When she stopped crying, he rested his chin on the top of her head and finally said, "You okay?"

From that day forward, he had been her friend, the only one who never asked for a thing from her, until much later, when he asked her to leave with him. The only one who could be trusted to sit with Boyd when she hurt because of something that had happened to somebody else. The only one who didn't expect her to take away his pain. Isaac had been a refuge, and she had needed a refuge.

Of course, Boyd hadn't done anything real for the girl besides embarrass her, hadn't fixed anything at all. Later, when the girl didn't come back, Isaac had permanently moved to Boyd's table in the cafeteria, just their two lunches on the table's long surface in that packed space, Boyd fundamentally different, having lost some sense of safety in the world. Later, when the rumors about the girl started—*It's not true, stop making stuff up*—how they had found her in the bathtub, water tinged pink, Isaac was there for Boyd again, sitting beside her after school in Mr. King's classroom, asking nothing from her, just letting her sit with her discovery that a pain was in the world that broke people, a pain against which she, too, could be broken, if she let herself, because she was powerless against that vast scope. The world beautiful and lovely and joyous, yes, but molten as its core, capable of such utter destruction.

May 21

Two days before the drought broke, Boyd carried the first load down to the water's edge. In two days, Boyd's grandfather was getting married to his longtime girlfriend, Sylvia, and Boyd would have to go to the wedding, but until then, she would camp a night or two down by the water with Isaac. She carried her pack down across the pink granite dome of rock and through the old pecan orchard and the retama and pin oak that grew along the river's edge. She wore a pair of faded cargo pants and a linen fishing shirt, nothing bright or flashy, so she looked as if she could be from any time around here, either from now or from a hundred years ago. The flat green plastic of the sluice pan hanging from her backpack caught no light, but every now and then it bumped against a carabiner with a leaden thud. She came out onto the lake, the sandstone gravel crunching underfoot, and she liked the sound so much she took a few steps more than necessary.

First she pitched her tent, smoothing the gravel bed with the handle of her pickax. The gravel—big disks of sandstone, spheres of honeycombed limestone, clamshells both ancient and modern—would be hell to sleep on, but Isaac was bringing two air mattresses later in the truck. She threaded the poles through and staked the tent, driving the stakes deep enough to catch the ground underneath the gravel, knowing the stakes would slide out if she didn't. She hung the electric lantern from the hook inside the tent.

Isaac would borrow Carla's truck to drive his equipment down because he had a lot. He would bring his tent, a big four-person affair, the air mattresses and bedding, and both a grill and a camp stove, just in case he couldn't start a fire, and an ice chest full of beer and groceries. He was bringing two camp chairs, the kind that collapsed into a single column, and a folding table, and three electric lanterns and a row of tiki torches with citronella oil. There were clothes, too, in a suitcase, and his canoe and oars, and all of his panning equipment. A battery-operated radio. Some fishing gear. A tarp to string up in the trees for shade. He was planning to stay the entire summer, pull what gold he could from the lake. She was not.

She untied the sluice pan, setting it in a corner of the tent with care. Next the books from the backpack: the *Audubon Society Field Guide to North American Birds*, a star guide, and one slim novel, Muriel Spark's *The Girls of Slender Means*, lit in the late-afternoon light, filtered by the nylon, the titles already falling into shadow. She knew she cast a silhouette through the nylon; if anybody was out there, the person would see her. But she knew there was nobody. Most lakes and the rivers that fed them were empty, and they were several weeks yet from being full of the summer people. Lake Travis was less than 40 percent full, and Lake Buchanan the same, and so, in this fourth year of drought, nobody went swimming there. Those two lakes stank of catfish and mud and had rings higher than a man's head, and those rings showed where the water should have been. The lake bottom being exposed led to a melancholy feeling, almost apocalyptic, and most people didn't care for it.

She stepped outside, becoming part of the landscape again instead of something set apart by nylon. The moon rose in the eastern sky, and after her eyes adjusted, she saw a water moccasin, head raised about four inches, slide along the bank of the river. She couldn't resist that briny smell of water, so she gave the snake a wide berth, waded in, and ducked her head under, feeling the way she always did when she was in a natural body of water, that here she was in the earth's bloodstream.

In her pocket was the first gold of the summer, only this bit of gold had been stolen and not panned. Her mother's wedding ring, tricolored gold roses in a band, bought twenty years ago in the Dakota badlands by a father who seemed to have been a different man entirely from the one Boyd had known all her life. Her father had asked for the ring so that he could give it to his new girlfriend, and Lucy Maud had said she would consider it. But Boyd had not been able to bear this, so when her mother had been at the library bickering with the other part-timers, Boyd had gone into her mother's room and taken it from the dish at the back of the sink. The pocket where it rested was zipped so that the ring would not slide out.

Now back across the gravel field, through the shadow of the pecan orchard, the leaves whispering as she walked, and across the granite dome, a rock the size of a school bus, rising several feet into the air. Ghosts of white lichen unfolded across it, and dark rust spots stained the color of dried blood. Her footfalls, gravelly and brittle. The pencil cactus that caught at her pant legs. The smell of the river, which was really the smell of the earth, the scent when spring dirt was turned over and the dark dwellers scurried away from the sun. No sun now—a break for the sedge grass, the yucca, the white-tailed deer. The respite of night.

The light of the house ahead, the windows along the back where the house faced the lake illuminated and active, a giant moving-picture set apart from the night like a drive-in movie. Isaac was already there, moving with Boyd's mother, setting a dish of something on the table, and Boyd realized she would be expected to stay for dinner, instead of driving the truck down to the campsite and settling in to the swish of water on pebbles.

She knocked on the back door, locked because Lucy Maud hardly ever used it, and they both looked up at her, Isaac placing forks on the left sides of plates, Boyd's mother straining a pot of potatoes at the sink, the cloud of steam rising around her face, turning the tendrils at her temples damp and curly. Boyd came in, for that one last dinner, two days before her grandfather's wedding, and two days before the storm.

Later, she and Isaac drove down to the lake in Carla's truck, and she helped him pitch his tent in darkness. They inflated the air mattresses, two of them, and put one in each tent. Even if they were something, and Boyd still did not know, it would be too much for either of them to share a single tent. There had been that one time, before he had left Marble Falls, but it had been awkward, and neither had forgotten that awkwardness, how their relationship had been one thing but was not yet something new.

"You ever decide what you're going to do next year?" he asked. He knew she wasn't headed to UT, that was for sure, but he still wanted her to take classes at Austin Community College.

"No." She didn't want to talk about it, but no college was in her near future. Her parents would make her a homeschooled diploma and that would be that: she'd be done with school, perhaps forever. She did not know what she would end up being, but she knew where: for as long as it was possible, she would remain here, with her garden and her lake and the pecans and live oaks of the old riverbeds.

"If you went to ACC, you'd be in Austin." He let the statement stand and she followed it to its conclusion on her own.

"Yeah, I'm not going to Austin." She could not handle cities, those concentrated places of humanity, and they overwhelmed her with a certain knowledge of the world's sadness. In a city, Boyd was far more aware of what a person would do for a place to sleep, of the way addiction severed families, of the harsh edge of struggle on buses and subways and street corners. Not only was she more aware of this situation in cities, but she was also aware of how helpless she was to stop it. In cities, too, the loss of the natural world was a heavy blow to Boyd—she needed that green as ballast, as a grounding. In the city, she was too aware of what had been cut down, what had been polluted, what was lost.

"What have you got against it?" She knew him so well, but he sometimes seemed to know nothing about her. "Boyd, I have to be there."

"Are you asking me to come?"

"I'm asking you why you're not."

She thought he knew why she wasn't, but that he wanted her to say it. "If you asked me, maybe I'd go." It was true, too; if he asked her, if he told her that he wanted her to be there, she'd have no choice. She felt incomplete—all flounder-y—without him, as if every experience she would have in her life would only be for the story she could tell him. For it to be as if it had really happened, she felt, Isaac would have to be there.

Isaac twisted, finishing his beer and crumpling the can before tossing it back in the ice chest. "I'll miss you." He hadn't asked her to go. She knew why, too—he couldn't stand to be poor like his father, who was a teacher, yes, but who had been given to get-rich-quick schemes Isaac's entire life. They'd talked about the people who stayed: *How do they make money?* Isaac asked. This wasn't farming country. They were cops, managers at Walmart, and some were teachers. But it wasn't enough for him, he who wanted to transcend, he who wanted to be better and richer, and if he ever came back, he'd live in Horseshoe Bay with a boat and a nice car and a private practice in town.

He shook himself, a move originating in his shoulders and traveling down to his fingers. "What if I pulled enough money out of this lake to pay for medical school? What if I got out of this whole thing without any debt and we could just go from there?" Isaac, who was fascinated by the insides of things; Isaac, who, yes, wanted to be a surgeon because of money, having been raised a hippie's son in a Texas backwater, but who was truly interested in the zipping open of skin, in the baring of muscle, tendon, bone, in the silver membrane encasing organs. In another life, he would have dissected Victorian corpses to catalog the parts. But it wasn't quite as morbid as all that, she thought. Isaac was genuinely interested in helping people. She didn't know what a future together would look like—he wanted to leave so badly, and she wanted to stay.

"You might could," Boyd said, imagining a medical school tuition's worth of gold dust.

"That's not even the real money around here."

"Nope."

He was talking about the stories they'd heard all their lives: the mines, the buried treasure, the prospectors thwarted and disappointed and dead. On this side of the lake alone, somewhere on or near Boyd's family's property, there was supposed to be an old silver mine. A hundred years ago, an unnamed man had wandered into town to spend silver ingots, saying he had a mine full of them, already pulled from the earth. He'd left town, having spent a fortune in three nights, and was never seen again. Nobody had ever found that mine, but everybody wondered if it had been the silver mine Jim Bowie had come to Texas to find, long before he died at the Alamo, sick in bed but shooting with both hands nonetheless. The real treasure, however, was the Mexican gold that Maximilian had buried somewhere in San Saba County.

"You coming to my grandfather's wedding?" she asked eventually.

He nodded and opened another beer. "Yeah, of course. I want him to come to mine, right?" It was such an odd remark—Isaac wasn't close to her grandfather whatsoever, had only met him once—and Boyd's grandfather had no reason to be at Isaac's wedding unless Isaac was marrying Boyd. It wasn't the first time he had done this—he acted as if their getting married was an inevitability, that what was happening right now was temporary, that Boyd would change her mind and join him in Austin or wherever he was. And she knew that she probably would eventually, that she would leave this lake and these hills and go live with Isaac in an apartment in some distant place. The thought exhausted her. She said nothing, raising her hand to say good night, and she went inside her tent and zipped it up, stripping to her underwear in the light of the electric lantern. She lay on her air mattress with her flashlight, listening to the night and holding the Muriel Spark novel as if she were reading. Her neck and collarbone felt a phantom ache of bee stings, even though it was six weeks later, and she wanted to tell Ruben King how the tendrils had pulled at her wrists and shoulders. She heard the barn owls and the cricket frogs and the wind running its fingers through her trees.

Isaac, still by the fire, was thinking about how Boyd wanted him to somehow stay here, to find a way to be who they were right now for the rest of their lives. Truthfully, he saw an appeal to this: what a safe life, to be Boyd and Isaac in the Hill Country, staying the same, just growing a little older.

The problem was, he didn't want to stay the same, or at least he didn't want the same life he'd had growing up. He wanted a nice house—a new one, maybe custom-built—in suburbia. A clean porcelain bathtub, not the yellowed vinyl tub of his father's. He wanted drawers in the kitchen that rolled open easily, carpet that didn't carry the smell of last year's rain. He wanted a house that didn't have a coffee can of bacon grease on the back of the stovetop. Heavy stainless steel pans instead of one crusted cast-iron skillet. Multiple sets of sheets.

There would be children—one boy and one girl—and his wife would drive a minivan for at least a decade of her life, but she would complain about driving it. The boy would play soccer, the girl would study ballet. Both of them would play an instrument. His wife would be a good cook—though he would be in charge of the grill—and on Saturdays he would play golf. He'd have his own set of clubs that he would keep in the trunk of his car.

Where would Boyd's vision fit into all of this? He did not know. He wasn't even willing to consider staying because right now he had nothing—no money, no nothing—and this staying put, this stasis, would postpone his having something. He loved Boyd in a way he could not describe, with a sort of feral matter-of-factness, but what they each wanted from their lives seemed incompatible when meshed together. Boyd was his best friend, and he realized now that his feelings toward Boyd had something paternal and maybe a bit condescending: he wanted to protect her. He remembered that day he'd seen her give that man medicine at H-E-B, and he'd never seen anything else like that—a person who was attuned to and who anticipated the needs of other people, and who worked hard to meet these needs. Boyd was endlessly, infinitely giving, and it exhausted her. It exhausted him. He wanted to help people, too, but he knew how to draw a line for himself. He'd never been in a situation in which he'd been unable to turn off his emotions—he'd been confronted with heartbreak, but he'd done everything he could and, in so doing, satisfied his conscience.

He remembered, too, the one time they'd slept together, one night last summer, when they'd been camping at the lake, and he'd heard her crying in her tent. He'd had a girlfriend at the time—Mae, a fellow premed student, with whom he volunteered at Seton Hospital. But he had gone into the tent to comfort Boyd, and she had clung to him in such a way, and when it was over, neither of them could believe it, but she still wouldn't let go. Much later, it occurred to him that it was likely Boyd's first time, but in that moment when he held her in the middle of the night on her air mattress, he'd realized that no matter what he felt, he was too careless for her, too unready for a relationship that would fundamentally close off parts of his life.

He felt a need to disentangle himself from Boyd, the opposite of ripping off a Band-Aid, a nearly imperceptible drawing back that would nevertheless result in separation, though he didn't want her to realize that it was happening. At the same time, this thought was unbearable: there would never be another Boyd. He pictured them in their different lives, both married to other people. When he pictured this, he saw Boyd and himself across a room, exchanging glances. He thought that their spouses would just have to understand, that his wife would have to be okay with Boyd always coming first because she always had. But no. No wife would put up with this. And how could he bear the thought of Boyd's husband?

He thought, too, of the girls he'd dated this year in Austin, mostly sorority girls, though this didn't mean empty-headed and shallow, dressed in cardigans and UGGs. Taylor, hair the color of roasted almonds, studying finance. She knew so much about food, and Isaac had lapped this up; she'd taught him *cava* and *manchego* and *gnocchi* and *prix fixe*, and the differences in glassware. Brooke, a gymnast, whose muscled body had been painfully hard against his, had helped him figure out how to dress himself, had even taught him how to tie a tie. The one not-sorority girl, Carrie, waited tables at the Crown and Anchor and was unbeatable at foosball. All of these possibilities, plus a million more, and not one of them was Boyd. But Boyd was Boyd, wanting out of life what she wanted, and he would not impose upon this Boyd-ness because in twenty years she would hate him for the imposition. Nor could he resign himself to a life of sameness in the Hill Country: the same grass, the same people, the same Dollar General and H-E-B and Whataburger and Walmart. He loved it here—he truly did—but he wanted to see what else there was in the world.

Things You Would Know If You Grew Up Around Here

*There's More Gold in the Ground in San Saba County
Than There Is in Circulation in the World*

Another thing the old-timers will tell you. Stories? Maybe, but good ones. And there's evidence, too. It's not just as if they made it up out of whole cloth. The *San Saba News* reported on that capitalist out of Mexico, the miner Edward Fitzgerald, who in 1887 showed up to Hoover's Valley, went straight to Mr. Rufe Hoover, and offered him ten thousand dollars, take it or leave it, for a specific 640 acres, with what he suspected was two miles of inexhaustible fissure veins of rich gold and silver both. Then, in 1899, a Dr. Kelso dug in the yard of John Haas of Bowser Country in search of the six million dollars of gold that Maximilian buried in the Hill Country when he invaded Mexico in the nineteenth century. Dr. Kelso found a map in Mexico, dug up poor Mr. Haas's yard, and found a boat, a coffin, a tray, and three hearts built of masonry. This is what the San Saba paper said: "three hearts built of masonry." In 1901, Kelso disappeared, leaving only a hole. From the *San Saba News*, July 19, 1901: "And this hole is no little thing either; it is 130 feet long, 70 feet wide and on an average about 12 feet deep."

Then, in Detroit, Michigan, in the *News Tribune*, October 4, 1901, news about a different find: "The buried treasure of the ruins of San Saba, Tex., for which Texans have been seeking for more than a century, has been found and some of it carried away by a small party of Mexicans." This was the first time—at least that I know of—that Pedro Yorba was named, and we only have a partial story of that one ingot, and what happened, and how those men died under the wall at Fort Bowie. How, under attack, they fled and threw the treasure into a deep well. One hundred feet deep, the single eyewitness said. Nobody would ever find it, and it would remain in the ground for eternity.

May 22

In the morning, Boyd made coffee before Isaac was even awake, using his camp stove and her cast-iron percolator. It was that hour when the rising sun drives the wind before it, and mist rose off the lake, too low for the wind to catch it. The coffee steamed in her flecked porcelain cup; she blew on it and sipped gingerly.

Still before Isaac woke, she took her sluice pan to the water's edge and scooped gravel, shucking her shoes and standing in the cool water. She squatted on her heels, though she wouldn't be able to maintain this position all day, and stroked the gravel with her right palm, then tipped the edge of the pan into the water and began the stratification: swirl, shake, swirl, shake. Before long, Isaac joined her. No need to say a thing—a quick nod and a smile was enough. Shake, swirl, then she lightly washed the top layer of dirt back into the lake.

She had started earlier so she reached the black sand more quickly. He glanced over at her pan, interested to see what she had, though it was still too early. "Boyd," he said when she caught the black sand in the dents at the edge of the pan. "Things come to you so easily."

It wasn't true. She just didn't do the things that didn't come to her. She was not, for example, much interested in sports or cooking or art. But here with the sluice pan, she was better than him, and she'd pull more out in half the time. Isaac was patient, however, and that's how he paid his tuition bill. Boyd didn't mess with the black sand, the sand where the iron rested. But Isaac, by the end of the summer, would spend the evenings with mortar and pestle, grinding this sand, then pulling it out with a magnet, leaving the tiniest gold, the micron gold, behind. Boyd's interest would, by then, have moved on.

She fanned the last bit of sand in the pan and saw the tiny nugget, the size of a peppercorn. She palmed it, a quick thrill tightening her throat, and Isaac nodded his approval of her. His nod made her both inordinately pleased and sharply irritable.

They heard the engine and the gravel popping underneath the tires; Boyd's mom and Carla were there to pick up the truck. When the car stopped and Lucy Maud got out, she looked pointedly at the stack of crushed beer cans. Boyd reluctantly left the water, dripping as she went.

"They're predicting rain," Lucy Maud said, looking up at the sky as if she were expecting a thunderbolt right then. The sky was a flat blue, the light both muted and sharp. "Boyd, we have the wedding tomorrow."

Boyd, crouched over the camp stove, nodded. "I'll be there in plenty of time." The hearts of the coals glowed, heating her shins and forearms.

"No."

Boyd looked up.

"I mean," Lucy Maud clarified, "I think you should spend the night at home tonight. You should go to the rehearsal dinner."

"Yeah, okay."

"I watered your garden last night. Your pole beans are coming in nice, running right up those stakes."

Boyd was annoyed; she'd been planning on watering the garden later that morning. You didn't water in the afternoon here; experienced gardeners said you'd burn the plant in the afternoon sun, but Boyd knew for sure that a plant left wet overnight would attract slugs. She felt a sense of property over her garden; somehow her mother watering it diffused Boyd's efforts, made it less hers. "Thanks," she said.

"Some rain will fill that barrel of yours, you think?"

"Half an inch is supposed to fill the whole drum."

Carla, whose barrel it had originally been, shifted, and Boyd wondered if she wanted her barrel back, if she was mad that Boyd had found it and kept it without asking permission. Boyd knew the soap business was not as good as it had been.

Isaac finally spoke. "Might come up in a bit with Boyd and charge my phone."

Lucy Maud brightened. "I'll make y'all some lunch."

Boyd had planned a day sluicing, especially if she was going to miss tomorrow for her granddad's wedding. "Bring me some back, will you?"

Lucy Maud said, "You can't come for lunch?"

"I'll be home for the rehearsal dinner. I'd like to hang out down here as long as possible if I'm spending the night at the house." Boyd's hair smelled like a campfire, and she was reluctant to wash it.

Lucy Maud said, "They're predicting maybe five inches. Y'all might want to pack everything up for the weekend, come back down on Monday. The Memorial Day floods are always the worst. It was a Memorial Day flood that broke the banks of Shoal Creek. Your dad and I were in Austin when that happened, and it was something to see."

"I said I was spending the night. This lake's so empty it'd take an ocean to flood it." Even the ground on which they were standing, covered as it was in rocks, shells, and gravel, revealed the drought: waves of silt crusted where the water had last stood, cracks in the earth, the space between the cracks concave as a bowl, meant to hold water.

"That's when the worst floods happen."

Boyd could feel her mother's concern, see it in the way she shifted from foot to foot. A flood seemed so unlikely at the moment, with the world as dry as it was. "I'll spend the night at the house tonight," she repeated.

Lucy Maud let it go.

Carla spoke up. "You got a cup of coffee to spare?"

Boyd poured coffee from the percolator into Isaac's mug and handed it to Carla, who cupped it with both hands. She was wearing a knit cap she'd made herself, and gloves with no fingertips. It was already seventy-five degrees.

"I'll come eat," Isaac volunteered, grinning at Lucy Maud as if she had really meant to ask him. "I'm not in a hurry to stay down here. I've got all summer."

Lucy Maud looked at him. "Yeah, I figured you'd be there." Boyd knew her mother was wary of Isaac whenever he came back, wary of what would happen to Boyd when he left again.

They stood for a minute, silent, listening to the mockingbirds and the jays and the sound of the water barely lapping the shore. The morning smelled newer than the night had, fresher, and the scent of coffee added to that impression. Isaac got a camp chair for Carla, and she sat, crossing her legs at the knees and swinging her foot, which was clad in a hand-knit sock. With each movement, she shed a scent of patchouli and sandalwood.

Inside Isaac's tent, a phone rang. He fetched it and answered, then mouthed to Boyd, *My dad*. "Uh-huh," Isaac said, tucking the phone between chin and shoulder and looking out over the lake. "You were listening to the radio?"

It seemed a normal conversation, but they all eavesdropped. They could hear the sound of Ruben King's voice but couldn't make out what he was saying. Isaac nodded as if his father could see him. "How do you know it was him?" Isaac said when his father took a breath, and then: "Dad, you realize this is crazy." Isaac shook his head at Boyd, dismayed by whatever Ruben was saying, but Isaac was smiling, so it couldn't be that bad. "Yeah, all right. I'll be there in an hour." Isaac hung up.

They all looked at him.

"I won't be going to the rehearsal dinner tonight."

"I didn't think you were anyway," Boyd said.

"Free food at Dahlia's?" Lucy Maud asked. "I thought for sure you would make it."

"My dad wants me to come home for the day, help with some stuff in the yard."

"Okay." Lucy Maud didn't seem that interested, but Boyd could tell Isaac wasn't telling the truth, or at least not all of the truth. He wasn't as open to her as other people were, but she could still tell.

"Can you give me a ride back up to your house?" he asked Carla.

When she nodded and stood to go, Boyd said, "Isaac, can you help me with something real quick?"

She grabbed the tarp so she could string it up and walked twenty yards to a copse of pin oak. Isaac reached for it, and she unfurled the blue square, shaking it free in the wind like the parachute she used to play with on the good days in elementary PE. "Help me with this." She handed him a length of twine and a pocketknife. "What did your dad really want?"

He shook his head, holding the end of the burlap twine in his teeth while he unrolled it with one hand and opened his pocketknife with the other. "He's crazy, you know. They all get crazy if they live out here too long by themselves." Isaac spoke around the twine, out of the corner of his mouth.

"How so?" She held the tarp and he slid the twine through the grommet.

"That gold. You know, we were just talking about it last night, and I hadn't heard anything about it in years."

"He think he found something?"

"No." Isaac twisted his mouth in disappointment. "He was listening to the radio. He thinks someone else found the gold from Mexico." Isaac paused, reaching up and wrapping the other end of the twine around a branch. "He thinks he knows who it is."

"What?" She spread the tarp, bringing another corner to another branch.

"He's so crazy, Boyd. We all are. Thinking this is *The Goonies* or something, like there's an actual treasure out there. There isn't."

"I know." Boyd looked back to her mother and Carla, both watching them, her mother poking the fire as if she owned it, the same way she'd watered Boyd's garden. "What'd he say?"

Isaac leaned his head far back, looking up at the sky. "He said he was listening to the radio, that call-in show out of San Saba, you know?" He had stubble dotted over his jaw, a new development this summer.

She knew: pecan futures and river depths and what kind of fish were biting where and with what lures, and drought, drought, drought like the end-time.

"Well, somebody called in and asked, 'If I found something on my property, does it belong to me?' And the host said, 'Now, it depends on what it is.' And the caller said something about something that would make him rich. The host said, 'Now, what would that be?' And the caller hung up." Isaac brought his head back up, looked down at the twine and the knife in his hands and cut another length.

"So?"

"Exactly. Some dude calls in to a radio show and says literally nothing, and my dad is ready to track him down because it sounds like the man down the road."

"You're not helping him in the yard, are you?"

"Of course not. We're driving up to see this guy, and then who knows what. 'Did you find Maximilian's gold and then call in to a radio show?' The guy's going to call the cops."

"Unless he really found something."

Isaac looked at her, grimacing in disbelief. "If he found something, Boyd, he's going to shoot us for trespassers." Isaac jerked the twine tight, taking all of the slack out of the tarp. It was about a foot over Boyd's head and provided a good fifteen square feet of shade. "I don't have time for this shit." When he reached up to cut the last bit of twine free from the roll, he sliced his thumb with the pocketknife. "Goddamnit." He stuck his thumb in his mouth, then pulled it free, examining. The cut was deep, the blood welling up from its core. He stuck a fingernail in and pried it open, and for a second Boyd could see bulbs of yellow fat. "Well, that's fucking great." He looked at her as if it were her fault. "There's nothing to find and I'm losing a day of panning. You know how much I got to pull out this summer to pay my tuition bill?" He stalked back to the fire, tossed the now-closed pocketknife on his camp chair, and grabbed a T-shirt out of his tent, which he wrapped around his thumb. It was far too big of a bandage, but Boyd could see the scarlet blooming through the white fabric.

Lucy Maud, who'd been watching the whole thing, though Boyd could tell that she hadn't heard a bit of it, said, "You're going to need to go to a doctor, get that sewn up."

"If there's time, maybe." He took a deep breath, got control of himself. "I'll probably go as soon as I get out to my dad's."

Carla got the hint and struggled to rise from the camp chair. She set the coffee mug in the dirt beside her. Lucy Maud said to Boyd, "See you after a while."

Boyd nodded, squinting into the sun, which was beginning to burn off the haze. Before Isaac got in the bed of the truck to get a ride back to his car, he turned once more toward her. She considered him for a minute, how much he'd changed: legs too long for his body, stomach and chest somehow packed more full of flesh than they'd once been, a restlessness visible in the set of his lips, in the way he ran idle fingers through hair that was just a bit too long, jeans half tucked into Carhartt boots. If she were only just meeting him, if she hadn't known him all these years, would she still feel this way about him, this compulsion almost?

Isaac, as if reading her mind this time, came and planted that one last kiss on her forehead, more brotherly than anything else. Then he hitched up one of those too-long legs, climbed into the back of the pickup truck, and they were gone, dust hanging in the space where they had been.

Boyd slung the rest of Carla's coffee out over the gravel and sat down to drink the little she had left. But it was cold, and the coals had already died out. The morning was gone.

Things You Would Know If You Grew Up Around Here

There Are Things Buried in the Lake

There are no natural lakes in Texas. None. Well, there's one, Caddo Lake, way out in East Texas, but that lake's naturalness is disputed, or maybe it's more of a bayou. By and large, lakes are a glacial phenomenon, and Texas has never been known for her glaciers.

In Texas, lakes are dammed river valleys. People used to live in those river valleys. This means that when you swim in a lake in Texas, you're swimming over the remnants of someone's life. Houses. Churches. Schools. Windmills. Wood doesn't deteriorate quickly in water, so these things will stand for ages. When dams were built by the Tennessee Valley Authority, the government moved cemeteries, but not here in Texas. But does it matter that these cemeteries weren't moved? This ground is full of the people who came before. Just last year, when Cottonwood Shores was building a public boat ramp, they uncovered a grave more than two thousand years old.

I guess what I'm trying to say is we were never the first.

After Carla drove Isaac back to her house to get his car, she wasn't ready to leave Lucy Maud's house. Carla thrived on solitude, but now, something was different. She'd spent so much time alone that company had started to be a novelty again. And something about Lucy Maud entertained Carla and made her feel at home all at the same time.

Lucy Maud was estranged from her husband, and Carla knew that Kevin was having an affair. The other woman was younger, one of his students at the university, but that was all Carla knew. It wasn't one of Lucy Maud's favorite subjects.

What was one of Lucy Maud's favorite subjects was her father's wedding, and how he was letting her plan it. Lucy Maud's father, Homer, was getting married to his longtime girlfriend, Sylvia, and Lucy Maud was thinking she'd be good at being a wedding planner, and her father's wedding was as good a time as any to get some practice. The rehearsal dinner was that evening, and Lucy Maud was a bundle of nerves.

"They didn't even want a rehearsal dinner," she told Carla as Lucy Maud swept the kitchen. "Can you imagine? They didn't even want to rehearse. They wanted to go to the courthouse and get it over with, but after all that they've been through? They've known each other for nearly fifty years. I got them a minister, and they're having a real wedding." Lucy Maud knelt to hold the dustpan and swept the pile in. "And when you have a real wedding, you have to rehearse. What if something were to go wrong?"

Carla nodded, sitting on one of the barstools at the marble countertop, feet dangling, just listening to the sound of Lucy Maud's voice. It was heavenly, the kind of thing that you didn't have to pay too much attention to, a sort of unimportant background noise, but you couldn't help it anyway. "Right?" Carla said, because she sensed a lull in the monologue and wanted to hear more.

"I mean, not that it's a catastrophe if somebody says something at the wrong time, and there are only going to be about thirty people there, but think about it on my end. Who would recommend me as a wedding planner if my only prior experience is one where somebody messed up?"

This was an excellent point, Carla thought, then she realized that in another life, her Austin life, Carla would have rolled her eyes at the unimportant concerns of a woman such as Lucy Maud. But here—here, something was different. Out here, Carla understood people better somehow, had more pity or something.

"I need to go to the grocery store." Lucy Maud put the broom away and took off her apron. "Want to go?"

They got in Lucy Maud's car and headed down River Road, back out to the main highway, on their way into Marble Falls. Despite the drought, the wildflowers were high on the roadsides, bluebonnets giving way to the verbena and purple nightshade of late spring. The light was strange, Carla noticed, and then Lucy Maud pulled over to the side of the road.

"Look at that," she said, resting one hand on Carla's headrest and twisting her body so she could see out the back. "I could see it in the rearview, but, man."

Carla, too, turned to look, though she had to peer over Lucy Maud's forearm. The sky, black like dark water, as if night were fresh on their heels and running them down. Carla shuddered, thinking no car was fast enough, thinking the only safe place was home.

Without saying anything else, Lucy Maud turned the car around and headed back. The rain would soon start, and they could see the storm on the horizon, but right now the world was golden, and the air from a dream. Whatever Lucy Maud had needed to get from the store was forgotten, and they were the only car on the road. But it didn't rain yet.

Boyd took her field guides with her because what else was she going to do? Her mother was planning the whole thing, wedding included, for Boyd's grandfather and his longtime sweetheart, Sylvia, and Lucy Maud, frankly, was a mess. The details were too many for her, and she was feeling pulled in all directions, and she didn't have a good handle on any of it. She was nervous, apt to bite back if spoken to, so Boyd knew to lie low. And when Boyd's father, Kevin, arrived at the restaurant, Lucy Maud's face went pale except for two crimson circles high on the cheekbones, and Lucy Maud did her best to ignore the man who was still technically her husband but who hadn't *actually* been in almost a year. Lucy Maud had made the mistake over one painfully hopeful weekend that Kevin had spent out at the lake of asking him to be her father's best man.

When they'd arrived at the restaurant, Lucy Maud's twin sister had already been there and had been for some time, drinking wine and decorating. Boyd was surprised by this; Lou wasn't one to drink. In fact, every morning Lou attended an AA meeting down at the community center, but not because she was an alcoholic. Lou was lonely. At forty-seven, she had never married and was still living with Boyd's great-great-aunt Fern, and so every morning that Lou could, she headed down to the meeting and said that she was there for support, though nobody needed it. Truthfully, Lou never touched the stuff, which was why Boyd was surprised to see her putting them back, swaying on her feet as she decorated, draping white plastic over tables and strewing white beads over the plastic. When she finished, she went out to the patio, where a bluegrass band was playing, and she took off her shoes and stomped her feet as if she'd seen one too many mountain movies. Boyd was fascinated by this display and came to stand against a post, watching, trying to understand. Lou always had a vulnerability, but somehow it was now more exposed, a wound, open and weeping, and Boyd caught from Lou a ragged edge, a sense of something submerged, a certain gasping for breath. Boyd pitied her and stood close, ready to go to her aunt if Lou should suddenly realize that people were watching her in a not-kind way. Boyd couldn't bear for Aunt Lou to feel that people were laughing at her. After a moment, Boyd realized that the brown hair of the fiddle player was floating on the wind, and it had been a long time since Boyd had known an afternoon wind. She looked up at the sky, surprised by the black on the horizon.

When Lou went back inside, Boyd followed, and Boyd's grandfather arrived, along with his bride-to-be, Sylvia, and they both looked as if they didn't know where they were supposed to be. Sylvia wore a green wrap dress and Boyd's grandfather a bolo tie, and Boyd could feel their unease. "We didn't ask for this," Sylvia whispered to Boyd's grandfather, Homer. "Who is paying for this?"

Boyd saw Sylvia's eyebrows rise even higher when the group was seated and, after the salad, rib eyes were served, eight giant slabs of beef going around the table, an absolute fortune's worth of dead cow, and Sylvia said, "We could have just had a barbecue." Meanwhile, Lucy Maud's eyes had taken on a fearsome sheen, and she moved around Dahlia's banquet room as if animated by puppet strings, redraping Lou's tablecloths and pushing in chairs. "Sit down and eat your food," Lou told her, and Boyd grimaced. Lucy Maud did not like to be bossed around by her twin sister.

After everyone was well filled with steak, it looked, for a moment, as if there would be calm for a little while, as if everybody had settled in and could just enjoy one another's company. Sylvia—now in her late sixties and still stylish and trim, with big Sophia Loren glasses—leaned against Homer, which intrigued Boyd, because they'd been dating since the early seventies.

The history was too complicated sometimes, and it seemed crazy to Boyd that all of that drama had resulted in this calm rehearsal dinner decades later. Karen was gone and her husband was gone, and only Sylvia and Homer remained. At the end of the table, Boyd's great-great-aunt Fern, tiny and folded into herself, smiled privately, tapping her lip with an index finger, remembering something that Boyd could not read. Boyd's father, Kevin, had his phone out, checking baseball scores. Lou had a finger hooked into her chardonnay, fishing out what looked like a piece of cork, one eye narrowed so that she could see better. The pastor was there from the Lutheran church, and Boyd knew he was there only because her mother had insisted. Homer and Sylvia had wanted to go to the justice of the peace.

Boyd got out her bird guide, remembering a black-and-blue jay she'd seen on the lake that morning. It was, for the moment, quiet and pleasant, and she wished that Isaac had come. That afternoon, she'd felt a pain in her left thumb and she'd thought of him then and thought again of him now. He would have loved that rib eye, oozing blood and marbled with fat.

But that morning Isaac had headed back toward San Saba. He'd ridden up the hill with Carla and then gotten in his Corolla and gone home, going the long way, going over the low-water crossing by Cottonwood Shores. No other houses were this way until the crossing, and then came a whole neighborhood, which had gone up in nine months in the early eighties. Not many houses were the other way, either, the way with the bridge. A land developer owned much of that scrubland, waiting for the time when it would be worth enough to build on. Isaac knew that it was a weird way for Boyd's mother to live, thinking that she had this whole side of the lake practically to herself, but knowing that one day, they'd be squeezing in houses over here, too.

No water was in the low-water crossing, and though the depth gauge at the side of the road stated that the water could rise to six feet, Isaac could not imagine that amount of water covering this crossing. His car eased up the other side, and then two right turns and he was on the main highway, headed toward home, and running dangerously low on gas. But he was in a hurry, and he passed the last station without stopping, knowing he had enough to come back this way once he'd reached his father and found out what was going on, and what his father's plan was.

But his father wasn't home when Isaac got there. He pulled into the yard and killed the engine, the heat of the day just now waxing, warming the car. His father's Subaru wasn't in the yard, and the front door was shut, which meant nobody was home. This time of year, it was too hot to close doors and windows, and usually Isaac's father had the door wide open but the screen door shut and a box fan propped up right inside.

He called his dad's cell phone and heard it ring inside the house. Isaac went in, his phone still at his ear, following the sound of his father's. He found it in the living room, on the table by the brown velour easy chair, next to a full ashtray. Balanced on the edge of the ashtray was the burnt end of his dad's roach, pinched tight by a clip. Isaac picked up his father's phone and looked at it for a minute before setting it down again.

He wandered into the kitchen, where his father's breakfast dishes sat on the table next to an open issue of *Omni* magazine. The magazine's pages were well-worn; it had been defunct for decades, but his dad kept all of the issues he'd ever received, despite the information in them being nearly obsolete. It didn't matter, though, to Ruben King; a thing's age was a marker of value, too. Ruben King had eaten eggs and chorizo for breakfast; a smear of chile remained on the plate. Isaac picked up the plate and put it on the counter next to the sink. The wood-look laminate of the countertop was buckling, and Isaac shook his head. Ruben's careless attitude toward house-keeping had contributed to his parents' divorce, and Isaac's mom was now in California. It was not likely that Isaac's mom's breakfast dishes were still on the counter.

Isaac didn't know what to do. He looked down at his thumb, which had only recently stopped bleeding. The wound hung open, thick and fleshy, almost labial. He sniffed; it smelled like rust. His father had said he'd known the voice on the radio, that it had been a neighbor, but Isaac didn't know which one. Not that they had that many neighbors out here. Nobody wanted to live out here in the mesquite and the limestone dust, far from the water. Allen Potivar lived up the road, but he was on oxygen these days, and Isaac didn't imagine that he did much tramping around the country. John and Roger, down the road in the other direction, spent most of their time in Austin, but Isaac guessed that one or the other of them could be out here for the long weekend. The other neighbors were farther away, and Isaac didn't know how well his father knew them. It'd be different if Isaac had gotten gas, if he had enough to drive around the countryside hunting Ruben's Subaru. But Isaac hadn't, and his father had told him to meet him at home, so Isaac decided to wait.

And after a few minutes of waiting, sitting in his dad's easy chair, smoking the rest of his dad's joint, Isaac decided he should probably head to a doctor. But the same concerns stopped him: his dad's whereabouts, the fuel gauge resting on *E*. So he decided to sew up the wound himself and brought the first aid kit to the kitchen table.

The first aid kit was not well-kept. It had an Ace bandage, some ancient Pepto-Bismol pills in plastic packaging, three Band-Aids decorated with Peanuts characters, two sealed alcohol wipes, and a roll of surgical tape. He took the tape and the Band-Aids and left the kit on the kitchen table. Flies circled his father's breakfast plate on the counter. Isaac had been gone a year, Isaac's mother, Melissa, nearly a decade, and everything seemed coated in grime.

He needed a needle and had no idea where to find one. He dug through the drawers of his dad's desk and found playing cards, drafting pencils, a slide rule. A sliver of geode, purple shards dusty. In one drawer was a mass of bread-wrapper ties, and Isaac didn't know what his dad was saving those for. No needle, no thread.

Next his father's medicine cabinet: an orange prescription bottle of hydrocodone, a container of Tums, calamine lotion. The drawer next to the bathroom sink: tweezers, toenail clippers, and finally, a travel sewing kit. Isaac poured rubbing alcohol over the gash in his thumb, wincing and blowing on the wound, then he carried the sewing kit back to his dad's chair.

He threaded the needle with black thread, tied a knot at the end. This last part was tricky because the thread was so flimsy and his left thumb so tender. He pinched the wound shut with the thumb and index finger of his right hand, having to set down the needle. How was he going to do this when he only had one free hand? He could wrap it up in surgical tape, he guessed, but no. He'd decided he was going to sew it shut, so here he was, needle threaded, mind steeled against the pain he imagined was coming, and he was going to do it.

He tried counterpressure, pressing his left thumb into the table, and still the wound gaped. He flattened his thumb between his knees, but the angle was too awkward; he couldn't sew the wound shut like this. Finally he put his left thumb in his mouth, squeezing the end of the wound shut with his teeth, the other end of the wound clear of his mouth. Then he closed his eyes and shoved the needle through.

Insane the amount of pain. He gasped, losing his tight grasp on the wound. How could a needle feel like this, as if he were pushing fire into his skin? The needle was a sliver, the wound hardly threatening or serious, but he felt the needle up his arm, in his armpit, in the socket of his shoulder. He closed his teeth again, bringing the thread around for another pass, and tasted a thin stream of blood draining through his teeth onto his tongue. Another pass, this time slower, and it was worse. He hesitated, letting go of his tight hold on the needle, and he pushed it through with the heel of his hand. Another sickening pain, and the needle dangled on its thread from his thumb. He didn't know if he could do another stitch.

But he did and then he was done, and then the pain subsided when the needle was clear. He tied the thread as best he could with teeth and right hand, then went into the bathroom and poured alcohol over his thumb again. Now a dull throb was centered in his bone, and he opened the bottle of hydrocodone and chewed two, the bitter taste a comfort on his tongue.

He went in the kitchen and opened a Shiner, taking the beer back to his father's easy chair, and settled down to wait for his father. Across the county, Boyd had been getting ready for her grandfather's rehearsal dinner. When he finished the first beer, he drank another, then he fell asleep, his head and heart slowed by the medication. He would sleep through this night, exhausted, and almost through the next. Eight hours from this moment in the chair, when his father called, his cell phone would ring in the dim house, and Isaac would not wake up.

Things You Would Know If You Grew Up Around Here

The Gold Isn't the Only Thing People Want

But this story is not a treasure hunt. Not really. Something about the gold fascinates, doesn't it? Something about being buried and recovered. That's why all of those people are looking for that art dealer's treasure in the Rockies, why people still get excited if we find a bag of money that might once, briefly, have belonged to D. B. Cooper, that hijacker who parachuted away with hundreds of thousands of dollars.

But other things are here, a latent richness of earth and water, and in Texas, we've believed ever since oil geysered out of Spindletop in 1901 that our fortunes are to be made underground. To be hauled out of the earth, drilled, fracked, mined. Did you know that Llano County contains every naturally occurring element known to man? Even if you didn't, some people do. It's some people's job to know these things, to reduce the earth to resources, to know where to find them. The earth subdivided into parts, and some of those parts are worth a lot of money. When the dam was built, when the lake was filled, we buried two of the most valuable hills in the country, hills full of uranium. And still, when the lake falls enough, people come out to fetch it.

May 23

6:00 P.M.

It started to rain during the ceremony.

Boyd had still not heard from Isaac. She'd called him when she'd returned to her mother's house, protective of Lucy Maud, setting up for bed in her own bedroom instead of heading down to her campsite. He didn't answer—his phone ringing eight, nine times—and she wondered if he'd gone somewhere with his father, if Ruben King had tracked down the neighbor. She wondered if the neighbor had been the one to call in to the radio show.

That morning had dawned humid and thick, the sky the color of unbleached cotton, the air dense enough to pull legs and arms into torpor. She and her mother had headed over to Aunt Fern's late morning, on the far side of the lake. Boyd had gone inside, sat down at the kitchen table, and put her forehead on the cool oak surface. Lou, who seemed not to be hungover, came to her and put her hand on Boyd's shoulder blade. Boyd knew Lou felt sorry for her, felt that Boyd didn't have any kind of childhood, felt that Lucy Maud was a tough mother and that Kevin was an absent father. Boyd raised her head with a jerk, looked through the kitchen window off into the distance, blinking. She got up without saying a word and went to the living room for her backpack full of field guides. When she left the house and walked across the yard, out toward the lake, she could feel Lou watching her through the window.

After a while, though, they came and got her to help set up for the wedding. They worked in the heat, in the low nineties, for close to an hour, arranging the chairs and wrapping them in tulle. Boyd's mother had hot-glued hundreds of white silk flowers to the gazebo, and a wasp's nest was tucked into the eave.

Later that afternoon, with the wedding party assembled in the gazebo, the wind picked up and raindrops fell, heavy and fat, splatting on the sidewalk from the porch to the driveway. The sky was yellow, bruised and golden, and the heaviest rain held off for a minute.

The preacher felt the urgency and rushed them through the ceremony. Boyd stood with the tiny pillow, her face blank when the preacher asked for the ring. The bride's dress blew against Boyd's grandfather's suit pants, pasting itself, and Homer took Sylvia's hand, uncomfortable with the big to-do. The wasps slumbered in their nest, and down the little hill, the lake's surface was gray. A lily blew from Sylvia's bouquet, and Boyd chased it. Sylvia's hand went to her head to secure the tiny veil pinned there, and the wind knocked over a chair.

Soon, the white silk flowers came loose and blew away, at first one by one, but then in concert. When the preacher pronounced the couple man and wife, the flowers circled and danced in the air around them, and the sky roared with the first of the thunder. Boyd breathed the smell of rain on the leading edge of air, watched those flowers floating.

"Everybody inside," Lucy Maud shouted. "Bring your chairs!" Beside Lucy Maud, Boyd's father carried four chairs, two in each arm.

Inside, Kevin tapped the keg of Lone Star. Aunt Lou took a sip from a red plastic cup, then handed it to Boyd. An elderly couple held hands on the sofa, and Aunt Fern went to them, talking quietly, and their faces revealed their confusion. Aunt Fern these days was still earnest and kind, but she no longer made any sense. Fern recognized their confusion, however, and said instead, loud enough for Boyd to hear, "But wasn't the wedding pretty, all those flowers flying around?"

The phones of the elderly couple chirped, one after the other, and the man pulled his phone out. "Tornado warning," he said as phones around the party buzzed and vibrated. The woman said, "Is that the one where there's really a tornado? Or is that a watch?"

"Turn on the TV," Boyd's dad said, and Boyd was stunned when he wrapped his arm around the waist of Lucy Maud, who was drinking Asti Spumante out of a plastic flute and grinning. Boyd knew her dad was genuine, but she also knew that this reconciliation would be short-lived. Her heart hurt for her mother. Somebody handed him the remote and they flipped through the channels, every local station giving a weather report.

A man Boyd didn't know whistled, good and drunk. "That's right across the lake from here." She could feel what they were thinking: they were not scared and wanted the storm to come closer. The man said, "Let's go see if we can't see it."

They stood on the porch, the group of them, and they could see nothing in the sky because of the dark cloud cover. The wind had stripped the gazebo of its ornaments, and everywhere the loose, light leaves of summer strafed the air. The chairs had been folded and propped on the porch, but white bits of plastic had caught in the trees, and that plastic would line birds' nests for months. The wind pulled at her, and she wanted to go wherever it wanted her to. They all felt that way.

"Shhhh," Lucy Maud said. "Everybody shut up. Y'all hear that?" It took a while to get everybody to be quiet, a full minute of shushing and elbowing, and when the group was silent, nobody could hear anything.

"What?" a woman asked, head cocked to hear better.

"You hear that roar, that freight-train roar?"

Everybody was silent again, nobody hearing what Lucy Maud referred to.

"Y'all don't hear that?" Lucy Maud regarded them and then heard something different. "Get in the storm cellar!"

Faces turned to Fern, and she pointed to the back of the house. Every one of them walked off the porch and into the rain, keeping close to the shelter of the structure, still listening, still hearing nothing. Lucy Maud held the door up and open, and they all filed downstairs, still clutching drinks or napkins. The older folks needed extra help on the stairs, so Boyd got out of the way and found a seat on the dirt floor, in the corner of the basement. When Lucy Maud climbed in last and shut the door, the light winked out with it, and for a few seconds they were all in total darkness, until Sylvia pulled the string on the bare lightbulb and once again they could see.

"I never did hear what you were talking about," Homer said, looking awkward in his suit in the swaying yellow light.

Boyd's dad checked his phone, as did the drunk man. "Oh, there's something all right," said Kevin, but the other man looked skeptical: "That ain't anywhere around here, though."

The rain came harder and faster and Lucy Maud said, "Just everybody make themselves comfortable. It'll all be over soon." To Lou, she whispered, "I'm not losing anybody on my first wedding." Lou shrugged; Boyd knew it didn't bother her to be in the storm cellar.

All told, they were down there for less than half an hour, even though Lucy Maud kept them in the cellar far longer than she needed to because, in the excitement of the storm, Kevin had held her hand. When she did release them, they emerged into hot sunshine and to a humidity that told them the heart of the storm had not passed through here. They did not yet know how close it had been, how it had blown through Lucy Maud's house on the other side of the lake, not five miles as the crow flies. They laughed at each other, at how ridiculous they had been in the basement when there had been a keg to drink upstairs, hiding from nothing but electronic messages from their cell phones. They traded stories of how the weathermen never got anything right, how if the weathermen said that it was going to be a sunny day, they'd better bring an umbrella. The keg was halfway finished when the elderly couple left, and after them two ladies from Abilene, and the drunk man not far behind. Nobody saw Kevin pull Lucy Maud around the corner of the house or saw the way he placed his face in her neck, just breathing. She had pulled him backward by the hair, gently, and her eyes had met his, and the storm meant that their relationship was both more permanent and more temporary than they had ever before realized, a thing they would always return to but that would never again be primary. Behind them, in the house, the remnants of the wedding party: Italian cream cake on clear plastic plates, gold-rimmed napkins crumpled and discarded, cheap champagne left in the wells of plastic champagne flutes, red Solo cups with the rest of the Shiner. Lou and Aunt Fern were unscathed and silly, drunk from beer and on the memory of those flowers swirling around a bride and groom in the last days of their middle age. But they didn't know about that first part of the rain, how bad that storm had been for some people.

Everywhere in the Hill Country, that night the drought broke and the lakes began to fill back in, things were lost. In Hutto, Brushy Creek broke its banks and a mother and daughter were swept away in their Toyota. In Victoria, a man was struck by lightning while sitting under a tree drinking beer out of a can wrapped in a paper sack. The papers reported that one of his eyeballs exploded when the lightning traveled through him, but it was too quick; he had never known. In Wimberley, a vacation house was torn from its foundation as the Blanco River rose from five feet to forty in a few hours. The father was pulled out of the river twelve miles away in San Marcos with a broken sternum and a punctured lung, the mother found much later in a cypress tree. The children were not found for years.

Also that night, Lucy Maud was raw, emotional, and when her husband looked at her, her hand full of his hair, she met that gaze eagerly, even though she knew he would not be her husband for much longer. When he pulled her to him and said that he was too drunk to drive back to Austin that night, she could not help herself; she put off the heartache for a little while longer. He'd been so unhappy with her aging, with the way that her body had not wanted another body, and so she couldn't blame him for leaving. Tonight, however, her body remembered the old ways, and she had not been touched in so long. Boyd was staying at Aunt Fern's, and Lucy Maud and Kevin left separately, because Lucy Maud didn't want anybody else to know.

In the morning, the newlyweds were off to San Saba, sticking to the main highways, unaware of the extent of the storm. Kevin and Lucy Maud were in a hotel room in downtown Marble Falls. Lou, Fern, and Boyd sat on the front porch drinking their coffee and orange juice, Boyd thinking of Isaac, who had missed the wedding. The women were unaware yet that the storm had been what it had been, that to many folks it was pretty much the end of the world. Unaware that it wasn't yet over, that it was coming for them, too. In the sky were the remnants of that early line of storms, clouds the three of them would never again see: lenticular and mammatus, stippled and peaked, like putty, or cake icing, only ever seen when the sky has ripped apart and sewn itself back together.

For the moment, a pause in the rain.

May 24

8:30 A.M.

Isaac woke in his father's easy chair, the air swollen and tumescent, over-filled. His tongue was dry and large in his mouth. When he rubbed his eyes, the lip of his wound caught with a shot of pain, but not the same kind of pain as before. Not heat tunneling down into his bedrock, but the prick of a flu shot. It was early, morning giving way to full day. He did not yet realize that he had lost a day and almost two nights. His arms were quick to lose their stiffness, but his legs were reluctant to move, the bone ache of his thumb now translated bodily, something he could feel in his core even as he stretched and moved.

A glass of water first, then food: the rest of the cylindrical package of chorizo, turned out into his dad's grimy skillet with two eggs over the top. With a curiosity about everything, and yet still a detachment, his eye cast over the contents of his father's fridge. He registered the contents, intending to remind his father about the dangers of margarine, the nutritional worth-lessness of canned biscuits. He pictured his father's heart, oversize in a stringy body, strangled by trans fats. This train of thought had no real emotion, was simply a filing away of information, something to be handled later.

He ate his own fatty breakfast, thinking of Boyd, thinking it was the morning after the rehearsal dinner and that he needed to make sure he had a clean shirt for her grandfather's wedding today. She, too, would likely wear something clean, but that would be the extent of what he could expect from her, style-wise. She would likely not even wear a dress, and he thought that he had never seen her in a dress, and that this might be something he would like. Boyd of the freckled angles, her head perched just forward of her neck, her eternal watching and measurement. She caught things about people, and he did not know how she did this, but when she was with someone, she was so often only a reaction, an eternal observation, evaluation, and its subsequent response. He thought she was this way even with him but knew of no way to prove it. In the life he wanted for himself, his wife would have occasion to wear a dress. This was important to him.

He picked up his phone, intending to check his email, but the internet was out and his phone would not connect. A voice mail from his father, somehow retrievable even with the loss of network:

Hey, Isaac, where are you? I thought you might be at the house by now. I had to run when Allen Potivar came by, if you can believe it. You already took so long. Meet me here. Or call me at this number, at Allen Potivar's. Yeah. Better to call first.

Isaac was more surprised by this message than he had been about the radio show. His father, in general not one to hate at all, hated Allen Potivar, ever since Allen's grandkid had failed Texas history in middle school and Allen had wanted to actually fight his father, to meet him in the parking lot after school as if they had been the seventh graders. His father thought people such as Allen Potivar were *what is wrong with the world*. People such as Allen Potivar *had no personal responsibility*. And though Ruben King never spoke of it, Isaac disliked the look of Allen's house down by the dry creek, stucco painted to seem like adobe, with a defunct satellite dish in the front yard. And now he'd have to go there, because Ruben's phone was here, and Isaac couldn't call his father.

First, coffee made quickly and orange juice whipped up from a can in the freezer. Isaac's body needed something, but he couldn't figure out what. Now in his Corolla with both drinks in cup holders, the fuel light came on as soon as he started the car. He headed the short way to Allen Potivar's: back down the long road on this side of the hill, then around and up. Another way was down the main road past the Texaco station, where an ancient bloodhound sprawled on the painted concrete underneath the awning, taking in the coolness of the stone, but Isaac didn't go that way because it was more than twice as far.

The things he saw as he drove surprised him: mesquite trees upended and on their sides, gouges in the white earth, animals—deer, dogs, goats, even a wild boar—standing in the road as if they did not even hear him driving through. In an old live oak, a girl's yellow princess dress, caught on a branch and twisting in the wind as if being led in a monstrously quick waltz. The light had a quality he could not name; the world was overly bright, yet, when he turned to look at any one thing, the thing appeared too dim to examine. Birds in the sky, headed south, and he thought, *Fleeing*. Too high to tell what they were, but Boyd would know. Nobody was on the road, not a soul. A pecan tree partially blocked the way, and he drove around it.

As the Corolla climbed the other side of the hill, he caught every now and again a glimpse of the valley floor: empty, as if no human had ever crossed it, as if he were the first. When Allen Potivar's road gave up being asphalt and became gravel, Isaac knew he was close. There was a sound, but he couldn't place it, so he rolled down his window, thinking something was wrong with his car, but it was coming from outside.

Around a bend, he saw the source of the sound: the water coursing down the hill, the dry creek overflowing. It covered the low-water crossing that led to Allen Potivar's house, and Isaac stopped his car and got out.

He couldn't tell how deep the water was, but he knew he was close to Allen Potivar's house. He climbed on top of his car, shielding his eyes from the yellow glare, and looked down the road on the opposite side. A glint of silver down there, and Isaac was sure the silver was his father's Subaru. So close. A glance back at the river: swift and filthy with the earth it had taken on its journey. He tried to remember where the road was. He thought the water was no more than a foot deep. A glance behind him: such a long way back down the hill, coming back up the other side. His father right there.

So he got in the Corolla and drove slowly forward, inching the car's tires into that moving water. Things from books appeared to him: the nest of water moccasins in *Lonesome Dove*, the part in another book where the narrator said that water moccasins smelled not only like death but also like something that feeds on death.

The car didn't make it all the way in before the front wheels were lifted and taken downstream, and so this was how he ended up: car pointed with the river, as if he had chosen to drive that way instead of across. His hands on the steering wheel, he turned back toward the road but could get no purchase. The smell of earth and water, and a coldness on his feet: water rising, soaking his socks.

Things You Would Know If You Grew Up Around Here

Most Deaths in Storms Are from Flash Floods

In places where there is soil, the soil takes the water up first. Especially in times of drought. The earth then is so parched that it will take on inches and inches of rainfall before the water begins to stand.

Not so in the rocky places. In rocky places, in gulches or washes or wadis, water has nowhere to go but down. Once it reaches the lowest place, and the water is left to stand for a long time, it will sift down, honeycombing the limestone because it is softer than the stone that has already metamorphosed: the granite, the marble. But in the short term, the water flows down and picks up the world as it goes: boulders, trees, dirt, animals. Anything in its way. Within a couple of hours, a flash flood formed like this can reach a height of thirty feet, rising into the air like a three-story building, barreling its way downstream.

Because nobody could get ahold of Lucy Maud, Aunt Lou drove Boyd home once the breakfast dishes were washed up. Aunt Lou tried to get Boyd to stay at Aunt Fern's, but Boyd was convinced that the reason she couldn't get in touch with Isaac was because he had returned to their campsite and he wasn't getting a signal. Aunt Lou told her no, that the campsite was likely rained in, but Boyd knew Isaac would be quick to go inspect it and set things to rights.

Everywhere the signs of devastation, but the things they didn't yet know were worse. In the tornado's path, a car spring wound through a torso, a body facedown on a roof. The low-water crossing leading to her house was gushing, the rain gauge reading five feet, and Aunt Lou sucked her teeth at how fast the water was moving. "Some fool's going to get washed away today," she told Boyd. "But it will be somebody from out of town, somebody who doesn't know better." She turned the car around and headed the other way, the way with the bridge.

When they reached the bridge, Boyd quickly caught her breath of surprise—if she betrayed herself now, if she showed fear, Aunt Lou would take her back to Aunt Fern's to wait for her mother. She didn't want to do that because she wanted to check on Isaac, so when she saw what awaited them, she trapped that breath and pressed her lips together.

On the bridge, an enormous cypress tree was wedged in the railing. The canopy trailed in the water still, but the roots, dripping and brown, went through and over the slats on the bridge. The trunk seemed almost redwood in scale, here, in such a surprising place. It must have been pulled on the storm's current, because no cypress trees were on the lake. They were to be found much farther upriver. Here, where this tree should not have been, the astounding size was even more upsetting: juxtaposed against this massive trunk, the scale of the bridge was all wrong, was for a different size of human and car entirely. And on the bridge, presumably there to deal with the tree, were two army trucks, canvas hoisted from the truck beds by ropes on metal frames. The soldiers who had ridden in those trucks were busily fussing over the problem on the bridge.

Again, Aunt Lou stopped, sucking her teeth. Boyd knew Aunt Lou wasn't sure how to handle this new information, or what her responsibility regarding her niece was. Well, Boyd didn't particularly want to be Aunt Lou's responsibility, so Boyd let go of her held breath and smiled. "Wow," Boyd said innocently. "It must be the Army Corps of Engineers." It wasn't—they both knew it was the National Guard—but the statement allowed both women the freedom to pretend.

Boyd unbuckled her seat belt and got out. Already, a man in desert camouflage was heading in her direction, holding an M16 service rifle as if it was a part of his uniform, which, Boyd guessed, it was. Aunt Lou was right behind her, and together they stood on the bridge to Boyd's house as the wind nearly knocked them over.

"No through traffic," the soldier said, and it sounded rehearsed. Boyd knew he'd said the same sentence to somebody else who had recently passed—or had tried to—this way.

Again, that innocent smile. "Wow," she said, marveling at the tree that lay across nearly the entire width of road. "That was some storm." She cast a look at Aunt Lou, who was examining the soldier, and said, "But we're not through traffic."

"There's another approach to this neighborhood," the soldier told Boyd. "Nobody's coming this way." She saw his hesitation in the way he glanced backward, and she sensed that he didn't feel quite capable of making any major decisions.

Now Aunt Lou spoke up. "The other approach has five feet of rushing water over the road. We have to come through here." Aunt Lou, much like her twin sister, didn't like to be told what to do.

The man drummed his fingers on the black body of the service rifle. "I can't let you drive through here until they clear that tree." Boyd, startled, caught a brief glimpse of something more from the soldier: It wasn't just the tree. The army men were worried about the bridge.

"We can drive around the tree," she said, and the way he twisted his mouth, choosing his next words, confirmed her suspicion.

"Look," the soldier said, and they were attracting attention now, as other men wandered over their direction. "We're evacuating along the Blanco, but we're not yet evacuating here. Even so, we don't recommend that you cross this bridge. You got somewhere else to go?" He was addressing Aunt Lou now.

Boyd turned away from him, addressing the other National Guard members coming their way. "We've got people down there. If I have to walk across this bridge, I will."

"And have more people down there?"

"I'm not leaving my mother," Boyd said, knowing that this wasn't quite the truth. "Or my neighbor. Or my friend."

"Sam," one of the other soldiers said. This man was slightly older, black, with three stripes on his sleeve. "This isn't a hurricane. We're not keeping people out. We're only keeping them off the bridge."

"You can't drive across this bridge, ma'am," the soldier named Sam said, as if Boyd hadn't heard the other man.

To Aunt Lou, the other man said, "How far you got to go?"

Aunt Lou jumped, surprised to be addressed. "Not me." She pointed at Boyd. "Her. She's trying to get home."

The sergeant thought about this for a minute. At last he said, "Sam, why don't you drive this girl on home?" He nodded at Boyd and Aunt Lou, then trotted away to the conversation about the massive cypress. The private, Sam, watched Boyd. She guessed they were about the same age.

"You're not coming, ma'am?"

Aunt Lou, dazed, looked back toward her car. "I can't. I've got to get back to Aunt Fern," she said, as if Sam the soldier knew Aunt Fern. To

Boyd, Aunt Lou said, "Go straight home, now, okay? Call me when you get there."

Squeezing Aunt Lou's elbow, Boyd nodded, then ran to get her stuff from the car. When she returned, Sam led her across the bridge as Aunt Lou waved, and Boyd felt as if she crossed some threshold then: the world as she knew it before, and the world as she was to know it now. This world looked similar, but with subtle differences, and Boyd felt that the new one was governed differently, that it had rules that were just a bit off-kilter. The new world had teeth, and in just a matter of time it would bite her.

They stepped through waves of mud come to rest on the bridge. She knelt and palmed a handful, trying to locate the source, but the earth did not give up this information. Now, on the bridge, she only thought that the mud was silty, like the bottom of a riverbed, and she thought of the great rivers of the earth, the way they flooded regularly before we dammed them, the way they carried this rich silt out into the fields. Here, two National Guardsmen swept the silt from the bridge with straight brooms, service rifles strapped to their backs. In other lives, these men were salesmen: one sold Nissans, the other Dell servers. Both of them felt that what they were doing now—simply sweeping, wearing desert camo—was far more real of a thing than what they did at home: work and wives and, for one of them, a daughter, and domestic routines over and over until the grave. It did a man good, they both thought, to be out here like this, to reconnect to what the world was like, to see what it was capable of.

Indeed, they were all men, except for Boyd, and except for Aunt Lou, whose car was now in reverse, and who waved tentatively as she backed up.

Men with chain saws were shearing branches from the old cypress, the newly opened ends bleeding sap. She saw, suddenly, the cypress by the side of a riverbank, and underneath the cypress, other men: Comanche, the Spanish, the Germans. When her vision was gone, she stepped over the long fingers of the tree, which was older than the lake, an ancient thing now leaving the world. Standing water was on the bridge, and where the tree's roots trailed in this water, the tannins turned the water the color of blood.

Sam told her to wait next to the truck, and he ran back to the sergeant, rifle bouncing in his hands. She saw them talking—*Keys are in the vehicle, We're gonna need more help down here, this thing's cracked straight through, who knows how old it is*—then Sam ran back and motioned for her to get in. She climbed in the truck, tossing her backpack onto the floor, and Sam turned on the engine, leaving the bridge, heading out toward the lake. The white-tailed deer were everywhere, wandering, and they hightailed it when they heard the truck pass. She saw, without exaggeration, a hundred deer in the half mile between the bridge and her house, and she also saw two armadillos, a host of rabbits, dogs set loose and roaming.

She motioned the soldier toward her house and he stopped the truck, looking at her doubtfully. "You sure you want to be out here all by yourself? You probably don't have power. Maybe not even water."

"I'm not all by myself."

He nodded, not believing her exactly. "Yeah, okay." A minute watching her, then: "Listen, let me give you my cell phone number. You get in trouble, you call me, promise?" He fiddled around in the console and pulled out a scrap of paper and a pen. When he handed her his number, she saw the paper was something official, some orders she probably shouldn't be allowed to have.

"I didn't know soldiers could carry phones."

Sam waved his hand in denial, smiling a not-real smile. "We're not soldiers. I study accounting at UTSA and work at H-E-B. This isn't real life. You just call me . . ." He paused.

"Boyd."

He nodded. "Good name. You just call me, Boyd, if you need me."

His hands, she saw, were small and well-kept, his grip on the steering wheel easy. What would it be like to go somewhere with him, to be with someone not Isaac?

He drove away, massive tires popping fallen pecans. She looked for a minute at the phone number in her hand. Then she turned around and went into the house.

Nobody was there and the electricity was indeed off. When she realized Isaac was not inside, a sliver of fear took her, the thought that Isaac might have been at their campsite during the storm. No, he wouldn't have been at the site. But why had he not come to the wedding?

She went back outside, heading toward the water, but the first footprints she saw in the mud led not to the lake but to her garden. She followed, curious.

Her garden seemed not to have been affected by the storm. No. That wasn't true. Her garden seemed not to have been *destroyed* by the storm. Instead, it seemed to have burgeoned, to have multiplied. She realized as she stood there, stunned, she could *see* the vines on the pole beans growing, lengthening nearly imperceptibly toward her, reaching as they had on that first day when she had knelt to guide the beans up the stakes. A constellation of white dots was on the soil where the pods had cast off blossoms, and she remembered her grandfather's wedding.

The garden had a smell that she couldn't place: feral, meat eating, alive. Her tomatoes had blended into the beans—there were no longer orderly rows anywhere—and she pulled at a yellow plum tomato. The plant did not let go at first, stretching toward her before the fruit came loose. She placed it between her teeth and bit down, the juice overflowing her mouth so ripe that it tasted rotten.

She had planted this garden—why? Not necessarily to feed herself or her mother; they had enough food. She liked beans and tomatoes well enough, and a garden tomato did taste better. But no—she remembered herself in those early weeks of spring, wrestling with the barrel, scratching that desiccated surface of earth, and she thought that maybe she had wanted to know the plenty the earth could provide if she stewarded it; she wanted to walk her short rows and see the beans dangling like earrings on their stems, to see the tomatoes lit from within. She had started this—whatever this was— on the day she had told the garden to multiply, her words an incantation.

But she couldn't remember what she'd told the scarecrow. There was no head, just a shirt tied off at the hands, jeans tucked into her mother's old Nikes. Only one Nike now, crusted with mud, the other shoe missing, who knew where. She recognized the Swoosh in the footprints that had led her here, in the footprints all over this garden, lining the rows, yes, but more than that: circling the house, stopping at the windows as if looking in, walking down to the lake, even approaching the road. For a moment, she imagined the scarecrow covering this distance, then laughed at herself. It was two crossed sticks. Nothing there but some old clothes.

Then the answer came to her, even as she stood there and noted the mud on the jean cuffs, the streaks across the shirt where someone had wiped muddy hands (hands! There were only sleeves): Isaac had done this. He had felt bad about missing her grandfather's wedding and so he'd played a joke on her. Isaac was joking, which was sometimes funny, sometimes not, but he was never mean-spirited. Nothing about Isaac was mean-spirited: he fancied himself a protector of all that was weak, some Texas knight-errant off to medical school (he hoped) instead of some quest, and she admired this about him. She smiled in utter relief that Isaac was here somewhere, safe and accounted for, her Isaac even when he wasn't always hers. For a second, she wondered why the soldiers hadn't mentioned that he had passed this way, then she realized he must have crossed the bridge before they arrived. When Isaac crossed, had the old cypress been there, bleeding into the water?

She left the garden reluctantly, unwilling to leave behind this feeling of life, this feeling that she was connected to something much greater than just her little self. She could have lain on the space that remained in the rows and been happy for ages—but turned toward the lake, following the Nike footprints, sometimes deliberately placing her feet within them. This earth was now more hers, she thought, but could not say why she thought this. This sky, gray with the day's rain, belonged to her, or she to it. She thought of how she'd questioned the scarecrow, before she'd realized that it had been Isaac, and how despite having been raised on horror movies that would have suggested otherwise, she had known that the scarecrow had meant her no harm. The worst thing it would have done was to pull her into this world, Hades to her Persephone, but this world was only a deeper, more vivid version of her own.

Debris was caught in mesquite trees that were forty feet from the water-line, and she saw the trail that the water had made when it receded. Her tennis shoes stuck in the mud, her steps harder because of the suction. The ground was scattered with bits of Styrofoam coolers and plastic grocery bags, summer detritus coughed up and deposited here. She felt responsible for this mess and knew that she would clean it up as soon as she could.

But nobody was at the campsite, and one glance told her that nobody had been since the storm. Isaac's tent was caved in, water pooling in the giant depression in the top, the inside still dry but disturbed, as if the storm had picked up the tent, shaken it like a snow globe, then set it back down. Her tent was still perfect, stakes intact and everything. The tarp on which he'd cut his thumb hung from the trees, shredded, one grommet trailing the ground. The camp stove and chairs were missing.

She unzipped her tent. Everything was still in place, even her bed still neatly made. But the floor was muddy with footprints. She looked closer: the Nike Swoosh in the ball of the foot, and now, despite what she believed to be the essential harmlessness of those two crossed sticks, dressed to scare the grackles, a chill took her. How could Isaac have done this and not fixed his own tent?

Outside, low thunder, and then against the tent's nylon, heavy drops, the next wave of rain. The sky, too heavy to hold itself longer, gave way.

Things You Would Know If You Grew Up Around Here

Every Religion Has a Story of the Flood

Here are the ones that apply to this part of the world:

To the Germans, those Protestant lovers of the hard life, the flood washed away the sinners. We are all of us fallen, all of us deserving of punishment. Noah was a sinner, too, but not as bad, enough to save. The rainbow is not God's promise to us but God's promise to God: no matter how bad people get, God has drawn a line for himself.

To the Spaniards, carrying the long arm of Catholicism, the facts of the flood are questioned, leading to an interesting paradox: the flood may not be fact, but it is definitely true. How is it possible that a man lived to be six hundred? How is it possible a man could gather two of every living creature and feed them and house them on a boat for forty days? The message is sacred, however: we have all sinned and fallen short, and God reserves the right to drown us.

To the Comanche, who were here before anyone else, the flood was how the world started. They believe that this area was the first dry land in the world. This place was the first place to rise.

9:00 A.M.

Isaac could not open the door. The water pressed against it from the outside, and the water was stronger than he was. The car's electrical system was unresponsive, something probably wet, so he could not roll down the window. Meanwhile, the water was now midthigh, the brown of cardboard or packing tape, and cold, cold. Once, he'd done a polar bear swim at Barton Springs in Austin, but that had been different. That water had invigorated him, had made him emerge from the water hopping gingerly on his toes. This cold numbed him, robbing him of life, settling deep and quick, tethering. He felt that if the water rose above his heart, his heart would stop.

He pivoted in his seat, his back on the emergency brake, and brought his knees to his chest. The water, heavy with collected earth, grasped at him, weighing down his jeans, sending rivulets across his torso. He kicked.

Nothing the first time: not a crack or a shard. Just the squeak of his boots on the window tint. Again. A line appeared, alive, running obliquely from his heel to the side mirror, continuing to crack even after he'd pulled his feet back for another go. In the water, things: a McDonald's cup, paper, a UT baseball cap. These things came from inside the car, but what was on the other side?

Another kick and now a whole network of splinters and shards, held together by the black film of tint. He kicked again and again, and now the water helped, came rushing in, crumbling what had once been his window. At first, it pushed him back and pinned him to his seat, the shattered glass fanning over him, scoring his cheeks and the backs of his hands. The water was everywhere now, even in his mouth, gritty against his teeth, and how easy it would be to let the water win. It was raw and somehow hot against the surface of his eyeballs, prying his fingernails back, entering the slit in his thumb, loosening the stitches. His body rose now, lifted by the torrent, and as he came loose, he was able to pull his feet underneath him, to press his toes against the passenger door, and push.

The water now streamed in underneath, as well as through the window, and as he passed through, there was just enough room. He only just grabbed the side mirror as he went by. If he had missed this, he would surely have drowned, turned over and over in that tide. But he did grab it, his fingers catching in the gap between mirror and case, and before it gave way and came off, he grabbed the window frame, the glass rendered dull by the tint. He pulled himself onto the roof, which had not yet gone under.

The car twisted in the current, not spinning exactly, but bumping into things and reacting. He was no longer on Allen Potivar's hill. He could see the upper halves of pecan trees ahead and knew he was close to the Colorado River, down toward the valley. He would pass under one of those pecan trees soon, and when he did, he took his chance.

He jumped, as much as he could with the water pulling at his legs, and felt the rough bark in his hands. He swung his feet up and put his face against the tree. His car kept going without him, and he could not know this then, but he would never see it again. The car would be swept past San Saba, coming to rest on a rancher's piece of the river. In the dry years that followed, cattle would surround it, watching it rust into the dirt.

Now, though, Isaac clung to the pecan, safe for the moment, thinking of all those years of childhood when he'd wanted a tree house, thinking that Boyd would think this turn of events a great joke. He laughed himself at the relief of it all. The wind chilled him further, and he reached for his phone, though he already knew it was not there.

9:35 A.M.

Abruptly, Boyd felt Isaac, tasted the copper fear in his mouth, felt the shivering of his chilled limbs, threatening to rattle right off the branch. She saw him in the tree—not the chain of events that had led him there, not whatever had happened with his father—but enough to know she could find him if she looked. She did not know how long he had been there, nor how much longer he could hang on. Getting such a clear vision from Isaac was a shock—he had never given her so much, and he had certainly never needed anything from her. But now Isaac was in trouble—she felt his panic as her own, felt his chills as goose bumps on her arms, felt his heart race in the high pitch of her blood.

There was something else, too, something she could not name, just a vision of a splash in the water, a thing she was meant to save being lost in the flood. She imagined, suddenly, her life without Isaac somewhere out there, and this idea also quickened her pulse—the thought was unthinkable. Even when they were separated, which was most of the time, the idea that he was out there was a comfort.

She headed to Carla's to borrow the truck, needing a vehicle and not knowing what she would encounter out there. She didn't know if the army men would let her pass, but she imagined if that bridge could hold those two Humvees, it could bear a Ford Ranger. There was standing water in the floodplain between Carla's house and the water, moving but with nowhere to go, quivering like Jell-O, so she had to walk up to the road. She was afraid that she would waste all this time and that Carla would not even be there, but Boyd had no choice—no car was at home, and anyway, she needed a truck.

Carla's house was dark, also without electricity, and in the front yard the mimosa tree had been stripped: red blossoms punctuated the slimy green pile of leaves on the ground, and the blacks of the branches and the trunk were wintery scratches, stark against the stucco. Boyd knocked on the door, and when there was no answer, she went in. "Carla?"

The smell of sage and sweetgrass burning, the air thick with smoke. Carla wandered out into the foyer, a wide black stripe painted across her face, temple to temple, her body burly with layers of extra clothing: sweatshirts and leggings and jeans. Relief spread across her frightened features. "Boyd!" she exclaimed, taking Boyd's face in her hands, hands that were slick with cold sweat. She smiled. "I didn't even realize that I needed you, but here you came anyway."

Boyd rested her own hands over Carla's, not pulling those damp palms off her face exactly, but getting ready to. "Carla, I need to borrow your truck."

Carla nodded as if she hadn't heard. "Of course, of course. But first . . ." She removed her hands from Boyd's cheeks and led Boyd into the living room.

The furniture—two couches and a coffee table—had been pushed back against the wall, and in the center of the polished concrete floor was the source of the smell: a pile of herbs and grasses, not quite on fire. A black spot was spreading on the concrete's varnish, a spot that would remain long after this time, long after the electricity came back on and the water fell. The subtle scent of sage would be a permanent resident of the house from this point forward. Boyd looked at Carla, at the black stripe on her face, at the extra clothes.

Carla caught the look. "It's a sweating ritual. I can't turn on the heat—there's no power—but I'm cleansing this house, protecting it." She shrugged sheepishly. "It sounds stupid. But it's true."

Boyd said nothing.

"And of course you can take the truck. But first, Boyd, help me do something really quickly, even if you think it's stupid." Carla motioned for Boyd to sit by her, on the floor next to the smoking grass.

Boyd glanced over her shoulder. "I—I can't. I have to go."

Carla took Boyd's hand. "Boyd. You won't be successful until conditions are set right." Carla smiled, knowing that Boyd would not believe her. "Sit, and I'll let you have the truck in a minute."

So, despite the urgency of Isaac caught in a tree, Boyd sat, cross-legged, and Carla continued, "I don't know how to do whatever it is I'm doing exactly. But it doesn't matter. It's the invocation that counts. It's one that I've never done before, but I saw the snakes this morning and I knew."

"Carla," Boyd stopped her, thinking of the Nike footprints in her tent. "What are you invoking?"

Carla blinked, surprised not to be talking for a second. "Why, the serpent." At Boyd's jump, Carla said, "Not the serpent in the Garden of Eden, if you're worried. Or maybe it's the same serpent. It's the serpent that created the world."

"I beg your pardon?"

"Oh, I could tell you stories, but I won't. You have to go and I'm too busy. Here, Boyd, put your face over the smoke." Carla pushed Boyd's nose inches from the smoldering pile. Smoke stung her eyes and tears fell, great drops, landing with a faint sizzle, sending up steam. The tears were from the stinging, not any emotion, though she felt Carla's tinny nervousness as flutters in her fingers.

Carla was not crazy, Boyd didn't think, although this ritual was far beyond what Boyd had expected, dedication-wise. A book was open on the floor beside Carla, a fat, large paperback, and Carla read from this book now: "'She who observes the water, who studies the dew from the drop, who knows the course of the stars. Her heart is like a serpent.'" Carla closed the book and Boyd saw the title: *The Great Cosmic Mother*. Underneath this, it said *Rediscovering the Religion of the Earth*. Carla reached into the smoking pile and pulled out a stem of smoldering sage. Showing no evidence of pain, she ran her fingers over the black part, staining them with soot, then she leaned forward and traced a spiral in the center of Boyd's forehead. Another swipe of the sage, then a spiral on her own forehead, above the black stripe at her eye line. "There."

"Why are we doing this?"

"This morning, outside, the snakes in the front yard. A hundred of them, maybe more. I stepped outside to see if there was any damage, and there they were, all headed the same direction, toward the dam. Toward the high water."

"What kind?"

Carla sat back on her heels and shrugged. "I didn't know them all. Hell, I didn't know half of them. But there were king snakes and rat snakes and skinny little garter snakes, and you could tell the coral snakes because they were so bright. Water moccasins, too, headed down to the water, so who knows where they've been. Rattlers. I've never seen a rattler uncoiled, on the move. It looked like it was naked."

Boyd said nothing, thinking of her own morning discoveries.

"Boyd, I have never seen anything like that in my life. They were running to something, or from something. I tried to think what it was like, and you know what I thought of? Indiana Jones in the Egyptian temple. He would have hated this. They were like their own water, flowing. And this"—Carla waved her arm to the herb pile—"I don't know. The serpent, she is evil or not evil, depending on who you ask. But she's always female." Carla reached over and traced the spiral on Boyd's forehead. "She may or may not hurt you. But she's here."

Boyd rose, wading through the hypnosis of Carla's steady voice, the smoke, the house stale with a lack of electricity, the air uncirculated by fan or air-conditioning.

"The truck keys are on the kitchen counter. I'd offer to make you some coffee, but, well . . ." Carla opened her palms. "If you want some water, though."

"I'm fine." Boyd swayed on her feet. It was darker in the house than when she'd first come in.

"Where are you going?"

Boyd was suddenly aware that her own mission would sound just as absurd as a serpent ritual in a living room. "I'm going to get Isaac. I'll bring your truck right back."

Carla smiled again, tilting her head as if she was deciding whether to believe Boyd. "Of course. What's a truck, really? Just a thing." Carla studied

Boyd for a minute. "You're really something, aren't you, Boyd? I don't know what. There's something about you. Was I ever like you? No, I don't think I was." Carla pushed her glasses up her nose. "I've loved it out here. You and your mom, you guys have been kind to me."

Boyd didn't know what to say. She didn't know why they would be anything different.

Carla walked her to the door, and before Boyd got in to the truck, she turned back to look at Carla framed in the doorway: thin, wiry with years of yoga, curly hair going every which way. When *had* Carla first appeared? Boyd wondered, and then she remembered: Carla at their dining room table after Boyd's father had left. Carla in Kevin's spot. Boyd headed to bed to read Stephen King and Larry McMurtry, and Carla and Lucy Maud halfway through another bottle of red. In the morning, the empty bottles on the counter next to the sink.

The army men and their trucks were gone, along with the cypress. So was the bridge.

The two arched supports were still standing like sentries in the cascade. But the concrete of the bridge had fragmented into the water, rebar dangling like the spines of prickly pear cactus. The gravel aggregate was exposed at the broken edges and still flaking off, looking to Boyd like a crumbling granola bar. Boyd stopped Carla's Ranger and got out.

She could not cross here. Boyd knew better than that. Water frothed around the two remaining pillars, filled with branches and debris. Boyd saw the body of a possum go by, tail limp and naked, and she shuddered in revulsion. The rain still fell; the wetness that had marked her jeans at her ankles was now at her knees and still climbing.

She drove to the low-water crossing, but immediately gave this idea up. Water was still several feet over the road. One foot of fast water could take a car, and this gauge said that five feet of water was across the road. If she tried to drive across, she would never come back out.

How, then, to get off what had essentially become an island? To get above the dam and up the river? She had no doubt she could find Isaac; she was drawn to him like a magnetic pole, reading his distress like a Geiger counter. She could find him, she thought, as long as he held on. She hadn't been able to sense him for so long, and then, suddenly, he'd been there. He would try to get off the tree soon, she was sure, and she wished she could tell him to stay put. That image again—a stone dropped in the floodwater, the wake left behind when something she loved slipped from sight.

She went back to the bridge, or what was once the bridge. When had it crumbled, breaking apart? All of that stone now in the water, heading toward the lake, the remnants of a bridge that had stood for three quarters of a century. She'd read once that many, if not most, of the bridges in the United States were too old to be structurally sound, were disintegrating just as this bridge had, only at a much slower rate. Waiting for one final stress to bring them down. Had it been the cypress? And now, was that cypress in the water, or had the army men cut it up enough to pull it out? She saw a pile of lesser branches on the opposite shore, but no sign of the central trunk.

In her pocket was the soldier's phone number. She pulled out her phone and dialed. It rang four, five, six times and then disconnected. Of course. Hadn't she known that she was not yet going back to the other world? Hadn't she known that this raw wetness would keep her for a while yet?

But her phone rang in her hand, and when she looked down, she recognized the number she'd just dialed. When she answered, the voice on the other end said, "I missed a call?"

She nearly wept with relief. "Sam! It's Boyd. The girl from the bridge. I'm trapped and I need out. My friend needs help up the river. Can you get me across? Or can you help him?"

Silence on the other end, then: "Yeah, I can probably do that. I don't know how we'll get you across, but we'll figure something out. Let me talk to my sergeant."

Again, relief that watered her eyes. "Thank you." She leaned her forehead against the steering wheel, sure for a second that things were going to work out. "Should I just wait here? I'm on the other side of the bridge, in a truck."

Quiet as the man calculated. "You better go on home and wait. I . . . I'll be a while. Maybe first thing in the morning? I don't know when I can get out there."

A coldness in her throat. She lifted her head from the steering wheel, looking out over the space where the bridge had once stood. "Tomorrow?" Fear crept over her. "Tomorrow will be too late." The water was rising, and she had to find him.

"Hang tight at your house. Nobody can come today, but I promise—*promise*—to try to get to you tomorrow. The storm was bad. The things we're seeing . . . Unless you're in distress, like life-threatening distress, we need the resources for those who are. Boyd, there are kids missing. Old people in wheelchairs. Stay where you are."

She could not tell him why she needed to get across, how she knew Isaac was in trouble. But she had to tell him about Isaac. "My friend needs help. I need to help him. He'll die if I don't."

Silence as he considered this. "You need to call the fire department and tell them where he is. If they have somebody, they'll send rescue personnel."

"I don't know where he is."

"Boyd, I can't get there today. Even if I could, I don't know how I'd get you across that bridge. I tried to get you to stay on this side of it." He breathed heavily into the phone. "You have to hang tight."

Already her mind was working: sheets of plywood, she thought, spanning from bank to pillar to pillar to bank. The downed trunk of a tree. She'd walk out to the main road and beg for a ride. Sam was still on the phone, but she'd forgotten him until he spoke again.

"Boyd, go in your house and lock the doors. I will call you first thing in the morning."

Her battery was at 20 percent with no way to plug in her phone. It wouldn't be working in the morning unless the power came back on. "Yeah, okay. Take care of yourself." She hung up, still assessing the river.

She half slid, half scrambled down the bank and stuck a tentative toe in the water, gauging how difficult—how dangerous—it would be to cross the river.

Her toe, still in its shoe, hardly felt any pressure from the river. Almost as if there were no current at all, no difference between the slow river of late August and this churning beast from the end of May. So she put weight on the foot in the water, lifted her other foot, and took a large stride across.

The river took her, and for a second, her head was underwater, her feet higher than her face. The current had been like a hand that had reached out and grabbed her, like fingers on her ankle. She tumbled along the bottom and then spread her fingers wide on the riverbed and dug for purchase as the river pulled her away. But she held, and she drug herself out, and when she lay gasping on the bank, several yards from where she'd started but still on the same side, she realized that she had, at most, been in two feet of water. If the river had pulled her just a bit farther out, she would have been much deeper, with no hope of pulling herself free.

Now the river seemed to lap at her feet, and she noticed she was missing a shoe. She tucked her feet up under her and regarded the river. It was stupid, she knew, but she felt as if the river were alive. As if it were hungry. As if it wanted her especially.

And, too—she thought she heard something, like men shouting and working, like the grinding of a mill wheel. She tried to follow the river up, but the trees blocked both her way and her sight. She abandoned the crazy idea that something was up there, but she could not shake this feeling that the river was somehow sentient. She walked back to the truck, drove to her house, and sat in the driveway, thinking.

There were fresh footprints, and she could see from where she sat that the scarecrow was no longer in the garden. Taken by the wind, maybe. Washed out, maybe. But the size 7 Nike was walking away from the house this time, heading up the river toward the dam. Up the river. The shortest distance, as the crow flies, between her and Isaac. She went inside and packed a bag: water, a lighter, almonds, and granola bars. She changed into her mother's L.L.Bean duck boots, then went outside and followed the prints. The boots were the same size as the tennis shoes, and then she thought, of course they were. Both pairs of shoes had once belonged to her mother. Rain fell into the prints, threatening to wash them away.

Isaac, in the pecan tree, was unaware that Boyd knew he was there. He was alone and felt certain that he would remain alone. His thumb pulsed with intermittent pain, a worse situation than if it had just hurt continuously in one solid block of aching. He had not yet made it to med school—though he had done an internship at Seton Hospital on Shoal Creek—but he knew this water was not good for his thumb and that he needed antiseptic. Even with the stitches, the wound had a gap where the edges had dried out, hardened, and shrunk back. He needed to get out of this tree.

But the thumb wound was the least of his problems. The water beneath him churned with a ferocity that seemed like hunger. Today, he was sure someone would go under and never come back up. This was not a prediction—Isaac was not given to predictions, preferring instead hard certainties—but a fact.

He would cling to this branch as long as he could, and he hoped that this would be long enough. Here he was: windswept, wet, cold, worried about the gap in his thumb. But he was not under that brown and roaring water.

When he looked down, he started, nearly knocking himself out of the pecan tree's canopy. The lower branches were filling up as every animal that could tried to escape the water. Rabbits, raccoons, possums, daddy longlegs, field mice, cockroaches. All hanging on and sharing real estate. Soon, he imagined, they'd rise higher in the tree, so he looked up in the canopy and climbed. He came to rest on a slimmer branch, unsure how long it would support his weight.

Things You Would Know If You Grew Up Around Here

So Many People Came and Went in Those Days

Also in the Hill Country was the counterpart to the hard-drinking, hard-fighting American West: the remnants of a Mormon colony, founded by Lyman Wight and his followers in 1851. They'd moved throughout the region, hounded by debt collectors, but they'd settled between Burnet and Marble Falls and built a mill, both gristmill and sawmill. They disbanded in 1858, when Wight died, but the mill remained until 1901. In 1902, the wooden part of the mill—the flume—burned, and in 1915, so did the homes of the remaining Mormons. If you were to go there now, if you found that forgotten historical marker on that lonely old road, you could walk among the foundations, grown over with crabgrass, and visit the cemetery. You could listen to the mesquite rustle in that cemetery and imagine that it sounded like whispers, as if those few people left behind when the world moved on had things to say, but could only say them to one another. Nobody living goes there these days.

All over the Hill Country are things begun and abandoned: a colony of freedmen down the road at Peyton Colony, an old army post at Camp Verde, the old town of Calf Creek, the place where Jim Bowie had that fight with the Tawakoni in 1831. Nothing more than a bunch of abandoned buildings, slowly being bleached by the sun.

12:45 P.M.

In a Holiday Inn Express in Marble Falls, Lucy Maud sat on one of two queen beds, showered and teeth brushed, as her soon-to-be ex-husband called his new girlfriend, now fiancée. Lucy Maud didn't know much about her, other than that she was one of her husband's grad students. Kevin was in the bathroom, seeking privacy, but the door was ajar and she heard what he said:

"That storm was something else. Glad I rode it out in Marble Falls." Lucy Maud realized suddenly that he was in the bathroom because he didn't want the woman to hear Lucy Maud if she said something.

Why was she doing this to herself? Kevin had for so long been so much to her. He still was. She wondered for a minute if they would still be together if she hadn't brought the infidelity accusations to him, if she had looked the other way. But no. Get real. She couldn't have let it go. Something had been off, but not seismically off, in the marriage for a long time. She had reached an age when she didn't want to be touched, and she had pushed him away, and so she felt that she bore much of the responsibility of the dissolution of her marriage. The final blow, however, was all his. An instinct had dinged, but no alarm bells had sounded. One evening, Boyd had mentioned Kevin's girlfriend, and from that moment, confrontation had been inevitable.

Lucy Maud remembered the afternoon she'd followed her husband, already knowing what she would find. She had gone into Austin around three on a Tuesday. She was going to a doctor's appointment first, a meeting with an allergist whose nurse had pricked a grid full of needles into her back. The nurse had said they would call with the results, but both of them could plainly see and Lucy Maud could plainly feel that she was allergic to ragweed and mold. Lucy Maud and her tender back headed to campus next, determined to see whatever was to be seen.

She bought a coffee at the union and sat outside his building, Batts Hall. She felt stupid. Did she expect him to walk out of Batts, arm around his grad student? But she had seen him, not quite like that, emerging from the building alone, walking quickly, body pitched forward over his toes, hurrying. He'd walked down the west mall, stopping in front of the fountain with the bronze horses, and he cast one look behind him. She'd ducked, sure he was going to see her, but he'd only looked back toward the tower. Then he stepped into the street, opened the door of a waiting car, and embraced the driver. Lucy Maud tried to see that driver but only got a glimpse of blond hair and slender forearms draped around Lucy Maud's husband. Then the car was gone, and Lucy Maud supposed that she could have had more incontrovertible proof, but what was the point? She'd known as soon as Boyd told her. Boyd was never wrong.

Now she leaned against the headboard and tried not to cry. She assumed that the woman to whom Kevin was speaking was the woman in the car that day. It would be worse if she was not. Lucy Maud would rather Kevin have left her for the great love of his life than for a series of affairs or shallow connections.

He came out of the bathroom, sheepish, and lay down beside her, his face in the pillow, and she began to cry. He was planning a wedding. He put a hand on her knee, comforting. The air in the room seemed curdled.

Her phone rang and she let it. She did not want to move the hand from the knee. After a second, however, Kevin raised his head and crossed the room to her purse, reaching in as if he had the right, reading the screen. Good. Let him have the question.

She closed her eyes, unwilling to take the call. Then she thought: Boyd might be trying to reach her. She held out her hand, eyes still closed, and he put the phone into her palm. Finally, on the sixth ring, she answered, "Hello?"

"Lucy Maud," Ruben said. They'd met a handful of times, a casual relationship, but one with mutual respect. "Can you go get Isaac from the water and tell him to call me?"

"I'm not at the water. And I doubt he came back last night. That was some storm."

"Came back? Where'd he go?"

She shrugged as if he could see her. "He went home. Two days ago now."

Silence. "Okay," Ruben said after a minute. "I guess I'll try him there." A pause. "If you see him, tell him we found something. Tell him I was right."

"About what?"

"Just tell him Maximilian. Tell him Pedro Yorba. He'll know."

She hung up, wondering if Boyd would know about Pedro Yorba, if Boyd knew where Isaac was. But no. Boyd had stayed with her aunt Lou, was probably even now sitting at Aunt Fern's dining room table, doing the crossword puzzle.

"We should go see if Boyd's at home," she told Kevin, who stood beside her waiting to put the phone back in her purse.

"All right. We'll go together."

She looked up at him and started to cry again. Outside, thunder.

Boyd, spiral on forehead, backpack on, marched in step behind the scare-crow (who knew how far), calculating distance: roughly a quarter mile to the dam, then up and over, then maybe five miles up the river, depending on where Isaac was. Crossing the dam would be hard; the field of boulders at its foot would be covered with water, water coursing over and through the spillway. The prints she followed veered right, and it took her a minute to see where they headed: the hanging tree was submerged, only the canopy visible and looking like a tuft of broccoli. The last Nike Swoosh was inches from the water, then the prints were gone. Reluctantly, she left the foot-prints, taking instead to the line of mesquite and juniper that skirted the dam. She could see the concrete structure through these trees, massive, making for the landscape a new horizon.

The first thing she passed: the little pioneer cemetery in its cast-iron fence. The earliest graves were only 150 years old, from the middle of the nineteenth century. These markers were hard to read; the elements had worn the engraving thin, rendering the limestone dark and smooth as adobe. The graves from the beginning of the twentieth century were marked with much larger stones, often made of local granite peppered with veins of iron flecking orange rust. So many small grave markers with lambs resting on top: the final places for infants and small children. She knew the story of one of these children because Ruben King had told her. Caleb Muller, age five, laid in a grave marked in German, had wandered into the scrub in the years before the First World War. The moon was ringed with ice that night, a rare late-November freeze. Caleb's family searched for him, calling, and discovered his body the next morning not steps from where his mother had walked, in between rows in the kitchen garden, between the last row of hibiscus-like okra and the great perennial stand of dill, the child smiling and stiff. The smile, Ruben had suggested, was false, the boy's lips pulled back in cold and fear. Now, Boyd knelt in front of Caleb's grave, nearly heartbroken, and said, "I wish I could help you." She thought of the boy, scared and alone, growing slowly colder.

At least two other graves had no name. INFANT SON one said, and showed a life span of six days at the end of 1893. Another was simply blank. Ruben had said that these children had not been named, that the mothers had known not to get attached. Sometimes Boyd walked the cemetery, and cemetery math was a peculiar thing, revealing, if not answers, clues. One of the women, Ella Hotz, died within a day of one of the lambs. A group of graves, including what looked like an entire family, were dated 1918. The last one in that family, the father, had outlived the rest by three days. Who had buried them, then, after the Spanish flu? Who had gathered the bodies and erected the stones?

The INFANT SON being mossed over on the marble made her think, briefly, of someone she hardly ever thought about: her great-uncle William, her grandfather Homer's twin. He'd been buried as an infant in 1951, and then the dam had been built in 1953, and his grave had been covered for more than half a century. These last few years, the drought had exposed these old towns and all of their churches and windmills and houses and post offices, and, yes, sometimes even their dead. Last summer, Boyd and her mother and Aunt Lou had taken a johnboat to see the place exposed, and Boyd had not liked it. The place did not belong to the air but to the water, and when Lou had stood in front of a grave similar to this one, with even a similar lamb, Boyd had imagined that this was how she would feel if she were to ever visit Pompeii or Herculaneum or to board the *Flying Dutchman*: here was a place that did not belong to her.

Rain fell now on these graves in the pioneer cemetery, big drops splashing back up because the ground was saturated. Boyd paused only a second, leaning on the fence, the cast iron biting into her forearms. Roughly thirty people here, laid to rest in what still felt like the middle of nowhere, and in what must have felt then like the edge of the world. Lives so different from the ones people lived now, and wouldn't these deceased have been surprised? But then, from this spot, they would have no idea: not much around here. Only the occasional car, once a week or so, traveled the dirt road Boyd now walked. The world had not yet reached them here, in the shadow of the dam.

She turned away and kept walking, knowing she had miles to go, still facing the obstacles ahead. Rain fell on her face and she pulled her hood up, marching, crunching the pink gravel, feet dry in boots. The soldier Sam had said, *Children are missing. Old people in wheelchairs.* Here, at the side of the lake, she was on high enough ground that this seemed impossible. But she knew that wherever Isaac was, there was another version of possibility.

She thought of him now, tried to see what he was seeing. She felt some vague panic but was not sure whether it was his or just her own projection, some vestige of feeling. Wherever he was, he'd settled in, no longer broadcasting that panicked edge.

As she walked, she startled things. Grasshoppers the size of her fist, jumping, in their confusion, toward her. White-tailed deer, families, tucked into the mesquite. Mice in the tall grass. Raccoons, though it was day, waddling a safe distance away and then stopping to peer at her. As she approached the dam, she heard stones skittering behind her, and when she turned, she thought that she could see that they were all there, the wet grass moving with a mass of hidden bodies. What did they want?

When she reached the foot of the dam, she knew she had to be careful. The view expanded; trees were unable to grow in the field of boulders. The floodgates to the right of the dam were open: brown water churned white rushed through and added to the water in the basin. A smooth, glassy sheet of water poured over the spillway. Above the dam, in the two towers, she knew, engineers would be overseeing. They would not let her pass, would tell her to go away, and they might even arrest her. She would have to avoid detection as well as water. She lay on her belly on a chunk of granite, wishing she'd brought binoculars, and decided to skirt the structure, climb the ridges of the canyon, come back to the river once clear of the dam.

She guessed it was now around one P.M., and the heaviest rain was letting up. A mist clung to everything, primordial but cold, and even as she watched, the two towers on the dam started to shimmer and recede. She slid off her belly and began the walk up and out of the valley, away from the dam.

Soon, the fog was so thick she was disoriented, and her only directional marker was uphill. She kept walking, as she was not in wilderness but was instead in settled country and would not get hopelessly lost. As she walked, she remembered one of her favorite Stephen King books, *The Girl Who Loved Tom Gordon*, about a girl who stepped off a path in Maine and almost never made it home. Too, Boyd remembered an article she'd read in some magazine about a man, a finder man, who was called every time someone disappeared in the Appalachians. Some people he found, some he didn't. Forests swallowed people sometimes. There was the woman who left the Appalachian Trail and whose body was found twenty years later, her diary revealing that she had survived for weeks, one of her last entries mentioning all the people she loved because she knew the diary would eventually be found. This was not that. This was central Texas, populated, trees low-slung and often sparse. Only the pecans and ancient live oaks were any kind of real trees. The mesquite was feathery and short; this species had only been here a century or so, brought up from Mexico by cattle during the cattle-drive years. The Ashe juniper was spindly and twisted and, she'd been told more than once, spectacularly unsuited for this landscape: rumor was each tree required as much as sixty-five gallons of water a day, and this in a country that knew drought. Ranchers told tales of clearing the juniper and, the next year, dry creeks running wet again. This group of trees was not the sort to get lost in.

But the fog increased, blooming, and eventually she'd gone as high as the land would let her. If she was at the top of the dam, at the top of the box canyon, then the terrain would level off and she would find herself close to the water again. But this was not the case; instead, she found herself at the peak of a hill, and she turned back to look around.

A young boy stood there. He was close enough that she could see details on his clothes: he wore no pants, and his shirt was rough spun and long. No shoes. His hair was long, too, curly and pale. Fingers of mist rose off him, as if he'd just arisen from a hot bath on a cold day. He was shivering.

Her first instinct: to care for the boy, to help him find his family. The only emotion she could get from him was fear, but it was blind fear, not nuanced: a single tone, like a television after programming has turned off for the evening, or when the station does a test of the emergency broadcast system. Something about that fear was dead, machinelike. "Are you lost?" she asked. "I might be lost, too."

He turned and pointed back in the direction she thought he'd come from.

"Do you live around here?"

The boy looked at her, pale eyes big in a child's face. He said something in German, and she didn't understand it. His voice was high-pitched, childlike.

"I don't speak German." She knew why he did but would not admit it to herself. "I'm trying to remember. *Sprechen Sie Englisch?*"

At this, he cocked his head, listening as a dog would listen. Only his head, only that curious angle of the neck, the rest of his body mechanically still.

"I'm lost, too. I'm trying to get over the dam." She pointed left, out into the gray, in the direction she imagined the dam might lie.

Now he cocked his head to the other side, his curly hair falling away. His bare feet were dirty, as if he'd been walking for some time. His toes curled underneath his feet. He was cold.

She had her hoodie, and now she dropped her backpack so that she could take it off. "Do you want my jacket?" She held it at arm's length, resisting the urge to throw it. When he hesitated, she dropped the jacket and took a step back.

He approached the jacket gingerly, skittishly, as if he were some wild thing and she were offering food. He pulled the jacket on and it engulfed him, falling below his long shirt, swallowing his arms in their homespun sleeves. She remembered that in the pocket was the soldier's number, but it was also in her phone. *Children are missing.*

She couldn't stand here and stare at this kid all day. "Do you need help finding your family?" Could she leave a child out here?

Again he pointed behind him, but when he turned back, he pointed at her.

"Oh, I'm not your family." But he knew that. That's not what he was saying. "You mean you want to help me."

She didn't know if he understood her, but he nodded. His one-note fear had abated, and she wondered if he'd been scared of her. "I'm looking for the river." She hesitated, grasping for the German word. "*Der Fluss*. The river."

He nodded again, and in his eyes, the blue iris was nearly all pupil. "The river," he said, with an accent. It was not his word for it, but he knew it.

She flinched when he took her hand, afraid he was coming in for a hug. But he didn't. Instead, he pulled her forward, down the side of the hill, and she fully trusted that he could take her where she wanted to go, even if she didn't particularly want to make the journey with him.

But then, she thought, as his cold hand let hers go and as she continued to follow, the dam was built in the fifties, long after the First World War. And this thought revealed her own mind to her, revealed how she had been hiding things from herself—suppressing them—and now she was forced to admit that the storm had changed something. The world had slipped from its track. She thought about this, too, for a moment, life as a train rail or a song on a record, but the metaphor wasn't quite right. No, to Boyd the storm had been more like the part of an eye exam when the optometrist lowers the circular lenses and asks, *Which is better? One*—pause—*or two?* The storm was like this: a different lens had now snapped into place, and now some things were less visible, and some things—things that had been present all along—more. She followed the boy, hearing only her own footfalls.

2:45 P.M.

Carla sat cross-legged and draped with a blanket, looking for something in the smoke as the herbs smoldered on her floor. *What am I?* she thought. *What do I believe?*

Marriage-less, childless, nearly friendless. Only Lucy Maud and her family. Carla was out here to escape the rat race, the materialism of life, the grueling Austin commute. Her heart had pinched every time new concrete was poured, mired in nostalgia, gripped with the sense that progress, while it might once have been good, was now evil, a force of ruin and subversion, Shiva the destroyer of the beautiful world. She now made everything she could, had even acquired a spinning wheel in a plan to spin wool, and she cut ties to the destructive force ruthlessly, ferociously. She was, she thought, a daughter of the earth.

She believed that the primordial ooze was amniotic. She believed that the earliest religions of the earth were woman centered. She believed that the nearly spherical figurines of women from prehistory were images of the Goddess. She believed that she, too, was a goddess, only with a lowercase *g*. Because she had never given birth, she believed her divinity was stunted, would never quite grow to fruition.

It was she who'd encouraged Boyd to garden, who had shared a copy of *Animal, Vegetable, Miracle* with Lucy Maud and Boyd as a sort of mandate:

here is what we must do. She knew when Lucy Maud's marriage ended long before there was any actual talk of divorce: she recognized the signs of betrayal on her friend, recognized the traces that shadowed Lucy Maud, knew the moments when her friend was occupied and forgot the betrayal, knew the moments when she remembered, saw her expression change. From Lucy Maud, Carla relearned the value of the moment, the heartbreak incurred when the present moment is lost, those times when Lucy Maud remembered her past and caught sight of her future. Carla found something with Lucy Maud: a mirror, a hope. Like Boyd, Carla was drawn to the pain of others, but for a different reason. Carla, as someone who had suffered trauma, looked for those who wore their pain visibly. Those who had been hurt would no longer hurt others, at least not on purpose. (There were exceptions to this, of course; some hurt people turned to hurting others even more, but Carla knew how to avoid these people.) Pain pried open a secret spot of empathy.

Lucy Maud's daughter, too, was kind and would not hurt Carla. But Boyd was too naïve for Carla's taste. Boyd's empathy came not from any particular history but from some fine-tuning mistake made by the universe.

A beautiful girl: freckled, angled. Boyd's center of gravity seemed lower than other people's; her balance came from the base of her spine. Her posture seemed crouched, primed, as if at any minute she could unspool herself and be more than she appeared. A latent possibility there. Yet so young. Still so hung up on pleasing.

Carla breathed in the smoke, tingeing her insides with sage, infusing this modern house with ancient things that had almost been forgotten. What would it hurt, she thought, if she truly awakened the serpent?

She was crazy. She knew it. But she also knew she was no more crazy than the fundamentalists upriver, who had also come to the Hill Country for refuge. The women who were not allowed to wear pants, the home-schooled children who never went anywhere but church. She saw them in the Walmart on 281; she recognized the similarity between them but doubted that they did the same. They looked at her with suspicion, as a bearer of iniquity, but she looked at them as kindred spirits.

If she had an apple, she would eat it, though historians suggested that it had been a pomegranate in the Garden of Eden. They—she and the fundamentalists—believed in the same things, only she believed in those things and more, and in those things in a different way. Multiplicity, she told herself. The possibility of the infinite.

She was meant to see the snakes headed to the water. She was meant to know that something had changed or was changing. That the earth was in charge again.

She rose, curious to see where the snakes had gone and what other wonders there were to behold. How she wished that Lucy Maud were at home, but Boyd had indicated that she was not. In Carla's dark house, she was lonely, her eyes hooded in the dim, her body calcifying cross-legged.

Her knees and ankles cracked as she unfolded herself. She did not yet know why she felt this sense that the world was ending, or why the snakes had stirred in her such a sense of calamity. There was the lack of electricity and Boyd's worry about her friend, but none of that added up to the dread Carla felt, the certainty that something had gone quite seriously wrong. In nearly every religion is a sense that balance must be restored by a sacrifice.

She opened the door, letting the smoke inside the house dissipate. Outside, the sky was yellow, and the rain still dripped heavily from the eaves. Her feet were immediately soaked, but she kept walking, her face to the wind. She walked up her driveway and out onto the road, then she walked toward the dam, toward Lucy Maud's house. She spread her arms, palms up, and she lifted her face. A ghost whiff of sage clung to her. She saw no sign of life, and certainly not the snakes she was seeking: the animals had all fled.

But Boyd had not, she saw. When she approached Lucy Maud's house, she saw her own truck, the one Boyd had borrowed to go get her friend. For a second, she forgot the snakes. She turned toward Lucy Maud's house, curious to see how Boyd had helped her friend and returned so quickly. She thought about how, in the old days, if they were going to sacrifice something to restore a balance, it would be someone or something like Boyd: young, good, someone whose loss would be felt. In that regard, Carla was in no danger.

Things You Would Know If You Grew Up Around Here

We Are Entering the Sixth Great Extinction

It is hard not to paint this world in elegy. We have melted the poles and raised the seas, and we are the last who will see what we have seen. In our lifetimes, the ocean will be equal parts plastic and fish. We can expect three quarters of species to disappear over the next century. Look out your window. Imagine the loss. Who can say what is to come next? The world will not end, perhaps, but what you and I have known, what my son and his friend have known, is passing, and will not come again.

The little boy had pulled Boyd off the trail. Lichen unfolded across the boulders they crossed, and burrs clung to the legs of her pants. A smell of wet. No trees in this spot. The sky should have been open, the world visible beyond a few yards. But Boyd could see nothing past a short stone's throw; the world's tone was muted.

She watched the boy in front of her, one minute walking solemnly, the next scampering up a large piece of granite. His bare feet were calloused, used to going unshod. When she'd first encountered him at what she'd thought was the foot of the dam, he'd been missing a tooth. She even thought she could remember which one: the top center one, the one to her left. Now when he grinned at her, she saw he was missing several: both front, both bottom. The gums beneath were not full and pink, either. She could see the sockets, tipped white and pale, drying. She looked at the ground, instinctively searching for the fallen teeth, but she saw nothing.

She could remember little German. As a homeschooled student, she'd studied several languages: French and Spanish in particular, but also Greek, Turkish, Latin, and, yes, some German. These last she'd studied as part of her library's digital collection, a software program with lessons in a hundred languages. Of all of these, German had been the toughest, the least intuitive for Boyd. The cognates seemed to make little sense when placed in sentences. Now she could not remember how to say *Where are you taking me? Where are we going?* She could hardly remember how to say *where*, though she remembered that it did not sound like the English *where*. "*Wo?*" she tried.

The boy stopped, his hands placed flatly against a boulder he was about to scale. He pointed vaguely up and forward. "*Das Fluss.*"

"*Sie,*" she said. *You.* "*Mutter? Vater? Nein?*" Where was his family?

He shook his head. In his eyes, the iris seemed to be overtaking the white. His skin had a flat affect. Gray. "*Sie sind zu Hause. Sie suchen mich.*"

She caught none of it. They did not have a language between them. "You speak no English?" She saw his forearms had goose bumps, though the day was warm. "*Sprechen Sie Englisch?*"

"*Nein.*" Then he reconsidered. "I can speak a little. The river is close." He pointed again, this time over the boulder where his hands now rested. "See. See for your own self."

She hesitated, her weight shifting beneath her. She knew what he was, didn't she? But she'd followed him anyway. Or maybe she'd followed him because she'd known. His low level of pain, constant but flat, out of her realm of helping. He helped her, yes, or at least he thought he did, but he also wanted something from her. She thought she knew what this was, and she knew she'd be unable to give it. The time for helping this child had passed more than a hundred years ago. Did he know?

He smiled at her, his mouth now missing even more teeth. "Oh, no," he said, as if he could read her mind. Was he speaking English or did she now understand his German? "All time is the same now. Come. Look at the river."

He took her by the elbow, and the place where his hand rested seared cold. She felt for a second his panic, saw the night and cold settling in around him as he stopped to wait for his parents. He was still waiting. She moved forward, put her hands on the granite, climbed.

He'd led her to the river, swollen with rain. The dam must have been far below them now: she couldn't even see it. She saw nothing to indicate settlement or civilization, save for one faint curl of smoke to the west. She had not realized that the stretch between the dam and Horseshoe Bay was so large. Multimillion-dollar homes should have been here, boat docks, golf course greens. Instead there was a long swath of nothing: water and trees and her familiar river looking like the Mississippi, unbounded and bestial. Somewhere out there was Isaac.

She turned, a question on her lips. But the boy was gone.

She pulled her hands away from the stone and slid down, walking over to where the boy had been. No trace. She looked back the way they had come and could not see the trail. She could have sworn that there had been no trees, but now the trees had closed behind them after their passage through. She could not guess the path of return.

But there was no need to return. She called for the boy briefly, not even knowing his name, but then she turned back to the rock and started to climb. She was not sure how she could dismiss a lost child so easily, but as she reached the top of the boulder and dusted her hands off, she realized that it was because the child had been so emotionally flat. Nothing had been there. She had never met a person like this, not in all her eighteen years. Even when she could not *feel* the emotion or sense what a person thought— telling what a person thought was such a rare exception—she could tell why somebody was doing whatever he or she was doing. She could sense motivation. The world was endlessly fascinating to her because of this, and she felt it was splayed open, both obvious and profoundly unknowable. But the child had not been or done or felt like any of that. He had long since given up hope. She hadn't reached him at all. She hadn't even known his name. Oh, but she had, hadn't she? Didn't she know his name was Caleb?

Then what had he been doing here? Where had he come from and how? And the only answer she could honestly give herself was the storm. The things that she had seen in the last day—it was, only now, approaching twenty-four hours!—were things that could not have happened before. She'd had a preview when the garden had grabbed her wrists that day toward the end of the drought. And Caleb, this ghost child looking for his parents, had come to get her over the dam, up the river as quickly as possible.

She knew enough about herself and about others to know she was somehow different. But everybody was different in some way. Ruben King had the ability to nearly see the past, to see history walking. Lucy Maud was a pleaser, a server, a thin layer spread wide, giving, giving, giving, then taking it back in shrill bursts that shocked everyone around her. At war in Lucy Maud were these two things: what she imagined that others needed and what she needed herself. These two things could not coexist; they were instead like children's hands in the game where two people stacked them, pulling the bottom one out and placing it on the top, repeating, repeating, until the game devolved into a series of furious slaps. Boyd found it revealing that nobody could play that game for longer than a few seconds, as if everybody recognized the futility. Rather than making people just stop, the futility accelerated the game. Nobody could stand to end up on the bottom. Lucy Maud's ability to hold this self-subversion in suspension astounded Boyd.

Carla, too, could sense things others could not, but Carla's intuition was different, earthy, like a third eye. Carla's gift came from looking, from a natural curiosity, from an innate femaleness, a certain view of the world. Carla called the earth Mother.

But what was Isaac's ability? Isaac had a calm matter-of-factness, a cold eye for logic. It wasn't that he was emotionless, exactly, but more that emotions were the lesser part of his makeup. On good days, Boyd found this calculation to be a ballast to her own overprimed sensitivity. On bad days, well . . .

But what were the bad days with Isaac? He never lost his temper, was never unpleasant to be around. The worst that ever happened with him was an occasional low-grade irritability, as there had been two mornings ago at the campsite when he'd snapped at Lucy Maud, and he'd immediately felt bad about it. But this cold logic was not an ability, and instead more of a way of being, and Boyd found this coldness was often a relief to her, a source of support: Isaac was always Isaac.

She shimmied down the other side of the rock feetfirst on her belly, sending shards flying as the granite exfoliated beneath her fingers, the outer layer hardened and sloughing off. She was going downhill now, this boulder at the tip of a hill of them. Her toes flexed in her mother's boots, seeking purchase, and soon she was breathing heavily. The sky, rainless and cloudy for several hours now, shimmered with the promise of more rain. In the distance, black streaks in the sky revealed that Horseshoe Bay was getting pounded. The world's edges had become clearer, and she saw that she was coming to the end of the field of boulders, coming abruptly up to the river and to its line of trees. In between the rocks now, the ground was wet, water repelled by the saturated ground. She was on the other side of the dam, but she wasn't quite sure how, and she still could not see it. She thought again about the lack of civilization in her immediate view, how nothing man-made seemed to be in her field of vision. But no, she thought suddenly, picking up her pace as she hopped from rock to rock. She smelled the mesquite smoke now: sweet and close. She saw, too, in the trees ahead, a clapboard house, white but streaked with rain. The smoke she smelled curled out of the chimney, and in the muddy front yard, a black dog watched her draw closer.

2:45 P.M.

Lucy Maud and Kevin had reached the washed-out bridge and had, without even bothering to call, turned around and headed back to Aunt Fern's. After a silent moment in which both thought about the bridge but said nothing, Lucy Maud realized that the reason she didn't call her twin sister, Lou, or their aunt Fern was because Lucy Maud didn't want to tell them that she was with Kevin, the implication being that she'd been with Kevin for all those hours in the interim, too. Not that Lou or Aunt Fern would say anything. It was the looks they would give each other, looks saying that the weakness of the heart could be painful, that what makes a heart happy in the short term could well undermine it later. And Lucy Maud knew the pain was coming. She knew Kevin was engaged to another woman, that that other woman did not know that Lucy Maud was with her fiancé (how much did that word hurt?). No, Lucy Maud knew that *this*—whatever *this* was—was temporary and would last only until they found Boyd, who was probably still at Aunt Fern's. Lucy Maud was not worried about Boyd. Lucy Maud had raised a resourceful, competent child. Boyd, now eighteen, could handle pretty much whatever. Boyd was fine.

But Lucy Maud was not. She was reacting to an afternoon, evening, and morning with her soon-to-be ex-husband, and she knew it was a worn and overused cliché, but she felt like an addict relapsing. She was gorging on this time with him after so long without, returning to that source of relief again and again, her left hand resting on his right thigh even now as he drove, unable to sever the connection. She pictured this hand on thigh as an IV connection, and, God, how did she feel when he stopped at a red light and absently rested his own hand on top of hers? The withdrawal would be painful. In a few hours she would be even lower than she had been before and was even now bracing herself. She could not believe that, not long ago, she had turned him away, that at times in the night when he had turned to her, she had pretended to be asleep.

But was it so wrong to believe that this separation would not come? Oh, she knew it would; she was not stupid. But was it so wrong to pretend? She tried to think of normal things she could say to him—things about dinner or taking out the trash or putting the laundry in the dryer—just normal, domestic things that would make her feel for a moment as if they still had a life together. But she could come up with nothing. If she even said, "Let's stop by the grocery store for milk," he would look at her and know, spell broken. She was convinced the only reason his hand had rested on hers was to comfort her because the bridge was out and they weren't sure which side Boyd was on. He was comforting her, she thought, but she didn't need comfort because of Boyd. Boyd was fine.

They turned off the highway and headed toward Fern's piece of the lake. Kevin didn't seem worried either, Lucy Maud noted. He seemed excited, and Lucy Maud analyzed this excitement: Perhaps she had let their lives become too boring. Perhaps all she had needed to do to keep her husband was to be more lively, more adventurous. Nobody wanted to live the same old life day in and day out for decades.

The other woman was his graduate student. Lucy Maud couldn't imagine that the woman was that much more adventurous, but she was younger for sure. She still had that drive, that ambition, that Lucy Maud had once had but had abandoned long ago, first because they had moved so much—to Kevin's MA program in Oxford, Mississippi, then to Nashville for the PhD, then to Knoxville for a visiting professorship, then finally to Austin—and second, because of Boyd. After leaving jobs in so many towns, Lucy Maud felt nearly unemployable, and when Boyd was born, the net difference between wages and child care had not made it seem worth being employed. Boyd had been born in Nashville, and by then Kevin's teaching stipend had been large enough for them to scrape by, so she'd stayed at home and had never gone back to work full-time. When they'd separated, Kevin had let her stay in the lake house and left her an allowance, though now she hoped to earn money from wedding planning. She had no room for a sense of adventure anymore; she lived too close to the bone to crave that sort of excitement. But to get her husband back, she was willing to do just about anything.

"Pull over here," she said, inching her hand up his thigh. They were on the highway, passing a historical marker. Cars were flying by.

He jerked his leg away from her hand, swerving as he did so. "Jesus Christ, Lucy Maud! You almost made me hit that eighteen-wheeler." He looked at her sideways and kept driving.

The humiliation stung. In their marriage, he'd always complained that she had never initiated sex. Well, it was true. She didn't know how. Even when she'd felt like doing so, she couldn't bear the possibility of rejection. Then, when she'd gone through menopause, she had felt that part of her life was over, that she had lost all interest.

She thought about unzipping his pants and lowering her face to his lap. He was not likely to turn that down, after having begged for it on so many road trips. But, no, it was only half-hearted anyway, because she was trying to prove something and was not genuinely interested, and besides, here they were turning into Aunt Fern's driveway. Lou's car was out front, and Fern was in her chair on the front porch. She raised a hand as they approached, and Lucy Maud couldn't tell if she knew who they were. But no, if Aunt Fern was having a bad day, Lou was usually right there next to her, sitting and swinging her foot, drinking coffee all the way until dinnertime.

But Lou had heard the car pull into the drive and emerged now from the house, waving with one hand and cradling her phone to her ear with the other. As Lucy Maud and Kevin got out of the car, Lou hung up the phone and set it on the porch railing. Her face was lined with worry: two diagonal slashes between her eyebrows, parentheses around her mouth.

"Y'all heard from Boyd? I left her with the army men. But I can't reach her now."

"What army men?" Kevin asked.

"The army men on the bridge to your house. Moving a giant tree. She wanted to go home and they said they would take her, so I left her with them."

Kevin and Lucy Maud looked at each other. "There are no army men," Lucy Maud said.

Kevin said, "There's no bridge either."

Lucy Maud felt a small niggle of worry, now as the rain started again, and as Aunt Fern sat, smiling to herself about something only she could see, as Kevin's car engine ticked, and as Lou paced the porch. Boyd, separated from all of them, on her own and cut off. Lucy Maud pulled out her own phone and called Carla.

Things You Would Know If You Grew Up Around Here

Purple Blazes Mean No Trespassing

This only became law in 1997. But I remember purple paint on tree trunks even when I was a kid, so who knows how long the rule was around before they made it legal.

But here's the gist: purple paint on a fence post or tree means NO TRESPASSING. The blazes must be fewer than a hundred feet apart in timberland and fewer than a thousand feet apart in open country. Even people who are color-blind can see purple blazes, so no excuses. Technically, the penalty for trespassing falls to the law: Class B misdemeanor, unless you're armed, and then it's Class A. In reality, though, everybody knows that a landowner's not likely to go through so long a process as arrest and prosecution. Everybody knows that the real danger when you pass this boundary is that you take your life into your own hands. You could hardly blame somebody for shooting a trespasser, right?

Boyd stood frozen, trying to decide whether the dog meant her any harm. He yelped once and stood tense, ready to spring, but he didn't growl. Instead, he watched her, barking every now and then, his legs stiff.

She thought about going around and did try to skirt the house, stepping to the right and walking through the brush. The dog followed her, and it was harder going out here. The scrub Ashe juniper had not been cleared and scratched her face as she walked. Grapevines and thorns pulled at her pant legs, and still the dog followed her.

As she walked, she saw the fence posts painted purple, that color between lavender and royalty that was so familiar around these parts. She saw a windmill, blades spinning, but she wasn't sure a pump was attached, and on a clothesline hung a single white sheet, heavy with moisture, waving thickly in the wind. The house was two-story, tall and narrow, looking to Boyd as if it were tilting into the mud. An outbuilding, board and batten, double doors closed with a wooden bar. Too big to be a garage, but not quite a barn. A stable. In the mud, hundreds of horseshoe prints. A wide front porch wrapped around the side of the house, and on the porch was a jumble of wood scraps and old furniture. She looked around and realized there was no car.

A whistle and the dog ran away. Boyd turned, and standing on the porch was a woman in a long skirt, her hair piled on her head in a bun. In her left hand, she held a rolling pin, and in her right, something she fed to the dog, who then took up a post by the porch steps. Behind the woman, the door hung open.

"Hello?" Boyd said tentatively. The woman's clothing unnerved Boyd, and she thought of the boy who had led her across the dam, and how he'd said that all time was the same now. Boyd saw that it was not a skirt but a long dress, made of what looked to be gray lawn, with a thin border of lace at the collar and a few inches above the hem of the skirt. The woman seemed expressionless to Boyd: not curious, not afraid.

Boyd realized that what she had thought was a rolling pin was instead a miniature baseball bat, a foot and a half long, meant for a child. The woman now palmed this bat, a hand on each end, one over and one under. It was a makeshift weapon, meant for self-defense.

"What are you doing here?" The woman's accent was clipped, vaguely Dutch English. "This is private property." Boyd remembered the purple blazes and thought she was lucky she hadn't been shot.

"I'm passing through." Boyd moved a step closer to the woman, a gesture of friendliness more than anything else. The dog rose to its feet. "I'm"—Boyd pointed in the direction she'd been headed—"going to find a friend."

Silence as the woman regarded her, then: "That way's flooded out. But then"—the woman pointed in the direction from which Boyd had come—"it's flooded that way, too." Now she took in Boyd's appearance: the duck boots, the backpack, the jeans wicked with rainwater.

Boyd glanced down at her mother's boots, wondering about the shoes hidden underneath the woman's dress. Maybe they were old-fashioned leather with hook-and-eye closures, rising above her ankle. Maybe they were flip-flops. Maybe they were tennis shoes. "I went around the flooded areas," Boyd said.

The woman nodded. "Indeed." She dropped the small bat to her side, her skirts folding around it. "Such strange things happening. But I reckon you're not much of a threat." Boyd could not imagine that anybody had ever counted her as a threat. "You want to come in for a cup of coffee?"

Boyd felt the urgency of Isaac in the tree pulling her upriver. A tick of insistence, but also a sense that she had not yet reached the part of the journey where she would be allowed to reach him, that she needed to discover something here. "Sure. But I can't stay long." She stepped past the purple-blazed pickets, the dog now unconcerned, Boyd having been given the woman's tacit approval. It raised its black head from its paws as Boyd walked around it. When Boyd was on the porch, the woman turned and went inside, the screen door left open, and Boyd followed, passing the jumble of scrap wood.

It was dim inside, dust floating down through shafts of light filtering through lace curtains. There was no foyer: Boyd found herself immediately in a room she would call a parlor. A Victorian sofa sat in the center of the room, complete with red velvet upholstery, carved legs stained mahogany. A knotted rug on the hardwood floors. A curio shelf, triangular, in the corner of the room, filled with china so thin that Boyd saw the light marbled through it, like mother-of-pearl. In another corner of the room, a console television set, seated on the floor. Boyd's grandmother had once had an RCA set like this: a piece of furniture in itself, the case wooden and solid.

The television surprised Boyd. She had not expected it, and for a moment, she faltered. She would have been less surprised by a spinning wheel. The world had turned crazy.

The woman stood in the kitchen doorway. "In here."

Turning in her direction, Boyd saw the kudzu climbing in through the window, snaking across the wall that had been to her back. The vines had entered benignly, fingers exploring, but now the wallpaper puckered under the green.

Boyd's quick intake of breath made the woman turn back. "Oh, that. That happened yesterday." The woman stepped over and pulled the vines free, tossing them out the window. Brown spots remained like little check marks, evidence, as if the plant had been a green centipede. "I keep doing this and it keeps coming back." She shucked the final strand out, her hands sinking as if it were heavy; Boyd thought of an elephant's trunk, leathery and thick. The woman slapped her hands together, dusting them off. "There."

In the kitchen, Boyd was even more confused. The woman had no oven, but instead an old-fashioned wood cookstove. The refrigerator was old-fashioned, too, a rounded one with the freezer door inside, the kind of freezer that needed to be defrosted. On the counter, however—really a long farmhouse table against a wall underneath a window—a KitchenAid mixer and a Keurig. The sink was lemon yellow and deep. Already the woman was putting a pod in the Keurig; soon Boyd heard the hiss of the water warming.

"It's hazelnut." The woman shrugged. "I like it. I hope it's okay."

"Of course." Boyd didn't know where to stand, and she put her fists into her pockets because she didn't know what to do with her arms.

The coffee poured into the mug and the woman handed it to Boyd. "Cream or sugar?"

"Both."

The woman fetched a bag of sugar from a cabinet, milk from the fridge, and a spoon from a drawer. She turned back to the Keurig to make her own cup. "I'm Laurie."

"Boyd."

Laurie smiled over her shoulder. "Nice to meet you, Boyd. You doing some traveling?" She nodded at Boyd's backpack, propped against the wall.

"My friend is upriver. I haven't seen him since the storm started. And I—the bridge to my house was washed out and I—"

Another hiss as the coffee brewed. Laurie nodded and leaned against the counter, as if Boyd's reason for walking across country wasn't preposterous. "Weird storm, wasn't it?" Laurie pointed back through the kitchen doorway, and Boyd could see that the vines had returned to the living room, fingers reaching out into the woman's house. "And I bet you can't call her."

"Him. No, I can't call him."

"Ah. Him. You can't call him." The coffee was ready and Laurie motioned for them to sit at the kitchen table. "Where do you think he is? What makes you think you'll find him?"

Boyd watched her, trying to determine the woman's age. Her face was unlined but something about her seemed older: the hook of chin, perhaps, or the slightly hooded eyes.

"I just will."

They sipped their coffees in silence, Boyd feeling a pressing need to move on, but also feeling as if she might need something in this house. And not just food, though hunger pulled at her insides, and she wished the woman had offered her a sandwich instead of coffee. In the kitchen window, the tip of a vine appeared, inching across a white sill. "Do you live out here by yourself?"

The woman, after staring into her black coffee for a moment, glanced over her shoulder toward the front room, toward the stairs. "No," she said at last, and then, a crash from upstairs, something falling to the floor. Three vines on the sill now, one long enough to begin climbing the wall.

Boyd set her feet firmly on the floor, pushing her weight into her toes, ready to rise. She had not sensed another person upstairs; suddenly, she felt exposed and untethered. One hand cupped her mug while the other fell to her backpack, now propped against her chair. Laurie closed hands around Boyd's left hand, the one holding the mug, and Boyd did not know what to feel: a low-grade terror because something important was not out in the open, mixed with an adrenaline-filled relief at the kindness of the woman's touch.

"Don't be afraid. Here, there is nothing to fear." Laurie dropped her hands from circling Boyd's and grabbed Boyd's wrist instead. "I want to show you something. Someone. My daughter. Then I'll fix you some lunch and you can go find your friend."

Boyd hesitated. Laurie had said she would *show* Boyd her daughter, not that Boyd would meet her. Boyd could not get anything from the woman other than a supreme calm, a calm that robbed Boyd of a similar feeling. Yet Boyd, shouldering her backpack in case—in case of what?—followed the woman and stepped over a board where the floor had started to crumble into the white limestone beneath it.

Laurie led Boyd through the parlor, where vines had already started again, and a thin one came in underneath the door. They stepped over this vine and climbed the stairs, Boyd's hand resting on the deeply polished banister. As they walked, thin puffs of dust rose from beneath their feet, not from outside, but from the house itself disintegrating. Boyd noticed cracks in the risers. It was an old house, after all.

At the top of the stairs was a small landing, and light streamed in through a hexagonal stained glass window, sending amethyst and turquoise darts across the rug. A bookshelf to the right held books with embossed leather bindings and porcelain dolls dressed in pinafores and crinolines. One of them was on the floor, its porcelain hand shattered beneath it. Laurie picked up the doll—was this what they had heard fall?—and put it back on the shelf, unperturbed. "Nobody plays with these anymore," she told Boyd, and led her into the first bedroom on the right.

Light poured in through three windows; this bedroom was at the corner of the house. High ceilings, a Queen Anne–style wardrobe, a rocking chair with a quilt overlaid. In the center of the room, a hospital bed, a person, a patient, asleep, IV line and catheter running out from beneath the sheet. The patient: pale, puffy but not fat, a shock of red hair beginning to tangle at the skull.

Boyd turned to Laurie. "This is your daughter?"

Laurie, biting the bottom of her lip, eyes wide, nodded. "Her name is Angie."

Boyd went to the bed and stood beside it. Angie was so pale that Boyd could see veins through her papery eyelids. Her chest rose and fell and rose, and Boyd noted a thin sheen of hospital: anodyne, urine. Angie was an adult—that much Boyd could tell—but Boyd couldn't say if Angie was twenty or forty. She had the same timeless and worn quality as her mother. The braided rug underneath the bed was threadbare at the wheels. The bed had been there a long time.

"What happened to her?"

"Car accident. Driving home one night after her shift at H-E-B. She hit a deer and drove off the road."

"May I?" Boyd reached for Angie's hand, and Laurie nodded.

Boyd took the girl's hand in her own, her right palm against Angie's and her left palm cradling the top, enveloping the weak fingers. A fecund, almost tropical warmth traveled up Boyd's arm: first her wrist, then her elbow, then her shoulder, until it reached the top of Boyd's head and relaxed her for the first time in a few days. It radiated down now, a sensation almost like a hot shower, wet without being wet, a sultry sort of peace. The girl's body thrummed.

"How long has she been here?"

"Here?" Laurie moved closer so that she was standing beside Boyd. "I brought her home four years ago. I pay a nurse part-time, but Angie just needs an IV and she has a hep-lock. Before that, she was in a facility for two years, and in the hospital for two months."

Boyd was silent, turning the girl's hand in her own.

"She was always just the most extraordinary child. Not smart exactly, but brilliant in a way that I can't really explain. She knew what you were talking about before you did, almost. She was kind." Laurie waved a hand toward the window where the stable was just visible. "When she was better, we had all kinds of animals running around here: goats, raccoons, rabbits, even a possum and a feral pig. They just followed her, you know?"

Boyd did. For a moment, Boyd wondered if this was the person she had always suspected was out there, the person who would be able to understand Boyd because she was like Boyd. What if Boyd was finally to meet this person, and the person was no longer the same?

"There's still hope, the doctors say. There's always hope. Her brain function is normal. There was no loss of oxygen, no severe trauma. She's just asleep. She's been asleep for almost seven years."

Boyd still held the girl's hand. She didn't feel anything but that lush warmth. No thoughts were in that head; the girl had just gone. Yet, here her body lay, and this was not a thing without life; Angie's hand had a weight that seemed almost like a grip, and her eyelids fluttered as if she were in the middle of some REM dream.

"Most of the time, I just sit up here." Laurie pointed to the rocking chair and to the stack of books beside it. "I read to her every afternoon. I think she likes it."

Boyd didn't know if Angie knew her mom was reading. The separation between body and spirit seemed complete to Boyd, the body an inanimate object, but, of course, Boyd didn't really know. "I wish—I wish that she would wake up. That you could have your daughter back in some way."

Laurie blinked, then acted as if she hadn't heard, as if she had heard similar things from other people. "Sometimes I read her favorites over and over again. She loved *Terms of Endearment*." Laurie shrugged. She folded her arms in front of her, resting her palms on her elbows.

"How did they let you bring her home?" Boyd had never heard of a coma patient in an upstairs bedroom.

Another shrug. "I just took her home. I have power of attorney for her. It's no crime to refuse medical care. Even cancer patients can walk out of the hospital anytime they want. I could care for her here, so there's no neglect. She doesn't need intubation or anything like that."

Boyd gave one last squeeze to the girl's hand, then set it down gently among the bedclothes, clean and bleached white. "I should be going."

Laurie started. "I forgot! I was going to fix you a sandwich."

Boyd almost told her not to worry about it, but she was so hungry. After one last look at Angie, they made their way downstairs. Boyd watched Laurie spread peanut butter on white bread. It wasn't Boyd's favorite, but then, this wasn't a restaurant. Laurie wrapped two sandwiches in a paper towel, and Boyd put them in her backpack. Then Laurie handed the third one to Boyd for eating now.

"It's not much, I know. I'm on a fixed income out here." Laurie wiped the counter with a dishrag. "It's so crazy how your whole life can change in one night." She swallowed and closed her eyes. "It's lonely out here. I feel—I feel adrift."

Boyd went to her and hugged her, peanut butter sandwich still in one hand, and over Laurie's shoulder Boyd saw the kudzu and grapevines, the moss spreading along the sill. In the night, the house would be taken, the woman and her daughter unmoored in time and space, lost to what, for the rest of her life, Boyd would call "the days after the storm." Laurie in the room upstairs, in her long prairie dress, reading library books aloud to a girl who had been turned loose from her body. Rocking and reading. The dog on the front porch and the horse in the stable the only other creatures.

Tears welled at the corners of Laurie's eyes. A naked need. Boyd did not want to walk away. But Isaac was in the tree, Isaac whom she did and did not love, and who did and did not love her.

Laurie walked her to the porch and pointed her in the direction of the river. "Keep going west and you'll hit it." The porch rails had begun to crumble, the barn to sink into the ground. The land a slow quicksand, reclaiming and erasing. And Laurie—did she notice? Boyd made a promise to herself that after she found Isaac, she would make her way back here, that she would sit in the chair and read to Angie, speaking the words of others, both dead and alive, into a palimpsest of time and place. Boyd was starting to learn how this earth worked: everything that came before bleeds through.

She waved and set out walking, and the dog followed her, but only to the fence. Then she was untethered again, waist-high in bloodweed, heading in the direction of the river smell.

Things You Would Know If You Grew Up Around Here

So Many Animals Are Already Extinct Here

Well, of course there are a bunch. There was another time, practically another earth, once. A time of, as they call it, megafauna. The animals larger than the ones we have now, the oxygen concentration so high that it would support extraordinarily large life.

In this era alone, this time of megafauna after the land had emerged from the ocean, we had the great Columbian mammoths, an animal hard for a modern human to imagine: thirteen feet high at the shoulder, with hulking, curving tusks. The *Camelops*, a genus of camel so ancient that we cannot determine whether it was humped. Dire wolves. A crazy animal called a glyptodont, basically an armadillo the size of a Volkswagen. Saber-toothed cats and scimitar cats, and short-faced bears. All of these things disappeared before 5000 B.C.E., and most faltered in what we call the Quaternary extinction event. Storks and eagles and owls and woodpeckers.

There is a cave north of Austin, discovered when a highway was built. They drilled down to take core samples, trying to see if the spot could support an overpass embankment. Thirty-three and a half feet down, the drill bit hit open air. They drilled a bigger hole and lowered a man down, and he alighted on a patch of petrified bat guano in a vast room, part of a series of underground caverns that stretched for miles.

In the cave are bone sinks, the remains of prehistoric sinkholes. Animals fell into these and didn't come back out. Forty-four species of bones, eleven of which are now extinct: a leopard frog, a saber-toothed cat, dire wolves, spectacled bears, mammoth, equus, peccary, glyptodont, ground sloth, four-horned antelope, camel. All of these animals were once here, and now they're not. In this case, they have been preserved for us to study, bones underneath a highway.

Carla followed in Boyd's footsteps, trailing the scarecrow, too, though she didn't yet know it. In her haste, she had stupidly worn yoga slings out of the house, and they were spectacularly unsuited for the mud, remaining behind for a split second after her foot. She had gone first to Boyd's house, knocking on doors and windows. Getting no answer, she had tried the doorknob, and it had given way underneath her fingertips. Inside had been the dead air of an empty house: a stillness, a staleness. She crossed the threshold and knew at once that neither Lucy Maud nor Boyd was there.

Behind her, her own house waited, but what was there for her? No one. She didn't know how, but Boyd was somehow bound up in this storm, along with the snakes and the lack of electricity and the way the sage smoke had hung in the air. More than anything else, Carla was curious—where had Boyd gone? More than this, however, was the sense of being propelled forward by the atmosphere itself.

That unnamed dread remained, that trick of the low air pressure that had driven her from her house, the sick feeling that had gotten her thinking that the world was out of balance and would need something to put it right. Now there was a mystery: the empty house but her own truck in the front yard. So she'd gone outside, seen the footsteps, and followed them. At some point, she'd become aware that there were two sets of footprints. Now she stood at the waterline, one hundred yards up the slope from where it usually stood, and the prints diverged: one set headed to the left, toward the dam, and one set headed into the bowl at the foot of the dam.

She couldn't very well head into the water, so she followed the set of footprints that headed upriver, and soon she found herself in the field of boulders at the foot of the dam. Though it still drizzled, the water here was beginning to recede, and she was able to hop from great stone to great stone despite her poor choice in footwear. The dam was five hundred yards in front of here, slightly to her right, and the floodgates were open, a sight she hadn't seen in years. The two twin towers on the dam were manned, she knew, and when she came within a certain distance to the dam, some warning system would be activated and she could be arrested. She veered left, just enough so that she could climb to the crest and see what she could see. With no footprints on the boulders, Carla had no way of knowing which way Boyd had gone.

The climb was arduous, and soon Carla found herself on her hands and knees, scrambling up a granite face, coming to the top, and finding herself face-to-face with pencil cactus and raccoon scat. She stood and dusted her hands and looked for the ways to scale the next bit of hill. Finally, she reached the top, looking first upriver toward Horseshoe Bay, then down to the lake, seeing her own house, along with Lucy Maud's, on the finger of cove where the lake began. Nobody had come to get her, and brown water still coursed merrily through the floodgates, and the high windows at the twin towers of the dam were just as blind as ever, revealing nothing about who was inside or what those people thought or did.

Above her, the river was swollen, choppy like surf. The banks were submerged and the place where the river met the land was unused to this contact: it crumbled like a cookie dipped in milk. Ahead of her was Horseshoe Bay, and she knew that around a bend or two, she would find a house and a boat ramp. Carla faced a choice: forward, or back toward her house, toward the long stretch of river before it opened into Lake Marble Falls, and the river bend before her held such a possibility that, without much thought at all, she moved in that direction. Behind her was dread, the trick of the air pressure, the way she felt the storm before she saw it.

Ahead was, if not hope, relief. She patted her pockets. She had nothing: no ID, no phone, not even her keys. She certainly had no water or sustenance, which seemed important only because she had no actual destination, only a direction that felt perpetual: up. Her first step off the limestone and granite found her shoulder deep in bloodweed, still able to see the river but just barely.

She heard them before she saw them and certainly before she felt them, their silky coursing bellies, the flicks of rattle-less tails. It was if the weeds were whispering to her. She could almost understand the language. Boyd would have understood it, understood what the earth was trying to say. Carla was so close to being that person, that conduit, but she must have gotten something wrong. Some communication wires must have been crossed, because with the next step, a flash of black, a flash of pain, and then two bright drops of crimson on her heel where the fangs had sunk. The snake gone, unidentified, Carla bleeding into the ground.

3:50 P.M.

Carla had not answered her phone, of course. Lucy Maud stood in Aunt Fern's front yard, her soon-to-be ex-husband's hand on her shoulder, Aunt Fern in her own little world on the porch, nodding to herself, Louisa May standing next to her, towering over. The bridge was out, the army had been there but was now gone, and Boyd was nowhere to be found.

"Well, now—" Kevin was gearing up to make a speech. Lucy Maud knew him too well, knew he didn't have anything particular to add to their situation, but that he didn't like this raw emotion that felt like panic, and he considered it his job to orate them out of it.

She placed her flat palm on his chest. "Listen, Boyd is probably at home. For whatever reason, she's not getting a signal. I'm sure it's just the weather." She sensed her soon-to-be ex-husband deflating, the air in his chest releasing, a relief that he didn't have to take control. "I'm going to call 911 and see if they can't get someone out there to check on her. Lou, can I use your house phone?" Lucy Maud didn't wait for an answer but headed right inside.

They trailed her like cans stuck to a newlywed's bumper, except for Fern, who laughed aloud, quick and staccato, then looked up to the sky. They milled around Lucy Maud in the kitchen as she dialed, resting her elbows on the countertop.

The dispatcher answered after the third ring. "Nine one one, what's your emergency?"

Lucy Maud hesitated. "My daughter is stranded. A bridge is out."

The woman, clinical and efficient, paused. Lucy Maud imagined her typing something, headset on. "Where is she stranded?"

"She's at my house, down on River Road, but I can't get to her because the bridge has washed out."

Another pause. "Age of the child, please."

"She's eighteen."

Another pause, and this time Lucy Maud sensed judgment. When the woman replied again, Lucy Maud sensed that the woman had gone off script. "Is the house underwater or something? Is it flooded, or about to be?"

Lucy Maud knew from this that no help was coming. "I don't know. I don't think so. I can't get down there."

A beat. "Ma'am, I understand your concern, and on any other day I'd send somebody down there. But we are stretched thin this afternoon. With real emergencies. Did you know houses washed away in Wimberley? Whole houses. With people in them."

The description of a real emergency did not make Lucy Maud feel better.

"Ma'am, unless there's a real emergency, with a person in imminent danger, it's not a call for 911. You might try 311, the nonemergency assistance line, but resources are being triaged. You're not likely to get a welfare check today."

Lucy Maud rested her forehead on Aunt Fern's cabinet. "Can you take my information, just in case?"

The woman hesitated. "Sure. But nothing will come of it."

When Lucy Maud gave her name and address, then a brief description of what Boyd looked like, she wondered if the dispatcher was even writing anything down. She thanked the woman—for nothing, she thought—and turned back to the group.

Kevin had his back to her, staring out the window. Fern was still on the front porch. But Lou stood with her hands clasped at her waist, eyebrows drawn together in worry. "I should never have left her by herself on the bridge."

Lucy Maud shook her head. "You didn't leave her by herself, though. You left her with the army."

Interrupted from his window staring, Kevin said, "National Guard," as if it made a difference.

"National Guard, then." Lucy Maud tried to hide her frustration, then wondered why. Hiding her frustration with this man had not kept him faithful. "What the hell difference does it make?"

Kevin looked up, surprised. "They're not the same."

Lou said, "I left her with a soldier named Sam."

"Thank you," Lucy Maud said in exasperation. "And that soldier likely took her home, right? And he wouldn't have left her anywhere it wasn't safe. Wherever she is, which is probably home, she's safe."

Lou nodded, the movement both quick and grave. "I wouldn't have left her otherwise."

"I know you wouldn't have. She's fine." Lucy Maud had hoped that Lou would reassure her, but instead, Lou's hesitation had the opposite effect.

Lou nodded again, and outside, Aunt Fern laughed at who knew what, the sound musical and sharp, entirely out of context. What to do? What to do? Lucy Maud felt the need to pace, felt there would be some relief in a measured walk of the room, hands clasped behind her back. But she didn't, and instead she thought of Ruben King, calling to get her to contact Isaac, spouting a bunch of nonsense about Maximilian and Pedro Yorba, names she'd heard before but couldn't remember from where. She would call Ruben.

She patted her pockets, then searched through the purse slung over her shoulder. He had been so secretive on the phone. He'd found something, he'd said. Maximilian, he'd said. Pedro Yorba. When she pulled out her phone, she googled the name. She got nothing on Pedro Yorba, only pages about the Nigerian Yoruba diaspora. Then she googled Maximilian and Texas and she found a message board that simply read "Maximilian's Treasure Found?" When she clicked through, she found a post that said that Maximilian's treasure had been found by Jesse James and a group called Knights of the Golden Circle. The post's author claimed that Maximilian had survived the firing-squad execution, that he had been saved by Dr. Frank James, that he paid the Knights of the Golden Circle ten million dollars to help him recover his treasure, and that he changed his name to John B. Maxey. The rest of the thread mocked this original poster.

Good Lord, was this what Ruben King had been talking about? She'd never taken him for a nutcase, just an old hippie who had fled to the Hill Country when Austin had changed, as so many of them had done. Was she supposed to take him seriously? And what if Boyd had gone looking for Isaac, who had been looking for Ruben? She dialed the last number in her phone.

"Isaac?" Ruben answered on the second ring, his voice breathy and high-pitched. She thought he was a fool for treasure hunting now, as the world was ending.

"No, it's Lucy Maud, Boyd's mother." She made eye contact with Kevin, who watched her. She thought he might be impressed with her decisive nature, with how completely she'd taken charge. Well, fine. She liked to take charge, was good at it, even. He had just never let her.

"Is Isaac with you? How did you know to call me here?"

"You called me from this number earlier. And Isaac is not with me."

A hesitation. "When you see him, will you tell him to call me? Listen, I found—I need to talk to him. I'm at Allen Potivar's, on Nameless Road. We found something, but we don't know what it is."

Had Ruben always been like this? She didn't remember thinking before he was so flaky. Eccentric, yes—to Lucy Maud, Ruben's obsession with history bore an amateur mark; he was not the scholar that Kevin was. "Ruben, I haven't seen Isaac. And to tell you the truth, I haven't seen Boyd. I'm looking for them."

On the other end of the phone, he sucked in a breath. "Oh, yes, if you see Boyd, tell her to come, too. This is really quite a find out here, and I want Boyd to be part of it. Even if it's not exactly treasure *per se*, it's something. It's history. Boyd would—well, I don't have to tell you that she would love to be part of it."

Lucy Maud rolled her eyes, but Ruben couldn't see. She couldn't imagine being married to this man. "Yes, Ruben, I understand that she might be excited about whatever it is that you're doing right now, but the fact remains that I have not seen her." Lucy Maud decided not to tell him about the bridge, or even too much about the storm, but she couldn't resist a passive-aggressive dig. "And it's raining, if you haven't noticed."

A silence on the other end as he considered this point. "I left a message for him," Ruben said finally. "I expect him to be here soon. We've hardly slept or eaten out here. We're trying to get down to this thing. Isaac should be here anytime."

"Ruben," she cut him off. "When did you leave the message? When was the last time you heard from Isaac?"

Another silence. "I haven't talked to him for a couple of mornings. I left that message—well, I guess I left it yesterday."

Isaac had left on the morning of the rehearsal dinner, and as far as Lucy Maud knew, he had not been seen since. Something was dreadfully wrong, and Lucy Maud didn't know what to do about it.

She felt a restlessness born of frustration. "I'll call you if I hear anything." Before she hung up, she added, "You do the same." Then, absently, her thoughts elsewhere, she went back to the message thread.

>*—Does the treasure even exist? Would anybody know it if they found it? Do we even know what it was?*
>
>*—It was supposed to be 45 large barrels filled almost to the top with gold. Some jewels and some silver. On top of this was a layer of flour in case the group was caught. This was Maximilian's own fortune, the one he wanted to smuggle it out of Mexico and to Europe. But of course, he never made it.*
>
>*—Do any of the stories say where it is buried?*
>
>*—Where the mountains make a V. You look through a window rock that lines up with Castle Mountain, and this window will tell you where the treasure is buried.*

Again she thought, *That old fool.* These hills weren't mountains. She'd never even heard of a Castle Mountain. Yet it was hard to ignore that high pitch in his voice, a voice that usually had the slow and pleasant drawl of a longtime stoner. She closed her eyes and shook her head, trying to figure out what to do next.

Boyd came across the body just as it was getting dark, the light low, centered behind the trees. For some time, she had noted debris in the canopies: twigs and sticks and branches and trash all caught in the short mesquite, all pointing the same direction, washed by the flood and laced almost deliberately wherever they had caught. An order to the chaos, but then, there had always been.

And then there was the man, draped around the trunk of mesquite, caught on what her mother called river teeth, the place where stuff snags. His shirt was missing, but his pants were still there, cornflower-blue jeans with Wrangler tabs sewn to the pocket, and his shoes were still on, leather chukkas of a nondescript taupe and no particular brand. The body was swollen with water and facedown, but Boyd knelt to look at the open eyes, brown and clouded over. The man's mouth was agape, revealing the silver line of a dental bridge, the glint of golden molars. A smell to the open mouth, almost like respiration, but the body otherwise odorless, despite what she would have expected. She circled the body, wondering what to do, noticing the hook-shaped scar on the shoulder blade, glossy yet precise, almost surgical, though she couldn't imagine what surgery had been performed in such a location. She guessed his age to be late sixties, the size of the belly revealing something about his health, though nothing else did, except for the scar.

She glanced up at the sky, rocking back on her heels. She could not carry him. She would have a hard time finding this place again and could only note it in reference to the river, a river that did and did not resemble the one she'd known for much of her life. How, then, to remember him, to let anybody know? One of his hands was wedged beside him but the other dangled free, fingers pudgy and waterlogged. No wedding ring, she thought, but the man was someone, was defined in part by his relationship to other people: brother, father, son, ex-husband, friend. Whatever he had been was now gone, but there was still this shell, this body.

She took her phone from her bag, noted the 17 percent battery, and photographed the man, his face first, then his whole body, caught ignominiously in the tree, then his tattoo and the scar on his back. Her phone beeped at her, telling her to plug it in, that it was now below 15 percent. The sound caused a brief second of panic, and she decided to call somebody, to let someone know where she was and what she was doing, but she saw immediately that there was no signal. She examined the photos she had taken—clinical, the light almost fluorescent in the photo but yellow-gray in real life—then she rested her hand on the man's scar for a minute.

He might have identification, and she lifted her hand to his waist, hesitating before she slipped it inside his front pocket, looking at his face as if he might object. The fabric was wet, and she could feel his body through the thin layer, and she imagined that he was still warm. She pressed her lips together, not wanting to inhale, and when she couldn't pull the wallet cleanly out, she pressed his shoulder with her other hand, lifting him. A deep breath slid from him, the last of this world's air leaving.

But the wallet was in her hands, and she flipped it open. The leather was disintegrating, saturated, rotting in the floodwater. Behind the plastic, the man's driver's license. The water had turned it sepia toned, made it look like a daguerreotype. She couldn't see it through the plastic window, and she slid it out, wanting to note the man's name so that later she could tell the authorities that a body was in the woods, a loved one's questions answered.

But the driver's license was different from her own, and she held it up to the light. Laminated, the plastic thicker at the middle, it had a thin ring of clear plastic on the edges. The photograph was raised—she could feel it with her thumb—and she realized that an actual photo was under the lamination. The typeface was weird as well; an actual typewriter had made this license.

`Roy Spires. Marble Falls, TX. Expiration Date: September 2, 1989.` The man's driver's license had expired almost ten years before she was born. She looked further in the wallet, and now she saw that the money was older, too, two fives and a one in the old-fashioned baroque style, the kind she occasionally saw as a child. An outdated American Express card, green with a white border, and a Shell credit card.

A breath while she decided what to do. She couldn't take the wallet with her; she would feel as if she were robbing the dead. She didn't want that old wallet with her, anyway. How long had that man carried an expired driver's license? Or else, she thought, wiping her palm on her pants, how long ago had he died? She grasped the man's hand as she slid the wallet back into his pocket, then she moved on.

She had not known when she started how long it would take to find Isaac, but she'd estimated five miles as the crow flies, and she'd thought that she could surely accomplish that in an afternoon. But she had not counted on the small child Caleb, nor on the circuitous nature of her route, nor on the clapboard house on no visible road where a woman tried to keep the vines at bay and in the afternoons read novels to a woman-child who was neither there nor gone.

She could not guess how much farther she had to go because she was so at sea in the terrain. She'd been walking for hours and she could not even say that she'd made it halfway. She no longer felt Isaac as a compass point, but she remembered him in the river, caught in a tree, as the other man had been, and that was her navigation: Go this way, far enough, and she would find him.

In the day's last light, she came upon the flood's version of a tidal pool, a bit of river separated when the water withdrew. A bowl at the bottom of a grove of pin oak, a rocky chunk of the earth removed. In the bowl, brown water was settling clear, particulates sinking; they were now part of this piece of earth and would be even after the water evaporated. The movement of water was a mechanism, the earth rearranging herself.

In the bowl, silver to the brown, were a handful of river perch, maybe four or five, undulating and silky. She thought they sensed their new limitations, knew that they had been left behind by some greater machinery, trapped in a foreign place that to them might as well be the moon. This was the last place they would ever be, and Boyd thought they knew that.

She was hungry, and river perch were delicious fish, even though they were so bony that each bite was a great deal of work. She thought for a second of eating them, knowing that it was well past dinnertime and that her backpack held few provisions. But she was reluctant in some odd way, feeling that this was too easy, that these captive fish were not a gift but would somehow be an exploitation. Besides, she realized, looking around, if she did eat them, she'd have to eat them raw: every bit of kindling around her was too wet to burn. She'd never get anything going in this sodden world.

She couldn't stomach the idea of raw perch and realized that for all of her outdoor ambitions, all of her feelings of being somehow aligned with this geography, she had not even packed a pocketknife. She could not even clean the fish, and this realization stopped her. She had a couple of Kind bars in her backpack, and the sandwiches the woman had given her, and a plastic bottle of water that had been in their kitchen even though her mother thought the world had no need for more throwaway plastic. Boyd knew now with little question that she'd spend the night in these woods, sparse as they were, but surely she'd find civilization early the next morning. And if she didn't? She had not imagined that she could disappear in this part of the world, but clearly what she'd known about her home was only a small part, the reality of it being prismatic and insanely complicated, and certain things she had thought of as natural law seemed to be broken. The past, for one. Things from the past had wandered into the present—that boy Caleb, that strange and timeless quality of the clapboard house, that man from thirty years ago—bleeding through some temporal barrier that she had taken for granted. She'd known that the earth was in some sense alive; all of this held life: plants and animals and even the wind and rain that still fell. But she now believed, in some sense, that the earth was sentient. That the earth was aware and was even trying to communicate in some fashion.

She thought about the river's fingers on her ankle, and how the earth had tried to take her.

She stopped herself there, still standing beside the little pool of doomed fish. This was a new thought to her, not necessarily unwelcome but certainly surprising. She could not pinpoint what made her feel this way, but she remembered the bean tendrils on her wrist so long ago now, and the way the bees had stung her when she had tried to break free. She remembered the footprints of the scarecrow, and how she had believed that it had come to life, believed this so much that she had imagined that she was following in these prints.

The light had winked out on the fish bodies, and darkness was settling with an audible murmur over the pin oaks. Underneath the trees, the fallen leaves, ridged at their edges like a coin, yes, but not the stiff, nearly ever-green of the live oak, formed a dense carpet. She pulled one of the Kind bars from her pack, then nestled the pack against a tree and leaned against it, slumping down until she was almost supine. She ate the bar, body nearly horizontal, but her head upright, as if the only thing she was missing were a cowboy hat. Next to her, the fish swam in their temporary bowl, knowing, she thought again, that their time was finite, was even now running down.

Dark came on, but the blackness was brief. In this time of year, the moon rose quickly after the sun fell, and as it rose, it was huge. Now the moon was truly full, and through the silvered and slivered mesquite leaves, she could see its pocked and pitted surface.

This was a different thing from camping on the lake. For one, there was no Isaac, nor the backup plan of going home should she decide to sleep in a bed for the evening. There was no proximity to refrigerator and kitchen, and despite her recent snack bar, her stomach felt hollowed. She'd learned in elementary school that hunger pangs were the sides of her stomach touching, and she felt now that her stomach had collapsed in upon itself.

She also remembered a quote from *Charlotte's Web*, and maybe she didn't get it exactly right, but the gist of it was that it was hard to sleep with a full head and an empty stomach, and it was true for her, for a little while at least. That morning, she had left Aunt Lou, crossed the bridge with Sam the soldier, discovered her garden had vivified or incarnated, been almost taken by the river, saw footprints that may have belonged to a scarecrow she had raised not six weeks ago to guard that garden, participated in some serpent-waking ritual with Carla—here Boyd raised her hand to her forehead—been led around the dam by the ghost of a child buried in a pioneer cemetery, and discovered Texas's own version of sleeping beauty in a house Boyd was not sure she could ever find again. Now she lay here at the base of a tree, famished, wondering if she would see Isaac, or anyone, again.

She fell asleep under the pin oak, despite the full mind and empty stomach, her hands falling to her side, palms up, her mouth slightly ajar. The forest, such as it was, went on around her. Raccoons inspected her pack and turned away disappointed. A fat opossum with a bald tail watched her chest rise and fall, and field mice ran over her shins, so that she moved in her sleep and cradled herself into a fetal position.

A short-nosed bear trundled by, taller than she would have believed, had she been awake to see it. Not long after, a saber-toothed cat stalked through the underbrush on heavy paws, its hour come round at last. It regarded her, considering, but turned away. Later, when the moon was higher in the sky, smaller, and the night darker but still not dark: a glyptodont, armored, tail articulated, huge and lumbering, the ground trembling under the sloth-like toes. Its short face extended and retracted, like a turtle's, and it, too, saw the girl under the tree and recognized her for what she was.

Things You Would Know If You Grew Up Around Here

The World Has Changed Everywhere

The pace of warming in the Arctic is almost twice the global average. Glaciers are disappearing, melting into the seas. In the tropics, the seas are rising, and the nations that have contributed the least to global warming will pay the highest and earliest price. Europe, too, has experienced record heat in winter, archaeological sites being revealed across the continent, from a lost German village to an Irish prehistoric henge.

Now, in the Czech Republic, the rivers have fallen so much that boulders are revealed, especially in the Elbe River. These rocks hold dates, going as far back as 1616, warning people of what happens when the water falls, when drought takes the countryside. The locals call them hunger stones, noting that such droughts signal a harvest so meager that people will die. On one of the rocks, the inscription WHEN YOU SEE ME, WEEP.

Lucy Maud had still not been able to reach Carla and was quickly nearing the end of her rope. Two hours had passed since she had spoken to Ruben, and nothing had happened other than time ticking away. No word on Isaac, who had now been missing since the rehearsal dinner. No word on Boyd.

Lucy Maud was not a person who did nothing; stillness was an impossibility for her. Now stillness was even less of an option. Who could be still when her daughter was unaccounted for? Especially in this weather.

And Kevin and Lou—Lucy Maud did not think that they were particularly helpful. They *said* a lot of stuff about how Boyd was fine—Boyd was resourceful, Boyd could take care of herself—but then their tone of voice and body language revealed that they, too, were worried. They bantered as they always had, as if there were nothing to be worried about, but Lucy Maud could see through them.

They were all sitting at Aunt Fern's table, Lou drinking a Dr Pepper as if it weren't six o'clock in the afternoon and Kevin playing a game of solitaire. Lucy Maud watched him cheat a couple of times—when he couldn't play, he just turned a card over—and she thought she should have noticed this detail about him long ago.

At last, she picked up her phone and called Ruben again. Despite his silliness about buried treasure, he was Isaac's last known destination, and thus the only real lead for finding Boyd. But the phone simply rang—no answer from anybody on Nameless Road. She hung up, closing her eyes, irritation curling her insides like paper burnt at the edges.

"Y'all," she said because she had to say something, "I think I'm going to head out to Ruben King's."

They both looked up, surprised at the exasperation in her voice but not at the news. For two hours, they had all been waiting for Lucy Maud to do something, and here it was finally, the last resort that Lucy Maud had at the moment. Where Isaac was, Boyd would not be far behind, and Isaac had been heading to find Ruben King out on Nameless Road. It was a long shot, but Lucy Maud was determined to do something.

"Okay," Lou said, and Lucy Maud saw Lou exchange a look with Kevin, some private judgment about Lucy Maud's behavior. But part of Lucy Maud—most of her—did not care. She remembered how it had felt in that Holiday Inn Express bed when Kevin had been on the phone in the bathroom. She got up from the table.

"Well, let's go." Kevin gathered the playing cards into a stack.

Lucy Maud nodded.

"I'm coming, too," Lou said, and though Lucy Maud wasn't entirely sure about this, she said nothing.

They followed her outside and she got in Kevin's car, Kevin in his own passenger seat, and Lou stood for a moment in the yard. "Well, come on, I guess," Lucy Maud told her sister, and was surprised when Lou turned around and went back in the house, raising her index finger as if to say, *One second.* Lucy Maud was surprised again by the realities of Lou's life, because Lucy Maud had completely forgotten about Aunt Fern, but Lou had not. They couldn't leave Aunt Fern behind. She would wander off. But she was going to be more hindrance than help in whatever adventure they were about to have. For a second, Lucy Maud hesitated—she didn't think it was a good idea to bring Aunt Fern. But then she remembered that Lou would be with them, watching Aunt Fern as she always did. They would all be fine, if they could only find Boyd.

8:00 P.M.

Carla, still walking, even more unprepared for a night in the elements than Boyd, saw lights ahead of her, electric lights that drew her forward. She didn't hesitate; it was much better to look for a person than to sleep on the ground. She had no plan, just an idea that the person might offer a ride home or a telephone, though she wasn't sure she wanted either.

Her heel had stopped bleeding, but two twin spots remained, so red that they were black. She knew from the elapsed time that the snake had not been a rattlesnake, or if it had been, the bite had been dry, venom-less. Otherwise, her leg and foot would have swollen within minutes, and it had now been more than an hour, and nothing had happened other than the blood clotting thickly, her body staunching the wound.

She knew, too, that it had not been a coral snake, another of the poisonous snakes in the area, because the pain had been manageable, then quickly forgettable. A coral snake's bite was said to be one of the most painful experiences a body could experience. She also knew that the bite was wrong for a coral snake—fast—whereas a coral snake chewed to deliver its venom. She was glad for this; she had read an article in the *Statesman* that said coral snake antivenom was no longer made, being too expensive to make and to store.

That left copperhead and cottonmouth, or water moccasin, as the other possible poisonous snakes in the region, and she didn't think it was a water moccasin. She'd never heard of somebody being bitten so far from the water. And if it was a copperhead, she wasn't too worried. That bite wouldn't kill her, though it would hurt for weeks. But this bite didn't hurt, and the fear that had gripped her when she had looked down at those two twin dots was slowly fading and being replaced by something else.

This something else—what was it? For a while, she walked toward the lights and asked herself this question. Power, she thought for the first few hundred yards, but that was not it, or at least it wasn't nuanced enough. Power made her think of the radioactive spider that had bitten Spider-Man, and this was not that. It was more a steady drumbeat of boldness, a sense that her relentless self-questioning was abating. She remembered reading Gloria Anzaldúa's *Borderlands* in college and recalled that the serpent was the symbol of the feminine body, and of *la facultad*, the ability to see the deep core of things. She hoped, fervently, that this was true. She would, she thought, be able to handle whatever came her way.

Soon she reached a fence, the outer perimeter that enclosed the lights she'd been following. The fence was barbed wire, with cedar posts with a purple blaze every twenty yards or so. She skirted it, seeing what she could see in the near dark. Three large pole barns were triangulated on the outer edges of the property. Nestled in the middle were several houses of varying sizes, one painted white, one brown and turquoise to look like adobe, and one shingled cottage that looked as if it would be more at home on the seashore. Another house, a larger one, two stories and wide, was centered in the middle of the compound. On each front porch, a light, and several sodium lamps on tall poles scattered at regular intervals. She saw an open area beyond the houses that was too dark to check out, but she imagined field or paddock, then a dip in the land, and beyond this she saw the canopies of pecan trees, even in the dark. Those trees were unmistakable in this country, towering over everything else as they did, looking like the trees of some greener and more hospitable place, transplanted to central Texas.

This was a commune. Enough of them were in the Hill Country that Carla could recognize one when she saw it. What type of commune she could not say. As Austin had changed over the years—as the hippie culture

THINGS YOU WOULD KNOW IF YOU GREW UP AROUND HERE 153

of the sixties and seventies had been replaced by the eighties yuppie culture and the grunge culture and was now nearly subsumed by a money-driven hipster culture—the original Armadillo World Headquarters hippies had fled west, and you could still find them here, with long white beards and Magellan fishing shirts, growing their own marijuana in greenhouses, worshipping the sun. There were also family compounds, communes that happened more accidentally, when somebody with a piece of land hosted their relatives, keeping sons and daughters and sisters and brothers close. Carla, however, guessed that this was a religious commune, despite not seeing a chapel.

The religious communes had been popping up more and more out here lately, though some had been well established for decades. She'd heard teachers—Isaac's father, for one—talking about children who had been born on these communes and for whom no record existed—no birth certificate, no Social Security number, no nothing—who would never go to a public school or fly on a plane or have a driver's license, credit card, or checkbook. Some of the religious groups out here—Mennonites and Quakers and their offshoots—practiced a faith that made a lot of sense to Carla. They respected their land, and they rejected material, capitalist lives. But some of these groups were more sinister to Carla, practicing a dangerous sort of patriarchy as a religion, and every once in a while, some shocking news would get out, such as the nearly four hundred women authorities removed from the compound near Eldorado in 2008, when underage girls were forced to marry much older men.

She could still not say what made her guess that this was a religious commune, other than the general tidiness and that tall house in the middle, a house that seemed to Carla to be the main house on a plantation. Except for the Mennonites, Carla had a deep-seated distrust of those so religious as to sequester themselves; to her, these communities often seemed like little dictatorships in which one person controlled the lives of everybody else. She knew this wasn't always true, but this was her view. However, she was hungry and didn't want to sleep on the ground, so she tried to find the gate. At the very least, they might have a phone so she could call someone, maybe Lucy Maud. And then what? Go home for the night and come right back here in the morning?

She didn't know how to make it happen, but she wanted to spend the night in a bed and then wake up exactly here, still walking in this direction. She had no idea where she was headed but thought that she would eventually get there and would run into Boyd along the way. Carla felt led, an inexplicable pull west, and had the idea, ridiculous though it was, that the serpents wanted her to follow Boyd.

It was not late, just dark, and though darkness was indeed coming later these days, she guessed it was still only around eight P.M., in these last days of spring. She would not be rousing people from sleep or getting them out of their beds. If she could only find a gate, she could make her way in and find somebody. Tell them she was lost, which was not untrue. Those purple blazes, though, they stopped her. Getting shot was a real possibility if she wasn't careful. If this was a religious group, out here for privacy, for a lack of eyes, then they would want to get rid of her as quickly as possible.

When she found the gate—a long cattle gate closed with a chain—it was locked. An intercom was on the fence next to it, a fence of spindly Ashe juniper with the bark still on. But the intercom looked ancient for an intercom—from the eighties, maybe—and when she tried to push the buttons, nothing happened. They just rattled around in their spaces as if they weren't connected to anything. Meanwhile, it grew darker.

She twisted her mouth to one side, wondering what to do. "Hello?" she yelled. It would be nothing to climb over this gate, but those purple blazes suggested that she should not. Wouldn't it be something, she thought, to come this far and to get shot by a bunch of religious zealots. "Hello?" she yelled again, and at the closest house, the shingled one that looked as if it belonged on the seashore, a door opened, spreading a windowpane of yellow light upon the front porch. Music escaped, too, classical strings, and even from here, Carla thought she could place the melody—Dvořák's "Humoresque." She smelled somebody's dinner, and a longing overtook her. What would it be like to live like this, among people who cared about you? But she also believed that most religions were a form of patriarchy, a means for men to control women and children. Here she was a woman, and she had once been a controlled child, but she would never be a man.

The figure at the door was lanky in trousers and a tank top. In the figure's hands, cutting obliquely across the body, the silhouette of a rifle. Carla could not tell what make, but it was a hunting rifle and not something more sinister. Still, she rocked back on her heels, unsure whether this was hospitality, unsure what she'd stumbled upon out here where the way to answer a visitor was with a gun.

She could tell by the way the man walked—measured, light, and wincing—that he was barefoot, that she had taken him from his supper table. "Here," she said, waving so she did not startle him so that he would not shoot her, and he stepped in her direction. When he was finally in front of her, he looked up from the ground. Carla was surprised to find herself looking not at a man but at a woman, neither old nor young, with a weathered face and dark hair cropped close to the skull. The woman's build was indeed lanky, as Carla had noted, wiry and strong, nearly vibrating with a latent potential energy. Carla could not guess her age; the woman could be anywhere from thirty to fifty.

"Yes?" The woman's tone of voice made it seem as if it were not unusual for Carla to be standing at her gate. The woman's stance, however, was wary.

"Hi." Carla reached a hand across the gate as if to shake, but the woman only looked at it and held fast to the rifle. Carla tried a different tack. "I'm lost. I was looking for someone and it's been hours and I haven't found the person and now I have no idea where I am." She gestured around her. "And now it's dark." Another moment, then: "Can I use your phone?"

The lanky woman glanced behind her, toward that square of light on the shingled house's porch, toward the suddenly serious bridge of "Humoresque." "Um," she said, considering, then she cast a long look up and down Carla, her gaze stopping at last on Carla's face. "What's on your forehead?"

Carla's fingertips went to the space above and between her eyes that she called *the third eye.* "Oh, that." She reluctantly wiped as much as she could off. "Just some ashes." She realized how strange that sounded. "From earlier," she added, as if that would be helpful.

The woman just watched her. "You alone?"

"Yes." Carla felt the cumulative ridiculousness of the choices she'd made all through that long afternoon. If she showed up on her own doorstep like this, what would she do? "Look, I know how this sounds."

The woman nodded. "Are you armed? Before I let you in here, I want to know if you are armed."

Carla stepped back, shocked. "No," she said, bewildered that someone could think she would carry a firearm. "I am not armed. I don't even own a gun."

A smile from the woman, and the rifle was dropped to one side. "Well, come on, then." She opened the gate, unwrapping the chain, and Carla saw that the padlock had not even been closed. "You can use our phone."

Carla walked through the gate, hearing her yoga slings—which she was surprised had made it this far—crunching the gravel. The woman stood to one side, not quite ready to turn her back on Carla, and now she finally put a hand forward. "Kim."

Carla shook the hand. "Carla. I live down toward Cottonwood Shores, down below the dam."

"Below the dam? You walked all that way?"

"Yes. It's a long story."

Kim took Carla into the shingled house, where three other women sat around a dinner table. A roast chicken was in the center, and while it hadn't quite been picked clean, not much was left. Beside the chicken was a sheet pan of vegetables: potatoes, red peppers, onions. Tortillas—to Carla's eye homemade—on a dinner plate beside this. The women looked up at her when she came in: one had pushed back from the table and was knitting something with blue yarn, one had her elbows on the table and her chin in her hands, and the other swirled a glass of wine, the red liquid hypnotic to Carla in this yellow light.

"Y'all," Kim said, "this is Carla. She's lost." They raised a hand, a knitting needle, and a wineglass in her direction, their expressions curious and, Carla thought, welcoming. Kim turned and handed Carla a cell phone she'd produced from her pocket. "She needs to use the phone." Kim pointed toward a living room to the right of the short entry and dining room. "You can go in there if you need privacy."

It was a flip phone, not a smartphone at all, and Carla did not know how to get a number for a taxi company. She did not even know if there was a taxi company out here. She tried to remember Lucy Maud's number and couldn't; she hadn't dialed it since she'd programmed it into her phone. Carla felt acutely the small size of her world: she had a friend in Austin,

Donna, who lived off Shoal Creek and with whom Carla drank margaritas on occasion. But, again, she had no idea what Donna's number was. She had a brother in Oklahoma, Trevor, to whom she hadn't spoken in months, not since his wife had had their fourth child in as many years. She should really go see him, Carla thought, and sat down on the couch, still holding the phone.

Kim watched her from the doorway. "You okay?"

Carla looked up at her, tears starting as she realized how lonely, how alone, she was. She closed her eyes so that Kim wouldn't see them, swallowing hard. After a minute, she had control of herself. "I don't have anybody's number."

Kim's lower back rested on the doorjamb, her body bent at the waist, that same latent energy that Carla had noticed before and that, she realized, was similar to Boyd's. "Hey," Kim said after a minute, "why don't you eat something while we figure out who to call."

Carla, grateful, nodded.

Kim led her back into the dining room, and the knitting woman looked up and gave up her chair for Carla, Kim fetching the woman a stool so that she could stay close to the table. The wine-drinking woman got Carla a glass, too, and the third woman got Carla a plate and tried to get some of the remaining meat off the chicken. Carla sat and let herself be served, and the tears came now again, slow but relentless. "I'm just tired," she told the women, and then the one fixing a plate said, "Oh, you're vegetarian," as if that was what was wrong with Carla, and then she scraped the chicken back into the roasting pan.

Carla shook her head. "No, no, it's not that. I eat meat. I mean, still, for now, though I keep meaning to stop but I just never do."

They all looked at her, and she knew she hadn't answered their question. "I just—I just don't know what I'm doing out here, and I'm lost and tired and hungry. So thank you."

The woman hesitated, then scooped the chicken back up with a serving spoon. "Well, okay." She moved on to the vegetables. "You can cry all you want, then."

The statement stopped Carla. It was so similar to what her stepdad would have said to her once, the exact same words but with a different tone. *You can cry all you want*, he'd said as he pulled the belt from his pants, the *shhhh* of the belt loops a chilling sound, as she'd braced her knuckles on the back of a chair for the blow. But this woman—her words were the same but the meaning was different. This woman's words—an echo from another part of Carla's life—meant something, the way the snakebite had meant something. "I'm sorry," she said, though she didn't think she needed to.

"I'm Imogene," the woman said, and put the plate down in front of Carla.

Kim got her some silverware.

The knitting woman, whose needles had paused while Kim had fetched the stool but who had otherwise kept steadily clicking, said, "Bess."

And the wine drinker: "Annie."

Carla picked up a chicken leg with her hands. She was ravenous and ate, she felt, like a maniac. Juice dripped down her arms. "Sorry," she said again.

"Nothing to be sorry for," Kim said. They watched her eat for a moment, then got back to their own conversation.

"There are two broken panes on the greenhouse," Annie said. "We lost some of the aloe vera. But not much."

"Okay." Kim took a minute to think. "We'll get somebody out here to fix it. But all of those panes are the same size, right?"

"I think so," Anne said.

"Well, I want you to watch how it gets fixed, and if we can buy extra panes and store them, let's do that. Then we won't have to call somebody next time."

They chatted like this for some time, pleasantly and productively, mostly about the stewardship of the property. Imogene talked about rabbits and Bess about sheep, while Kim nodded along and listened and responded. They talked about the care of an elderly woman, and Carla remembered the other houses on the property. More people were here, she realized with disappointment. She didn't want there to be any more people than these four women who were feeding her, who had told her to go ahead and cry if she wanted.

She tried to get a sense from the conversation how many others there were. There were children because Bess had mentioned knitting crib blankets, and Annie had talked about teaching junior master gardeners. Carla got the impression that maybe many more people were here, having similar dinners and conversations in the other houses.

At last, after Carla's plate had been refilled and Carla finally slowed down eating, Kim turned to her. "If you want, I can drive you home. You don't need to call anybody." Carla felt panic, thinking of her house, the polished concrete floors, the quiet. After a minute Kim continued, "Or you can just stay here for the night and we can get you home in the morning."

Hope—a flying, blooming thing—in Carla's chest. Carla resisted the urge to reach for Kim, to touch her, to know with her own fingertips that Kim was real. "Yes. Yes." When the other three looked up, nodding, Carla had some feeling that this was how they'd come here, too. Wanderers, lost and hungry, come to rest for a night, but the night had stretched out to something much longer.

Lucy Maud was trying to find Nameless Road in the dark, while in the back seat, Aunt Fern was telling Lou a story about the time before the dam, only Aunt Fern was calling Lou *Bea* instead. "Albert cried that day we decided not to dig her up," Aunt Fern said, talking to Lou as if Lou's own grandfather were her husband, and Lucy Maud couldn't figure out whom Fern was talking about. Fern took Lou's hand and stroked it. "But it wasn't because he was weak or bad, Bea. You know that better than anybody, don't you? Albert was a good man—the best." Albert was Fern's brother, dead for fifty years, Homer and William's father, though William, too, was long gone. Lou, patient, just nodded, and Lucy Maud wondered when Lou had stopped trying to explain that the world was not what Aunt Fern thought it was. It seemed a sad thing to give up that argument, as if acknowledging that Aunt Fern would never be in the real world again. Kevin, beside Lucy Maud in the front seat, flipped through the radio channels, finally stopping on some Fleetwood Mac and singing along under his breath: "'If I could, baby, I'd give you my world . . .'" And Lucy Maud thought again that Kevin was looking at her in a different way, that maybe that grad student in Austin wasn't so appealing right now.

They had turned off the main road some time ago, and the GPS had led them to a dead end. They'd seen water off to the side of the road, water covering one of the approaches, and Lucy Maud had been glad they hadn't come that way. But still, she couldn't be sure she was on the right path now, and what would she do when she showed up wherever Ruben King was? It was getting late—it had to be around nine P.M.—and obviously neither Isaac nor Boyd was with Lucy Maud. Instead, she had her soon-to-be ex-husband, her twin sister, and a great-aunt with midstage Alzheimer's in the back seat. Fern said, "*Shhhh,*" with her finger to her lips, and they all listened to nothing but the radio, obedience to their aunt ingrained into them. "Did you hear that?" Fern whispered. They heard nothing, but then Fern started talking again. "Of course, she was buried in the same cemetery that William was, that long field under the Douglas firs. Homer was so little then. He didn't even realize he'd lost his brother, but you did, didn't you? You knew your baby had died." Aunt Fern still thought Lou was Lou's grandmother Bea. Lucy Maud imagined Douglas firs and cemeteries and half-level tombstones rising out of the mists.

They passed several small roads, all nameless, but not, she didn't think, Nameless. But for the lack of mailboxes at the turnoffs, she would have thought them to be driveways. At last, she could tell that they had skirted the hill and were about to come back out on the main road, and she knew that was not what she wanted. She stopped the car in the middle of the road, white limestone dust hanging in the headlight beams, and reached over and switched off the radio.

"Hey," Kevin said.

In the back seat, Aunt Fern sat straight up. "Do you hear that?"

They turned and she pointed out Lou's window. When their gazes followed the direction of Fern's index finger, she clicked off her seat belt and it slid across her lap. "Don't you hear that man? I thought it sounded like Albert, but—" She didn't say anything else, and Lucy Maud wondered if Fern realized that Albert was dead and had been for decades. While Lucy Maud and Lou were looking out the window, thinking about their dead grandfather, Aunt Fern opened the door and got out.

"What?" Lou scrambled to get her seat belt off and go after Aunt Fern.

When Lou got out, Lucy Maud stayed put, drumming the steering wheel lightly with loosely closed fists. "What do we do now?" she asked herself.

Kevin thought she was speaking to him and seized her phone from the cup holder to poke around on the map. She let him, even as irritated as she was. Wouldn't do them any good for her to snap at him.

Lou banged briefly on the window: "Help." Then she ran away again in Aunt Fern's direction. Lucy Maud and Kevin exchanged glances and got out of the car. Lucy Maud saw her twin sister running away, but Aunt Fern was too far away to see.

They followed Lou about twenty yards down the road before Lucy Maud realized she should have turned off the engine. With each step, the sound of its running seemed farther away, as if the night were an insulation, the acoustics not quite what she'd expected. Thank God she'd turned off that Fleetwood Mac song, as that would have been unbearable, that music hanging in this thick air, feeling a mile away instead of a hundred yards.

They could no longer see Lou. In fact, they could see little, their eyes not having adjusted to this dark.

"Kevin, there's a flashlight in the glove compartment."

"All right." He turned back. Lucy Maud kept walking, picking up speed, wanting to catch her sister but scared of tripping on something. She could tell by the wet sound of the gravel on the asphalt that rain had recently passed through here. The whole world was wet now.

"Lou?" she called, her feet sliding on the gravel because, in the dark, she was not sure where to put them. "Fern?" She looked back but could not see Kevin, even though she could see the car's headlights illuminating twin beams of limestone dust. "Lou?" Nothing. On the air, the sound of running water and the night.

She stopped on the road, her hands on her hips. She couldn't walk forward anymore; she couldn't see a thing. But how could Lou and Aunt Fern see anything either? Aunt Fern was old and not so quick. How far could she have gotten? Surely they were still on the road. Surely Aunt Fern would not have ducked off into the underbrush or gone down the hill.

Lucy Maud realized that she could not be sure what Aunt Fern would do. She hadn't been around her in so long. Lou was the caretaker. But Lucy Maud wouldn't have called her twin that before now. Until the moment when Fern stepped out of the car, Lucy Maud would have called Lou Aunt Fern's companion. Until this moment, Lucy Maud hadn't realized the extent to which her aunt needed help. But the signs had been there: that story at the rehearsal dinner, which nobody knew and which was obviously from a movie or a book. And just a few days ago, Fern had stripped naked and ambled down to the lake. Boyd had brought her back. Lucy Maud hadn't realized how like a child Aunt Fern was. She knew Lou left Fern every morning to go to her AA meetings, and Lou also worked part-time at H-E-B. What happened to Aunt Fern when Lou was away? Did Fern wander off then?

Lucy Maud could not go any farther in the dark, and Kevin had not returned with the flashlight. She turned around. She would get the car, drive slowly back down this road, headlights on and windows down, calling for her twin and aunt. She didn't know if she should be worried about Kevin, who was a perfectly capable adult but who should definitely have returned by now.

When she reached the car and opened the door, she saw him, sitting in the passenger seat, on the phone. She knew with whom, too, even without the guilty look on his face when she opened the door and the dome light illuminated him. She stopped.

A betrayal, certainly, but of what magnitude? Lucy Maud knew about the graduate student. But no. Now Lucy Maud was the woman on the side, and the graduate student didn't know about her. She could tell by the way Kevin exited the car in a hurry and walked away, before Lucy Maud could say anything. He was afraid his Austin girlfriend would hear her.

She got in and leaned her head on the steering wheel. What was she so upset about? She knew him for what he was, knew that so much of what had happened between them could be said to be her own fault. But this betrayal hurt her anew, and after a minute she figured out why. He was supposed to be helping her. This was an emergency. Boyd was missing, and now Lou and Aunt Fern were out there in the dark. And Lucy Maud herself had been standing in the dark, waiting for Kevin to bring her a flashlight. But here he'd been, seizing the moment to reassure the Austin girl that he wasn't doing exactly what he had been doing.

Lucy Maud put the car in reverse, turning around. Her sister and her great-aunt were out there. She wasn't going to sit here and ponder her soon-to-be ex-husband's latest betrayal. She rested her right hand on the passenger headrest, looking over her shoulder. She hit the gas a little harder than she meant to, and the car bucked backward. She heard Kevin's footsteps as he realized what was happening and ran to get in. "Love you, too," she heard him say, then he hung up.

"Jeez, Lucy Maud, what are you doing?" He shut the door and put his seat belt on as if they were going for a long drive.

"Well, I couldn't very well keep going in the dark." She refused to look at him and instead rolled down her window. Still without looking, she rolled his down, too.

"Lou?" she yelled, driving back the way they'd come. She didn't know how fast to go; Lou had been running after she'd banged on the car. Lucy Maud had no idea how fast Aunt Fern would be but didn't want to run over one of them in the dark. She increased her speed to fifteen miles per hour, thinking that was a four-minute mile. No way Lou or Aunt Fern was that fast. But they'd had a head start. How many minutes had passed since Lou had banged on the car asking for help?

They continued down the road, paved once but mostly gone to gravel, like so many of the other roads around here. Nothing in the headlights: no trace of the two women. After a mile or so, Lucy Maud grew frustrated with only being able to see in front of her, so she reached in the glove compartment and got the flashlight she'd sent Kevin for. Here she finally looked at him, hoping he could read her contempt. Useless, she thought, narrowing her eyes. She could never depend on him.

They drove for a bit, calling and seeing nothing. After ten minutes, she calculated that they had gone two to three miles. They'd seen no sign of Lou and Fern. Lucy Maud knew, too, that they were coming to the end of this section of road, and she was reluctant to leave it, knowing as she did that her sister and her aunt were somewhere behind her. To her left was a wet-weather creek, a gully that would normally be dry but that now coursed with water. She hoped that Aunt Fern had not wandered into that.

She stopped and reversed again, ready to go back down the road. As she turned around, her headlights fell on a silver Subaru in front of an A-frame cabin. A cabin just off the road, down one of the long driveways. "Hey, isn't that Ruben King's car?"

Kevin looked at her. "I haven't seen Ruben King in five years. I have no idea what he drives." When Lucy Maud was silent for a minute, thinking

THINGS YOU WOULD KNOW IF YOU GREW UP AROUND HERE 165

about how much of Boyd's life he had missed, he added, "You did a good job, Lucy Maud. You always were a good mother." It was almost as if he could read her mind.

She softened. She knew she was being manipulated, but what did it matter? He was a supremely flawed human being, but she loved him anyway. For years—decades—they had been so much to each other, often, other than for Boyd, the only thing. It was hard to believe now, but she'd once been astonished at his tenderness, at how solicitous he had been. The way he'd waited on her when she'd been sick, giving her a bell in the bedroom so that she could call him as he worked in the kitchen. The time in Austin when she'd offhandedly remarked that she'd always wanted a swing, and her surprise to see one hanging from the live oak the very next day. The way he'd reach over in the night, both of them sleeping, just to make sure that she was there. All of this before she'd aged, before he, too, had aged but had not yet come to admit it. "Sweet-talking your way out of everything," she said, and let it drop. There were the two missing people to worry about, and now she was 90 percent sure that was Ruben King's car. Even in the dark, she could see the black rectangle of a bumper sticker. She thought she knew what that sticker said: YOU MAY ALL GO TO HELL AND I WILL GO TO TEXAS. DAVY CROCKETT. She could not see the window where Ruben King had a Wheatsville Co-op sticker.

Now the dilemma. Did she go knock on that door or did she keep looking for Lou and Fern? She thought about sending Kevin back down the road one more time, but part of her thought that if she let him go, if they split up, she'd lose him, too. She felt that there was something about the night that she couldn't trust.

"Kevin, I know that car belongs to Isaac's father. I'm going to knock on that door to see if he will help us find them." She thought for a second, then turned the car around so that the headlights shone back up the road. Then she turned to him. "Stay here." *I don't want you getting lost, too.*

He nodded, not taking much convincing.

She added, "Watch for them," and got out of the car. She didn't even want him to get in the driver's seat, sure that if he did, he would drive off.

She lingered for a moment, bent at the hip, head inside the car, body outside. Who could explain why you loved a person? How many years had she known this man, and still, her heart quickened when she saw him. She remembered him: gangly, before he'd grown into his height, finishing undergrad. He'd tried to take her to an Ayn Rand objectivist meeting. She should have known then that one of his defining characteristics was a self-centeredness that was not quite meanness. The man had always looked out for number one. Ah, but how she'd loved him, and how she still did.

She nodded once, resolutely, stood up, and closed the door. She walked away, headed to the A-frame cabin. They'd come out here to find someone because they'd lost someone else—and lost two more people. The math was not on their side. She should never have let Lou bring Aunt Fern.

Boyd, asleep on the ground. A smell on the air. The sea. The ancient animals passing through, stopping to gaze at the pool of trapped river perch. And Boyd, dreaming of rafts on the Rio Grande and Guadalupe, the bats of the summer dusks, the carpet of bluebonnets in the late spring. Sleeping deeply until the man knelt beside her and shook her by the shoulder.

Still, she was reluctant to wake. She felt adrift in something amniotic, as though parts of her were still being formed. A sense of starlight and fusion. The golden heart of ore on an anvil, dotted with the black specks of the exterior's quick cooling. But the man continued his shaking, urgent and undeterred.

"Miss?"

In the place between sleep and wakefulness, she perceived that he spoke an old-fashioned German and that she understood it. She stretched and her shoulder slid out of his hand. When she opened her eyes, she saw him, rocked back on his heels in a squat, his elbows resting on his knees. His face was lined around the eyes but still young, his beard and mustache neat, his sideburns robust, his clothes homemade and worn.

She sat up and saw beyond him a woman, hair so light that it seemed silver in the moonlight. She wore a long dress of dark calico, and bare toes peeked out from the hem. Boyd thought the woman drew the moonlight. The woman opened her mouth to speak, but nothing came out.

Boyd sat up, scratching her head and shifting to chase the sleep from her limbs. She didn't know what time it was; the moon was still high, but the woman held a lantern.

"So sorry to wake you," the man said. "Have you seen a child? A small boy?"

Boyd got her feet under her and rose. She was taller than the man, and she was only five feet four inches. She was still unsure about the world, still remembering the strange events of the day before. The air had a quality she could not describe; it spoke of storm, of a rift in sky and space, the atmosphere knitting itself back together.

"Please," the woman said, taking a step forward. "You must help us. Have you seen a little boy come through here?"

Boyd had not seen a little boy. She did not know how to help. She looked into the darkness, her head turning first this way, then another. Then she remembered.

"Oh, Mother," the man said to the woman. "We must find him. The ground is already crisp with frost."

Boyd looked now at the ground and stepped in place a couple of times to test it. It was the end of May in central Texas. There was no danger—no possibility—of frost.

Of course Boyd would help them, though she was nearly positive the search was futile. She shouldered her backpack anyway. "I'll help you look."

The man and woman glanced at each other. Boyd did not know what they were thinking; their faces were expressionless. "Thank you," the man said, and the woman walked forward, past the pool of trapped perch. "Caleb," the man yelled. Boyd fell in line behind them, though they had just confirmed her suspicion: the search for this boy would not bear fruit. The search had had exactly one chance to be successful, a night more than a century ago, and having failed that night, it was doomed to fail this night as well. Nevertheless, she joined them, cupping her hands around her mouth and calling the boy's name into the forest. The thought came to her that she was counting on their not finding him. What would it be like to be alone in the dark with these two people when they came across what was left of their child, with his toothless mouth revealing his decay, and his constant hum of fear? Would their discovery end his discomfort?

She tripped, stumbling as she stepped on her own shoelace, but caught herself, her hands reaching out instinctively to brace her fall before she tumbled forward under the weight of her pack. When she'd righted herself, she knelt to tie the shoe, feeling as well as she could in the dark. The woman marched forward, carrying the lantern light.

When Boyd stood, the light was gone, and so were the man and woman. "Hello?" Boyd called. She hadn't gotten their names and couldn't remember them from the pioneer graveyard. "Hello?" she shouted again, though the couple had vanished. Instead, the forest answered her: wind in pin oaks, the drip of rainwater from Ashe juniper, the hiss of night wings on the sky.

She had not been afraid before, not really, and was not sure she was afraid now, but she felt suddenly how unprotected she was here, how out in the open. She had only followed the couple for ten minutes or so, maybe a quarter of a mile, but she was certainly in a different place from when she had started.

She removed her pack and sat, her back against a different tree now, a hackberry with gnarled bark, even though hackberry was a fence-line tree and here she was in the middle of the woods. She could not possibly go back to sleep; the night air had infiltrated.

A hand on her shoulder, and she jumped, startled. "Miss?" the man said.

She stood quickly, grabbing her pack. "You're back! I lost you."

"So sorry to wake you. Have you seen a child? A small boy?"

"No. Remember, we were looking for him?"

His figure, foregrounded, cut into the woman's circle of lantern light.

"Please," the woman said, taking a step forward, the light circle expanding. "You must help us. Have you seen a little boy come through here?"

Boyd, nonplussed, wondered if she was dreaming again. "But we were looking for him. Together. Just a second ago." Neither expression, dimly lit by flickering lantern light, responded. The woman raised the lantern, her arm parallel to the ground, her fist closed around the iron loop. Boyd saw she was missing a thumbnail, the nail bed raw and exposed. Things were falling off the woman.

"Oh, Mother," the man said to the woman. This time he did not turn his head to look at her but stayed fixed on Boyd. "We must find him. The ground is already crisp with frost."

Boyd hesitated, unsure what to do. It was not in her nature to refuse help to someone who asked for it. But these people appeared to have no knowledge of her helping them already, and she had been led so far from the river.

The woman, now sensing Boyd's hesitation, took her hand. Boyd flinched, but when she looked down, she saw that all of the fingernails on the hand not holding the lantern were accounted for.

She allowed herself to be led forward, stepping on ground that was decidedly not crisp with frost, falling in line behind the woman with the man bringing up the rear. Soon, Boyd found herself shouting into the night, "Caleb? Caleb!" She did not want to run across Caleb, and that made her wonder what these people were, whether they were ghosts or merely some record of a horrible night, some fabric of that time mis-woven into this.

After a few minutes of walking, Boyd realized that her footsteps crunched gravel and oak leaves, sometimes acorns or yucca pods, her weight enough to crack them. The woman in front of her made no such sound, but instead almost a tinkling, a sound of broken glass or ice. Now the woman in front of her was going faster, opening up a distance between them, and Boyd struggled to speed up. The gap between Boyd and the woman widened.

The tinkling sounds were also close on Boyd's heels, only a couple of inches behind her. She felt his breath on her neck, sensed that he would walk right through her, that his body would pass through hers, that she would bear this imprint of the past inside her for the rest of her life. She panicked and stepped briefly off the trail.

He went on, just missing her, a blur now matching the speed of his wife, the tinkling sounds of footfalls still audible, though she could not see his feet rise or fall. She stepped back on the path, following slowly, unsure she wanted to catch them. After a minute, the lantern light was gone, and she sat down to let her eyes readjust to the dark, noting the white cast to the landscape around her, limestone without much topsoil, and she wondered if they'd been climbing. Yes, she thought, considering this possibility, remembering how she had leaned forward as she walked, the rise of land here but nearly imperceptible. She felt exposed again, defenseless to a different wind and air. She could sense, too, the time that this would cost her, the urgency of Isaac in the tree, water rising around him. What that loss would mean to her. Whether she would end up wandering these woods, asking the rare passerby for help.

She had followed different footsteps from the garden to the lake, wondering how to get to Isaac. The river had seemed the most logical choice, a direct shot northwest, straight to where she had sensed Isaac in the tree. She guessed it was now around midnight; she would not be able to find the river again until sunrise. Isaac, too, must be alone in the night, assuming—which she did—that he was still holding on.

So she resolved to get whatever sleep she could, making sure she was ready for the morning, for the search for the river and the push toward Isaac. She could not sense him but felt that he must not be distant—she had traveled so far already. She still had the other sandwich for breakfast, and she would eat it while she walked. She was not in the wilderness here; though the Hill Country was rural, it was still fairly densely populated. If she headed much farther in this direction, she would run into the peach orchards and vineyards of Gillespie County.

She laid her pack on the ground as a pillow, settling her shoulders into the carpet of crabgrass. Then she closed her eyes against the night, remembering the bean tendrils around her wrists. When the hand gripped her shoulder again, in her dream she thought it was her garden, again making its claim. When she struggled to open her eyes—even as the man said "Miss?" again—she thought, who was to say that it wasn't?

Things You Would Know If You Grew Up Around Here

The Will-o'-the-Wisp Is Not Common Here, There Being No Bogs or Marshes

The will-o'-the-wisp does not often come to central Texas, belonging, as it does, to marsh and bog. You normally hear about them in Europe, leading travelers away from the safe paths.

But we do have stories of them in this part of America, too, in places not so far from here. West Texas has the Marfa ghost lights, and at night the highways fill up with sightseers trying to catch a glimpse of this phenomenon. Mexico has brujas, witches who turned into the lights. In Louisiana, where bayou takes the place of bog, they have the *feu-follet*, the succubus, a soul who comes back to seek vengeance, and who sucks the blood of children.

What is interesting about the Louisiana story is that some people believe the will-o'-the-wisp is the soul of an unbaptized child. This idea matches many versions of the European story. In Sweden, for example, people believe that the child is leading the traveler to water so that the traveler will finally baptize him.

We have all of these stories, but we don't know what happens to the wanderer. What does the wanderer do, having been lured into the marsh? Where does she go, when she steps out of this world and into another?

11:15 P.M.

Isaac tried to sleep, even though he'd reached the top limb in the pecan tree that would support him, even as spiders roamed over his closed eyelids.

He could not sleep like this, worried that he would roll off the branch and into the water, his skin literally crawling. He guessed that the tree was seventy feet tall, maybe six stories, and the water was half that distance below him.

The water had calmed a bit, no longer being funneled from rocky higher ground. It had receded; even in the dark, he thought that it seemed farther away, that the reflected, refracted moon was smaller and dimmer in the water's surface. In the morning, he hoped to see that the water was low enough and calm enough that he could climb down the tree.

In the morning, at the first good light, he might climb down this tree, swim across to dry higher land, try to walk down to Allen Potivar's house and find his dad. These arroyos funneled water when there was too much at once, but when the rain stopped, they were quick to dry up. Gravity pulled the floodwaters to a low area; these gullies were ramps, not ditches. He felt sure his adventure in the tree was in its final hours.

What a story this would be. He couldn't wait to tell Boyd about the raccoon family who huddled, blinking, across from him, or the garter snake that had slithered between his back and the trunk. A nine-banded arma-dillo was a foot below him, claws clicking, trying to burrow into one of the pecan tree's minor branches. And squirrels, so many of them: gray squirrels and fox squirrels and squirrels Isaac did not know the name of, darting suddenly from branch to branch, their movements jerky, chafing at their now-limited range. He thought they were like younger siblings at a sleepover, staying up long after the older kids went to bed.

Isaac, who had a horror of dirty things, who camped every summer by the lake but who did so as a driven man, a person who wanted to go to med school both to have money and to diagnose and understand the body, found himself unable to sustain a repugnance for this wildlife for the many hours between when this tree had started to fill with the refugees and now. His feet dangled on either side of the branch now, unconcerned with the beetles that explored the legs of his jeans. He would have thought trapped animals would be more dangerous, but so far, the inhabitants of the tree seemed wary at most. The red-eyed rabbit watched the rat snake, nose twitching, but did nothing except sit back on its haunches. There was, to Isaac, a sense of the lion lying down with the lamb.

In the tree, he thought of a moment in seventh grade, the last year Boyd had been in school. They had just become friends; it was only a couple of weeks after Boyd had grabbed that girl in the cafeteria and started screaming, and Isaac had taken her out of the cafeteria. That day was cloudy to him, but he had remembered how she had helped that old man at H-E-B, and somehow he had needed to help Boyd. On this day, not long after the incident in the cafeteria, Ruben King had led them in a discussion of "The Ones Who Walk Away from Omelas," a story by Ursula K. Le Guin. The whole class had been into the story, which had involved a society that was perfect, but only because a child had taken all of its pain and dirtiness. At the end of the discussion, his father had led them in a vote: Who would stay and be part of such a society? Who would leave because they could not live with this thought, even knowing that their departure would not help the child? Everybody said they would leave. Then Ruben King had asked them, though the story hadn't suggested this as a possibility, Who would volunteer to take the child's place? Nobody had answered, not even Boyd, though Isaac thought that he knew what Boyd would say. Had Isaac himself said anything? He didn't remember now.

In the morning, he thought, he would climb down. But now, he closed his eyes again to try to sleep. His palms rolled open, resting on his thighs. After a minute, a field mouse climbed in the bowl of his right palm, and Isaac, who was for this night a different Isaac from what he'd been before, let him. The mouse rested near the mound of his thumb, chewing on his stitches, and when he fell asleep, he dreamed of Carla knitting the wound closed. The night wore on.

Things You Would Know If You Grew Up Around Here

We Cannot Stop What Is Already Here

In May 2019, the Mauna Loa Observatory in Hawaii will measure the atmospheric carbon dioxide at 415 parts per million, a level not seen in eight hundred thousand years, not seen in the entire history of human beings. By the end of the decade, the planet in uncharted territory for humanity, for much of the life now existent.

The shingled cottage belonged to Annie and Bess, though later Carla would find out that the people here didn't think anything belonged to any one of them more than anyone else. But Annie and Bess, queenly women with queenly names, lived in this house where the cozy dinner had been held. They each occupied one of the two bedrooms, warm rooms in warm lamplight that Carla saw before they took her to the main house. In Annie's bedroom, a full-size iron bed with a white down comforter and a stack of books on a nightstand. In Bess's, a twin bed with a knitted throw laid across, a Turkish carpet on the floor, and a basket with a yoga mat and block in the corner. In between the two bedrooms, a bathroom, the only one in the house, with a strong smell of lavender and rosemary.

After Carla ate, Kim took her to the long house in the middle of the compound. This house was open, virtually wall-less, and on the ground floor, three long wooden tables were surrounded by mismatched chairs and benches. On the back wall was a large fireplace with a brick hearth, couches and chairs arrayed around it, though there was no fire at the moment. A woman of about sixty, long hair dyed red with henna, wiped the long tables with a dishrag.

To the far right of the room was a kitchen with two double ovens on the wall and a stovetop with eight industrial burners. The refrigerator, too, was industrial. In front of all of this was a long island with a countertop and sink. The countertop was full of dishes, the sink was full of soapy water, and a woman and a boy of late middle school or early high school age was washing the stack of plates, the woman wiping them clean in a basin of bubbles, the boy rinsing in a basin of water. Next to them, a woman dried the dishes and stacked them at the end of the counter, clean and ready to put away.

Carla understood that there had been a dinner here, too, and she saw by the stack of dishes that this dinner had fed quite a few people. Only a few people were in the room now—the woman wiping the tables, the mother and son. At the sink, the woman drying—but Carla got the impression that perhaps two or three times that number had dined.

Kim introduced Carla to everyone: Caroline wiped the tables, Lisa and Scott washed dishes, Sara dried and stacked. They all looked up at her, expressions curious and friendly, Caroline's gaze lingering on Carla's forehead, looking at the ashes she kept forgetting she wore. Carla waved back, suddenly shy. This house felt industrious, not quite as cozy as the shingled cottage. It didn't, she realized, even feel much like a house, but instead like a community meeting hall.

Kim led her upstairs to another open room, though this floor was more partitioned. At least a couple of bedrooms were closed off, and one huge dormitory-style bathroom, with stalls for toilets and stalls for showers and a row of sinks underneath a long mirror. The countertop here was empty—no toothpaste or hairbrushes, no toiletries whatsoever. Just a counter wiped clean.

In the main room, the landing was lined with full bookcases, and beyond this was a communal bedroom with twin and full and bunk beds scattered around, chests of drawers and trunks at their feet and by their sides. Curtains and sheets hung from the low ceiling around some of the beds, a measure of privacy, and around at least two of them was a triptych screen. Carla estimated that a dozen or so beds total were in the large room, and on many of these, a person stretched out, reading or writing or listening to music.

Again, Carla was shy. She almost regretted taking Kim up on the offer of a bed for the night. She dealt with few people in her life at the lake and interacted regularly only with Lucy Maud and Boyd. This room was more like what she'd left behind in Austin: cubicle land, only for sleeping instead of working.

Kim took her to a bed behind one of the screens, a full bed with a wooden frame and a cover that looked hand quilted. A nightstand on either side, each with a lamp on top and two drawers underneath. A beautiful antique steamer trunk at the foot.

"Do you think this will be okay for one night?" Kim sat on the end of the bed, her hand resting on the footboard. "I want you to be comfortable."

Carla felt as if she should set luggage down, but she didn't have any. Kim noticed the way Carla looked down at the trunk and said, "But of course! You need things! What do you need? A toothbrush and toothpaste? A T-shirt or a nightgown, maybe?"

Carla shrugged, unwilling to say anything. There was something off about the whole situation, something she could not quite articulate. How had she wandered upon a place that was so prepared to give her everything she needed?

"I'll get you toothpaste and a toothbrush and some clothes to sleep in. Don't even worry about it." Kim got off the bed and motioned for Carla to take her spot. "I'll bring you some books, too." Kim watched her for a minute, nodded, then slipped away behind the screen.

Carla looked around once Kim was gone, then sat down on the bed. She poked at one of the two pillows and picked it up and fluffed it. It seemed like a nice pillow, and the green-and-white gingham pillowcase was soft from good use. Around her, she heard voices, people discussing the day, people settling in, and those voices had a kind timbre, though Carla could not pick out an actual conversation.

She opened the top drawer of the nightstand nearest her, looking for a Bible. Nothing, so she opened the bottom drawer. When she didn't find one there, she rolled across the bed and searched the two drawers of the other nightstand. No Bible. Somehow, she'd known that. She was not yet sure what the organizing principle of this commune was, but she no longer thought it was religious. She slipped off her yoga slings and lay back on the bed, her body tired from the walking she'd done. Her feet were filthy from the mud she'd walked through, now dried to her ankles and calves.

She stared at her toes. They would need a wash before she got beneath the covers.

Kim returned, a full canvas sack slung over one shoulder. "I gathered some things from the closet." She set the bag on the bed next to Carla and started pulling things out. "A toothbrush. Don't worry—it's brand-new. We stock a bunch of them. A T-shirt-slash-nightgown that somebody left. A couple of books to read"—an Agatha Christie novel and *Animal, Vegetable, Miracle*—"and a towel if you want to take a shower." Kim looked at her now, and Carla got the sense Kim wanted her to be pleased.

Carla picked up the T-shirt, white but gone to gray, with an American flag across the chest. It would reach her knees when she put it on. "Whose was this? Where did they go?"

Kim blinked. "Um, I think that shirt belonged to a woman named Liz. She—well, she left after her husband died."

Carla tilted her head, surprised.

"He had a heart attack." Kim thought for a bit, deciding whether to say more. "We're far from a hospital out here, you know."

Carla was quiet.

After a minute, Kim went on, "His name was Aaron, and he was very young to die. Midforties. But when they came to us, they were so unhealthy, Liz and Aaron." Kim pointed at the T-shirt Carla still held. "Liz must have been three hundred pounds. They were one of the few who didn't walk here, didn't just show up on our doorstep."

At this, Carla's eyes widened and she covered her mouth with one hand. She could not imagine that other people had found this place on foot, and yet, yesterday, she would never have believed it of herself.

"Aaron was a vet tech. Really good with the animals. We took his loss hard. Then Liz left for the funeral in Kingsland and never came back." Kim's stare was unfocused, and she nodded to herself, remembering. Carla watched her, thinking she'd cut her short hair herself, watched the way Kim's taut skin moved over her cheekbones. She was a tight, compact woman. "Liz was an excellent cook." Whatever Kim was remembering had her. At last, she caught herself and reached in the bag, pulling out a bar of soap. She handed it to Carla. "In case you wanted to take a shower."

"Thanks."

Now Kim watched her. "You know, if you like this bed, you can sleep in it for as long as you want."

"I have to find my friend." It was more defensive than anything else—Carla wasn't even sure she was still following Boyd or why she'd done so in the first place.

"Of course. Maybe we'll help you."

What would Carla tell them about her search? How crazy would she sound? "Maybe."

"Anyway, you don't have to decide tonight. You can shower or whatever and get some sleep. Read a book or something. If you don't like these, there are more on the bookshelves." Kim pointed behind her, in the direction of the stairs.

"Thanks."

"Sure." Kim rose. "You need anything, tell any one of us. We were all new once, too."

When Kim left, Carla took the soap, T-shirt, and towel to the dormitory-style bathroom. Inside the shower stall was a bench for her clothes, but the bench was long enough for her to sit on and to be in the water, too. She sat in the warm shower, thinking that here she was, wet again, after all that time in the mud and the rain. But this was a different wet, a warming one, and she turned her face up and felt the water on her forehead, washing away the serpentine coil of ashes. She shifted on the bench, her feet at the dry end, her face in the water, her eyes closed and her hair falling all around her. Her hands fell to her side and her feet turned out in a kind of shower Savasana. Corpse pose. She felt splayed open—physically exhausted and emotionally vivisected—unsure of where she'd landed. This place, with Kim and Annie and Bess and Imogene and Caroline and all of the other people she'd met, felt too beautiful to be trusted, like a siren's song, and she, eternally skeptical, was looking for evidence of rocks. What would a single sailor do in that case? She could not tie and untie herself to and from her own mast. So far, she had sailed her ship well around the dangers. But what that meant was that she had sailed her ship around everything: around every possibility of siren, around every possibility of safe haven. After being dashed against the rocks in her earlier life, Carla had sought a calm ocean, a boat on a mirrored surface, alone with the sea and the sky.

Lucy Maud was glad that Kevin had left the car door open: the dome light revealed that he had not yet disappeared into the fuzzy night. She saw he was on his phone, but he wasn't necessarily texting, she told herself.

She stopped watching him because the going was treacherous: the front yard was full of container gardens, and she came close to tripping and falling face-first into white limestone gravel. They weren't neat and tidy container gardens, either. Most had been repurposed from a jumble of old and defunct things: a fiberglass canoe; a set of kitchen cabinets turned on their backs, doors removed; a claw-foot bathtub, enamel flaked away. She turned the flashlight on these shapes one by one, even though a bright sodium lamp lit the whole place, just to verify each thing's identity. When she moved the light away, she imagined that each thing morphed, that it became something monstrous just out of her line of vision, hulking to three times its normal size. Her steps quickened and she reached the front porch, climbing the stairs quickly, feeling the way she had as a child swimming in the dark lake, the sense when she emerged that she had pulled her feet out just in time, that something was just under the surface, a millisecond—a millimeter—from striking.

Before she even had a chance to knock, the door opened, and a shirt-less man stood there, pointing a .22 rifle at her. A light in his house backlit him, and she saw clear oxygen tubing running from his nose, looping behind his ears, then disappearing behind the front door. The thought of a rifle and an oxygen tank scared her. She took a step back but didn't say anything.

She wondered what good it had been to come here. They hadn't broken down, and this man would not be helping them find Lou and Fern, not with his oxygen tank. Instead, Lucy Maud pointed to the Subaru. "Is that Ruben King's car?"

The man lowered the barrel and looked behind her as if he didn't know what she was talking about. "Who's asking?"

Lucy Maud didn't see any point in concealing her identity, though the unusual greeting had her disoriented. "I'm a friend of his son's. Well, the mother of a friend of his son's." She thought for a minute. "I need his help. Is he here? My daughter and his son are missing. I think they're together."

His mouth fell open as he considered this news. "Huh." He dropped the rifle to his side. "Well, I guess you better come in." He opened the door wide for her.

She glanced back. She could still see Kevin. "Sure, just for a second. They're not the only ones missing."

The man brought her in and directed her to a striped velvet couch that she guessed was from the seventies. She sat, back straight, on the edge, feet tucked underneath her, looking around.

The house looked as if an old bachelor lived here alone. The ancient cathode ray television had a La-Z-Boy in front of it. Next to the La-Z-Boy sat a TV tray stacked high with newspapers, some unfolded and refolded, some still in their plastic sleeves. A pillbox was on the TV tray, too, a long clear one, with separate compartments for each day of the week. Leaned up against the La-Z-Boy were three containers of oxygen.

Lucy Maud noted all of this, perched as she was on the sofa's edge, while the man fiddled with his oxygen tubing and sat back in the easy chair. When he put up the footrest, she said, "I can't stay long. I'm just looking for Ruben King."

The man cocked an eyebrow. "Do you know who I am?"

She shook her head.

"I'm Allen Potivar. Known Ruben for decades." He watched her. "How'd you know to come down here if you don't know who I am?" One eye was narrower than the other; she felt she was being interrogated. So what? she thought. None of this was a secret.

"Ruben told me to come down Nameless Road when I found Isaac. But I can't find either Isaac or Boyd. My daughter. I thought he could help." She looked away, the man's gaze too much for her. "I saw his car from the road."

He nodded. He was, she thought, deciding if she was telling the truth. She wished she had Boyd's ability with people, but Lucy Maud had never had that understanding or ease. He still didn't say anything, and she recognized his silence as another interrogation technique; he wanted her to be uncomfortable with this silence and to fill it.

"Look, is he here?"

He twisted his mouth, unprepared for the question. "Sort of."

She exhaled, unable to control her impatience. "I don't have time for this. Either he's here or he's not. Isaac and Boyd are both missing, and now I've got two more people missing, too." She waved a hand behind her. "My twin sister and my senile aunt are wandering around out there. The authorities won't help us. I don't even know that Ruben can. But we need help from somewhere because I don't know what else to do." She ran a hand over her face. "And I've got my estranged husband in the car watching for them, but if I don't hurry up, pretty soon he'll be missing, too." It seemed overwhelming suddenly, just an impossible situation.

Allen Potivar put the footrest down and leaned toward her. "Ruben King is here, on my property. Or at least he was an hour or two ago. He might be missing now, too. He doesn't have a flashlight or anything, so he should have been back soon as it turned dark."

She turned toward the open door, noting that he'd set the rifle down just inside. "He's out there?"

Allen nodded. "Yep." She shifted, leaning into the conversation, one elbow on the armrest. "And I got to decide what to tell you because, listen, if I tell you why he's out there—what he's after—you'll go running out into the night, too." Allen took a quick, deep breath through his oxygen nosepiece. "And you'll want a piece of my pie, too, and I don't yet know how much pie there is to go around."

She blinked. "I don't want any of your pie. I don't know what pie you're even talking about. I want to find my daughter. And my sister and my aunt." She felt bad that Lou and Aunt Fern were almost afterthoughts.

"Okay. I'm going to hold you to that. Because you promised. Even when you find out what it is, it's still mine. Not yours. And I agreed to share a little with Ruben King because he's helping me." Allen gestured to the oxygen tanks. "I can't carry all of this stuff out there. I've got a portable oxygen concentrator—like a little pump—I carry with me, but the battery only lasts a couple of hours. I had to come back to the house to charge it, but he wanted to stay working. In the meantime, it got dark." Allen fixed his gaze on hers. "He don't even have a flashlight, like I said. That was the first thing we should have done when we opened the mine: come back up to the house and get a flashlight or a lantern or something."

She laughed, finally putting two and two together. "A mine? That's what he was going on about then when I talked to him? Maximilian and Pedro Zamora."

"Yorba," Allen corrected her. "Pedro Yorba."

"Whatever. Y'all know that's—" She didn't finish the statement. What did they or she or any of them know? Rumors of gold that, if it had existed at all, would have been found a hundred years ago. "Are you saying that you have a mine on your property and that Ruben King is there?"

He reached out a hand, fingers splayed, then closed it quickly into a fist, drawing back. It wasn't a threatening gesture but one of dismay, trying to grab his own words and shove them back in. "Now, you can't tell anybody, you understand?"

She stood, breathing deeply so that he would take her seriously, would not dismiss her as hysterical. "Who am I going to tell? I can't get anybody to listen to me. And this"—she gestured to the misty night beyond the open front door—"is about the craziest thing I've ever seen. You know what happens during a normal rain?" He didn't answer. "Everybody stays home. They sit on their couch with a blanket and a frozen pizza and they watch TV. They don't all go out in it and disappear." She snapped her fingers, raising her hand above her head. "Why in the hell are people wandering off in this weather? One after another?" Even herself, she thought, even though she knew better.

He nodded, thinking about this. "Well, I know why Ruben King is out there. I'd be out there, too, if I could breathe. I smoked for just under fifty years, and let me tell you, that was a mistake."

"Is your pump charged now?"

He glanced at the machine next to the wall. To Lucy Maud, it looked like a large lunch box. "Yes. But it's dark. I only get two, maybe two and a half hours on that pump, and if it runs out, I might die. You ever stop breathing for a few minutes? It's likely to kill you." He sat back in his chair, straightening his arms for leverage, palms planted firmly on the armrests. "I almost come close enough to know a couple of times."

She walked to the door and glanced out. Kevin still scrolled through his phone in her passenger seat, his face top-lit, everything below his glasses cast in shadow. She felt, again, how much she'd missed him, even with all of his pretend helping and general uselessness. She'd drag him through this life if she got the chance. She thought that he, too, felt some pull. He'd been with her now for close to thirty hours, and yes, he was helping find Boyd, but there was something more, something urgent and essential between the two of them, like a drink of water when you were thirsty. She knew that she was no competition for the grad student, but here he was, with Lucy Maud and lying to the grad student. She thought of the way forward, and she decided that she was grown-up now, well accustomed to life's amalgam of bitter and sweet, and she wondered if they would be able to reach some kind of time-share-husband deal, where she had Kevin part of the time and where he lived his Austin full-professor life the rest of the time. She didn't want that part of his life anymore, anyway: the endless infighting of academia and the perpetual complaints about students, but also the hero worship, where every year a new crop of acolytes convened at the feet of a man who hadn't written a book—or even a journal article—in seven years. In that world, and maybe in this one, too, his favorite thing to do was to love himself. But she didn't care that he was Narcissus by the mountain pool. She just wanted him around some of the time.

She turned back to Allen Potivar. What a waste it had been to come after Ruben King—she had only been needing to do *something*. Now she needed to see about Aunt Fern and Lou, whose last whereabouts were a lot more clear. But this was Allen's road, this Nameless Road. "Listen, we were driving down this road and we came to a dead end. Maybe three, four miles up? You know where I'm talking about?" He nodded. "My aunt—she's got dementia but it's aggressive—she got out of the car and wandered off while we were stopped. My sister followed her to bring her back. But neither one came back and it's been a good hour or two. You have any idea what could've happened to them, or how I might go about finding them?" She remembered the sound of rainwater rushing down the gully. What could be swept away on a night like this? What things could go awry and never be put back quite right?

He shook his head. "There's nothing between here and there. An old cistern for cattle, but no houses or people."

She nodded, expecting as much. "Well," she said, thinking as she talked, "I guess I better get back to finding them. When—if—I do, I'll come back to help look for Ruben. And then"—she laughed, a bitter sound, remembering what had originally started this wild-goose chase—"maybe he can help me find Boyd and Isaac."

Allen got up slowly, adjusting the oxygen tubing. "Let me—" He unplugged the oxygen generator from the wall. "Let me come with you. I'll ride in the car with my pump and I'll help you."

She looked at him, doubting how much help he'd be. At the least, he'd know the area.

He caught the look. "Oh, you think I need a shirt?" White hair sprouted from his nipples and traced a line up over his belly button.

"Yes."

"Well, all right." He disappeared into the back room, carrying the condenser, then came back wearing a flannel work shirt, unbuttoned, put on like a jacket instead of a shirt.

"Okay. Thank you." It seemed like the wrong thing to say.

He followed her to the car, grabbing the rifle as they filed out the door. She could not say whether this made her more nervous or less; her main thought was that at least now he wasn't connected to a canister of pure oxygen, but merely to a machine that condensed the oxygen already present in the air. She wasn't worried that he'd set himself ablaze if he fired the gun. He did not lock the door as he left, which surprised her, but then she considered that what he really cared about protecting was out there in the mist.

When she got in the car, Kevin squeezed her hand, then Allen Potivar opened the door and slid into the back seat. Kevin turned to look and she said, "Allen here is going to help us." The clock on the dash said it was 12:34.

Once in the car, all the doors closed, they sat silently for a minute. Lucy Maud was unsure where to go or what to do. The only rational thought she had was that she must keep all of them together, that if any one of them wandered away from the others, the problem would only be compounded. "I guess we should drive up this road again," she said, hoping Allen Potivar would say something, would have some bit of advice, tell her something she'd overlooked. She heard the soft whir and click of the oxygen condenser and Allen's shallow breaths.

It was Kevin who finally spoke. "Let's drive up to where we last saw them."

Lucy Maud, thinking she should have left Lou and Aunt Fern at home, headed back up Nameless Road, her Taurus moving through mist thick as cotton.

Things You Would Know If You Grew Up Around Here

We Cannot Stop What Is Already Here

We knew. We knew and did nothing. In my youth, we talked about the earth heating. The UN addressed the rise in temperature in 1988, creating the Intergovernmental Panel on Climate Change.

We changed nothing, instead increasing the use of fossil fuels, adding more carbon dioxide to the atmosphere. We lived our lives recklessly and with abandon, and we will see only the beginning of what we have done and what will happen. The rest we've left to our children, their inheritance this uncharted world.

May 25

12:15 A.M.

Boyd, on the night's fourth iteration of the search for Caleb, trying to decide what to do. She walked between the parents, the mother going in front with the lantern, the father behind her, tinkling like bells. She walked quickly because she didn't want the bells to overtake her.

But what could she do? She had been shaken awake twice; the fourth time she had been expecting the cold hand on her shoulder and so had been waiting. No matter what Boyd said, the man and the woman said the same things they had in the first encounter, as if the first conversation had been recorded and was just being replayed. By the third time that the man had asked for Boyd's help, Boyd started to pay attention to how the body stood, to where the gaze fell. At some point, she realized he was reacting to an earlier version of her, that he was watching her where she'd stood during that first encounter, and she did not think that he saw her now. It was unsettling to see his gaze focus on a place beyond her, to see him conversing with some trace, some ghost of a Boyd now left in the night.

She stepped aside to let the father pass, and she walked behind them slowly, the fairy twinkling and lantern light outpacing her in the night. When she could no longer see or hear them, she sat, back against a granite outcrop, the stone exfoliating and brittle, the least comfortable seat she'd had all night.

It was now the deepest part of night. The stillness was a weight, pinning her to the earth, and the air had a blackness, a sense of swimming through deep water. She heard a ratcheting noise in the trees, and it made her think of the earth as a clock, winding herself.

She remembered again the bean tendrils around her wrist, then she thought of the shadows twisting on the branches in the shape of cocoons, the moon revelatory, the beat of earth and time synchronizing in a way with which she was not familiar.

The tendrils on her wrists had felt restrictive, like manacles. But the night—while the night was a weight on her shoulders, it was not burdensome or unwelcome, but was instead the ballast of a life that was in danger of floating away. It was a tether to something beautiful, something life-giving, a lifeline tossed from a greater vessel.

She could not explain what was happening now with time. She knew that Caleb and his parents were wisps of something that had come before, impressions left on soft clay that had hardened into fossils. But she could not say where in time she was now, nor even if time was a thing she could pin down.

She remembered Ruben King trying to explain the theory of relativity to her, and she had pictured the universe as a panel of fabric, warped by the gravity of the objects it contained. But Mr. King had lost her when he had tried to explain that time and space were on a spectrum, that time bled into space and vice versa. This had made no sense to her, this image of a spectrum. How could a point be more time than space, or more space than time? He had seen her confusion and suggested another image, not spectrum but grid, and her Cartesian mind had grasped this, had seen the grid laid over the universe, had been able to understand a point as *here in space, here in time*, no one without the other. The idea had snapped into place, much like the grid across the universe, but still, she'd found herself unable to follow TV shows or movies that had talked about rips in the time-space continuum. No matter. Now she thought of the grid of the universe as three-dimensional, of the axis of time as being exceedingly tall, with all time layered upon a place.

The bean tendrils. The riotous roar of a garden alive. The scarecrow walking—where? Footprints she had followed until they had disappeared into the water. The incantation when she had planted: *Be fruitful. Multiply.* The sense that something had awoken, that she had come to rest on an island that was really the back of a whale. The body of the thing submerged, its scope only visible in its proportions.

She watched for the man, hoping to see him approach, but he did not come for such a long time. Finally, she laid her head back on the crumbling rock, and when her eyes closed, she felt the hand on her shoulder. She would not be allowed to see him coming. His arrival must always be a surprise.

He asked her the usual questions, but she didn't even bother to answer. It didn't matter. He and the woman responded as if she did. They continued their little drama without her, but when it came time to move on in search of Caleb, with Boyd in the middle, she remained seated. She would not go with them this time, would not wander the hills chased by tinkling feet, would sit here and wait for the next time the hand touched her shoulder.

But they froze when she didn't join them. They got stuck, caught on their track, and she thought, ominously somehow, of a vinyl record that was not cut in a spiral but in a series of concentric circles, the needle stuck in the same groove until it could manually be moved. She did not know how to do this and was waiting for dawn to somehow break the pattern.

A breath. Two. Still they waited for her. This part of the drama would not be allowed to continue until she got up and went with them. Another pause as she figured out what to do. She could not bear their stillness, nor the sense that all life had stopped. She listened and heard insects in trees, wind in the pin oaks. It was just them. If she turned now and walked away, would some hunter or hiker wander across them one day, still stuck here, waiting for Boyd to join them?

Boyd stood, gathering her backpack. She wondered how long she would have to walk with them to start the movement again. She stepped in their direction, falling into place between them. The record started again, and the lantern swung in the woman's clawlike hand.

A sense of breathing, of heart beating: everything coming back to life. The earth made round and whole. The light glancing over the stone: tick, tock, tick, tock. The long, slow exhale of the night. Boyd walked two, three steps between them—tinkling, tinkling, ice breaking on a lake's surface—and

196 NANCY WAYSON DINAN

their ghost engines revved and here they all went, a procession across the countryside, lit by the lurching light.

A few steps—one, two, three—and she stepped to the side to let Caleb's father pass. She thought he would continue into the night, following the woman's siren song, and for a moment he did.

He tinkled on, his gaze forward, his feet moving but not moving, and she thought she would return to the rock and rest for a while, until she felt the hand on her shoulder again. She thought they probably had three more enactments of this drama before dawn, at which time, Boyd assumed, the couple would disappear and she would continue her search for Isaac, though she imagined she'd be pretty tired. She had been close, she thought, to Isaac when night had fallen, but she could not say how far or in what direction he lay now.

The tinkling—now, for Boyd, the background noise of the deep night—so ubiquitous that it had become texture. When it stopped, she thought that they had gone. But no. The man was still there to her left.

And now his head swiveled to face hers, making eye contact for the first time in hours.

She stepped back, swallowing, exposed and unprepared to be acknowledged. A fear lodged deep in her chest: here she was, set loose in the world, unarmed and vulnerable. Here was the world, neither good nor evil, coming for her.

Eye contact—two, three seconds—and Boyd was so frightened that tears leaked from the corners of her eyes. She could not read his expression in the dark and felt nothing from him emotionally.

He said, "Go back. This way is not for you." A new track on that vinyl record, one she wasn't supposed to see, and she understood that if she followed them, the night would never end. He turned away, tinkling, moving forward, gliding again, but not quite slipping neatly back into the groove in which he was supposed to travel. "It's almost too late for you."

Things You Would Know If You Grew Up Around Here

The Stories Are Many, and They Don't All Agree

If we start to tell the story of the Lost San Saba Mine, a good place to start is with *Coronado's Children*, a book written almost a hundred years ago, in 1930, by J. Frank Dobie and subtitled *Tales of Lost Mines and Buried Treasures of the Southwest*:

> Sometimes the name of the fabled source of wealth is Los Almagres; sometimes Las Amarillas; again, La Mina de las Iguanas, or Lizard Mine, from the fact that the ore is said to have been found in chunks called *iguanas* (lizards); oftener the name is simply the Lost San Saba Mine or the Lost Bowie Mine. In seeking it, generations of men have disemboweled mountains, drained lakes, and turned rivers out of their courses. It has been found—and lost—in many places under many conditions. It is here; it is there; it is nowhere. Generally it is silver; sometimes it is gold. Sometimes it is in a cave; sometimes in water; again on top of a mountain. Now it is not a mine at all but an immense storage of bullion. It changes its place like will-o'-the-wisp and it has more shapes than Jupiter assumed in playing lover.
>
> Only the land that hides it does not change. Except that it is brushier, groomed down in a few places by little fields, and cut across by fences, it is today essentially as the Spaniards found it.

A soil that cannot be plowed under keeps its traditions—and its secrets. Wherever the mine may be, however it may appear, it has lured, it lures, and it will lure men on. It is bright Glamour, and it is dark and thwarting Fate.

1:30 A.M.

Lucy Maud, having gone up and down the road a few times, thought that they were getting nowhere. "Y'all," she told the two men riding with her, "we're going to have to get out of the car."

In the back seat, Allen shifted. "I've only got about an hour left on this thing. And I don't move fast these days."

She looked at him in the rearview mirror. "How many people are out there right now? Three?" She gestured to the open window. "And Boyd's somewhere out there, too. Sitting in this car and driving up and down this road feels like it's doing something. But it's not."

Kevin, called into the appearance of action, spoke up. "What's out here? Could they have ended up at someone's house?"

Click, whir. "Nothing. Nobody lives out here. It's miserable on this road. Damn near close to a desert. All rock and scrub trees."

"Then where the hell could they have gone?" She felt on the verge of some outburst, not quite panic, but absolute frustration that she didn't know what to do or how to fix this.

"I guess it's possible that they ran into Ruben King," Allen said after a minute. "They might all be together right now."

"At the mine shaft?" When Lucy Maud said it, Allen Potivar kicked the back of her seat.

Kevin caught the kick and started paying more attention.

Allen sighed and then, having released too much oxygen, took quick breaths through his cannula nosepiece. "See, this is why I didn't want to tell anybody."

"Tell anybody what?" Kevin blinked at him, all innocence. She knew that face. *You can trust me*, that face said.

Lucy Maud hit the steering wheel. "What am I supposed to say about Ruben's whereabouts? You just said they might be together."

"I don't want anybody else knowing about it." In the back seat, Allen crossed his arms across his chest. She thought he might be pouting.

"In case you didn't know," she said, knowing very well that he didn't, "Kevin is a classics professor. He's been on a few archaeological digs in his time."

"Ah, yes," Kevin said, putting on a professor's voice. "Quite a few. All over the Mediterranean world, actually, though I'm not an archaeologist. The most interesting one was on Thera, a Greek island many believe might be Atlantis, and where the project was excavating an archaic site—"

"Kevin"—she put a hand on his knee—"give it a rest." She left her hand there and looked at Allen in the rearview mirror. "Kevin's not after your money."

Allen squinted at her, his expression asking her to please give him a break. "It'd be just as bad to have a bunch of professors out here poking around." After a minute he added, "It's not artifacts. It's silver." He shook his head, disgusted with himself that he'd said that much.

She took off her seat belt. "Silver?" She put one hand on Kevin's headrest, turning to look at Allen. "But Maximilian's treasure is supposed to be gold."

"You don't think there's silver, too?"

"And isn't it supposed to be in barrels? Is the stuff you found in barrels?"

Another exasperated sigh and then the sharp intakes of breath. "You know you can't believe everything you hear." He said *can't* "cain't," the way her aunt Fern did.

"I know I believe we're getting out of this car." She turned off the engine and opened the door.

"I only got an hour left on this thing," Allen said again.

"Well, we better hurry." Kevin wasn't moving. "You coming?"

He jumped and unsnapped his seat belt. "Oh, you want me to come this time?"

"Yes." Otherwise he'd be another soul adrift in this mist. She turned back to Allen. "Once you take us to Ruben, you can head back." She thought for a minute and added, "As long as I think we can find our way back." It hadn't yet occurred to her that she might become one of the lost people, but this new thought made her nervous. She wondered again if Lou had found Aunt Fern, if they were now together.

She thought about leaving her car door open so Lou and Fern would see the light if they stumbled this way. But no, a raccoon or a possum might crawl into the car seeking dinner or refuge. Then she thought about just leaving the dome light on, but she didn't do this either. She knew, even if they were only gone half an hour, that if she left the light on, she'd return to a dead battery, to a car stuck in the night. She hoped that if Fern and Lou came this way, they would stay at the car and wait for Lucy Maud and Kevin, and she left a note under the windshield wiper, hoping that they would see it. She didn't want them found and then lost again.

Allen Potivar led the way slowly, taking measured breaths and carrying his oxygen generator like a lunch box. "We're still going out here without a damn flashlight," he said, "making the same mistake twice."

Kevin ran back for the flashlight from the glove compartment.

But the flashlight was no match for the night, illuminating a tiny fraction of their path, and she could see Allen getting frustrated by Kevin's unsteady hand with it. If this were a movie, they'd all be carrying torches, a column of fire lighting their way, but this was no movie and she was skeptical about those movie torches anyway. She took the flashlight from Kevin and handed it to Allen. "Thanks," she told Kevin, as if that had been his plan with the flashlight all along.

They left the road and cut across open country, and when the flashlight's beam fell on the ground, she saw the distinctive needles of pine trees, though she knew of no pines in this area. They were thick, swollen with rain, all pointing more or less in the same direction, washed by floodwaters and come to rest on this limestone floor. The air was thick, rich with velvet moisture. It would be a lake summer; they hadn't had one in years. Last year, Lake Travis had been at 31 percent of capacity, and what water had been left had pooled in the bottom, stagnant.

When they'd gone one hundred yards, Lucy Maud knew that she'd need Allen to find the way back to the road. She guessed she could turn around and walk in the opposite direction and hope, but nothing looked remarkable to her. They were on no clear path, and nothing indicated direction. The only thing keeping Lucy Maud and Kevin from being swallowed by the night was grumpy, territorial Allen Potivar, clicking and whirring in front of them. She wanted to talk to him, to ask him questions, but she could tell he was struggling to breathe.

Things You Would Know If You Grew Up Around Here

The Floods That Year Were Devastating

That year, the highways became rivers, and twenty-five hundred vehicles were left behind, a parking lot slowly sinking as the water rose, the clearest sign of apocalypse yet. In the countryside for weeks after, the vultures circled the river banks, pecking the eyes of the giant carp that had been caught in barbed wire when the rivers crested the fences.

Steve Thuber, the mayor of Wimberley, told CNN how unprecedented the rise of the Blanco River had been: "In 1929," he said, "we had a thirty-three-and-a-half foot surge come through. That was the highest on record. This one topped out at forty-four and a half feet before we lost communications with the gauge." Everywhere, records were broken, the collected highs and lows of a century discarded in a matter of days.

The first rain after so long without gives everything a different smell. It had been raining for two days now, but Allen Potivar's hill had been so sere before, it was as if this gravel, this inch or so of topsoil, were seeing rain, even now, for the first time, and the smell—the smell was of deep moss and algae, of secret life underneath the surface.

Lucy Maud thought about Ruben King, trying to remember anything about the man. That was unfair. There was plenty to remark upon. He was into history, for one; if he were walking with them now, he'd be able to tell her what had happened in this spot, whether it had been held by Comanche or Apache, whether Spain had set up a mission here, or how the Anglos had come into this country. When Boyd had been in school, she'd been quite taken with Ruben King; it was how she'd met Isaac. Texas history had been fascinating to Boyd, and Lucy Maud remembered that Boyd had borrowed so many books from Ruben: Roy Bedichek, John Graves, J. Frank Dobie. Lucy Maud, who had grown up in a little town outside San Antonio, had been shocked by Boyd's interest in the subject; to Lucy Maud, Jim Bowie was as distant and hard to imagine as George Washington or Benjamin Franklin. For Lucy Maud, the subject was academic: the books said this happened at this place on this day. But Boyd felt the presence of a real person who had been in the world and was now not. Boyd saw a chain of cause and effect that extended down to her—somebody did something so something happened so something else happened—and she knew, too, that she was both cause and effect. This long view of place had been something Ruben King had tapped into.

This image Lucy Maud had of Ruben aligned with the vision she held of so many other people in the Texas Hill Country. She knew he'd gone to UT in the late eighties, too old to be a real hippie, but following in those footsteps nevertheless. She imagined him as a student, eating the whole-wheat deep dish at Conans Pizza or a Greek salad at Miltos, wearing Birkenstocks while everybody else was wearing Keds, a joint tucked into his shirt pocket for in between classes. He could never have been anything but what he was, had made the kind of life he'd hoped for all along. She was not this person, but she had to admit she understood it; something in this sky and air, this low mix of tree and stone, was enough.

Why had he never remarried after divorcing Isaac's mother? She could not remember if she'd ever known the story and could only recall brief flashes of the woman: very blond with a round face and a heavy body.

Lucy Maud remembered picking Boyd up at Isaac's house once—Boyd must have been twelve or thirteen—and Ruben and his then wife—Melissa, maybe?—had been on the front porch playing "Uncle John's Band," both of them with acoustic guitars, though Lucy Maud could plainly see in the few seconds that elapsed before they stopped playing that Ruben was better at it, more natural with the guitar on his lap, his fingers more adept at picking out the bridge. Melissa's voice had been too high, but she had been enthusiastic in an endearing way. Boyd had heard Lucy Maud's car and had come out of the house, and Ruben and Melissa had turned toward her with such looks on their faces that Lucy Maud had felt a surprising pang of jealousy. How long ago had Melissa left? It occurred to Lucy Maud that she never asked Isaac about his family.

They had slowed to a crawl, Allen struggling with the flashlight, the oxygen generator, and breathing in general. She did not know how much farther they had to go, so she caught up to him, took the flashlight, and led him to a group of limestone boulders. They sat for a few minutes, the click and whir blending in with the sounds of the late-night insects, and after a while, Lucy Maud discovered that she could see better without the flashlight, her eyes having adjusted to the dim, so she switched it off.

Kevin was the first to speak. "Can you imagine being out here like this one hundred years ago?"

This was so close to what Lucy Maud had been thinking that she straightened in surprise.

Allen tried to answer, gasping between words. "Guess I'd've died a long time ago."

Lucy Maud tried to cheer him up. "Hey, we all would have. If we made it through childbirth. No antibiotics."

"But some people made it," Kevin said. "You hear all of these old stories about people, sometimes eighty or ninety, being taken off their land and put in nursing homes. Seems like I knew three or four people that happened to in the late seventies and early eighties."

"How horrible." Lucy Maud didn't know why she thought it was horrible; this felt like a knee-jerk reaction. If she thought about it objectively, a nursing home was probably better than living out on some road like this, all by yourself.

"You better shoot me first," Allen said. Lucy Maud thought he was probably close enough to eighty for this conversation to make him uncomfortable.

Now that the flashlight had been shut off, the moon was starting to be enough, and in some ways, it illuminated more. She could see the shine of scalp underneath Kevin's hair, something she would never have noticed in full daylight. Well, they were getting old, weren't they? For the past decade, she had felt older than him—though the opposite was true—and now he was catching up to her. She found some satisfaction in this: maybe the grad student would notice. The grad student was in her midtwenties, closer to Boyd's age than to Lucy Maud's, and would surely notice her fifty-year-old boyfriend aging.

Kevin, unaware that Lucy Maud was sizing him up, continued, "Can you imagine the pioneers who stopped here and said, 'This is as good a place as any'?"

"What I don't understand is that all the old stories said there was a rock that looked like a castle and two hills that formed a window," Allen said. "There's nothing like that out here."

She looked around. There were hills, but they didn't see anything in the dark that looked like a castle. She also wasn't as familiar with Nameless Road as he was. "How much longer you got?"

He glanced down at the condenser. "I can't see the gauge. But, oh, about forty-five minutes or so. I'll have to turn around in about fifteen. Y'all don't want me to die out here, do you?"

She nodded, taking in the information, not answering him. No, she didn't want him to die. "How much farther do you think we've got?"

He sighed. "I think we've got further than fifteen minutes." He stood. "Especially if I keep sitting here." He moved slowly forward, and they followed him. "I'm coming from a different direction this time you know. I'm not coming from my house. The road's not quite the same." She wanted to tell him to be quiet, to save the oxygen, but she didn't. "I found it two days ago. I saw smoke coming from my backcountry. Thought I had a squatter. Followed the smoke to a burned cedar brake. This was just before it started to rain." He was gasping now, his head and hands shaking with the effort. "But the damn thing was—no squatters, no fire. A cedar brake had been burned—there was a scorched spot and burned branches and a pile of ashes—but when I got to the spot, the smoke disappeared. But you could tell the place had burned. Just it seemed like a long time ago. Everything was cold." He rested his hands on his knees, his head hanging. "And then I saw that hole in the ground."

More time ticked away as he shuddered, his body moving quick and shallow, more an expression of discomfort than anything else. The whir and click seemed quieter, slower. She stood, willing patience, and she thought she heard the machine skip a beat.

But she heard something else, too. The wind—the night air—was speaking. It reminded her of when she was a child and she'd fallen asleep on the couch while Aunt Fern and Lou were talking, a conversation that seemed so far away, wrapped in cotton. How crazy, to think suddenly of her aunt Fern's couch and Lou and Aunt Fern sitting at the kitchen table, Aunt Fern drinking coffee and Lou doing a crossword puzzle, even at a young age. Crazy how Lucy Maud could now remember the nap of the couch, the marled green stripe on the white background, remembered it on her cheek, even, her face pressed into the couch pillow, her legs tucked underneath her. The wind—it sounded so much like Lou and Aunt Fern— and then, when Kevin turned to her, wide eyes revealing that he heard it, too, she realized that it was.

Carla, clean, exhausted, sprawled on borrowed sheets, dreamed of snakes in spirals. Sleeping in a room full of other sleepers, she came to rest for a time. Rain now on the roof of the long house, soothing for those inside. The long exhale of night, and Carla—now smiling, now frowning—wrapped in night's coil.

2:17 A.M.

Of course Boyd ran. She had let herself be led too far down the ghosts' path. She didn't know what it meant—the sudden eye contact or where Caleb's parents had been headed—but she knew that something had almost gotten her and she wasn't clear yet.

When she looked back, stumbling over granite outcrops, she saw the lantern light dancing over the stones, moving not only closer but swinging from side to side, as if the lantern lurched in the woman's unsteady hand, as if she was traveling at great speed.

Boyd didn't know where she was running, except that she was running away. She knew that it was just a matter of time before she fell, and what would they do if they caught her?

She came down from higher ground and found herself in a grove of Ashe juniper, the needles underneath her feet muffling all sound. It was cooler here, almost solemn. The air smelled fresher, too: green, like mowed grass. She didn't see the light for some time, but she kept running, though the moon was little help here in this grove.

After a minute, the thought came to her that she had lost them. What were they, anyway, but traces left in the world? Did they have agency or consciousness or will? The ability to hurt her? She was out of breath and exhausted, and she thought of sitting down, but how could she do that now? How would she not expect a hand on her shoulder as soon as she fell asleep?

She would have to keep going until dawn, until she saw the east cresting pink and gold, until she saw the clouds pearled with the yellow sun. She didn't know how long that would be; she'd lost all sense of time, and when she thought about it, she decided that dawn should have been hours ago. She had been living in this night forever.

But this grove of juniper was peaceful, quiet and still and sheltered, and she sensed an openness beyond the arc of trees. The ground was even dryer here, the trees absorbing much of the rain. How easy would it be to sit down?

A breath. Two. Her next few steps took her to the edge of the grove, and she suddenly understood that sense of emptiness—the ground sheared off here into open space, and she could not see the bottom, only the moonlit tops of more juniper trees, maybe twenty feet below her. It might as well have been a thousand; she could see no safe passage down.

She'd felt a sickening exposure throughout the night, a realization of fragility, a sense that what she had believed about the world before the storm was not quite right. The world felt red in tooth and claw, hungry. But, too, she remembered that after the storm, the garden had welcomed her, and she had lain on the rows between the beds and decided not to leave, and she wondered if these two things were essentially the same thing. The earth wore different faces, but it wanted her in whatever way it could get her. It sent her its ghosts, and its river fingers, and its tomatoes that had tasted like flesh, and now she found herself deep in the night, essentially alone. Fear overtook her, a cold clenching of the throat, and she began to cry silently.

Now came the swaying light, after she had imagined she'd outrun it. What would happen when they caught up to her, when they both closed cold fingers around her arms? She looked out over that open space. Behind her, the glow was dim, but it was getting closer. It was just a matter of time.

When the light was close enough that Boyd imagined it was at the edge of the grove, she turned, prepared to see the couple in the distance, the woman leading the way with the lantern.

The man was right in front of her. He could touch her if he only lifted his arm. Worse, his face was blurry, smudged with a giant thumb, erased until almost blank.

Now things happened as if underwater, a slow-motion and breathless series of acts. He raised his hand and disturbed the air around her face, but he couldn't quite reach her. She stepped backward, tripping over an outcrop of limestone. The woman was beside him now, having covered thirty yards in a gliding heartbeat, her mouth open, her eyes streaming tears.

Boyd went down, with two ghosts above her. They pushed forward and she closed her eyes and stepped into the open air, not entirely by accident.

She hung in the night, staring at the stars, garments fluttering up around her, and it was almost as if she were weightless. The lantern light telescoped away until it, too, seemed a star. As she fell, she thought about Isaac in the tree, and how he had finally needed her, and the girl in the bed, how she was there but not there, and about the person Boyd believed was out there who would understand Boyd for what she was. Her mom and dad and the way they'd held hands in Aunt Fern's storm shelter.

In a second she was through the canopy and in the dark again. She landed on her back, stunned, the breath knocked out of her, but alive and sunk in a bed of juniper and pine, and the needles disturbed by her impact settled around and over her, until they formed their own sort of blanket, surprisingly thick. She was unhurt and covered, and the terror she had felt upon seeing that smudged face left her in a surge of relief. She could feel how violently her heart beat in her chest.

But after a moment, underneath the needles, she breathed. The light that filtered down faded, and the needles above her were not disturbed. Caleb's parents could not reach her. She did not move for some time, her breath coming more slowly, more regularly. The earth had made a bed for her and she slept.

Isaac, finally at rest, the moon upon his face. His tree companions were also sleeping, unwilling and wary bedmates. The pecan tree was a palm outstretched, a haven in the storm.

All over the Hill Country, the trees had taken in travelers, like medieval monasteries opening doors. A pause here while the night wound on. The eye of the storm.

Allen Potivar was beginning to wheeze. He pulled out his inhaler, puffed twice, then put it back into his shirt pocket, patting it after it was deposited.

Lucy Maud hesitated, torn between wanting to take him back and wanting to find her sister and her aunt. He'd said an hour; there was at least half that yet. How long would it take them to get back to the house?

But the voices, Lou's and Aunt Fern's, the sound of the wind talking, a lighthearted bickering, though Lucy Maud knew Lou didn't like to argue with Aunt Fern anymore, didn't see the point to it. They were together at least, she thought as her step quickened, as she pushed past Allen Potivar and realized that they weren't on any particular path and had just been heading a certain direction. She would never make it back to the road without him, not in the dark. Let him go back rather than die, of course; she'd make Aunt Fern and Lou sit right down and wait until morning. The light would eventually come, and while this seemed like the middle of nowhere, it was settled land and, well, somebody would come find them. She slid on a rock in her haste and quickly caught herself.

Now she heard a man's voice in between the two women's. She glanced back at Allen, but she couldn't read his expression in this dim light. It was Ruben King; she knew it was Ruben King. What other fool would be out on a night like this?

As she moved forward, clouds in front of the moon shifted. The same wind that had carried the voices now revealed two figures on the ground.

Lou was kneeling, bending down as if shouting into a manhole, and Lucy Maud realized that the manhole was Allen Potivar's mine shaft. Lou's hair hung around her face, and Lucy Maud thought for a second that no middle-aged woman should have hair that long, especially not when it was so shot through with gray. Behind Lou, Fern lay sprawled on the ground, face and palms turned up to the brief flash of moonlight. Lucy Maud heard her voice now, singing softly—"Skinna marink a dink a dink, skinna marink a do. I. Love. You"—a song from Lucy Maud's childhood, carried to her now not across the thirty yards or so separating them but across the forty years between what they all were then and what they all were now. Lucy Maud felt a heaviness at her forehead, and she pressed her fingertips there— good Lord, had they all been those people once? Aunt Fern had cared for Lucy Maud and Lou when their parents had not been around, and though Lucy Maud thought of her mother with a sense of heartbreak and loss, it was with Aunt Fern that both girls had bonded. Those days— hard to think of them now because there had been such a possibility to their lives, so many things they should have done and been, so many ways that they should have loved and been loved. Such a lump in Lucy Maud's throat, so that she couldn't even swallow.

This same wind now took the clouds and piled them before the moon, damping the light again. Lou and Fern faded into blackness, but Lucy Maud still heard Fern's song. She stumbled forward, picking her way down the incline, and behind her, she heard footsteps and the oxygen condenser, but those things were falling behind.

The man's voice responded to something Lou said, and what a strange feeling for Lucy Maud to have Ruben King intrude upon her childhood like this. His tone was quiet, calm, as was Lou's, and it sounded like the sort of conversation a husband has with a wife in bed, just before sleep. *Did you remember to pay . . . ? You'll never guess who I ran into today . . . Have you seen the . . . ? I can't find it,* as if Ruben King weren't stuck in a mine shaft, and Lucy Maud felt an unreasonable stab of jealousy at how intimate it all sounded.

Fern, singing on the ground, sat up. "Here comes little Lucy Maud. Told you." Then she lay back down. "I wonder if a person could count the stars."

Almost to them and afraid of tripping in the dark, Lucy Maud never-theless looked up. The sky was clouded: not a star was visible. Fern was in another night, as she often was these days, a night that had come before, plus stars, minus clouds.

Lou was on her feet. "Jesus, what took you so long?" It was hard to pick out any detail in the darkness, but Lucy Maud could see a wild gesturing of arms.

Lucy Maud faltered. Lou was not usually the one to yell and demand answers, and Lucy Maud was not usually the one to apologize. "I—I didn't know where you were. I've been trying to find you."

"I can't take care of all of this by myself, Lucy Maud! Fern isn't even Fern half the time, and now this asshole's stuck in a hole in the ground."

Lucy Maud heard an indignant exhale from the hole.

"We have been trying to find you. This whole time, we've been wandering up and down the road."

"We weren't ever even on the road. Fern took off into the countryside." Lou's head swiveled, looking past Lucy Maud. Allen Potivar and Kevin had caught up. "Oh, hello," Lou said, torn between frustration and the need to use good manners.

Fern, still on her back, said, "I didn't take off into the countryside. I heard somebody stuck in the ground. He's been down there for a long time."

Lucy Maud drew her chin back in surprise. "Just since this afternoon, right?"

"No. For ages." Fern shook her head, a denial that vaguely spooked Lucy Maud, but there was no time to figure out what Fern meant. Allen, tears now streaming from the outer corners of his eyes, half sat, half fell to the ground next to Fern.

The rain, which had been heavy in the air since they left the road, started again, the clouds unzipping like a seam. Fern raised her palms to catch the drops, but Allen, chin shaking, let out a thin moan.

"We have to get you back," Lucy Maud said.

Allen, tears of fear and frustration making inroads in the lines of his cheeks, nodded.

"Kevin," Lucy Maud said. "You need to take Allen back."

Kevin pointed to himself. "Me?"

She tilted her head. "Who else?"

He considered. "Well, I thought you would do it. You're the only one who could find the way back."

Her mouth fell open, though she didn't know if he saw. And what would he do? She'd come back and he'd be on the ground next to Fern, looking at the nonvisible stars. Lou would still be shouting down into a hole.

"Kevin, take him back. If you don't feel comfortable, stay at his house with him. Lord knows we don't need another lost person wandering around." Lucy Maud thought of all of them out here, loose in the night. "In the morning, call the police. They won't come out here tonight. If they could even find us."

Kevin hesitated. After a minute he said, "Okay." She imagined him thinking of a couch and television, of a refrigerator full of food. He and Allen asleep, Kevin on the velvet couch, Allen in the recliner, *Andy Griffith* or *Gunsmoke* on the television.

"Kevin, you have to make sure he gets there. If he struggles, carry him. He only has a quarter of an hour or so."

"Carry him?"

"Carry him. A fireman's carry. A piggyback ride. Make sure he gets back and plugs in his condenser." Lucy Maud turned to Allen. "Go on." She gestured toward Kevin with her chin.

Kevin and Allen started back toward the house, Kevin swinging the unlit flashlight. "Wait," she said, and took it. "None of us are using it, but I bet it's dark in that mine."

Kevin let out a little breath, indignant and in disbelief, but she didn't give it back.

"If you come back, bring another one. I'd light a fire, but—" She looked at the sky and drops fell on her face.

Flashlight-less, Kevin and Allen disappeared over the ridge. Lucy Maud, with Lou next to her, watched them go. She imagined them during that long walk back, silent except for the condenser, two tiny beings loose in the great world.

Lucy Maud turned back to the scene in front of her: two women lying down, the hole in the ground. Fern still singing to herself. Lucy Maud nodded at Lou and went to the shaft, kneeling and shining the light down.

The shaft was deep, more like a well, and adding to the well impression was the standing water at the bottom of it. She saw Ruben King perched on a limestone boulder off to one side, an island in that underground lake, but she could not see the floor of the mine. She had no idea how deep the water was.

"Hi, Ruben," she said, as if they'd run into each other at H-E-B. "You find Maximilian's treasure?"

He covered his eyes with his forearm, unused to the light. "I don't think so." His tone was tired, disappointed. "But we did find something." His knees were tucked up almost to his chin, and he lifted his right hand. In it was a single silver ingot, already formed and, even underneath the tarnish, glittering in the flashlight's beam.

She looked at that ingot for a moment, and at the miserable wet man who held it. His posture revealed that he was exhausted, and they still had to find a way for him to climb out. "There any more of those where that came from?"

He was quiet. "A few for sure." After a minute, he said, "I haven't done much looking around."

"Oh?"

"Yeah. There's no light, there's all this water, and then there's . . ." He looked at something she couldn't see. "There's—there's this guy down here."

She fell to her stomach and dangled the arm with the flashlight. "There's somebody else down there?"

He nodded, eyes fixed on something she still could not see. "Yep. Or there was. At one point. Maybe a hundred years ago. He—he didn't make it."

She angled the flashlight but saw nothing. "A skeleton?"

Silence as Ruben considered. "Yes. I mean, there's clothes still."

"Anything in his pockets? Do you know who he is?" She didn't know why she asked this. There would be no record of this man; he was absolutely forgotten.

Ruben looked up and gave her a half smile, embarrassed. "I'm not touching his pockets. I wish I didn't have to look at him." But look at him he did, and he told Lucy Maud what he saw. "His clothes are wet, ripped. The skin on his hands is totally gone; that's all skeleton. He has no eyes, but there's something on his cheeks, something that looks like skin. Would there still be skin?"

She leaned farther until she almost fell in the hole, but she still could see nothing. "I have no idea."

"It's pretty dark down here." She thought he was hinting that she should toss the flashlight down. But what if she needed it for Fern and Lou? She said nothing.

After a minute, Ruben said, "The thing is—"

She waited until she couldn't stand it any longer. "The thing is what?"

He exhaled, grappling with how to say whatever he wanted to say. "I keep—I keep trying to figure out how he died. Starvation, maybe? Just being stuck and unable to get out?" He looked up at her, and she knew he was thinking that might be his fate.

"Maybe." How would one climb out of this mine shaft? The wall was concave, something impossible to scale.

"But—" He cupped his chin in his hand, considering, looking back at the skeleton that she could not see, and she knew that in these matters he was far more of an expert than anyone else she ever knew. "But—he's upside down. His head is on the ground, his feet up on the wall. He looks surprised more than anything else." Ruben shook his head, still looking at the man. "He wouldn't have done this himself. An animal, maybe?" He looked farther back into the mine, another area Lucy Maud couldn't see. "I just keep thinking, 'What else is in here with me? What is biding its time, just waiting to come out?'"

The rain fell into the mine shaft, but she thought he was sheltered where he was. "We're going to get you out." But she didn't know how. "It won't be night forever." It was meant to comfort him, but she wasn't entirely sure. Beside her, Aunt Fern had moved on to "Danny Boy," and Lucy Maud almost told her to stop singing because it sounded so much like a dirge.

Just below a juniper grove, just past where the cliff sheared off and the land fell away, not two miles from the mine shaft, the lantern light was gone. A wind stole through, lifting needles, a breath of the late night, getting on to morning. The trees breathed, too, and the earth. Rain fell outside the grove, but the juniper sealed its little world, keeping the ground dry.

In the dim, a sleeve trailed, pale pink cotton with buttons in the shapes of cat's head. Below the blouse was a pair of blue jeans, no-nonsense Levi's that blended into the dark. The blouse and jeans glided forward, as on a mobile clothesline. The shoe underneath, though—one Nike, a running shoe that had seen better days—took steps, walking solemnly forward like a windup toy. The footfalls were silent, the only sound the earthbound respiration. In. Out. In.

The garments stopped at a rectangular depression in the earth. Was it a grave? It was recent, convex not concave. The blouse bent forward, the jeans crumpled at nonexistent knees, the legs and sleeves deflated, a sighing motion toward the earth. The clothes fluttered to the ground, bits of straw stuck in the fabrics, while the one shoe came to rest next to them.

Things You Would Know If You Grew Up Around Here

What Those Rains Were Like

It's hard to tell you what it was like during and after those rains. Hard to explain the damage a flood can do. The whole world was like a snow globe, shaken and settled; things come to rest where they were never meant to be. Imagine finding the contents of your house in the trees. Look around. The bookshelves, emptied and splintered upon the rocks. The books, pages and spines turgid, disintegrating into the wilderness. Televisions and game consoles and cords like a new breed of snake. Broken china and mangled aluminum pans. Pencils and earrings and athletic socks and LEGOs. The wrought iron bench from your front porch stuck in the creek half a mile down the road, paint flecking into the mud, too heavy to move. Wrought iron beds, too, and sheets twisting in branches, the roots of everything exposed. In every canebrake, in every place where the debris caught, were tree roots, shocked to find themselves in open air.

3:05 A.M.

In a house three miles east of the juniper grove, a girl who hadn't risen in years stirred. Her mother was downstairs, sleeping on a sofa that was being overtaken by vines. Grass grew on the parlor floor, and vines pulled at the walls. They had nearly wrested the kitchen from the side of the house.

In her sleep, the mother's hand fell to the floor, sweeping over the grass, and more grass quickly sprouted between her fingers, in the space between index and thumb. The vines coming in under the door sprouted heart-shaped leaves the color of limes. Now, eyes looked in the window: yellow with a vertical pupil. The wild wanted in. There was no more safety here than there was out there. This place was the wilderness; it was the same. Soon the roof would crack open, the moonlight permitted entry. Soon the chimney would crumble into the ground. In the barn, the sleeping girl's horse, unridden now for years, leaving U-shaped hoofprints that will ossify as the mud dries, but now the horse stamps in the dark, sensing something not right. The stable, faded board and batten, would disintegrate under the weight of the natural world, would stagger and then fall, all of that timber carried from somewhere, settling into the Texas earth.

But now, the girl who hadn't moved in years moved. The index finger of her left hand tapped the bedsheet; the eyelids quivered, then opened.

Cloudy pupils, the eyes gone to cream, the same color as the fingernails that now gripped the hospital blanket. Toes stretched underneath the sheet, big toes reaching, remembering what it was like to move. With a rolling motion of the head, the neck awakened, the awakening continuing in a wave down the length of the spine. The girl's tongue curled upward in a yawn. A shoulder arched, then the other. Legs bent at the knee, the thin blanket gathering into a pool and then flowing to the ground like so much water. The girl moved slow thighs.

The feet, ponderous, heavy things, were on the floor now. The eyes had fully opened; were her mother awake, she would be surprised by the gray iris. When the eyes had last closed—on a rainy night in a December long past—the iris had been brown with flecks of green. If the mother were awake, she would remember the phone call in the middle of the night, the quick trip to the hospital in Marble Falls, the long stay while everybody decided what to do next, the two years at a residential facility. She would remember the move home, the hospital bed placed in the upstairs room, the quick training she had done, the catheters, the IV bag, the novels read in the heat and dust of late afternoon. She would remember her own loud barks of laughter, sudden and surprising, when she had forgotten she was reading *Terms of Endearment* or *The Phantom Tollbooth*, and the sound of her own voice acting without her command had pulled her back to the Texas afternoon, to her own daughter, trapped, mind and body no longer in communication. She would remember the times she wondered what had happened to the rest of the royal court, to the people who hadn't been pricked by the spinning wheel, whether they had aged and died while Sleeping Beauty slept on.

Now the girl's left hand unhooked herself from the apparatus keeping her alive; she no longer needed it. The hospital gown floated open at the back. She knew what she was doing with the medical equipment: How? Her fingers unhooked, untapped, slid the needle out. Blood dripped and flowered on the floor. Her movements were confident but exaggerated, her fingers overextended, lovely shapes despite the off-color nails. The wind on her face, in her red hair, the same wind that brushed an empty shirt on a mound of juniper needles, the same moonlight that crawled over faces sleeping in a second-story common room, the same air that followed the whir and click of two men walking home in the dark and three women kneeling over a hole in the ground. It snaked around a Noah's ark of a pecan tree, snuck into a house with a burned spot on the floor and a lingering smell of sage, rifled through a campsite by the lake where panning equipment and books swollen with rain lay in disarray inside a sodden tent.

This wind, this moonlight—they were part and parcel, the same—animated a girl nobody thought would ever rise again. Even her mother, somehow suspended in time, believed the night would go on without them, but now the night had come calling.

Here, now, the girl answered, stepping out of the room for the first time in years, feeling the creak of rusty parts, the knee unaccustomed to its bend, the ball and socket of shoulders unaccustomed to the swing of arms.

What did those gray eyes see? We cannot yet know. How was the world when last Angie Mason walked? Who was in charge and what did they do? Banks were collapsing, as was the market. It had been a leap year that started on a Tuesday, an election year. The things she would not know, mind and body severed so, and for so long. She would not know of the airplane that had come to rest on the river, passengers lined on wings in the water. She would not know of the deep-water leak in the Gulf, or the new princess across the ocean, or the tsunami that had melted the nuclear reactors. That year, an ancient calendar had ticked down, and people who had never followed it were suddenly convinced that the absence of ancient time meant that our time, too, was spooling out. No. There was still some time left. We were now so far into the future that we were inconceivable to those ancients; only think of them imagining us, imagining the world at the end of their allotted time. Impossible. This world would persist yet a little while.

All of these things Angie Mason did not know. She walked through the hallway, head straight, gaze not falling upon her mother growing mossy upon the parlor sofa. Hand on the doorknob, turning, delicate bones arching at the wrist. The door swung open, and she stepped past the bridle and tack on the front porch, leather beginning to rot, and she stepped on the two stairs, already collapsing in the middle. The black dog watched her but did not rise. Her head was empty of a swath of history, oh, but full of so much more: of the spin of the earth, of the dust of planets.

She did not know about this rain, about the bridge that was out and the houses that had floated away. Another storm was in her head, even more devastating, a swirl of wind and salt, a scouring of coast in no one's memory but her own.

Stones pressed into her soles, tender from years in a bed, but Angie Mason didn't flinch. The night air brushed against her bare back, but she was not cold. She raised her face to the stars as she walked, all of those books her mother had read still in the deep recesses of her brain. Clouds were in front of the stars and then not, and she had not yet returned to herself.

Things You Would Know If You Grew Up Around Here

We Loved This Place

We loved the canyons, the limestone, the smell of the creeks in spring. The trees that had stood for centuries. The very ground we walked on.

Lucy Maud knelt at a hole in the ground and dangled a flashlight. The beam of light glanced off the limestone, chalky but not slick, and came to rest in the murky water pooled at the bottom. She could not tell how deep; without thinking she picked up a stone and dropped it. The shine of the surface broke—a small plunk—and the rock disappeared without revealing anything about the water's depth.

"How deep is it?" she shouted.

Ruben King, resting on the limestone outcrop, knees drawn tight, chin tilted up toward her, shrugged. "A few feet." She had thought the water was still; now, looking more closely, she imagined that it pulsed. Nothing disturbed the surface, she realized, but something was disturbing the body of it. After a minute, she thought she could see the surface almost burgeoning, the water doming as more was added to it from a source Lucy Maud was not able to discern. "If you stood in it, would your head be above water?"

"For now."

She could only see him when she shone the flashlight directly on him. His face was tired, the light catching in the hollows underneath his eyes, in the ridges of his forehead. Well, they were all getting old, weren't they? She'd hate to see what she would look like in a similar situation, trapped in the bottom of a mine shaft. The overhead light alone would age her twenty years. Even the usurper grad student would look terrible.

The thought made Lucy Maud smile, but she didn't hate the grad student. She had been young once; she understood Kevin's appeal, especially when he'd become Dr. Montgomery, intense and intent, reading Greek with one finger running along the words, spectacles slipping down his nose. When had he become this man? Lucy Maud had helped create him.

Now she looked down at Ruben King and thought she saw traces of her husband there, a sort of flicker of bone structure. God, what longing she felt, looking down the mine shaft, such a raw need to spend the love she had saved up inside her.

Clearly they needed a rope, and she wished she had told Kevin. She reached into her pocket and fished out her phone. But, no—Kevin wouldn't be back at Allen's house yet—what good would calling him do?

She should have sent Lou and Aunt Fern back with them, too. Now she felt responsible for all three of them, and Lou was—well, Lou had the potential to be less than helpful, more in the way.

"How did you get down there?" Lucy Maud asked Ruben. "Any chance of you climbing back out?"

He looked up to see if she was serious and then laughed. "You think I haven't tried that already?" He waved a hand toward the thing Lucy Maud couldn't see. "You think this guy hasn't tried it?"

"But you climbed down, right? You didn't just fall down this shaft?"

"I climbed down the first part. Fifteen feet or so. Then the room down here opens and I just dropped. That's about ten feet above me." He shifted, wanting to move but unwilling to put his feet back in the water. "If I could just get back up there—"

Lucy Maud sat back on her heels and looked at the clouded sky. Boyd and Isaac who knew where, and now this man. There was nothing she could do, and there was never nothing she could do. She was, above all other things, a doer. She could climb down, but then Lou and Fern would be adrift, and she would just be stuck at the bottom of a hole in the ground. She could walk Lou and Fern back to Allen's house—assuming she could find it—then come back with Kevin and a rope, again assuming she could find the mine shaft. But something stopped her. She felt that if she walked away from Ruben, the hole would become a grave, and she would come back to find Ruben and walk right past this place, and in a year his bones would be rattling around with the other poor guy's. She thought of all of those afternoons that Boyd had been at Ruben and Isaac's house, that year in seventh grade when Boyd's final Texas History grade had been 100.

"Ruben, I don't know how to get you out."

He laughed, though it wasn't funny. "That's okay. Unless you have a rope or a ladder, I don't imagine you could."

Lucy Maud adjusted so that she was flat on her stomach, her arm swinging the flashlight. "Do you want me to toss this down to you?"

"Sure."

She had visions of missing, of the flashlight sinking into the water, irretrievable. But Ruben caught it, and then she had a vision of André the Giant catching Robin Wright at the end of *The Princess Bride*. As the light had fallen, she'd imagined harp music.

He took the light and shined it back into the passage. She could no longer see his face. Then he switched it off to save the battery. "Do you have a phone with you?"

"Yes." Being prone was making her sleepy.

"Okay, good. In the morning, we'll call someone with a ladder, I guess."

She imagined carrying a ladder half a mile across gravel. "Or a rope."

"Um." Light shone on the walls of the shaft. She knew he was imagining scaling that wall, and she understood why he was worried. She doubted if she could do it, but then, she wouldn't have crawled into that hole in the first place.

Gravel bit through her clothes, but she settled in, the fatigue of the long night getting to her. Little was out here to stop the wind, but it was gentle, drifting over Fern, now asleep on the ground. Lou had tucked up her knees and wrapped her arms around them as if she was cold, the wind running over the cedar brake that had hidden the hole in the ground. The wind carried on it the knowledge of the flood, and the entire world was wet. How had they all—all of them—ended up out here? What in the storm had set them to wandering?

"I always thought about how Boyd and Isaac became friends." Ruben's voice was slow, in the mood to talk, not ready to go to sleep just yet. He didn't wait for a reply. "I'm glad they did, because I would have wondered what happened to her after she left school. A bright one, Boyd. And I don't mean smart bright. Bright bright."

Lucy Maud knew what he meant. Her daughter shone, some film of the universe still wrapped around her like a caul.

"Isaac, man"—she barely heard Ruben; he was now part of the warp and weft of the night that pressed down upon her—"I don't know where he came from. So ambitious. Wants so much out of life." Ruben was quiet for a minute. "But it's things. He wants a nice house, a certain kind of car."

"He's a good kid."

Ruben turned this over for a moment, as if he was surprised to hear her say it. "Sure. He is a good kid."

She laughed, a short, tired sound. "You think Isaac's too materialistic, but here you are on a treasure hunt."

He made a sound: half grunt, half laugh. Rueful. "You're right. But I'm not here because I really want things. Wouldn't you go after a treasure that was practically in your own backyard?"

She thought about this. "I might wait until it stopped raining."

A quiet was settling over them, the weight of deep night. She wondered how long it would be until dawn. But then she remembered her phone and checked the time: 3:21. The white light of the screen seemed out of place, jarring in the velvet dark, and when it finally turned off and she slid the phone back into her pocket, her eyes felt tender at the edges.

She rolled on her back, and for a few minutes she was the only thing that didn't belong in the landscape, a hard brick on the ground, her own contours not matching the contours of the earth. When the dark came back to her vision, when she could see the things around her, she was a small, small thing on the round earth's surface, granular. Then, somehow, she wasn't; she was absorbed, a part of something infinite, here on the surface of a dying planet, here with three others of her kind, untethered, a mitered gravity of existence, a swallowing. All four of them slept in the deep night, faces turned up, and the clouds revealed the starlight.

Things You Would Know If You Grew Up Around Here

What Lives in the Caves

In the caves of central Texas, the animals have adapted, growing eyeless in an eternal night. The blind salamander of San Marcos eats blind shrimp in the dark. The salamander's body is colorless, save for the bloodred gills it has in place of lungs. Bats live here, too, though only for part of the day, so they have kept some measure of sight, though most people don't know this. The bats of central Texas have become famous, with all those Mexican free-tailed bats pouring out from under the Congress Avenue Bridge in Austin at summer dusk. Millions of them. In caves, too, small mammals, reptiles, and birds find shelter from the heat at the entrance.

The mine shaft was not that kind of cave, the kind with a regular entrance. The difference between a cave and a mine is partly the degree to which man has carved it out and why. In this cave: the silver ingot, the man who had come before and never left, and the possibility of legend, of untold riches.

No birds, no mammals, were in this cave. They'd have to come down so far, like living at the bottom of a well. Pools of water might be farther down, might have cave fish, swimming blindly in pools, or crabs or shrimp or crawfish.

As the night wore on, the insects grew bolder: cave crickets with antennae longer than their bodies, beetles who lived on these crickets and their eggs. A scorpion that must have fallen in; scorpions prefer heat and sun. The things we call insects but are actually arthropods: centipedes and millipedes flowing like water over the walls, undisturbed when Boyd's mother's flashlight shone upon them. Not my favorite companions, sure, but the kind that makes you sad for what the world is losing.

In a hole in the ground, Boyd dreamed. Were they dreams? Of course they were. How else to explain the cacophony of voices? How else to explain all of these people wanting to talk to her, to tell her something they needed her to know? A woman—*Alice, Alice, Alice,* Boyd heard—saying her sister had poisoned her, had put antifreeze in the well. Another woman, nameless, needing Boyd to tell her husband that she'd loved him and she never told him and what a regret to carry with you forever. A man, sounding desperate and feverish, demanding that Boyd contact his grown children and let them know that there was no God, no Jesus, no heaven, that it had all been a lie. Another man, older sounding, saying the opposite, that it was not too late to repent. All of these voices, and many more, a din of the underground while Boyd slept.

Then there was the hum of other life—the trees, the grass, the spores and seeds and worms and snakes, all of it alive, and she was somehow part of it. She thought about how she'd known that another person like her was somewhere out there, someone who knew things in that inexplicable way that she did, and how Boyd knew that one day, she would find this person.

She did not dream of Caleb's parents, nor of their lantern, but she did dream of light and dark, of how dangerous light could be, of how safe was the dark. She dreamed of the world spinning, rabbits in their burrows, opossums dangling from trees like gray fruit. She saw her juniper grove flashing with the quick exposure of day, the turn back to night, the days and nights in such quick succession that the world seemed like an old-fashioned calliope, like the world flashing by outside H. G. Wells's time machine. So many days and nights in the history of the world, and in her dream she had gone so far back that the grove was gone, and cattle were driven above her. A few more flashes of light and dark, and the world started to fill with water.

What would remain if she stayed here long enough, if the clock wound back far enough? Would the water fill with plesiosaurs, would the ooze turn primordial? She was aligned, she felt, in some way with the earth, some magnetic core of her pointing true north, but she couldn't know everything, just that she was a small part of a larger universe. The voices still chattered in her head—all of the things left unsaid in a life, all of the news about what happened after the life had been lived. All of the stories about the afterlife were contradictory; the only common thread was that it was not what people had expected. She was struck by how many voices there were and yet how they could not seem to hear one another, could only detect her presence underground and speak to her.

How was she able to sense the earth and the thoughts of others in this way? Some accident of frequency and tuning, perhaps, but to her, it seemed so obvious. It was not even curiosity about others' lives—though she was curious—but a certain trick of empathy, a sense that it was possible to imagine another's life, that had developed into something more with Boyd.

But now, soothed by the flicker of night and day, lulled to sleep by the hum of the earth, Boyd rested for a while, safe for the moment in a bed of juniper and pine, breathing as the worms crawled through her fingers and the centipedes nested in her toes.

3:30 A.M.

In the night, the rain stole over the hills. The lakes undefined, edges gone. Their surfaces pocked by drops, swelling. Every river in Texas broken.

Darker, darker, darker. Later there will come a golden yellow, a blush, radiating from the east, but not yet. This side of the earth had not yet turned her face once more to the sun.

But these few hours between deepest night and morning were not empty. The nocturnal animals were awake and going about their business: skunks, opossums, coyotes. The night world hardly ever seen by us, but there nevertheless. Through the juniper grove, the prehistoric animals trundled, massive, already at home in this new world. These hours not any less important because we don't see them.

But they ticked down now, the globe spinning. At the moment, everyone accounted for, nearly everyone come to rest. Only the gray-eyed girl on the move, headed now toward the juniper grove, and the two men on a ridge trying to make it home before the air runs out.

Things You Would Know If You Grew Up Around Here

We All Fear the Deep Water

Thalassophobia, it's called, though this is technically the fear of the sea. But we all have this fear, even those of us who love to swim on the scorching-hot days of high summer. The water here in the Hill Country lakes is dark, though, and only imagine what could be down there. Some things we know about: the alligator gar, prehistoric remnant of a hundred million years ago, the fish with the long snout, the double row of teeth. The catfish, the old men of the lakes, rumored to grow to the size of VW Bugs at the feet of the dams. The houses and windmills and the churches with empty pews; only imagine how horrible to swim over these things, to have other lives in other eras playing out beneath your unprotected feet.

But more than this: the darkness. The sense, when you pull your feet from the water, that something has just missed you, that something is closing toothed jaws around a space only just vacated. Right up the road, the next lake in the chain of Highland Lakes is Lake Travis, the deepest lake in Texas. Twenty stories deep, a whole world just out of sight. Just for a moment, imagine yourself, all five or six feet of you, skimming the surface with all of that dark underneath. Twenty stories of dark extending past your legs, busy treading water. Imagine something happening; imagine your legs stopping, your arms no longer keeping you aloft. How long would it take for a body to fall? With what slow motion would it pass through the watery light, limbs outstretched, lifted slightly from the body, hair rising from the face? Soon in the dusk of water, in the twilight zone, the water mossy with sediment, the bubbles trailing upward. Then in the darkness for so long until coming to rest on the bottom with an inaudible thud, the body surprised by a bottom, by any barrier to the fall after so long without one. What has the body passed in its long descent? What stories could this body tell were it to rise once more to daylight?

3:35 A.M.

Two men struggled in the dark on a path that was not clearly marked. As the battery wound down, long after anyone had expected, each slow exhale could be the last. A rise and then Kevin saw Allen's porch light. Allen was crying again, tears soaking the front of his shirt. His hands rested on his knees and his body shook, chest trembling at a high, fevered frequency. Allen turned frightened eyes to Kevin, and a thin stream of urine trickled down Allen's leg. He was too scared to say anything, but Kevin knew. He remembered lifeguard training from a different time and place—a lifetime ago—and he bent and scooped Allen onto his shoulder. Urine trickled down his sleeve as the man shuddered above him. Kevin carried both of them home.

5:59 A.M.

And now the east was pink, the long horizon lit, revealing dew on the crabgrass. As happened in that part of the world, the sun pushed the wind before it. Leaves in the pin oaks lifted, and furrows appeared in all of the standing water, caressed into being like a crumpled length of silk. In Wimberley, crews and volunteers who had worked through the night to find the missing now ceded their posts to newcomers, fresh from a night's sleep, cupping coffee in hands that had not yet lost the chill of rest, slow to wake up. A National Guard soldier pushed a johnboat into the river, headed out to rescue people trapped on temporary islands, stranded and alone. The soldier, a redheaded man, young, worked at H-E-B in his real life. He wondered about a girl he'd met the day before, a girl who did not now answer her phone. In the boat were cases of bottled water. Ducks on the water, indignant at the activity. Doves keeping house in the trees.

And now the pink was yellow, the coal-blue dark thoroughly chased away, the smell different, bright and hopeful. Now flowers opened and leaves spread themselves. Now the black-capped vireos landed in the juniper grove, scolding one another from the treetops, a sharp *zhrrrreee*, until the sound gave way to birdsong.

6:00 A.M.

Next to the cliff, the ground burgeoned. Pine needles fell as Boyd sat up. She shook dust off her fingertips before she wiped the inside corners of her eyes. She blinked and felt dust in her lashes, saw the white limestone coating her forearms, giving her a pale sheen.

She kicked her legs, shaking earth and sleep from them, seeing her knees emerge, little mountain peaks that shed tiny avalanches of debris. A breath—she had been breathing all night, but this breath was different— cold, bracing, and instead of chasing dirt from lungs and trachea and nose, the breath settled the fine particles that remained, and would remain, part of her now. She opened her mouth to breathe more deeply and realized by the movement that her lips had been slightly parted all night. For the rest of her life, she would remember the fetid, fecund smell of the under-ground, ripe and wet and alive, crawling with the living of things too small to be seen.

Her knees hitched up, the soles of her feet getting their bearings. She got them under her and rose, rocking forward, and a shower of earth cascaded from her shoulders.

Her clothes were tattered, the convertible cargo pants shredded at the ankle. The linen shirt was thin to the point of transparency, wholly intact only at wrists, placket, and collar.

She could not say what had happened to her. The boy's parents had been nearly upon her, then she had fallen. Then what? She had been on her back in the pine needles, unhurt, as if the earth had swallowed her. She had somehow been able to breathe. Once buried in the earth, she'd become so sleepy, and she remembered little about what had happened next. She'd dreamed—she knew this because her head was full of crazy things—but she couldn't recall exactly what the dreams had been.

There had been a cacophony of voices. She could not remember what those voices had said, or if they'd said anything specific. It had been a white noise, background, urgent but indistinct. Boyd felt as if she'd been asleep at a party, the conversation distant.

As she'd risen, the earth had partially covered the pink blouse with the cat's-head buttons and the jeans. She stepped over these, their presence only just registering in her consciousness.

But she did dream of something, she knew, the person who she knew was out there. It seemed that if the earth somehow knew what Boyd was, then it knew what the other person was as well.

Thinking still about this person, she turned toward what she thought was the direction of the river, the direction of Isaac. She could not sense *him*—his thoughts, his feelings—but she could sense him, body in a pecan tree. If she turned her left shoulder to the rising sun and walked for a couple of hours, she would come close to finding him. In between, however, was the swollen Colorado River, and, oh, what devastation lay there. She remembered the water behind her: the bridge out, the cypress tree gone, and the way the water had wrapped around her ankles like fingers. She also remembered the pine needles against her cheeks and eyelids. The earth had had her, and it had let her go.

8:00 A.M.

Later than she would normally have, Carla opened her eyes behind her screen in the common room upstairs. The morning light had a friendly cast, an impression aided by the unintelligible chatter coming from the rest of the room. She stretched clean legs and arms underneath clean sheets.

When she rose, she left the big T-shirt on, but she put yesterday's pants on underneath. Already she was thinking long term: what clothes she'd need to bring, what books. She wondered if she'd be allowed to keep this bed or if she would end up in one of the little houses on the property.

In the bathroom, two women scrubbed the toilets, women Carla had not yet met, and she recognized the smell of purple Fabuloso. This seemed somehow out of place: she realized she'd expected homemade soap, lye from ashes. They wore yellow rubber gloves that reached almost to their elbows, and their presence—industrious and bustling—again gave Carla pause. Of course there would be dirty toilets on a commune. She just hadn't considered who would clean them. She had imagined something different: gardening in the sunshine, maybe, or knitting sweaters in a rocking chair. Maybe she could help them with their soap situation, as soap was one of her specialties.

She brushed her teeth with the donated toothbrush and wondered at her presumption. What made her think that they were going to invite her to *live* here? Sure, they'd taken her in on a rainy night when she'd been wandering the countryside in yoga slings, but that kindness did not necessarily extend to semipermanent room and board. And now she wanted to be here, but she didn't want to clean everybody's toilets. She remembered the warmth of the shingled house, the roast chicken on the table.

She headed downstairs to the long hall for breakfast, and it reminded her of the Lutheran church she'd attended as a child: an open kitchen on one end, full of women with aprons, a long counter between the work space and the dining room. Almost everyone she'd seen working so far had been a woman, and while this would normally have rankled—the domestic jobs relegated to the women—she saw that it was a necessity, that the women outnumbered the men to an astounding degree. She guessed maybe thirty people lived here all told, and she had seen one adult man and one adolescent. The commune was female, she thought, and then she thought, no, Amazonian. This adjective conveyed a certain fierceness that Carla believed women, when allowed, possessed.

Breakfast was eggs baked with vegetables, served in long pans with giant spoons. Homemade bread had been sliced, and next to it were jeweled preserves in Ball jars. She took a spoon of eggs, two slices of bread, which she spread with peach preserves, and she filled a mug with coffee. She wondered at the coffee; it could not be grown here. It felt a little like the purple Fabuloso: welcome but out of place. She sat at one of the long tables, feeling a bit like a college kid in a dorm.

The dining room was mostly empty; after a minute, she realized that the kitchen crew was doing more cleaning than cooking. At a place like this, everybody would have been up long ago. She guessed it was around eight A.M., judging by the sunlight, and it took her a moment to realize that she hadn't seen sun in a couple of days. The rain had stopped, at least for now. This was such a curiosity to her that she rose and went to one of the windows, coffee in hand, as if she meant to stand there for a while.

Outside, the ground was a mess, churned into what looked like chocolate pudding. People were indeed up, all women that Carla could see, going about the business of the morning, wearing rubber boots but still slipping in the wet. Carla saw Kim speaking to two other women, and she recognized Bess as one of them, she of the knitting needles in the shingled house. Kim stopped talking and gestured, pointing to something Carla couldn't see, though she leaned forward to look. Now all three women looked in that direction, and Carla read in their expressions a sense of alarm.

Carla hurried out into the yard, still holding her coffee, still wearing yoga slings. She looked in the direction the women looked, and for the first time she got a sense of the geography of the place—the Colorado River wound by and on the other side was a three-hundred-foot bluff, filled with Ashe juniper and pink granite—and against this backdrop, Carla was stunned to see a soldier banking a johnboat on the glassy river and fording the floodwaters to come ashore. Carla almost dropped her coffee cup. To her, a woman steeped in counterculture, the soldier meant nothing good.

The soldier had red hair. He stood in the shallow water in his army boots, looking ill at ease as a crowd gathered.

Kim stepped forward, squelching through the mud, sliding once but quickly regaining her balance. She was tiny next to the soldier, and Carla realized with a start that Kim was only about five feet tall. She had seemed short, maybe, but the coiled power in her wiry frame gave her a more imposing stature.

The redheaded soldier was tall, yes, but not unusually so. He seemed larger than he actually was because of an awkwardness, an unease in his body. When he walked out of the water toward Kim, his shoulders dropped and his palms faced forward, as if he were scooping air. The man hesitated, looking beyond Kim at the people assembling on the bank. Carla followed his gaze: to her left was a massive garden, sodden from the storm, at least an acre, sown with corn still only waist-high, rows and rows of tomatoes drooping at their stakes, peppers only a foot off the ground, a good quarter of the garden various shades of salad and leafy greens. Beyond this was a patch of cucurbits—Carla recognized the deep yellow flowers, open in the morning sun—melons and squash given free rein to spread their vines. Now she followed his gaze to her right, past the houses, to outbuildings and paddocks and goats that were white on top but brown with mud shoulder-down. Seeing these things as if through his eyes gave her an odd sensation; she considered them hers, yet they were just as new to her. Most of the few hours she'd passed here had been spent in darkness, sleeping.

The man stepped toward Kim and extended a hand. "National Guard, ma'am. How are you folks holding up out here?"

Carla saw in the base of the boat the cases of bottled water. He was here to help people, she realized, not to institute some sort of martial law.

Kim nodded. "We're pulling through." She jerked her chin back in the direction of the assembled crowd. "Everybody's accounted for." Now she saw Carla, making eye contact. "Plus one more."

The soldier pulled a pen and a notebook from his pocket. "You've got an extra? We're tracking down the missing. I'll check if they're on my list."

Kim beckoned Carla forward with a twist of an outstretched palm. "Carla here showed up in the middle of the night last night."

The soldier's pen was ready at the notebook, but he paused at this information. "In the middle of the night?" He looked up at Kim, who was looking at Carla, and he followed the direction of Kim's gaze until he and Carla were staring at each other, ten feet apart. Carla felt exposed, ridiculous. She crossed her arms in front of her, felt that this was too defensive a stance, and slid her hands into her pockets instead.

"I was looking for someone." Carla didn't want to tell the story; it wasn't even entirely true, she realized. If she was looking for someone, why had she stopped? It hadn't even occurred to her this morning to leave and start looking for Boyd. "I was lost," she said, trying to circumvent the question. Then she wondered what she had told Kim the night before because she couldn't now remember.

"Name?"

She didn't want to give it to the soldier. "Carla Brownwood."

He wrote it down. "I don't think you're one of the ones I'm looking for, but I'll double-check." He slid the pen and notebook back into his pocket. "It's a mess out there. I'm impressed you guys came through so well, y'all being so close to the river." He looked at the water's edge, appraising. Carla saw that the river here seemed full but enclosed, as if it had never burst its banks, and the slope leading up from the water lacked the little ridges of detritus left behind when water retreated, curved deposits that always reminded Carla of rice paddies or the arched lines of topographical maps.

Kim smiled with her lips but not with her eyes. "No, we've had very minor damage. We lost part of a greenhouse from high wind, but that's it. Well, and we're a little muddy." She looked down at her boots as if to demonstrate.

The soldier nodded, gaze distant. He was thinking about something else. After a minute, the distant gaze focused on Carla again. "You say you came in the middle of the night?"

Carla drew her chin back. "I don't know what time it was."

He considered this. "You drove?"

Now it would all come out. She looked at Kim, again trying to remember what she had told the women. Carla had done nothing wrong; why did she feel as if she were on trial? "No, I didn't drive. I—I walked."

"You walked." He nodded as if this information wasn't surprising at all. "From where?"

She rocked back on her heels. Everybody watched her now, all of the people she had met last night and this morning: Bess and Annie, and the two women in the bathroom with the purple Fabuloso. "From my house. On River Road."

His eyebrows rose. "That bridge is out. How did you get all the way here? Or did you cross before the bridge fell?" Now he was talking to himself. "No. I would remember."

She didn't answer until he looked at her again and took a step toward her. He was not threatening her; something she'd said had interested him, though she didn't know exactly what or why. "I followed someone. Down by the water. Across the dam." He had said, *No. I would remember.*

He was taking more steps toward her, closing the distance. "Who did you follow?"

She stepped back. "My neighbor. A teenaged girl. Her name is Boyd."

His lips parted and he drew in a breath. Carla could tell that he recognized Boyd's name. Boyd was on the list of the missing. "Look, is there some place you and I could talk? Just for a minute?"

This place was not Carla's, so she turned to Kim, and when she did, the soldier turned, too. Kim shrugged—*No big deal*—but as the people lined up behind her started to disperse, to go on about their daily business, they looked at Carla one last time, a new suspicion in their eyes. The morning sun rose in the sky, and the wet air hung heavy, the world's new weight.

The water had risen during the night, and Ruben King woke Lucy Maud up by shouting. The morning was cool. They were exposed on the ridge and the wind swept over her, the moisture in the air clinging to her skin. Ruben yelled again—"Hey! A little help?"—and she opened her eyes and struggled to place herself. The sunshine: unfamiliar. Clouds in a sky just beginning to take on the blue of day.

She heard another voice now, her twin sister, speaking quietly. Lucy Maud had been dreaming—about what? Something troubled her, some remnant of the dreamworld, and then she remembered the image in her dream. Boyd, the daughter she had carried for nearly ten months, three of those months over a brutal summer in a garage apartment in Austin with only a box fan and a swamp cooler as Kevin taught Greek to freshmen and worked on his dissertation on Linear B. Her own child—a part split off from her own body, the single most precious thing from a marriage whose loss she still mourned—lying on her back in a grave, loose clay and limestone piled above her. The dream had seemed so real, and Lucy Maud was having a hard time letting go of it. She sat up and dusted fine pebbles from the back of her hand.

"Are you still up there?" Ruben's voice was small and far away.

Aunt Fern, in an orange plaid housedress and tennis shoes, was in front of Lucy Maud, and Lou was up beside Fern, black T-shirt and unflattering jeans showing off her middle-aged spread. Lucy Maud blinked at them.

"Are you going to help that man?" Fern asked. When Lucy Maud didn't answer, Fern crouched beside her and took her shoulders. "Lucy Maud," Fern said with total recognition, and Lucy Maud almost cried. Aunt Fern was lucid, her memory slipped back on track. Lou said that it often happened in the morning, when it was just the two of them in the house on the other side of the lake, after Lou had returned from her AA meetings. Fern looked at Lucy Maud, let go of her shoulders, and reached out a hand, as if that waif of a woman could pull Lucy Maud off the ground.

Lucy Maud took the hand and rose, putting most of her weight in her heels so she wouldn't pull Aunt Fern over. Lou had also registered Fern's lucidity and had visibly relaxed, a nervous awareness replaced by a slumping weariness. They were all tired; they were all too old for sleeping on the ground.

Fern watched Lucy Maud for a minute, making sure she was okay, then turned to lean over the mine shaft. Fern cupped her mouth with her hands to amplify the sound: "We're all here. What do we need to do?"

A strangled noise from the bottom. Now Lucy Maud and Lou both leaned over, too, blocking out the light. Lucy Maud saw the flashlight's beam on the wet limestone walls looked thin and weak. She didn't know if it was because the morning sun was brighter in comparison or because the battery was wearing out, but the anemic light on the rock made her nervous.

The stone on which Ruben King had perched overnight was nearly submerged. The water lapped at his heels and toes, and he stood now, looking up at them from ten feet of open room and ten feet of narrowed shaft. They'd have to pull him up twenty feet.

Aunt Fern took a quick appraisal of the situation and said, "We'll have to get a rope," as if Lucy Maud had not suggested that same thing a few hours before. Lucy Maud found it hard not to roll her eyes.

"What are you going to do with a rope?" Ruben asked, eyeing the water that lapped at his shoes. "I don't remember anything to tie it to. Are y'all going to pull me up?" His tone was doubtful, frustrated. "Call somebody to pull me out. Call the authorities. Someone with a winch."

Lucy Maud could feel her blood pressure rise. Too many cooks. Stiff and achy after her night on the ground she rubbed sleep from her eyes and fished her phone from her pocket. But the battery was dead and she nearly chucked the phone down the shaft. "My phone is dead," she told the other three. "Do any of you have a signal?"

Fern shook her head.

Lou shrugged. "I left it at home. I didn't even think about it."

Lucy Maud swallowed her frustration with a sigh that she made sure her twin sister heard. "Well, we sure could have used it."

From the shaft, Ruben shouted, "I don't know where my phone is. I haven't seen it since yesterday."

Now there was nothing to do but go for help. Lucy Maud could not drum up much sympathy; of the two people she was worried about, Ruben King was the least important. Her dream about Boyd troubled her. The Texas Hill Country was one of the friendliest places on earth—the first letters of the names of the streets in sequence in Fredericksburg even spelled out the word *welcome*—but some people everywhere waited for an anarchy, waited until nobody was looking so they could do all the things their hearts secretly desired. Lucy Maud was afraid Boyd had run into one of those people, a person who seemed normal when the world was normal, but who privately couldn't wait for the world to slip. Lucy Maud had to figure out how to help Ruben because she needed to go find Boyd, though she didn't know where to start.

8:30 A.M.

Boyd, now backpack-less, ruined clothes barely covering her body, set out across the open country once again. The high ground—the ridge on which she found herself after leaving the juniper grove—had been scoured in the night, and everywhere she marked the path of water, the power of gravity. She had no way of knowing about the destruction on the Blanco River, just a little way up the road. She was headed to a different river, a river that had been tamed by a series of dams that corralled the water into a succession of highland lakes. Here, on the ridge, the destruction was minor and could be tallied by what was missing—and not much had been here to begin with—instead of what was moved or broken or added.

But that scrubbed-clean feeling started to vanish as she made her way down into the valley, guided by some internal compass that pointed her to Isaac. At first, things looked not quite right: tree branches lying on the ground, leaves still fluttering as if they did not yet know that they had been separated from the trunk; a child's pink plastic chair perfectly positioned and waiting for the missing little girl; a silverware drawer on its side in the mud, and over the forks and spoons and knives, a wild turkey, trotting. The bird was not afraid of Boyd, and she did not know if the bird didn't react because the world was different after the storm or because she was different after the night spent underground. If the bird hadn't turned its head a certain way as Boyd passed, she might have started to question her visibility, to wonder if her body had become as faded as her clothes.

She was pulled down, down from the high country to the riverbed, the pecan trees standing sentry in a nearly imperceptible grid, letting her know that here was the bottomland, the floodplain. Soon she would reach the river, but she knew that already: she could smell it, and she could see where the water had passed through. A stainless steel refrigerator lay on its side in the mud, sinking. She thought that in a day or so it would be submerged, the ground so soft, and then nobody would ever even know that it had been there. Only imagine: a family eating a picnic, a father and son hunting white-tailed deer, a kid on a four-wheeler. They would all be standing on top of a buried refrigerator and would never even know. Perhaps one day a metal detector might find it, and wouldn't the excavator be surprised: Someone buried a refrigerator? She remembered Ruben King telling her that whenever archaeologists didn't know what some artifact was for, they always said it was for a religious ritual: only think what crazy ritual could be invented to explain a buried refrigerator.

Now trees were on their sides, roots exposed, and in the canopies of the trees, which were also on the ground, were the contents of people's lives. Everything paper had started to disintegrate; a flaky paste of off-white wrapped itself around branches and twigs. Blankets and sheets, shredded and dirty, caught as if somebody had made a bed there. She saw a toothbrush on the ground, and the toothbrush seemed to go with the blankets; perhaps they shared a provenance; perhaps they had come from the same source.

As she walked, her clothes fluttering around her, she remembered suddenly the ring she had taken from her mother's bathroom. She had put the band of tricolored roses in her pocket only four nights ago, before she had pitched her tent with Isaac on the shore. Now she was certain that the ring had been lost, given what had transpired since then, both in the world and to her clothes. But when she felt her hip pocket, she felt the outline of the ring, and she slipped it on. It was the only thing in those pockets; her phone had been lost. It had been dead anyway. There was nobody to help her. She wondered whether her mother had yet noticed that she wasn't at home. Oh, she thought with an uncharacteristic absentmindedness, her mother was probably worried. But Lucy Maud knew how Boyd was, that Boyd could take care of herself.

The ring was now on Boyd's index finger; somehow she felt as if this would be safer. She held her hand before her face, palm out, examining the band that rested next to the tip of her thumb. What must her parents have once been like? Lucy Maud had been in high school when they met, Kevin finishing undergrad, and they had stayed together through her father's PhD, through the first years at UT, all the way up through his tenure process. The family had crumbled in the associate professor years; when Kevin had celebrated his promotion to full professor, there had been two celebrations: one with his department, to which he'd taken the grad student, and one at the lake with his former family, with an H-E-B cake in the shape of a mortarboard with a tassel, even though that wasn't quite right for the situation.

The ground sheared away—an old landslide—and Boyd had to climb down now, the wet limestone splintering under her hands. She would certainly meet the grad student at some point; the woman was to be her step-mother. Boyd thought the grad student was most likely pretty and stylish; Boyd thought this because the student was young, because her father had left her mother for her, and because her father had changed in the last year and a half, changed aesthetically. He'd turned in his old glasses with their nearly invisible frames for a dark, Buddy Holly–type pair. He'd started rolling his jeans at the ankles to show off his chukka boots. He'd attempted facial hair.

Ahead of Boyd, a house was caught in the debris—a single-wide trailer on its side, crumpled at one end. People were inside. She could not see them, or even sense and understand their emotions, as she had been accustomed to doing, but she could tell they were there, in the part of the trailer right before it crumpled, where the exterior was just beginning to bow. How did she know this? She stopped, unsure. This knowledge came as a surprise to her, as it was more than simply empathy. She looked around, trying out this newfound ability. This trailer had been in a hollow outside Kingsland until about two A.M. the night of the wedding. Boyd saw a shed and a four-wheeler next to it, and she knew those things still stood in the hollow outside Kingsland. She saw the trailer, too, how old it was, how it had once been derelict and a bobcat had found its way in through a hole in the floor, how it had been sold, and a woman had cleaned it up, had replaced the ratty carpet with linoleum, had scrubbed the walls and the counters. This woman was not the same woman who was now inside; Boyd could not seem to trace what had happened to the woman who had fixed up the trailer, only what had happened to the trailer itself. Wouldn't the Kingsland woman be surprised that the result of her labors had landed here in the bottomland?

Boyd could see, too, what this bottomland had looked like before the pecan trees were planted: rolling, waist-high grass here where the blackland prairie of East Texas broke up at the foot of the hills. She had heard all her life that the mesquite trees in this area had been carried as seeds in cattle manure, but recently she'd read an article that claimed this was not true. Now she saw the cattle drives pass through this bottomland, stripping a path of grass and pounding the earth underneath, and now she saw the Comanche trading with the Spanish before the Germans even came.

The history she'd apprehended through books and through Ruben King's stories now was so much more than just words on a page, and it came to her through a bodily knowledge and through a vision as if she were watching a movie. This movie now focused on a figure in the trailer, lying on the sodden floor, and on a baby, in a crib by the window, and Boyd imagined this baby watching her. Boyd raised her eyes to the window in question, seeing the blinds askew, but she could not see the baby that she knew was there.

The baby began to cry, and Boyd thought it sounded as if the baby was calling out to her, not as if it was in pain. She knew a woman was on the floor, but she also knew that the woman could not rise and help the child. The baby's calling to Boyd was nearly unbearable, and she bit her lip in frustration.

No windows were open, and the trailer must be burning up. Who knew what it looked like on the inside, having tumbled down to the bottomland? What must the woman on the floor smell like now, in that heat and stifled air?

Boyd could not bear the crying. She moved toward the trailer. She put her hand on the tilted door and, fighting gravity, she yanked the door open.

The soldier seemed like an ordinary guy. He just wore army fatigues. Even his hair wasn't quite soldier-ish, too long around the ears, and an un-army-like shade of red.

He hadn't taken Carla anywhere, just stepped to one side, while all the commune—she couldn't shake that word—residents filed back to whatever jobs they had been doing before the soldier had landed on the beach as if it were Normandy.

"This girl. This Boyd. On River Road." The soldier looked at Carla earnestly, a look that seemed incongruent with his desert fatigues.

"Yes?" It dawned on her that he knew Boyd, that he was asking after her in way that spoke of caretaking, or of property.

"I helped her, I think. She was with another woman and she crossed the River Road bridge before it went out. I took her to a house on River Road. Ranch-style, long, stucco maybe? A tile roof?"

Carla nodded. "I know the house." She had been there enough times. Carla had followed Boyd. She had traced those footsteps across the country-side. She remembered the snakes, how she had wanted to follow them, how one had gotten her in the heel.

She shook her head, a private message to herself. She wondered if she smelled like sage, remembered that burnt spot on her polished concrete floor, the spiral on her forehead—and Boyd's—in the place of her third eye. As Carla was thinking about all of the things she didn't want to tell this soldier, she realized suddenly that this commune, the place to which she'd been drawn in the middle of the night, was in the shape of a spiral. In the center, the long house, then rays of outbuildings trailing from it.

The soldier watched her, waiting to see if she was going to say anything else. What was there to say?

"Do you know this girl? Boyd?" He looked up at the sky for a second before turning back to her. "I don't even know her last name. Maybe Boyd *is* her last name." He tilted his chin as if Carla might corroborate.

But Carla was going through some things. She wanted to help Boyd, but she didn't want this soldier around. She didn't like soldiers and didn't want one to mess up her chances of becoming part of this community. She sighed overdramatically and said, "Her first name's Boyd."

The man raised his eyebrows. Carla could tell he'd almost given up on her and that she'd revived his interest. He was acting—well, he was acting unsoldierly. How well did he know Boyd? she wondered. Because it seemed as if he was now a Boyd acolyte, as if he had joined the Boyd cult. As if he had fallen under Boyd's spell, Carla thought, a clichéd statement but true nonetheless.

As usual, when she had these thoughts about her neighbor's daughter, Carla became annoyed. Boyd was no sorceress. Sorcery implied intent; Boyd was a wide-eyed ingenue, the kind of movie character that boiled Carla's blood. Lucy Maud was the one who should have bespelled people, but then, Lucy Maud was forty-seven. Women who were forty-seven were invisible. They did not often inspire acolytes.

"She said she was looking for a friend, a man. Were you also looking for that man?"

Carla had forgotten she'd told the soldier she was following Boyd. "It must have been her friend Isaac. They were camping down by the lake before the storm hit." Carla bit her lip, looking back over her shoulder at the efficient machine of the commune, people going about their daily jobs. She wanted to be a cog. "Oh, but Isaac left." She remembered that he'd cut himself with the tarp. She had driven him back up to his car. "I don't know anything."

Now Kim came striding up, mud flecked to the top of her rubber boots. "Did you work everything out?" Kim was business friendly, chirpy, but her underlying message was to wrap it up.

The soldier looked at Kim with fresh hope in his eyes. "Not really, not yet. But you could help," he said, turning back to Carla. "You could help me find Boyd. You were following her. You know where she was probably headed."

Now Kim looked at Carla, too, expectation etched across her features. Carla saw an evaluation: Kim was watching to see Carla's response in a crisis.

"Sure. I'll help. I can tell you where she might have been going." Carla remembered the footsteps disappearing into the floodwater. She had no idea where Boyd was. But this was not something she should say, not in front of Kim.

"Great." The soldier extended a hand as if this were a business deal. "I have an extra life jacket."

Kim put a hand on Carla's shoulder. "I'll keep your stuff on your bed."

Carla almost cried with gratitude. She thought about the weight of that hand as she followed the soldier down the bank, put the life jacket on, walked into the water in her battered yoga slings, and took a seat near the rear of the boat. *The aft?* Carla asked herself, and just before the man pushed off, Carla saw the water moccasins, weaving their way around the man's boots, as if he kept them as pets. He didn't react, almost as if he didn't see them, and then the snakes were gone, and he was in the boat, his boots dripping flood remnants and bits of the Colorado River onto the cases of bottled water. The sun, partway up the sky, warmed her face but blinded her, so she closed her eyes against it.

In the mine shaft, the water was at Ruben King's breastbone and rising more quickly now, all of the rain that had fallen now filtering through the limestone, filling in cavities, making its slow way to the aquifer. The sound of the cave had changed, now rounder and almost vibrato. A lush sound, a sound that spoke of the tropics. The corpse was gone now, under the water, and Ruben imagined him underneath in the dark, limbs rising as the water rose, newly animated and light. Ruben gasped as he realized why the bones had been upside down—the cave had flooded before, and the man had been lifted and set down in a different pose. Ruben wondered what position the man would be in when the water left again. He held the flashlight above his head and shone it in the corpse's direction; the light did not penetrate the dark surface.

Ruben, too, felt himself being lifted, buoyed. Soon he would not be able to touch the rock he stood upon; he wished the shaft would fill more quickly, so that he could tread water on the rising surface. He would rise, too, carried by the water to the chamber's ceiling, and then he would maneuver himself to the shaft, delivered to the surface by the floodwaters like some Venus on a half shell. He would not die in this dark water, trapped and cold; he would not be left behind to keep this man company. He wouldn't know what it would be like to lose the body's breath, the slow exhale without an inhale. He wouldn't know the floodwater, the last gasp that would fill his lungs with something other than air, that would return him to whatever had been before there had been life, that would complete a circle, lifelong, universal.

8:38 A.M.

Angie Mason in a hospital gown, gray eyes scanning the horizon, bare feet unfazed by the rough ground. Her head was full of something else, something that wasn't this, but she did not yet know how different these two realities were. Now she walked past the dark rectangle of a grave, and the discarded clothes of a scarecrow.

Angie Mason shed her hospital gown, her naked body crisscrossed with tape lines. Her flesh was flat in the places where it had pushed against a bed for a decade, rosy and surprised by the morning sun.

She pushed her arms through pink lawn sleeves. The cat's-head buttons were too difficult for her, so she only buttoned one, the one at her solar plexus. The jeans were too small for her soft body, tight around her hips and belly. She pulled one running shoe over a bare foot.

Had she registered these things? Not yet, not quite. There was a period of transition, a reentry. She had not yet coalesced, was a bit of double vision walking the countryside, refracted out of herself. Soon, she would come into focus, would be able to understand and evaluate, would be able to decide and not to just act. She was not quite a full person, not quite a thing with a mind or agency, instead still a piece of the storm, a part of a tempest brought to life. She left the hospital gown behind and continued in the direction to which she had been drawn.

Boyd, in the trailer, eyes adjusting. Light streamed in through the windows on the other side, and the curtains hung obliquely. The door had slammed behind her as she'd stepped across the threshold, and the floor tilted at such an angle she'd had to brace herself against the wall. In the darkness, her other senses were heightened: she heard the tick of the clock over the refrigerator, the drip of the water from the eaves, and she smelled mold and garbage, even a faint whiff of sewage. Underlying it all was the scent of baby powder and dish detergent, of a house that had been cared for until recently.

The woman—Boyd knew exactly where she was. She was on the floor in the doorway between bedroom and hall, and Boyd would have to step over her to get to the baby. But Boyd knew also where the woman had been, things she'd done before the storm. Boyd felt a kaleidoscope of iterations of the woman in this house: standing at the counter boiling water for macaroni and cheese, folding laundry on the dining room table, giving the baby a bottle on the couch while watching an episode of *Forensic Files*. There had been a life here before the storm, before the water had washed the home downstream.

The baby was silent, and Boyd wondered if she had imagined it, if the baby was also part of the film of the past laid over the current world.

Around her circled the ghost of the woman, doing the things that a mother would do, and Boyd was not entirely sure what was real and what was not.

Now the light inside became almost enough for Boyd, and she reached over to the closest window and pulled the cord, raising the blinds. The inside of the trailer came into focus.

On the floor, the woman was facedown, her blond ponytail flat and wet. Her knees were bent and her head was bowed in the position in which she'd come to rest so many hours ago.

Boyd moved forward in the canted space, trying hard to keep her balance, feeling somehow terrible when she stepped in a pile of dry spaghetti that had fallen from the open cabinets. She knew that it would never be cooked. The entire thing was unbearable: being in this house with the mother on the floor and her child in the room behind. Everything in the trailer spoke of poverty, but it also spoke of care.

Still no sound came from the bedroom, and Boyd knelt next to the woman. Boyd took the woman's chin in her hand and rested a moment before she turned the face upward. The woman's eyes were closed, but at the sudden movement, the lids fluttered open, and by some strange trick of the storm, she looked directly at Boyd. Boyd could sense her, still somewhere around, still somehow watching over her child, only recently abandoned.

And the woman—Boyd knew that she had tumbled end over end as the trailer had careened in the water, and that she had grasped the kitchen counters and the cabinet doors to hold herself in place as the water came in, and that she had finally been caught underneath the kitchen table, unable to escape. Despite the mother's fate, the baby had not fallen from the crib and had remained higher than the waterline in the bedroom.

Boyd had to step over the mother to get to the baby, and the bedroom was darker because the blinds had not yet been raised. The air was close and stale; Boyd smelled the baby's diaper before she saw the child. Then the baby made a sound, a crack in the back of its throat, as though it had been holding its breath and could no longer stand it. Boyd moved toward the crib, wanting to spend as little time as possible here, wanting to get the child and run.

Again she opened the blinds, and she saw first the diaper bag in the corner of the room, its contents emptied and saturated. The bag was made of a light blue toile, and on the flap was embroidered LILY. Lily. The baby was a girl. Now Boyd turned to the crib, afraid of what she might see.

But it was okay. Lily sat by the bars, one hand resting on the wood, and when Boyd looked at her, Lily blinked and pulled herself up. She stood at the edge of the crib and reached out her hand.

Boyd, ready to calm a crying child, was unsure how to react. She put her finger in the baby's outstretched hand, and Lily closed her fist around it. Sadness in that grip, *please* in that grip. The child couldn't know what had happened to her mother, but she knew that she had been left alone. Somebody should have come a long time ago and had not.

The child opened her mouth and started crying, a thin whimper, the sound of a child who had ceased expecting her cries to be answered. Boyd put her hands underneath the girl's arms and lifted her, and Lily stopped crying in surprise.

What would she need? Boyd hadn't ever been around babies, but she knew they needed formula and diapers and maybe powder or wipes or rattles. Boyd didn't know how old Lily was and couldn't begin to guess: less than three, probably, more than one. Diapers were on the floor, escaped from the overturned bag, and though most of them were wet, dry ones were still in a package, and Boyd thought that changing diapers was the first thing she should do.

Lily wore a tiny floral jersey dress, and it was easy enough to get the diaper off. Boyd used a package of wipes to clean the girl, then in a straight-forward operation got a new diaper on. When finished, Boyd rested the baby on her hip while she looked for formula, for bottles. She had never changed a diaper and, forgetting, briefly, about the rest of the circum-stances, felt something like pride.

In the diaper bag also: two bottles and a can of formula. A scoop was in the can and directions on the outside, and for Boyd, the hardest part was finding the water to mix with the formula. Obviously the tap was not working. But in the kitchen was a gallon of distilled water, and she filled the bottle with it, shaking it with the powdered formula, then she put the rest in her own water bottle, severely depleted after the trek across country.

Then she was ready, and the only thing to do was to say goodbye to the woman and to leave. Boyd knelt again, this time with a child on her hip, and said, "Say goodbye, Lily," the first words that Boyd had spoken since entering the trailer. Lily, holding her fresh bottle to her mouth, looked at Boyd in surprise. Had Lily been surprised to hear her name? Lily reached out her hand to the woman on the floor, spoke a noise that sounded to Boyd as if Lily realized that it was for the last time.

"Goodbye," Boyd said to the woman. "I'm sorry for what happened to you. I promise to take care of your baby." She touched the woman one last time, this time on the elbow, a solemn oath that Lily was in good hands, that Boyd would see her to safety on the other side of the storm. Boyd swore the woman nodded, thought she saw a barely perceptible tilt to her chin. Boyd thought suddenly of Carla burning those candles underneath the hanging tree, how the curse had been set aflame and transmuted to smoke. She thought of the Comanche blamed for the little girl on Babyhead Mountain—a girl who, in Boyd's imagination, now wore Lily's face—and of the woman Hettie Meyer, who had killed her own children.

Then Boyd left, gaining her footing again in the outside world, adjusting to the normal gravity and light. With Lily on her hip, Boyd set out once more, trying to find Isaac.

After too long talking about what to do, they still hadn't come up with a plan. Lucy Maud decided, as the sun came over the ridge and the early-morning wind died down, to take Lou and Aunt Fern back to Allen Potivar's. They were all starving, except for Aunt Fern, who was a bird you had to remind to eat.

Lucy Maud didn't want to leave Ruben King, but they weren't doing him any good sitting vigil at the surface. If they splintered away, it seemed less dire in the light of morning, with the rain finished and the sunshine crawling over the earth. Last night, it had seemed as if they were to leave Ruben, they would never find him again.

The morning light slanted just right above the shaft; she thought she would be able to find this spot again. She looked around and saw nothing that worked particularly well for a landmark. She tried to photograph the spot with her mind: the rise of land, the honeycombed limestone, the crab-grass. Allen had mentioned a cedar brake; she saw no sign of that now. Nothing much to distinguish it but the three women under the sun.

She knelt. "Ruben. We have to go get a ladder. Nobody's coming."

He didn't answer, and she knew that he had a hard time hearing with the water rising. But he'd responded only five minutes ago, trying to convince her to go get other people to help.

"Ruben."

When he still didn't reply, she stood and removed her light flannel blouse, leaving only the tank top underneath. When she unbuttoned the sleeves, she remembered a different blouse, one with cat's-head buttons, and she wondered briefly what had happened to it. She pinned the blouse to the ground with one of the stones, and before she rose, she yelled into the shaft, "Ruben! We'll be back soon!"

Her voice came back to her, dimmed by the water. There was another sound, but she didn't think it was him, and she wished she had the flashlight.

She rose reluctantly and motioned to Lou, who had positioned her body to keep the sun off a sleeping Aunt Fern. At Lucy Maud's cue, Lou shook Fern's shoulder gently, and the three of them set off in what they thought was the direction of Allen Potivar's.

They didn't get far, however—just to the line of juniper—when they saw Kevin, headed their way with a coil of yellow vinyl rope.

Lucy Maud, exhausted, felt her knees buckle at the sight of her soon-to-be ex-husband and the rope. She nearly fell forward. Kevin had always been an unlikely knight in shining armor, and she had always wanted one of those. Unlikely was better than not at all.

She turned to her twin sister. "Lou, you think you can get Aunt Fern back to civilization?" Lou nodded, took Fern by the elbow, and led her over the ridge.

Things You Would Know If You Grew Up Around Here

The Comanche Didn't Kill the Baby on Babyhead Mountain

Well, of course they didn't.

Nine and a half miles north of Llano lies the hill where the girl was found. Nobody quite agrees on the date. One history, given by a professor remembering local stories but writing much later, places the incident in connection with the Battle of Packsaddle Mountain, so after August of 1873. Many other historians, and a historical marker placed at Babyhead Cemetery, claim the girl was murdered in the 1850s. In any case, settlers found the dismembered body of a child who had gone missing, Mary Elizabeth, her head impaled on a stick near the summit of the mountain.

The story: the Comanche did it. Whites were not welcome in Indian territory. A pipe was found at the scene, evidence of Comanche. For years, this story was passed around. Every actual witness to the girl's body passed away, and so the tales became memories of memories.

But then the descendants of the settlers started to speak up, and their story was different. A man named Ned Cook, who still lives in Llano, told a story about his uncle David Webster, whose father, M. L. Webster, once told him a story about a mob of wealthy ranchers. They wanted to get rid of the homesteaders, and they went to M. L. and wanted him to take part. They said that the girl's family was "poor white trash" and that nobody would miss them. They said that if the U.S. Cavalry thought that the Comanche had done it, that they would send a unit to the area for protection. And also, Ned Cook said, the massacre would keep other settlers from coming in to the country, as the ranchers wanted all the land to themselves. Ned Cook's great-grandfather wanted no part in it, but it was done anyway.

Other descendants say the same, but there's no real evidence either way. Other than the pipe, easily planted.

But if your family has been in this area for years, you know about Mary Elizabeth—about Beth—and her head on the summit. A girl, an innocent, used. No cavalry ever came, but the settlers still did.

Lou and Aunt Fern went on ahead. Lucy Maud watched them go and silently wished them well. Kevin lifted a hand in a wave, much more concerned about rescuing Ruben King, though this was the last time he would ever see them.

Before they disappeared over the ridge, Lucy Maud and Kevin turned back to the task at hand. They knelt at the mine shaft and shouted, but they couldn't hear Ruben or he couldn't hear them.

Kevin looked at her, then looked around them, scanning the landscape for something. "If only there was a tree." He ran his gaze up and down Lucy Maud.

She blushed.

He rose and put his hands around her waist, measuring with the span of his fingers. "You're sturdy." He wrapped one end of the yellow vinyl rope around her. She raised her hands to give him better access as he jerked her body forward. She doubted that the grad student was sturdy, which was likely part of the grad student's appeal.

Kevin finished tying the rope around her. "I wish you were a tree." He rested his hands for a moment on the waist that was not as small as it had been. "Sit down." She sat on the poky gravel and he tugged. She jerked forward. He frowned. "Lie down. Like corpse pose in yoga."

She winced at the gravel on the back of her head. He saw and grabbed the shirt she'd left as landmark, balled it up, and put it behind her head. His hands were gentle as he lifted her skull.

"You do yoga?" Sometimes his whole life was a surprise to her.

He shrugged, sheepish. She realized whom he did yoga with and why he didn't want to talk about it. His fingertips were on her temple and she closed her eyes and tried not to think about anything. For a moment, Kevin blocked the sun, standing over her, legs wide, jerking his end of the rope until he was satisfied. "If it begins to pull you in, brace your feet on the edges of the mine shaft."

She nodded. "Okay." He was tying the other end of the rope around his own waist when he stopped suddenly and looked at the rope. "What am I doing? There will be too much slack. What do I do? Do I wrap it around my waist?"

"Boyd would know," Lucy Maud said from the ground.

"Yep." He was quiet for a minute, palming the end of the rope.

In the morning light, she saw the shadows in the creases of his face. In a different life, she would have seen these changes in him over their morning coffee. She hated the anger that accompanied this thought, so she lay back down, watching his unsteady, unsure hands.

"Tie it around your waist anyway," she said. "Even if there is too much slack. Use your arms to control the slack and your waist as a backup."

He looked at her, his brows pinched at the bridge of his nose, an expression he wanted her to read. After a second, she realized he was sorry. She'd take it, but it wasn't enough; she wanted him to really apologize for everything.

He said, "I wish we had a better plan. I don't know how we're going to pull him up."

"Go down. Get him over to the shaft. Come up one by one with the rope." She sat up suddenly. "I should go. I'm lighter."

She hated that look of hope in his eyes. He didn't think it was a good idea because it made more sense; he thought it was a good idea because it transferred the danger to her.

"No, no, I'll go." He waited for her to protest, to say it made more sense for her to go. But that look of hope in his eyes—that sense that he wanted her to save him again and would prefer for her to be in danger—she knew that look. She wondered if the grad student knew that look.

That look made her say, "Okay," in a bright and chirpy voice, despite knowing it would be more practical for her to go.

He emptied his pockets on the ground beside her: keys, ChapStick, his dead phone. He stood at the shaft's entrance for a moment, lost. The rope was nothing more than a tether, a way for him to find his way back out.

She stood and twisted, pulling the rope around her like a winch. The coil on the ground disappeared until only six feet or so was between them. She wrapped her hands around the rope at her waist. "I'll let it out as you go."

He nodded. His face looked like a different man's face—thin in the wrong places, silver stubble on his chin—with Kevin's old eyes. Then he sat on the ground with his feet dangling into the darkness of the shaft and turned and lowered himself, elbows at a strained angle as he held on to the edge for as long as he could.

Then he was gone. The rope still had slack, so though she couldn't see him well, she knew he was within a few feet of her, descending the wall. It had been half an hour since they had heard from Ruben.

Something You Couldn't Know,
No Matter Where You Grew Up

What Kevin Would Find in the Dark

Things You Would Know If You Grew Up Around Here

Different Kinds of Floods and How Long They Take to Dissipate

In central Texas, we have different types of floods. An overbank flood happens when a river cannot contain itself, when it spills out over its banks. A flash flood happens when water has nowhere to go, when it encounters resistance from concrete, saturated ground, or solid rock, then stacks up and finds itself a conduit. In man-made floods, water breaks or something like a dam fails. In those floods, there were failures, sure. In Bastrop State Park, thirty-five million gallons of water took out a century-old dam. The failure of this low-hazard dam killed nobody and affected no roads.

But mainly what we dealt with in the aftermath of the Memorial Day storms were overbank and flash floods, and the worst damage was when both phenomena combined. A flash flood is quick and deadly, but it dissipates in hours. An overbank flood, a flood where a body of water has forgotten its borders, lasts for days, even weeks. The body of water is slow to find its shape again, resists the limits it formerly knew, and wants more.

Isaac, who felt as if he'd been awake for hours, stiff and unfolding in the tree. He took a deep breath, and what should have been clean air was thick and fetid, humid to the point of mold. His skin was marked with the patchwork pattern of pecan bark, even underneath his clothes, a crisscrossed brand as if the tree had claimed him. Everything around him smelled and sounded like water; the leaves in the pecan trees rippled gently, like a stream unaware of the waterfall around the next bend.

His legs had become almost rigid during the night, as if he were a corpse on an embalming table. His back was kinked and his body L-shaped, and he wanted desperately to stand or to lie fully down, to unfold himself so that he would not be permanently bent.

He was amazed that he had made it through the night—the branch he was on was maybe a foot wide, and his back was to the trunk. Such a precarious position, yet not once had he felt himself about to tumble. Now, as he roused himself and shook whatever limbs he could, he took stock of his situation.

High in the tree, still about twenty feet above the water. The river looked less angry today, but more powerful. The current was still strong—he saw things float by: parts of boats and Jet Skis and water toys. But now, the river looked less roiling, more in control. Monolithic. If he fell into it now, he might never get out.

But he wouldn't fall—he would just wait it out, hanging on to his branch in the canopy. This flood wouldn't last forever. Already the rain had slowed and now here was the sun, glinting on the water. He didn't know how long he would have to be here, but he would stay as long as he needed to.

But no. After a night of peace, of lion and lamb, the denizens of the tree began to grow restless, as if they had only just now noticed him. A fire ant bit him in the webbing between thumb and index finger, and he jumped at the pain and in sheer surprise. They—he and all of the animals—had shared this tree all night without any confrontation or conflict, and to have such a thing introduced now seemed a betrayal. Another bite on the back of his neck, then the beetles on the branch above began to move toward him, clicking and in unison, and he felt for a second as if all of nature had turned on him.

He grabbed the branch on which he perched, fingers beneath his thighs, nails scraping the bark. Fire ant bites were acutely painful, but he held on, and the pain was temporary—each bite's sting would disappear in seconds. Hard, though, not to panic when they swarmed one hand en masse—he lifted that hand and shook the fingers, and the motion nearly caused him to fall before he caught himself. Now a fear bubbled up inside him, a sense that he had come so close—he had felt, for a moment, the open air, the pull of gravity.

He froze, trying to will himself stuck to the branch that for all that long night had been such a haven. The sound of the water below him was deeper than it had been, more bass and less treble, and he was keenly aware of the sun filtering through the leaves. It seemed, for a second, as if the earth were breathing, a measured calmness that felt like a long inhale.

The snake reared before him, coiled like a cobra, though he knew of no Texas snakes that could do such a thing, could contort in such a way. Through his shirt, he felt another one behind him, and this snake was the one that undid him. He rose in a panic, imagining that he could stand on that high branch, and when he fell, he could not say if the fall was accidental. Branches tore at his clothes and ripped his skin as the water rose up to claim him. He thought of Boyd, broadcast his panic, then felt it immediately lessen, and for the first time since he'd known her, he understood how she had such a hold on people, and what it was about her that made her hide from the world.

Boyd thought of her promise to the mother on the floor as she carried Lily, who made noises in the early morning that reminded Boyd of mourning doves. Boyd still felt the pull of Isaac, the compulsion to find her friend, but she was quickly being distracted by Lily's delight at the world, and by the way the child was trying to have a conversation with her.

They were under the canopy of a stand of juniper, and as always in this part of the country, the juniper tinged everything with a hint of magic, a sense of old-world forests, and hushed, other lives lived in the spaces between. The canopy had been thinned by the heavy rain, and light streamed down upon them, and when Lily became too heavy on one hip, Boyd shifted her to the other.

Half an hour after Boyd left the trailer behind, she was shocked to realize that she had been talking to the baby for some time. She thought back to what she'd said and could remember nothing but telling the baby stories: the story of the woman and her daughter in the house with the vines, the story of Babyhead Mountain, the birds in the hanging tree. The way the bridge had crumbled and disappeared down the river. Now she paid more attention, and what she said surprised her.

"When you get big enough to understand, Lily"—Boyd recognized the thought but not its articulation—"you'll see, I can't be around too many people at once. I couldn't go to school. It's hard even to go to the grocery store, unbearable to know that so many people are hungry." Boyd felt for a second that sharpness in the belly, the way other people's hollowness hurt her, and somehow, this longing made her think of the vines in her garden, of the way they'd grabbed her in the late spring. "They are not the only hungry ones either." The river had pulled on her ankle, trying to suck her down, and this near-sentient voracity reminded her of the Overlook Hotel in *The Shining*, as if she were a central Texas version of Danny Torrance. The world wanted something from her, but she didn't know what.

She looked at the baby. Lily's eyes were large in her face, rimmed in the longest lashes Boyd had ever seen. The pink to her cheeks went even to the ball of her chin. She was rosy and creamy and had hardly cried, some sort of dream child. Her blue eyes looked as if she understood what Boyd was saying, and her mouth was parted as if she wanted to reply. Indeed, she had for some time been replying, and though Boyd hadn't discerned actual words, she thought she knew what the baby wanted her to know. Boyd thought that she detected a sensitivity in the girl, a special understanding, and at this thought Boyd's step hitched in an even greater realization.

What must she herself have been like as a child? At what point did her mother realize that Boyd knew things about other people, that Boyd could pay attention in a way that was more than just paying attention? Boyd pulled Lily from her hip and held her at eye level, Boyd's hands underneath Lily's armpits, fingers wrapped around the child's shoulder blades. Boyd narrowed her eyes, then thought hard about the woman on the floor, examining the child as she did so, the baby's fingers cupping so that it looked as if she was reaching for Boyd.

She shook her head to clear the thought, but then had a thought that was somehow even less welcome. "If you are like me, you'll never be the kind of woman men want," she said, shifting Lily to the other hip because the girl had become too heavy. "You just won't. You have to understand this. You shouldn't let it bother you, but it will. It sucks. You can't ever really be independent of someone you love, and the other person will sense this. You can't ever be aloof, like the graduate student."

Lily opened her mouth and made a sound, and Boyd imagined that she understood the baby. "Oh, no, no, you won't hate her. Not quite. That idea will be there, but mostly you'll just feel kind of jealous, or aspirational, like you want to copy her. You'll wonder what it would be like to be that kind of woman, the kind of woman a man would leave his life for."

Boyd stopped short, surprised again by what she'd said, by how it seemed so out of nowhere. Something about Lily was making Boyd speak her deepest secrets. Lily took a hunk of Boyd's hair in her hands. Boyd felt a sudden press at the back of her throat, the beginning of tears, and she caught herself. "But don't worry, Lily. I will help you." Lily couldn't be the one Boyd had imagined was out there, could she? She was a baby, not even talking yet.

The child understood. Oh, she did not know that her mother was dead and that Boyd was carrying her across a wasted country. But she did understand that Boyd was now in charge, that Boyd was somehow in her own sort of pain, and that Boyd held the same trick of empathy and understanding. Boyd had never met a person like herself, a person who shared this quality, and even though Lily was a baby, Boyd did not know how to react. She blinked in the juniper-filtered sunshine, and Lily cooed again, trying to say something. Boyd thought that Lily was forgiving her, that the baby understood why they'd had to leave her mother in the trailer.

Boyd thought suddenly of a day in seventh-grade social studies when Ruben King had assigned them a story, "The Ones Who Walk Away from Omelas," by Ursula K. Le Guin. A society in that story was a utopia, a singularly amazing place to live, but for that society to exist, its pain had had to go somewhere. It went to a child who lived in a basement, who lived in filth and could not speak. When the citizens of that society came of age, they learned the truth about their own happiness. Some could not bear this truth, and these were the ones who left Omelas. Having Lily in her arms made the story somehow more real to Boyd: Would she walk away, knowing that she could not save a child like Lily, but could she live with the knowledge of the price of her own joy?

As Boyd was turning over this new information, a wave of panic buckled her, and she nearly dropped Lily. She felt wet again, as if she'd been submerged and the flood were pulling on her. She knew that Isaac was in the water, and Boyd gasped, feeling the press against her chest, imagining her lungs taking on the river, feeling Isaac's terror in the center of her torso. "Oh my

God," she whispered, seeing that wake on the water as something she loved sank beneath the surface. "Help. Please help." She did not know how far she was, or what she could do to help him.

Behind her at the edge of the juniper grove, though she didn't yet see it, pink lawn sleeves and cat's-head buttons were coming closer, trailing straw behind them.

And then people came out of the woods, displaced and bedraggled. Some had bags or suitcases; some had nothing but the muddy clothes they wore. They emerged on the bank like the sodden remnants of an apocalypse. Sam slowed the boat and brought it up along the bank, distributing bottled water, checking to see if anybody needed medical care. They took an old woman into the boat with them, her knuckles and wrists and ankles thick with arthritis. Carla made room for her in the bottom of the vessel. Patches of scalp showed through the woman's thin hair, and her mouth hung open in shock. Her white dress was streaked with sepia; in the night, she had been in the water. Boyd would know what the woman had been through, but Carla was astonished by the pain etched on her features.

Sam wrapped the woman in a scratchy green blanket, and Carla watched her eyes close briefly, pressed together in a mass of wrinkles. The woman's eyes opened suddenly, fixing Carla in their gaze, and the sudden eye contact startled Carla so much she nearly fell out of the boat.

Carla did not know how to feel, and so she just felt guilty, as she always had. She moved to sit beside the woman, and she was rendered helpless as usual by the sheer amount of the world's heartbreak. She was powerless against this tide: wave after wave of cruelty and sadness. What could a single person do? Carla had done nothing but isolate herself, but now she leaned her shoulder against the woman's, touching but just barely, a point of human contact. The sound of Carla's feet on the bottom of the boat was hollow, and it echoed up her legs, shivering into the joints of her knees and hips.

Sam said nothing, steering gravely from the back. Whenever they saw a new group of people, he drew the boat alongside them and made sure they were safe, that they weren't experiencing medical emergencies. He gave them bottled water and granola bars and held their babies for them. Carla watched how he nodded while he listened, head bent toward the people. He, too, was shocked by the suffering. Sweat beaded above his red eyebrows, a sheen slicking his entire freckled face. Carla hoped he'd put on sunscreen.

She had not known so many people were in the Hill Country, or that they were so different from her. They seemed from another time, standing on the banks in their bare feet, drawn to the river by the spectacle of the boat, the soft whir of the outboard motor a snake charmer's song. Some lacked teeth and one lacked a right hand and some were in wheelchairs and on crutches and others sucked at inhalers and others were covered in sores like a pox and some had eyes swollen shut. The farther the boat went down-river, the more Carla looked, and the worse the people got, until Carla thought that the Colorado was some sort of river Styx and the soldier some sort of Charon. Some she could see take their first steps to the edge of the water; some had feet sunk into the mud, as if they had been standing, waiting, for a very long time. Some looked at the johnboat and its occupants with hopeful eyes, some cynically, some blankly, tired and dead-eyed from what they had seen.

What had they seen? The storm had been odd, revealing how tenuous the layer of civilization stretched over the world was. Next to Carla, the woman began to shiver, even though it was warm, the humidity its own kind of blanket. Carla, in a move that surprised herself, put an arm around the woman's shoulder.

"She's in shock," the soldier said, as if the woman weren't there. "She'll need a doctor when we get back."

Carla wondered where they were getting back to, though she said nothing. She was unsure about the soldier's mission in general. He seemed to be intent on finding Boyd, but that could hardly be the goal of the U.S. National Guard. He seemed to have a lot of autonomy and little oversight. If he were a different man, a man with a scarier temperament, the type of man Carla was used to, then he could do some real damage out here with the full authority of the U.S. military. Instead, he was like some kind of benign helper, traveling up and down the river and distributing bottled water but no real aid, letting people know that civilization was on its way.

After a while: "How do you know Boyd?"

"I'm her neighbor."

The soldier was quiet. He already knew this. "Where do you think her friend is? The one she was following?"

Carla had tried to tell him that she had no idea. "I'm not sure."

"She okay, you think? She seemed pretty determined when I saw her."

Carla turned to look at him, lifting her chin stiffly over her shoulder. "I don't have any idea what she ran into. But Boyd can take care of herself. Boyd"—Carla hated to admit it—"Boyd is pretty resourceful."

The soldier nodded. Carla guessed that he was twenty-two, twenty-three tops, a baby. "So you think she's still alive?"

Carla blinked, drawing her chin back. "Alive? Why wouldn't she be alive?"

Sam tilted his head, wanting to say more than he ended up saying. "A lot of people aren't." He was quiet again, deciding what to say. "This storm, well—I've never seen anything like it."

Carla wanted to tell him to give it another twenty years. She didn't trust the absolutes of the young. They were uninformed, didn't have enough experience. "Okay."

He went on, "Yesterday—" He let the word hang there a minute. "Yesterday, I pulled two children out of a basement. A boy and a girl."

"Then you're a hero."

"No. We were too late. They didn't make it."

The three of them were quiet, listening to the outboard motor and the velvet sounds of water. Carla was shocked by the story of the dead children and turned this new information over in her mind.

The old woman, shivering in her army blanket, turned to Carla. "They're not the only ones either."

Carla, surprised to hear the woman's voice, met Sam's gaze. He felt the same way. After a minute, he looked back at the swollen river, and Carla, surprised at their connection, settled back into her seat, looking at the water with fresh eyes.

They watched the banks, avoiding the trees in the river. After another half hour, they ran out of bottled water and granola bars and no longer stopped for every group of storm refugees emerging from the wilderness. The soldier stopped for the infirm ones and rendered whatever medical attention he could, but they should have turned back by now. There was no point in their being on the water any longer; they should go back for more supplies, more men, more boats. It occurred to Carla that this was hardly a professional operation, and she realized suddenly that the boat was painted pale blue, almost white, no sort of army color at all. The gas can resting near the soldier's foot was one you could buy at a convenience store: red plastic with a black-and-yellow spigot. Back at the commune, he'd said there was a list of the missing and he'd written Carla's name down as if he were going to see if she was on it, but he had not checked his notebook or anything else since then, not with all these people, not even with the woman in the bottom of the boat. The National Guard hadn't sent him upriver at all; he'd worn his uniform for some other reason, but she didn't think he was a threat. She watched him; he was unaware that she'd realized he was not what he claimed to be.

The flies gathered around them now, sucking moisture from the corners of the old woman's eyes, though the world was full of moisture. Carla waved the flies away from both of them, and finally the woman, who stared at something none of the rest of them could see, began to talk.

The woman took a deep breath, readying herself. "I've seen it flood before but not like this. No, not like this."

Carla looked at her, surprised by the sudden conversation. She looked back at the impostor soldier, but his eyes were on the water.

"It always happens on Memorial Day weekend, too. I wonder how many people have died in Memorial Day floods around here. Hundreds, I bet, over the years." The woman nodded to herself, a private gesture. "Imagine all those people nobody ever found. All on Memorial Day weekends, but all those weekends years apart." Now she turned to Carla. "I ought to call my grandson. You got a phone?"

Carla shook her head—her phone was still at her house on River Road. But Sam the soldier fished his phone out of his pocket, keyed in his pass code, and handed it to the woman.

Carla watched her, unaware that there had been access to a phone this whole time. Whom did she call to report a rogue soldier?

The woman dialed and put the phone to her ear. Carla heard the muffled ring, how it went on for what seemed a good minute. The woman held out hope until the voice mail picked up, then she handed the phone back to the soldier without leaving a message. "Oh, well. He's in Houston. Probably not even raining there. He's probably out to breakfast."

Carla didn't have the heart to tell her that she had seen the news footage on the night of the wedding, that it had rained in Houston, too. Carla looked away, looked at the gray people lined up on the banks, trying to pin down exactly why they made her nervous.

9:10 A.M.

Isaac tumbling end over end in the water, less than twenty-four hours after his car had entered the low-water crossing. This time his head went under and he couldn't help it—he opened his mouth to breathe, and in the flood came. He knew from his hospital internship that he would not swallow too much of this—soon, his larynx would spasm and he would begin to choke, preventing the water from entering, but also preventing him from breathing. Next would come hypoxia, his brain and heart and all of his other tissues being starved of oxygen, the slow wasting of everything he had ever thought or learned, and that would be that for him—he would be just another piece of debris in the river.

After that first second of panic—the fall, the crash through the branches, the sinking into the water—he had become curiously detached. In that moment of panic, he had thought desperately of Boyd, with some odd belief that she could somehow help him. But the rational part of him knew better—whatever Boyd understood of the world, she was no superhero.

On one of his turns, his head breached the surface, and even in his detached state, even as he gasped for air, he was astonished to see the banks lined with people. He went under again quickly and didn't trust what he had seen. There had been so many—hundreds, even. And something about them was weird, was off, but he thought no more about them, preoccupied instead by the idea that he was drowning and by his curiosity about this process.

He was trying to swim but he couldn't. He had stopped turning, but he was still being pushed by the current: as he was swept forward, he was also swept under. Mostly, he tried to push himself to the surface, but this did little good. And there were things in the water with him—an unbelievable number of boat hulls and rafts, tarps and buoys and furniture, and at one point something huge bumped into him, and in the murk of the water, he thought it was a cow, but could not tell if it was dead or living.

He didn't know if he would lose consciousness before his larynx spasmed, but he knew he was close to something. What was happening was untenable—he could not continue to float on unharmed and under the water. What would happen when he lost consciousness? Would he know the moment when his soul or spirit or consciousness left his body?

How odd it was to lack emotion in such a circumstance. The only thing that made him feel anything at all was Boyd. He remembered the way he had looked forward to the comfort of this summer, to the time that they would have together. He remembered the light movements of her wrist as she had shaken the gold pan, the look on her face when she had palmed the small nugget. This was the real loss, he knew—not any fear about death or pain, just the end of possibility, all of those years left to them. Years of what? He did not know if they would have ended up together. But there would have been years of their both being out there in the same universe, years of hope and potential. If Boyd died, what a hole she would leave in his world. He couldn't help but wonder what his loss might mean to her, and this also made him sad—that he would never know.

The current swept him upward suddenly, some accident of river topography. His face above water again, his mouth open, sucking in as much air as he could. His eyes open, too, and he was shocked to see that the people on the bank were now in the water, and before he went under again, he was dismayed to see their arms extended, as if they were reaching for him.

Boyd, wondering if she had finally gone crazy, doubting what she had felt. Now Isaac was gone, as if he had never needed her at all, as if she had imagined all of it: the pressure on her chest, the feeling of being wet. A distressing emptiness in the wake of that feeling, but Lily was before her, so Boyd shook her head and turned her attention to the girl, though Isaac never left the back of her mind.

In the clearing, the light played over Lily's face. The child couldn't yet talk, but when she could—Boyd hesitated, because she didn't know what would happen then. But she wanted to be there because she wanted to protect Lily. The world would try to claim her, and Boyd would be the only one who understood. Boyd's mother had tried to help once she'd understood how the press of the world hurt Boyd, but by then it had almost been too late. Boyd would never be comfortable in any crowd, would certainly never be comfortable living in a city.

Who would take care of Lily? Boyd could not discern any answers, even after feeling for them. She had seen the vision of the trailer tumbling downstream, had seen the meals that the mother had prepared, but in these visions she had seen no other person present, no relative, no weekend father. This was not to say that there wasn't one—after the storm a person might come forward. Boyd didn't know what happened to unclaimed children, whether the law said that they went into the foster care system. But already Boyd was reordering her life: she would bring the child home to River Road, setting up a crib in her childhood bedroom.

As she considered all of this, she moved forward, still guided toward the river and to Isaac, still feeling that sense of urgency, but now, somehow, the feeling was muted. Whatever would happen had happened, and now they were living in the aftermath.

Somebody stepped in front of her, and Boyd was so startled that she almost dropped Lily. She had not realized that anyone was there, had not felt the person, had not sensed the person. Had she been so preoccupied with her own thoughts? Lily screeched in unhappiness; the stop had been abrupt.

Then Boyd saw what was before her, who had interrupted their pleasant reverie. It took her a minute to place the blouse with its cat's-head buttons, the old jeans, and the mud-encrusted Nike, and at last she looked into the face of the scarecrow she had made in the dry spring season, which already seemed so long ago. The face was surprisingly ordinary to Boyd: a girl in the last throes of girlhood, with red hair and gray eyes, but Boyd blinked when she looked at those gray eyes, which held such a storm. The scarecrow shed straw, though a body was inside the clothes. Its head swiveled to look at the baby, and Boyd felt its absolute hunger, the need to consume. Boyd let out a breath, remembering the fingers of river water on her ankle, and how the river had pulled her, had tried to take her under in the space where the bridge had once stood.

Angie Mason was not yet shed of the scarecrow, of the part of the world that had animated her. Some straw still clung to her forearms, to her ankles where they snaked out of her pant legs, placed there by Boyd in the late drought. The girl was also the one in the bed, risen but not yet whole, the girl Boyd had wished to return to her mother. The girl reached for Boyd, and Boyd stepped back. If Angie reached her—if Angie reached Lily—it would be as if Boyd were saving something drowning. It would pull her under, and she would never resurface.

She clutched Lily to her chest and ran. Behind her, footfalls. Two feet and one shoe. She smelled the river ahead of her, and she didn't know why she ran, except that she needed to.

Things You Would Know If You Grew Up Around Here

This Is All There Is

Carl Sagan, in *Pale Blue Dot*, referencing Earth in a photo from *Voyager 1*:

> Look again at that dot. That's here. That's home. That's us. On it
> everyone you love, everyone you know, everyone you ever heard of,
> every human being who ever was, lived out their lives. The aggregate
> of our joy and suffering, thousands of confident religions, ideolo-
> gies, and economic doctrines, every hunter and forager, every hero
> and coward, every creator and destroyer of civilization, every king
> and peasant, every young couple in love, every mother and father,
> hopeful child, inventor and explorer, every teacher of morals, every
> corrupt politician, every "superstar," every "supreme leader," every
> saint and sinner in the history of our species lived there—on a mote
> of dust suspended in a sunbeam.

Kevin inched his way down the wall of the mine shaft, using his fingers and toes to bear his weight for as long as he could. He couldn't put too much pressure on the rope around his waist; he didn't know how much Lucy Maud could hold. He didn't know how she was going to be able to pull two men up. He shouldn't have come down here. There was zero guarantee that he would come back up.

He'd been able to call Emily from Allen Potivar's house, and she'd been upset, which was understandable: he'd left to go to a rehearsal dinner and a wedding and he'd now been gone three nights. Also, he was with his ex-wife, which bothered Emily, and he didn't know that it should, because they were two different people and they fulfilled two different roles in his life, and he didn't think Emily should be jealous just because he thought Lucy Maud was a good mother and also a decent person to be around— "She got shit done," as he put it. He did think Lucy Maud might have a reason to be upset because what he got from Emily was that she was attractive, young, and small and a bit edgy, and also, she was brilliant, not just graduate-student brilliant, but actual brilliant, her obsessions with Iphigenia, Clytemnestra, and Agamemnon's House of Atreus wound around her like so much stardust, and that—well, that attracted Kevin very much. She and

Lucy Maud occupied different spots in heart and mind for him; he wished it were in the nature of women to understand this about men.

His face pressed against the rock as he climbed down, and it was cool and gritty on his cheek. He guessed that he was about ten feet down. Any second now and he would lose his foothold. He didn't know what he would find down here, nor how high the water had risen. He feared the drop when the shaft opened into the room: he would have to let go, hoping Lucy Maud could handle the sudden yank on the line, not knowing what he would land on, or whether he'd land in water. This last possibility scared him the most—water underground seemed like a horrible and dangerous thing. What if he was swept away and pinned somewhere, in some low place with no air pockets?

He reached it, the end of the shaft. He stretched his foot to find the next toehold and there was empty air. He closed his eyes and breathed in, cheek against the wall, smelling the wet earth in his nostrils, feeling the grit underneath his fingertips. Such a leap of faith this was—he'd either end up submerged in cave water or crumpled on the ground.

"Luce?" he called, the movement of his diaphragm pushing him away from the wall. He held on, but just barely. "I'm going down."

The shaft got darker as her head blocked the light. He couldn't look up, but he hoped she had her hands on the rope around her waist. "Are you going to let go?"

He didn't know what else to do. "Yes. Be ready." He shoved off the wall of the mine shaft so that he wouldn't scrape his cheek.

He hung in space for seconds, it seemed, like the coyote in a Road Runner cartoon, then gravity took him. He fell the height of a one-story house, and halfway through his fall, his torso was jerked upward because the slack in the rope had been played out. Light was almost totally blacked out then because Lucy Maud had fallen to her hands and knees above the opening to the shaft, and he recognized in the split second that only by great good fortune for him had she not fallen in after him. He hung in the darkness for that long second, then she pushed herself to her back and the shaft of light appeared again, and then the slack came as she unwound the rope from her waist.

He went down the rest of the way in jerks and starts, trying to pull himself upright instead of sprawling backward. When at last vertical, he grabbed the rope and his feet entered the water. A few more twists of the yellow rope, Lucy Maud unwinding herself, and he was chest-deep. He still had not touched bottom, and he could see nothing in the chamber; the sunlight reflected off the black water and did nothing but blind him and obscure whatever was underneath.

"Ruben?" he called, suddenly feeling the edge of panic. Entering the water had changed things for him. He finally understood that Ruben might be dead, and that he could die, too. The water had its own life; he felt pulled by a current, but in multiple directions. Something bumped against his shin and he shivered, thinking of the possibilities. And the smell—oh, God, it was as if he were inside the earth, as if he were already buried.

There was no answer. Boyd—what would she do? Ruben was likely already dead if he wasn't answering, right? Kevin should pull on the rope, yell for Lucy Maud to bring him back up. But she would think he was a coward. After a second in the black water, he decided that he might not care.

He felt something big in the water next to him, and he almost cried. What could live in a cave that was that large? A cave bear? A ghost of one of the dead miners?

Ruben King rose to the surface, arriving from wherever he had been hiding, and Kevin was livid because he wondered if Ruben had been playing some game. If he'd been here all along, why hadn't he answered? They could have tossed the rope down to him and Kevin would never have had to climb down here into this wet darkness. But when Kevin saw Ruben's face, he didn't blame the man anymore. Ruben looked as if he'd been through hell. He looked at once both red and pale, swollen with the flood, eyes haggard in a way that spoke of trauma. Kevin hugged him out of sheer relief that they could get out of here, and though it was not the right thing to do, Ruben hugged him back. Ruben's grip around his shoulders reminded Kevin of the first aid training he'd had as a kid, the warning that a drowning person couldn't help but drown you, too, if you tried to rescue them. If Kevin wasn't standing firmly on the ground, he would have gone under from the weight of Ruben's body. Kevin panicked for a second before he righted himself and pulled Ruben's arms off his neck.

Ruben seemed surprised that he could stand, and when he put his foot down, he pulled on the rope linking Kevin to the outside world. "Good idea. Wish I had thought to bring a rope."

"Where's the flashlight?" Kevin looked around. "Where were you? Why weren't you here?" Kevin looked up to the small circle of sunlight.

Ruben's gaze followed Kevin's. "There's a higher rock toward the back, and I was on it. I was mostly out of the water. For now." Turning back to Kevin, Ruben reached and rooted around in his fisherman's shirt. "When I heard you, I made my way over here."

"What are you doing?"

Ruben smiled and produced the flashlight Kevin had reluctantly handed to Lucy Maud in the dark, who had then tossed it down the shaft to Ruben.

"Does it work? After being underwater?"

Ruben passed the flashlight to Kevin, who shook it, both to hear the batteries rattle inside and to shed the water beading on the metal case. When he flicked the switch, the light shone weakly, and he pointed it into the dark recesses of the chamber, revealing how close the water was to the top of the cave. He laughed and was surprised by the sound. Nothing about this was funny. "Did you find any gold?" He wanted to know if all of this was worth it.

From some pocket under the water, Ruben produced a silver ingot, and he held it flat on his palm while Kevin shone the light on it. The ingot was nearly black with tarnish, but Ruben's fingers had already started to rub some of this blackness off.

"This isn't the gold. This isn't Maximilian. I don't—" Ruben swallowed and shook his head. "This is a few pieces of silver, for all I can tell, already shaped, and I don't know if they were even mined here."

Kevin nodded and reached a finger to touch the cold metal. "When the rain is over, when the water goes down, I'll come out here with a colleague from archaeology and we'll see what we can find."

"Colleague from archaeology?"

"I'm a classics professor." Kevin felt the usual pleasure at making the statement. "I'm at the university in Austin." He was careful not to brag, but of course Ruben knew which university. "We'll come out here, see whether it's worth exploring."

"Allen Potivar won't like that."

"No, but"—Kevin shrugged one shoulder and looked back up at the daylight—"let's worry about that later. When we're both dry."

"So what's the plan?"

"The plan is to get us both topside somehow. My wife"—Kevin caught himself—"my ex-wife is up there and will help, but she can't pull us up. The first person will have to climb out pretty much on his own."

Ruben nodded, considering. "Okay." He looked around, and Kevin knew that Ruben wanted to be first. He'd been down here so long already, essentially alone, and Kevin understood that Ruben wasn't eager to be alone again.

Kevin sucked in a breath. It didn't make any sense. The rope was already tied around Kevin's waist, and Kevin was fresher and stronger, more useful for both climbing up and pulling the other person out. But the look on Ruben King's face—haunted, almost as if he were holding his breath—made Kevin make his second decision of the day that went against his better judgment. It made no sense for him to untie the rope from his waist, yet he did. He fumbled with the knot under the water and uncinched and unwound himself, fingers slow and reluctant from the water's drag, then he moved to wrap the rope around Ruben's waist. Kevin couldn't help but study Ruben at this close angle, couldn't help but notice how one of his teeth needed a crown, how his face was jowly underneath the stubble.

Ruben must have been thinking something similar, because he said, "You think one day we'll be in-laws?"

"What?" Kevin stopped winding and pulled on the rope. Lucy Maud poked her head down and gave a thumbs-up, visible twenty feet above them.

"In-laws? You and me? You think Boyd and Isaac will get married one day?"

Kevin shrugged. They were so young. His daughter could be so much, if only she chose to be. "Maybe." He didn't know. Instead, he said, "Lucy Maud can't pull you up. You'll have to do it yourself."

Ruben nodded, pulling on the line to check it.

"I can give you a boost," Kevin said, considering the height of the open chamber. "Once you get to the shaft wall, you can climb it while using the rope."

Ruben agreed and climbed up Kevin because Kevin refused to kneel in the dark water, refused to put his head under. He shook underneath the other man's weight, but once Ruben stood on Kevin's shoulders, Ruben had only another ten feet or so to traverse. He pushed the balls of his feet into Kevin's shoulder and jumped, hitching his way a good third of the distance to the shaft wall, and Kevin, suddenly lighter, turned to watch him put one hand above the other on the rope, slowly, slowly making his way to the sunshine, to the surface of the earth. Kevin, left behind, was frustrated because it looked as if Ruben could barely hang on, was worried that any second Ruben's grip would slip and he would fall the length of the rope, crushing Kevin or splashing into the water. In a few minutes, though, Ruben reached the wall and began his tedious climb up that long section.

Kevin, frigid and bone soaked, wanted out. He was sick of the smell and sound and feel of water. He realized that the water had been halfway up his chest and was now about to cover his shoulders. It seethed around him, burgeoning and animate, and the surface moved in a different direction from the depths. He imagined a whirlpool, barely perceptible, taking him down. But solid rock was underneath him, and he knew with some relief that he could go no farther down. Ruben clung to the rock and inched higher. Soon the sun would be overhead, shining directly down into the mine shaft.

9:24 A.M.

The sunlight penetrated the surface of the water, and Isaac lay on his back as if in a dream. The hands reached for him, and he couldn't tell if the people wanted to help him or harm him, but it didn't seem to matter, because it seemed as if they couldn't quite reach him. Now his face was above the water and he stretched out his arms for more buoyancy and the people continued to reach out but not touch him. Then he realized that there was nothing to touch, that his outstretched arms passed right through the bodies of the people gathered around him.

He struggled to understand, trying to sit up in the swiftly moving current but unwilling to upset the equilibrium his body had found. He realized that he was again gasping for air, that he hadn't drowned yet, that here he was still in the land of the living but seemed to be surrounded by ghosts. He didn't believe in ghosts, of course, but here were these people, dressed in these strange clothes, their faces ashen and smudged. When he passed them—when his body passed through theirs—he felt something, some emotion that he knew was not his own, both because he could not discern the emotion's provenance and because he could never imagine feeling such things. The people were neither good nor bad—they just wanted what they wanted, and that was to claim whatever things they had wanted to claim before they left this earth, and they wanted a human connection again. Some had been killed by violence; some of these people wanted to respond with violence. All of them had wanted more from this life, had left unfinished business, and Isaac felt this longing as his fingers passed through their bodies, as he could not tell if ghosts or water pulled him forward, and it was because Boyd had somehow sent them. For a second, it was as if he could see what Boyd saw—he could feel another person's feelings.

And then a ghost boat was on the water, motoring down with a ghost engine. On the boat, the ghosts of a soldier and two women, one middle-aged, one old. The middle-aged ghost took up position at the back near the rudder, and the soldier ghost reached into the water, and this time, Isaac's arms did not pass through. The soldier gripped him by the biceps and pulled him over the side. Isaac was on his knees, racked with the effort to breathe—how had he not drowned when he had been so fully prepared?—and the middle-aged ghost said, "I don't believe it. That's Boyd's friend. His name is Isaac," and Isaac knew the voice but couldn't place it, couldn't yet make the effort to turn his head.

It was impossible to run with a baby, a being with a different center of gravity who had not yet learned to hold her body so it wouldn't bounce. Boyd pushed Lily's head to her collarbone with her free hand, now running without using her arms at all. She sensed the river, how near it was, from the way the leaves in the trees acted, as if they were reflecting water. The earth, too, sloped down, the ground soft beneath her feet, and she feared slipping, twisting her ankle, going down with a baby in her arms and a scarecrow girl baying at her heels. And if that scarecrow caught her? The pain of what that scarecrow knew was unbearable.

Lily was strangely silent amid all of this, and when Boyd glanced down, the baby was too still, and Boyd had an awful premonition, a feeling that she had smothered Lily. But no, the baby blinked up at her, head nestled into Boyd's collarbone, as if this flight were just another form of rocking.

Boyd had stretched the distance between them and the scarecrow, her shoes and open gait outmatching it, and though her body was pitched forward with the weight of the baby, she kept her feet as she stumbled down the slope, seeing at last the flat brown surface of the river.

And, oh, on that surface was a boat, and in that boat sat three people: a soldier, an old woman, and another woman Boyd could now see was her neighbor Carla. Then Carla moved her head and Boyd saw another person behind her—and Boyd almost sat on the bank and cried. The other person was Isaac, kneeling in the bottom of the boat.

He caught sight of her at almost the same instant and he stood, jostling the vessel, while the soldier at the back spread his arms, rebalancing everything. She recognized the soldier—he was Sam, the man from the bridge, the one she had called to help find Isaac—but she was so relieved that the long night was at an end that she hardly gave him a second thought, even though she had hoped that he would rescue both her and Isaac, and now, here they all were. How far had she wandered?

She heard footsteps behind her, and she turned to look. The scarecrow was coming down the hill. But Boyd thought, *It doesn't matter*. It could not control her here, not with Isaac and Carla and a soldier of the National Guard behind her. Nevertheless, she climbed out on a live oak branch that arced over the water. She would have swum out to meet the boat had it not been for Lily.

Sam steered the boat toward her, and Boyd went even farther out. The branch grew thinner now, and she balanced herself, cradling the child rather than embracing it, openly weeping in relief. She didn't care about being wet again, but she didn't want Lily to get wet. The child—Boyd didn't know what to think. Only that Lily would have a life where everyone would try to possess her, where everyone would want to be around her, simply because she would be able to meet needs and fill holes. Now even the earth made claims on Boyd—letting her know that it needed something from her, too, that it was in pain and struggling—and she wondered if it would do the same to Lily. The things Boyd had seen and felt lately—the distress, the history layered upon the world—and now she had the sense that there was only so much future, that the things we had done meant that the finite time that the human race would live here was far, far shorter than most people suspected. Boyd knew that Lily would feel these things, too. She was a baby—she couldn't possibly comprehend the intricacies of human emotion—but one day she would, and then the world would no longer be a place for her to discover and explore but would instead be a place for her to serve nearly against her will, a place of bondage and a constant low thrum of pain. The pain would not start as her own, exactly, but it would become hers, and the wish to stop it would be its own sort of need, one that would never be satisfied. The world's measure of misery was never in short supply.

The boat was nearly to the oak where Boyd and Lily perched, but the scarecrow girl scared Boyd. It wanted to own her and she was tired of being owned. More than anything else she wanted freedom, an existence that rode lightly on time and space, that did no harm, certainly, but was also not responsible for the harm done by others.

She clutched Lily to her and shimmied farther out onto the branch. The water churned beneath her; it was deeper than she'd thought. The boat adjusted course to catch her if she fell, the soldier staring and Isaac reaching out, and still the scarecrow girl came. Boyd realized suddenly that it wasn't after her but was instead after Lily. It, too, climbed the tree, surprisingly fast and agile. Boyd didn't know what to do. She pulled her feet underneath her, her knees bent, balancing herself and Lily on the arcing branch. In any second, the boat would be close enough for her to jump in, to hand over the baby. Carla was shouting, but Boyd couldn't tell what she was saying. The world wouldn't claim Boyd today. The only sound was from the outboard motor striking the water. Otherwise, everybody held his or her breath and blinked in the bright sunshine.

Kevin was thinking of Boyd, too, as he watched Ruben, now halfway up the wall. The going was extremely slow, and Kevin was getting nervous. More than nervous. He was on the tips of his toes because the water was now so high, and he didn't want to be on the tips of his toes because the water was now moving so much that any second it would take him.

Kevin was wondering what Boyd would do—what she would tell him to do—because he was certain that she would know. She'd cultivated this sort of knowledge in the same way he'd studied languages. She would tell him to get close to the chamber wall, maybe, so that he could hold on as the water rose. Or she would tell him to stay right there in the middle, so that he wouldn't get lost. He was afraid to shout for help, even, afraid that he would startle Ruben off the sheer wall and that they would have to start over. So he let the water rise to his chin and then past it. Now he tilted his head back to breathe, closing his eyes against that one bright patch of sunlight. Still Ruben climbed.

When it was too late, Kevin tried to shout, but when he opened his mouth, it filled with water. The mouthful of water weighted him down; his head fell back and his feet came up. He reached out both arms, flailed a bit, tried to regain his footing. He did—for a brief moment, he was on his toes again, though now several feet from where he'd started. His footing wasn't stable, however; the next second, he was once again on his back, once again swallowing the flood, and the current took him deeper into the cave, no matter how much he tried to swim against it. Soon he was in the dark, headed down, and his head no longer cleared the surface. He thought of a beach near Nafplio where he'd once gone with his grad student, and he wanted so badly to tell Emily some things about her career, wanted to help her puzzle out the two endings of Iphigenia, wanted her to mention him in the acknowledgments of the book she was writing. He thought, too, of a morning when he was in undergrad and Lucy Maud was eating oranges at the kitchen table, thought about an afternoon in South Dakota when he'd slipped a band of tricolored gold shaped into roses on Lucy Maud's ring finger. He would give anything right now to tell her that he knew how she had sacrificed, how she had made him Dr. Montgomery, how he had never been able to repay her. He thought of Boyd, knew the way she had been afraid to bother him, afraid to distract him from his work, which had always been more important. How horrible to come to the end and to know that your daughter believed this, and that you had never taken the time to correct this notion. Too, he remembered the way the tips of her cheekbones had grown red as the summers progressed, the way freckles had settled over her shins and the backs of her hands. Sunshine was in so many of these memories, a burnished and underappreciated happiness.

When Ruben at last reached the top and Lucy Maud untied him and tossed the rope back down, the yellow tip of nylon disappeared into the dark water. Nobody was left to pull up. The water, with a white noise that was its own kind of silence, had risen, until it was the only thing that remained.

9:27 A.M.

The live oak underneath Boyd was hundreds of years old, and she knew it had suffered these past few years, almost dying in the drought, and was now nearly submerged in the flood. It would be like this now forever: brief times between flood and drought, but the drought years growing longer and closer together. One day, maybe in Boyd's own lifetime and certainly in Lily's, this place would be a desert, the mesquite and juniper gone, the old live oaks crumbling into fields of dust.

The scarecrow girl was now close enough to see the fear in Boyd's eyes. It blinked and drew its chin back, surprised. Something about the girl was familiar, though Boyd could not say what.

Lily—silent, watching Lily—had wormed her way up, and now she dangled from Boyd's chest. Boyd, knowing what sort of life lay in store for the baby, held on to her even tighter. The child had no family that Boyd knew of—was there somewhere a father who falsely imagined that his daughter was safe?

Boyd thought of her own father, and she wondered where he was. He was imperceptible at the moment; she couldn't tell what he was doing or thinking. But he had never tried to possess Boyd in the way that other people had tried to possess her. He was bemused, standoffish, not given to emotion, and therefore not particularly impressed by Boyd's ability to read it. She remembered the staring eyes of the woman on the floor of the trailer; Lily no longer had a mother.

Now Sam pulled the boat underneath the live oak, as much as he could with the branch in the way. The water foamed here; it was deep and there was some obstruction. Boyd would have to jump as much as a foot, but Isaac and Carla both had arms outstretched.

She leaned toward Carla, the closest. The only sound was the outboard motor stirring the water and the slow chugging of the gas engine. The light seemed splintered, the way it reflected back at her. Boyd tasted something metallic and realized that she had bitten her tongue. The gas engine grumbled, and she lifted Lily away from her own body, the child's eyes registering alarm for the first time since Boyd had fled the trailer.

Lily's gaze on her, motherless Lily, Lily who possessed a certain understanding of the world, who would come to know so much more than she wanted to. Lily, here in a part of the world that was in trouble, a part that was at the moment drowning but would soon be parched and fissured again. Lily, here, in a time when the dead had awakened, when the earth wore its veneer of time only lightly, when there were rules of physics not necessary to follow. Lily, lying across Boyd's forearms, an offering, outstretched, breathing, eyes wide, a hand reaching out to circle Boyd's finger, the one that wore the band of tricolored golden roses. Lily, still and watching, an innocent on the cusp of life.

And Boyd let go, relinquished the baby into Carla's arms, into the safety of the boat. Only. Only Boyd let go too soon, and Carla didn't catch Lily. She fell through their arms in the silver light underneath the live oak, and she slipped beneath the surface of the deep and roiling water.

Here is what was lost under the water in the early years of the century, in a place that will look very different in the next: Entire families, washed away; property without measure; animals both loved and wild; a layer of earth scraped off. Parts of the past buried deeper, arrowheads and butter-churn shards and thimbles from pioneer homesteads and the silver of another era. Eyeglasses and books, including an eighteenth-century family Bible that had been brought to the New World from Bavaria by a man long dead. A bundle of letters from a man in the trenches of the First World War to a woman in Wimberley who had kept them long after she'd married someone else and had four children, then passed these letters to her eldest daughter. Another daughter's recipe collection, passed down from woman to woman to woman, the only history that family had, kept in the language of Watergate salads, sinsolo dips, shrimp-and-lettuce cups. A way of being passing undetectably before our eyes, the loss only visible in hindsight. Also lost: Human lives, hundreds of years' worth, old women who carried stories that were now gone forever, old men who carried old ways in hands now stilled. Children who left holes in both the present and the future. Babies. Among the babies, a girl. Slightly different, wound too tight, calibrated to the sun and stars. Lost by accident, by a miscalculation, and returned to where she came from.

Boyd, accustomed to everybody's grief but her own. Boyd diving into the water, boiled and bottomless. Boyd out of control, not knowing up from down, trying to find Lily but grasping only dark water. Boyd's mouth full of the flood, which was full of the earth and full of the sky. Boyd swallowing, but not yet breathing it in, taking the flood into her stomach but not yet into her lungs. Then the scarecrow girl was in the water, gripping Boyd from behind, Boyd's linen shirt tearing. The scarecrow girl did not let go right away; she held Boyd under, and Boyd bucked under her hands, pulling herself free momentarily, gasping for air when she surfaced.

Boyd heard a splash as Isaac went into the water to find Lily, but the scarecrow girl had her again, and the distraction of Isaac disappeared. The scarecrow girl pressed her spongy palms into Boyd's cheekbones, and again Boyd could not figure out why this touch felt so familiar. The fingers curled, the tips of her fingernails drawing half-moons into Boyd's cheeks.

The scarecrow girl's mouth was open in disbelief, so that Boyd could see the hollow in her cheeks. Boyd felt a need that was impossible to meet, a hunger that could not be satisfied. Not enough of the world was left. *Help me*, the scarecrow girl thought. Boyd had done this all of her life.

Then Boyd realized where she had seen the girl before—in the late-afternoon light of the sleeping-beauty house. In a hospital bed, and next

306 NANCY WAYSON DINAN

to it, a novel open facedown on an end table, a novel that had been read by a woman who had been endlessly faithful. Boyd had put her hands on the girl, had felt the girl's warmth travel up her arm, had said that she wished the girl would return to her mother.

But now Boyd could do nothing. This helplessness, this mindless vacancy, mingled with her own pain. She could not take back the baby's slip into the water, nor the call to this girl to come back from whatever darkness she had occupied; Boyd could do nothing to temper or assuage this.

And what pain it was. She had never before encountered anything like it. A grief to madden, unbearable to live with. Her breath hitched and her mouth hung open. Lily was lost.

The girl's dark brows were tensed, sloped down on the outside corners. Boyd could see the whites of her eyes, the pupils and irises riding high in those whites, as if they might roll back at any moment. The spongy palms were still on Boyd's face, and again they drew Boyd under. In a second, the world was muted and dark, and Boyd was gasping.

But then Isaac's arm went around her waist, and he wrenched her away from the scarecrow girl's grip, a colossal heave that bent Boyd double. The girl's fingernails on Boyd's face ripped deep gashes as the girl struggled to hold on.

Now Isaac had her against the boat, and Carla and Sam were pulling her up, ripping her shirt even further as they lifted her over the side. Isaac went under suddenly, and Boyd could tell that the girl had grabbed him from behind. She thought of Isaac's panic, how she had known that Isaac was in the water, and he had looked exhausted when she'd seen him, but he swam away quickly, reaching the other side of the boat, where an old woman sat still and watching.

The scarecrow girl came up once, gulped air, and headed back under, her head sloped down, eyes scanning. Then they didn't see her again.

Sam and Carla leaned on the edge of the boat, and instinctively the older woman leaned back to balance it.

Finally, Boyd climbed into Carla's arms, her own arms now empty. She lay back in the hull of the boat, and the old woman took the blanket off herself and laid it over Boyd. Boyd blinked, wide-eyed, and stared up into the canopy as Isaac said, "Let's go, let's go," and Sam turned the boat around and headed back down the river. It was too soon, Boyd thought, but none of them protested. They all knew that nobody was coming back up, that the river had taken what it wanted. They'd dangled something too close to greedy jaws, and the flood, hungry, bit. Boyd thought about the mothers involved: the woman on the floor in the trailer, the woman in the strange and sleeping house. Boyd had broken her promise to the woman on the floor, and the other woman, the one in the house, now completely alone, though she had been nearly so for years.

Carla knelt next to Boyd in the hull of the boat, though Boyd's eyes were closed. Boyd was dirty, and her clothes were shredded. She was scratched all to pieces, bleeding from scrapes on her forearm, the blood thinned by floodwater. Carla was happy to see her, relieved that she had made it through whatever adventure she had had.

This part of Carla was happy, but there was another part of her, too, a part that wanted more of Lucy Maud, which Carla could maybe have if Boyd was gone. But Carla was ashamed of herself for this thought, and then she remembered Kim and Bess and the shingled house. Lucy Maud was not the only thing anymore, and as Carla knelt beside Boyd, she took the girl's hand and shuddered at its heat.

Isaac knelt on the other side of Boyd, thinking of the mouse that had chewed his thumb in the night, the spiders on his eyelids. One of his hands rested on his own thigh, one on hers. Through her tattered pants, he could feel the incredible heat that rose from her body. He could hardly believe it was Boyd—what a gift from the universe to find her so easily, and after such a night—and he wondered how she'd ended up here, on this river, in such a state and carrying a baby. He remembered the splash the baby had made going under, the small wake of the body, the way the wake was swallowed almost immediately by turbulence.

When Boyd had gone in, some kind of instinct had kicked in for Isaac, and he'd found himself in the water before he'd realized it. But he'd been glad that he had when that girl had grabbed Boyd, had looked as if she was trying to drown Boyd. Now he dripped water on her, wanting to reach for the hand that Carla didn't hold. But he didn't. He was cautious as ever, sick with all of the possibilities of life, warming himself at the fire of his oldest friend.

On her back, headed down the river, Boyd did not see the people on the banks, but she knew they were there. She knew others were with them, too, people who had lived in other centuries. She knew these centuries went way back; people had been on this ground for millennia.

But it was too much, the knowledge of what she'd left behind in the water. A line of future truncated. A girl who could have listened, who could have helped. Who would have seen the suffering that Boyd saw, who would have done her best to take that suffering away. Already the earth was quieting; soon the communication would be severed altogether. Whatever had happened to Boyd the night she was buried was temporary; the earth wanted her to know something, but the window of knowing was finite and closing.

But the window had been enough. She knew. This drought and this flood may have been cyclical—a similar drought occurring in the fifties, a similar flood occurring in the eighties—but things were worse now; things were accelerating. She knew that in another few years, the storms in the Gulf would start: monster things that would flood a third of the state's inhabitants. This year's highest temperature would become the summer average, and the new high temperature would be something Texas had never seen. Boyd knew that she—well, that Lily—was born to see the end of a very long story. A part of Boyd thought that Lily was better off, that she would be lucky not to bear witness to what was coming. Already the water was taking something from Lily, siphoning off her body's heat until she was the same temperature as everything that surrounded her. Already, parts of her were oxidizing, skin cells were being shed; the water was underneath her fingernails and eyelids, flowing between all of the alveoli in her lungs. Boyd imagined the same thing happening with other bodies, but for them, the process was biological, physical, a result of the natural laws of the universe. For Lily, as it would one day be for Boyd, the process was a sentient hunger. To Boyd, it was like the guinea pig who ate her own children in Boyd's second-grade classroom. Blood and fur and bone on the wood chips, but whatever was important—whatever was alive—returned to the source.

What would it be like for Boyd to live in the pre-apocalypse? She didn't know. She wanted to cherish every moment, but she has not yet cherished *one*, not in her whole long life. She wanted to love the people she loved, but she wanted them to love her—*her*—back. She wanted to eat things where the grease ran down her forearms; she wanted to have a wedding cake.

But most of all, she wanted freedom. "Please," she said. "I wish not to know anymore." It was like that day in the cafeteria—unbearable—and she couldn't live with it. Was it selfish to cut the ties of pain here, on the threshold of the end? Or was it survival?

She didn't know. But now, on a river swollen to twice its normal size, she blinked up into the lacework of leaves and sunlight, and she turned her mind and heart away from the things she no longer wanted to see. Who would love her when she was only composed of herself, when she was not made up of the people who surrounded her?

She didn't know.

And as Boyd cut off this part of herself, as she closed down and shrank, as Isaac and Carla both jerked their hands away because Boyd's body suddenly scorched them, she imagined Lily, she of the red cheeks and chin, slipping through time, perhaps coming to rest in a house down by the old course of the river, a house where the tongue is German and the parents whisper about the young boy a neighboring family lost in the night. Perhaps teaching Latin to barefoot children in this hot country. Perhaps living with her family on that mountain north of Llano, in the last years of the Comanche, just before the ranchers found cause to change the mountain's name.

When Boyd started shivering, Isaac gathered her to him, surprised that the heat was gone, that she had off-loaded such energy, had spent something bodily. She was different—something was different about her—and he pulled her to him, one shoulder in his palm, the other nestled into his chest, and he wanted her to open her eyes and look at him. *Boyd, Boyd, open your eyes*, he thought, but there was no reaction. Something about Boyd was not the same.

The people on the bank disappeared. Not the real ones, not the ones who had come out for this flood. But the ones who had been there for a long time—for ages, from before any of the six flags flew over Texas, from before the rivers were dammed into lakes, from before cars were on the roads and airplanes were in the air—they were gone. Boyd did not see them go—she was still at the bottom of a boat, nearly catatonic. But she felt their departure like a drawing in of breath. Gone, gone, gone, breathing quickly in, until she began to hyperventilate.

Gone Boyd's grandmother Karen, who had died in a stranger's house in Galveston in 1978, a woman Boyd had never met but who had loomed large in Boyd's imagination simply because of the magnitude of Aunt Lou's heartbreak. Karen shimmered on the bank—not the woman of later years but the woman Homer had met so long ago—and held a hand out to her granddaughter as she passed, before Karen crumbled into the water like an airy pillar of salt.

Gone, too, Alice, who had been poisoned by her sister, antifreeze in the well, her mouth still moving as she disappeared, though no sound came out. Gone, too, the woman Hettie Meyer, huddled on the ground underneath the hanging tree with the bodies of a boy and a girl, still blue from the drowning, her wail unheard but felt as she took her sad burden with her. On Carla's dead acre, men rose from unmarked graves and pulled nooses from their necks. In another part of the county, Mary Elizabeth, a baby used as a pawn in a game with no results, straightening her head on her shoulders as she faded into a haze of speckled sunlight. Gone, too, the inhabitants of the pioneer cemetery, newly awake and confused, sitting on their own tombstones when they disappear, asking themselves, *What do we do now?*

* * *

Also departing, farther north in San Saba County, the men hurriedly trying to bury treasure underneath the wall of Fort Bowie, throwing down their shovels and turning their faces to the sun. Pedro Yorba, throwing silver into a deep well, let the coins and ingots fall through his fingers so that they looked like water. Is Maximilian with him? Hard to tell. Maximilian last seen in front of the firing squad in Querétaro City, Mexico, on the early morning of June 19, 1867, after paying his executioners gold coins not to shoot him in the head. The source of so many rumors, so many unanswered questions. All of them gone, briefly here and then not—resigned to a different set of suns, a different series of stars, a different spread on the axis.

Gone, too, the ancient animals, trundling around the countryside. The *Camelops* faded midstep, a giant glyptodont disintegrated into the heavy air. The eohippus, the antediluvian horse, disappeared as it trotted past a fence with purple blazes that surrounded a house in which a woman does not yet know her daughter is gone, gone in so many more ways than she could know, in a house that vines have ripped open to the sky. The vines also opening the stable, setting free a horse not ridden in years, but now the vines shrinking, retracting. A dire wolf, head slung low between shoulders, breached a compound of houses in the shape of a spiral, stalking a woman with short blond hair and mud boots. The dire wolf padded forward, teeth bared, but when the woman sensed something and turned, she saw only something that looked like a cloud of gnats. Strange. She turned back and continued to hang sheets on the wash line.

And Boyd would never know this, because she had chosen peace, but if one child was lost on this morning, another child was found. A German-speaking child, lost for more than a century, still bearing a chill and ice in his eyelashes, still wearing a jacket given to him by a girl seeking her friend, found his parents, who had lived long after him and never stopped looking. They folded together, and then they were on their way, reunited, to whatever comes next, Boyd's jacket fluttering, hollowed, to the ground.

* * *

Lucy Maud shouted down into a hole, the sound coming back to her tinged with water. The end of the yellow rope dripped. Ruben King stood beside her, his expression blank.

"Go get help," she told him, and he did. They would return—the authorities, the real experts this time, phones and roads and the world restored—but they would not be able to reach Kevin for two months, for the storm continued to drain into the aquifer long after the surface dried. Kevin would be found at the end of July by a team that Lucy Maud would hire after the excitement of the storm had passed. An EMT, a day laborer, a National Guard soldier, and Isaac, down in the muddy chamber, would unball Kevin's body and strap him to a board, lifting it to the surface where Lucy Maud and Boyd and Allen Potivar, oxygen whirring, would stand. In the soldier's pocket, the silver ingot, secreted away, a souvenir more than a theft, the object's value in the story. Allen Potivar would make Lucy Maud and Ruben promise not to tell why Kevin was down there, but the soldier would see the other body, pocket the ingot, and get an idea. One day he would return, but not for a very long time.

On this day, however, Ruben King ran back to Allen Potivar's, exhausted beyond measure, and Lucy Maud shouted into a textured darkness, a place where the film between this world and the next had rubbed thin, where someone had passed through.

She thought of their garage apartment in Austin in the mid-nineties, and she remembered a day so hot she had lain in her underwear on the floor by a box fan. He had come to lie next to her, their bodies separate because of the heat, his feet next to her head, and he had poked the pointy part of her ankle bone with his finger. Even in the heat, he had needed to touch her. Sweat had beaded in the space between her breasts, and she had closed her eyes to everything. The world had once contained such possibilities.

Sam handed the phone to Isaac and said, "You're the one they were looking for. Since yesterday. Does anybody know that you've been found?"

Isaac, with Boyd in his arms, looked at the man and blinked. Isaac sensed something between them, some competition that the soldier had decided to let go, and Isaac took the phone and dialed his father. No answer; then he remembered his father's phone by the easy chair at home.

Next he dialed Lucy Maud, and the phone rang for a moment before she answered.

Lucy Maud rocked, her head thrown back to the sun, her throat exposed, mourning a loss she had already mourned for so long. Only now the loss was more acute, and she rode this sharp wave of pain the way she had the contractions when she delivered Boyd. *It is not too much to bear*, she told herself. *It is only pain.* In through the nose and out through the mouth.

Her phone rang, a number she didn't know. "Yes?" she said, after she almost didn't answer.

"Lucy Maud." Isaac's was maybe the last voice she expected to hear. She was looking for him, and he found her instead. "I'm with Boyd. She's all right."

What a funny thing to say. There was something he was not saying, but she ignored this tiny doubt, lowered her head, and covered her eyes with the hand not holding the phone. "Thank God, thank God," she said as the pain crested, and she rode the back side of the wave into the trough, able to gather strength once again.

On Allen Potivar's porch, Aunt Fern and Louisa May sat on a dusty old swing that creaked in protest if they moved too much, drinking coffee as if nothing whatsoever were wrong. Lou thought that she was better off not going anywhere, better off just sitting here with Aunt Fern, who was likely to wander away and cause a bigger problem. Lou knew that Aunt Fern would not be living at her house on the lake much longer, that she would need a level of care that Lou could not provide, and she took Fern by the hand, but Fern just stared out over the scrub. What was she thinking about? Lou could not guess. She could only imagine herself alone in the house on the lake, the wind in the sheer curtains her only companion, the hollow life that was coming for her.

By the river, as a woman in wellies hung sheets on a clothesline in front of a low-slung shingled building, she heard footsteps behind her. She jumped—she was on edge, the world proven too strange. Just that morning, a soldier had arrived in a boat, then later she had imagined a huge beast, something like a wild dog, only impossibly large. She had felt its breath, even, but when she turned to see it, the figment of her imagination had disappeared, dissolving at the edges of her sight. Now she heard steps and was afraid to turn.

But whatever it was would be there, even if she didn't look; and if she did turn to look, perhaps it would melt away, as the dog creature had done. She breathed and pivoted, the clothespin in her mouth.

It was a girl, a wild girl, naked. She wore the wind in her red hair, and in her face—there was something Kim couldn't place: a fear, a roiling, almost as if another face were beneath it. Kim's throat went dry with her own sharp fear, then the girl stumbled forward and fell at Kim's feet next to the basket of wet sheets. The girl was soaking—she had just come from the river. Had the river taken her clothes?

Kim yelled for help, and help came running: Annie dropping a hoe from the kitchen garden, Bess dropping a shovel from where she'd been turning compost. The three of them picked up the girl, whose eyes flew open as she was lifted. She didn't speak, and Kim saw that she was not embarrassed by her nudity. The girl still said nothing, and Kim wondered if something was wrong about her. They carried her up to the main house and tucked her into bed, taking a washcloth to her limbs and face. They did not try to clothe her. They also could not place her age—somewhere between fourteen and thirty. They put her in her own room and closed the door behind her. What a strange time this was, this time after the storm.

The bride and groom, Homer and Sylvia, sat at their kitchen table, putting together a jigsaw puzzle. It had rained for days, so they had stayed inside, making a pot of chili and watching old movies on Netflix, even watching *My Man Godfrey* twice because Sylvia had wanted something funny. She felt depressed somehow, despite being just married, the clothes she had worn still in a ball on the floor. Something was off, something in the way it rained. She rested her bare foot on Homer's. He studied the puzzle and placed one of the few remaining pieces. She'd known him for decades, and what a history they'd had. His hands—the hands that had killed a man in the seventies—were knotted now and covered in spots. It had been in self-defense, and the story from another lifetime, a thing they hardly thought of these days. The world had moved on since then, and so many of the players in that original drama were dead. Only the two of them remained, in a house dry and warm while the rain fell outside. Soon she would rise from the table, maybe load the dishwasher. Soon Homer and Sylvia's respite would be over; soon they would again be part of the world. Their long march to marriage, the nuptials so far unconsummated after the ceremony, the companionship of half a century its own comfort. For a little bit longer, they would sit there.

Things You Would Know If You Grew Up Around Here

The Story Becomes Something Else

On the day I climbed out of a hole in the ground, my son fell out of a tree, and neither of us knew until later just how close we each had come to losing the other. Water had been involved in both cases, water the marker for that time, either too much or too little, flood and drought and flood and drought. In my hand I had held a silver ingot—I don't know whose hand had held it last, other than the upside-down man's. I should have put the ingot in my shirt, and maybe I would have gone into town to buy a shot of whiskey with it. I at least owed all of those treasure stories that small gesture, a nod to a way of living—to a place—that is gone. If I had tried to spend it—or just pretended to spend it, at the least—it would have been an act of remembrance, a hand raised in farewell at a funeral procession.

Something had been in the cave, some feeling that I might be the one who found what had been lost for so long. I must remember this now, remember how thin the frontier is between this world and the other, remember how easily it might have been me who crossed. The man who did had not even been seeking anything, and this feels unfair, as if I have taken something that does not belong to me.

Once, years ago, when Boyd was still in my class, I taught a short story, "The Ones Who Walk Away from Omelas," by Ursula K. Le Guin. In the story, there's this glorious civilization, wanting for nothing. But the trick is that at some point everyone in the civilization learns that his or her happiness has been bought with the misery of a child. When the citizens learn about the child—when they see the child—many of them decide to leave, even though they can't save anyone. I taught this story, and my son was in this class, and so was Boyd, and I remember that nearly all the students had said that they would leave, that they wouldn't stay knowing what they knew. Then I asked them: What if the choice was not to walk away, but to trade places? Then what? I said that this was the only way you could save the child, though Le Guin doesn't offer this option.

Everybody had been silent then, until Boyd had said, "Bulldoze it." Then Isaac—my own son—behind her, back before they became thick as thieves, said, "Yeah. Bulldoze it. Burn it down. Let the pain be in the open. Nothing less is real." Nothing less was real.

Let the sun in. Let the air in. Let the light snake into the corners and show the extent of the darkness. Let it be cleaned, regenerated through violence, purified, made new, sanctified, scorched, scrubbed, razed; let the world show its face. Let it show what we have done and continue to do and what we will not stop doing until the entire story is played out in the way that the course was set, and in the way from which it has never deviated, never wavered, not once, not even when we knew what was coming.

Nothing less is real.

Boyd did not yet know she had lost her father—what a strange feeling it would be when she knew only her own grief—did not know the world that awaited her. Isaac, brows knit together, both hands wrapped around one of hers, a man who would go through medical school, ministering to his oldest friend. Carla, watching Boyd's chest rise and fall in shallow breaths, remembered the spiral on Boyd's forehead, the snakes that had skated at her feet. Sam, manning the engine, heading back, already wondering why he had done this, why he'd gone after a girl who was, after all, only ordinary. Boyd—breathing, breathing, and Isaac turning the golden roses banded on her finger. The sunlight refracting into a rainbow over the back of the old woman, and the doves in the trees overhead.

ACKNOWLEDGMENTS

Thank you to the teachers, the friends, the encouragers, the readers.

Thank you to the Ohio State University MFA program, which first taught me what it looked like to be a writer; to Lee Martin, Michelle Herman, Erin McGraw, and the beautiful Lee K. Abbott, who changed my life forever. Thank you to the Texas Tech English Department; to Katie Cortese, Jill Patterson, Sara Spurgeon, and Marjean Purinton, for the lessons that you taught and for the examples that you set. Thank you, Katie, for the semester spent discussing domestic fabulism, a semester which shaped this book and any books that might follow. Thank you to Dennis Covington, and your lemon ice box pie, and thank you to Dennis Covington's last graduate workshop, to Matt and Mary, and to the tapas and sangria.

Thank you to friends and readers, and to LPG, which remains one of the most transformative experiences of my life. Thank you Jen Popa, Jessica Smith, Kate Simonian, Jasmine Bailey, Sarah Viren, Kathleen Blackburn, and Michael Palmer. I am beyond lucky to know you, and to read your writing, and to listen to your brilliant insights.

Thank you to Kerry D'Agostino, who is possessed of both an incredible editing eye and a deep kindness, and I feel so so privileged to work with you. I've learned so much, and I am so grateful for everything: all of the emails, all of the revisions, all of the questions and answers and support just when I needed it most.

Thank you to Lea Beresford and Grace McNamee, truly perceptive editors who asked tough questions and made the book so much better. Thank you, Laura Phillips, for your patience and expertise. Thank you, Bloomsbury, for giving this book a home.

Finally, thank you to my family: to mother, Jeri; father, Gene; and stepfather, Neil; and to my aunts and uncles. Thank you to Ben, James, and Paul, for the life that we have built, for the adventures that we've had, and for all of our future possibilities.

A NOTE ON THE AUTHOR

NANCY WAYSON DINAN is the managing editor of *Iron Horse Literary Review*. Her work has appeared or is forthcoming in the *Texas Observer*, *Arts & Letters*, *Crab Orchard Review*, the *Cincinnati Review*, and others. She earned her MFA from the Ohio State University in 2013 and is currently a PhD student in fiction at Texas Tech.